FRA[NK]... cated at Charterhouse and Balliol College, Oxford. He was an official in the education department from 1855 to 1884 and from 1885 to 1895 was professor of poetry at Oxford. He died in 1897. Himself a poet, and a good friend of the greatest poet of the day, Alfred Tennyson, Palgrave is now remembered, and will always be, for this incomparable anthology.

CHRISTOPHER RICKS has held a permanent post at Boston University since 1986. He was formerly a Fellow of Worcester College, Oxford, and later a professor first at Bristol and then King Edward VII Professor of English at Cambridge University, where he was a Fellow of Christ's College. He is a Fellow of the British Academy, and of the American Academy of Arts and Sciences.

His publications include *Milton's Grand Style* (1963), *Tennyson* (1972), *Keats and Embarrassment* (1974), *The Force of Poetry* (1984), *T. S. Eliot and Prejudice* (1988) and *Beckett's Dying Words* (1993). He has edited a collection of critical essays on A. E. Housman (1968), *The Poems of Tennyson* (1969, rev. 1987), *The New Oxford Book of Victorian Verse* (1987), Milton's *Paradise Lost* (Penguin Classics 1989) and *A. E. Housman: Collected Poems and Selected Prose* (Penguin Classics 1989). He was co-editor of *The State of the Language* (1980, and a new collection 1990). He is the general editor of the annotated Penguin English Poets and has also edited Volumes 2 and 3 in The Penguin History of Literature series, *English Poetry and Prose: 1540–1674* and *English Drama to 1710*.

THE
GOLDEN TREASURY
OF THE BEST SONGS AND LYRICAL POEMS
IN THE ENGLISH LANGUAGE

SELECTED AND ARRANGED WITH NOTES
BY
FRANCIS TURNER PALGRAVE

EDITED BY CHRISTOPHER RICKS

PENGUIN BOOKS

PENGUIN BOOKS

Published by the Penguin Group
Penguin Books Ltd, 27 Wrights Lane, London W8 5TZ, England
Penguin Putnam Inc., 375 Hudson Street, New York, New York 10014, USA
Penguin Books Australia Ltd, Ringwood, Victoria, Australia
Penguin Books Canada Ltd, 10 Alcorn Avenue, Toronto, Ontario, Canada M4V 3B2
Penguin Books (NZ) Ltd, 182–190 Wairau Road, Auckland 10, New Zealand

Penguin Books Ltd, Registered Offices: Harmondsworth, Middlesex, England

The Golden Treasury first published 1861
This edition published in Penguin Classics 1991
5 7 9 10 8 6 4

This edition copyright © Christopher Ricks, 1991
All rights reserved

The moral right of the editor has been asserted

Printed in England by Clays Ltd, St Ives plc
Set in Monophoto Baskerville

CONTENTS

PREFATORY NOTE TO THIS EDITION

Palgrave's *Golden Treasury* is the best-known and the best-selling anthology of English poetry ever. It is the best, too. A modern edition must not let anything come between a reader and the poems themselves. So all editorial material other than Palgrave's is placed at the back.

Only one decision requires clarification here. Between 1861 (the first edition) and 1891 (the last reconsideration by Palgrave), a few poems were dropped and a good many were added. Since *The Golden Treasury* is not only a masterpiece as an anthology but also a fascinating organism in the evolution of taste, the present editor has chosen to differ from others in two respects. First, there are reinstated within the one sequence the poems of 1861 which Palgrave later dropped, with a note of this at the head of the poem; and, second, there is supplied such a headnote for any poem which Palgrave added after 1861. The poems which Palgrave dropped are identified not only by the headnote but also by their not being numbered.

With the least of distractions on the page, the reader of this anthology, which evolved during thirty years of Queen Victoria's reign, can see at once which poems departed, which poems arrived, and when. Thus on p. 23, between poems XVIII and XIX, there is included a poem of 1861, headed

DIAPHENIA
[*Dropped 1891*]

And on p. 11:

II
THE FAIRY LIFE
[*Added 1883*]

Christopher Ricks

THE

GOLDEN TREASURY

OF THE BEST SONGS AND LYRICAL POEMS
IN THE ENGLISH LANGUAGE

SELECTED AND ARRANGED WITH NOTES BY
FRANCIS TURNER PALGRAVE
FELLOW OF EXETER COLLEGE OXFORD

Cambridge
MACMILLAN AND CO.
AND 23 HENRIETTA STREET COVENT GARDEN
London
1861

TO

ALFRED TENNYSON
POET LAUREATE

This book in its progress has recalled often to my memory a man with whose friendship we were once honoured, to whom no region of English Literature was unfamiliar, and who, whilst rich in all the noble gifts of Nature, was most eminently distinguished by the noblest and the rarest, – just judgment and high-hearted patriotism. It would have been hence a peculiar pleasure and pride to dedicate what I have endeavoured to make a true national Anthology of three centuries to Henry Hallam. But he is beyond the reach of any human tokens of love and reverence; and I desire therefore to place before it a name united with his by associations which, while Poetry retains her hold on the minds of Englishmen, are not likely to be forgotten.

Your encouragement, given while traversing the wild scenery of Treryn Dinas, led me to begin the work; and it has been completed under your advice and assistance. For the favour now asked I have thus a second reason: and to this I may add, the homage which is your right as Poet, and the gratitude due to a Friend, whose regard I rate at no common value.

Permit me then to inscribe to yourself a book which, I hope, may be found by many a lifelong fountain of innocent and exalted pleasure; a source of animation to friends when they meet; and able to sweeten solitude itself with best society, – with the companionship of the wise and the good, with the beauty which the eye cannot see, and the music only heard in silence. If this Collection proves a storehouse of delight to Labour and to Poverty, – if it teaches those indifferent to the Poets to love them, and those who love them to love them more, the aim and the desire entertained in framing it will be fully accomplished.

F.T.P.

MAY 1861

PREFACE

This little Collection differs, it is believed, from others in the attempt made to include in it all the best original Lyrical pieces and Songs in our language (save a very few regretfully omitted on account of length), by writers not living, – and none beside the best. Many familiar verses will hence be met with; many also which should be familiar: – the Editor will regard as his fittest readers those who love Poetry so well, that he can offer them nothing not already known and valued.

The Editor is acquainted with no strict and exhaustive definition of Lyrical Poetry; but he has found the task of practical decision increase in clearness and in facility as he advanced with the work, whilst keeping in view a few simple principles. Lyrical has been here held essentially to imply that each Poem shall turn on some single thought, feeling, or situation. In accordance with this, narrative, descriptive, and didactic poems, – unless accompanied by rapidity of movement, brevity, and the colouring of human passion, – have been excluded. Humorous poetry, except in the very unfrequent instances where a truly poetical tone pervades the whole, with what is strictly personal, occasional, and religious, has been considered foreign to the idea of the book. Blank verse and the ten-syllable couplet, with all pieces markedly dramatic, have been rejected as alien from what is commonly understood by Song, and rarely conforming to Lyrical conditions in treatment. But it is not anticipated, nor is it possible, that all readers shall think the line accurately drawn. Some poems, as Gray's Elegy, the Allegro and Penseroso, Wordsworth's Ruth or Campbell's Lord Ullin, might be claimed with perhaps equal justice for a narrative or descriptive selection: whilst with reference especially to Ballads and Sonnets, the Editor can only state that he has taken his utmost pains to decide without caprice or partiality.

This also is all he can plead in regard to a point even more liable to question; – what degree of merit should give rank among the Best. That a poem shall be worthy of the writer's genius, – that it shall reach a perfection commensurate with its aim, – that we should require finish in proportion to brevity, – that passion, colour, and originality cannot atone for serious imperfections in clearness, unity or truth, – that a few good lines do not make a good poem, that popular estimate is serviceable as a guidepost more than as a compass, – above all, that excellence should be looked for rather in the whole than in the parts, – such and other such canons have been always steadily regarded. He may however add that the pieces chosen, and a far larger number rejected, have been carefully and repeatedly considered; and that he has been aided throughout by two friends of independent and exercised judgment, besides the distinguished person addressed in the Dedication. It is hoped that by this procedure the volume has been freed from that one-sidedness which must beset individual decisions: – but for the final choice the Editor is alone responsible.

Chalmers' vast collection, with the whole works of all accessible poets not contained in it, and the best Anthologies of different periods, have been twice systematically read through: and it is hence improbable that any omissions which may be regretted are due to oversight. The poems are printed entire, except in a very few instances where a stanza or passage has been omitted. These omissions have been risked only when the piece could be thus brought to a closer lyrical unity: and, as essentially opposed to this unity, extracts, obviously such, are excluded. In regard to the text, the purpose of the book has appeared to justify the choice of the most poetical version, wherever more than one exists; and much labour has been given to present each poem, in disposition, spelling, and punctuation, to the greatest advantage.

In the arrangement, the most poetically-effective order has been attempted. The English mind has passed through phases of thought and cultivation so various and so opposed during these three centuries of Poetry, that a rapid passage between old and new, like rapid alteration of the eye's focus in looking at the landscape, will always be wearisome and hurtful to the sense of Beauty. The poems have been therefore distributed into Books corresponding, I to the ninety years closing about 1616, II thence to 1700, III to 1800, IV to the half century just ended. Or, looking at the Poets who more or less give each portion its distinctive character, they might be called the Books of Shakespeare, Milton, Gray, and Wordsworth. The volume, in this respect, so far as the limitations of its range allow, accurately reflects the natural growth and evolution of our Poetry. A rigidly chronological sequence, however, rather fits a collection aiming at instruction than at pleasure, and the wisdom which comes through pleasure: – within each book the pieces have therefore been arranged in gradations of feeling or subject. And it is hoped that the contents of this Anthology will thus be found to present a certain unity, 'as episodes,' in the noble language of Shelley, 'to that great Poem which all poets, like the co-operating thoughts of one great mind, have built up since the beginning of the world.'

As he closes his long survey, the Editor trusts he may add without egotism, that he has found the vague general verdict of popular Fame more just than those have thought, who, with too severe a criticism, would confine judgments on Poetry to 'the selected few of many generations.' Not many appear to have gained reputation without some gift or performance that, in due degree, deserved it: and if no verses by certain writers who show less strength than sweetness, or more thought than mastery of expression, are printed in this volume, it should not be imagined that they have been excluded without much hesitation and regret, – far less that they have been slighted. Throughout this vast and pathetic array of Singers now silent, few have been honoured with the name Poet, and have not possessed a skill in words, a sympathy with beauty, a tenderness of feeling, or seriousness in reflection, which render their works, although never perhaps attaining that loftier and finer excellence here required, – better worth reading than much of what fills the scanty hours that most men spare for self-improvement, or for pleasure in any of its more elevated and permanent forms. – And if this be true of even mediocre poetry, for how much more are we indebted to the best! Like the fabled fountain of the Azores, but with a more various power, the magic of this Art can confer on each period of life its appropriate blessing: on early years Experience, on maturity Calm, on age, Youthfulness. Poetry gives treasures 'more golden than gold,' leading us in higher and healthier ways than those of the world, and interpreting to us the lessons of Nature. But she speaks best for herself. Her true accents, if the plan has been executed with success, may be heard throughout the following pages: – wherever the Poets of England are honoured, wherever the dominant language of the world is spoken, it is hoped that they will find fit audience.

1861

Some poems, especially in Book I, have been added: – either on better acquaintance; – in deference to critical suggestions; – or unknown to the Editor when first gathering his harvest. For aid in these after-gleanings he is specially indebted to the excellent re-prints of rare early verse given us by Dr. Hannah, Dr. Grosart, Mr. Arber, Mr. Bullen, and others, – and (in regard to the additions of 1883) to the advice of that distinguished Friend, by whom the final choice has been so largely guided. The text has also been carefully revised from authoritative sources. It has still seemed best, for many reasons, to retain the original limit by which the selection was confined to those then no longer living. But the editor hopes that, so far as in him lies, a complete and definitive collection of our best Lyrics, to the central year of this fast-closing century, is now offered.

1883–1890–1891

Εἰς τὸν λειμῶνα καθίσας,
ἔδρεπεν ἕτερον ἐφ᾽ ἑτέρῳ
αἰρόμενος ἄγρευμ᾽ ἀνθέων
ἁδομένᾳ ψυχᾷ—

The Golden Treasury
Book First

I
SPRING

Spring, the sweet Spring, is the year's pleasant king;
Then blooms each thing, then maids dance in a ring,
Cold doth not sting, the pretty birds do sing,
   Cuckoo, jug-jug, pu-we, to-witta-woo!

The palm and may make country houses gay,
Lambs frisk and play, the shepherds pipe all day,
And we hear aye birds tune this merry lay,
   Cuckoo, jug-jug, pu-we, to-witta-woo.

The fields breathe sweet, the daisies kiss our feet,
Young lovers meet, old wives a-sunning sit,
In every street these tunes our ears do greet,
   Cuckoo, jug-jug, pu-we, to-witta-woo!
      Spring! the sweet Spring!

T. Nash

II
THE FAIRY LIFE
[Added 1883]

I

Where the bee sucks, there suck I:
In a cowslip's bell I lie;
There I couch, when owls do cry:
On the bat's back I do fly
After summer merrily.
    Merrily, merrily, shall I live now,
    Under the blossom that hangs on the bough!

W. Shakespeare

III
[*Added 1883*]

2

Come unto these yellow sands,
        And then take hands:
Courtsied when you have, and kiss'd
        The wild waves whist,
Foot it featly here and there;
And, sweet Sprites, the burthen bear.
        Hark, hark!
            Bow-bow.
        The watch-dogs bark:
            Bow-wow.
        Hark, hark! I hear
The strain of strutting chanticleer
        Cry, Cock-a-diddle-dow!

                            W. Shakespeare

IV
SUMMONS TO LOVE

Phoebus, arise!
And paint the sable skies
With azure, white, and red:
Rouse Memnon's mother from her Tithon's bed
That she may thy career with roses spread:
The nightingales thy coming each-where sing:
Make an eternal Spring!
Give life to this dark world which lieth dead;
Spread forth thy golden hair

In larger locks than thou wast wont before,
And emperor-like decore
With diadem of pearl thy temples fair:
Chase hence the ugly night
Which serves but to make dear thy glorious light.

– This is that happy morn,
That day, long-wishéd day
Of all my life so dark,
(If cruel stars have not my ruin sworn
And fates my hopes betray),
Which, purely white, deserves
An everlasting diamond should it mark.
This is the morn should bring unto this grove
My Love, to hear and recompense my love.
Fair King, who all preserves,
But show thy blushing beams,
And thou two sweeter eyes
Shalt see than those which by Penéus' streams
Did once thy heart surprize.
Now, Flora, deck thyself in fairest guise:
If that ye winds would hear
A voice surpassing far Amphion's lyre,
Your furious chiding stay;
Let Zephyr only breathe,
And with her tresses play.
– The winds all silent are,
And Phoebus in his chair
Ensaffroning sea and air
Makes vanish every star:
Night like a drunkard reels
Beyond the hills, to shun his flaming wheels:
The fields with flowers are deck'd in every hue,
The clouds with orient gold spangle their blue;
Here is the pleasant place –
And nothing wanting is, save She, alas!

W. Drummond of Hawthornden

V

TIME AND LOVE

1

When I have seen by Time's fell hand defaced
The rich proud cost of out-worn buried age;
When sometime lofty towers I see down-razed,
And brass eternal slave to mortal rage;

When I have seen the hungry ocean gain
Advantage on the kingdom of the shore,
And the firm soil win of the watery main,
Increasing store with loss, and loss with store;

When I have seen such interchange of state,
Or state itself confounded to decay,
Ruin hath taught me thus to ruminate –
That Time will come and take my Love away:

– This thought is as a death, which cannot choose
But weep to have that which it fears to lose.

W. Shakespeare

VI

2

Since brass, nor stone, nor earth, nor boundless sea,
But sad mortality o'ersways their power,
How with this rage shall beauty hold a plea,
Whose action is no stronger than a flower?

O how shall summer's honey breath hold out
Against the wreckful siege of battering days,
When rocks impregnable are not so stout
Nor gates of steel so strong, but time decays?

O fearful meditation! where, alack!
Shall Time's best jewel from Time's chest lie hid?
Or what strong hand can hold his swift foot back,
Or who his spoil of beauty can forbid?

O! none, unless this miracle have might,
That in black ink my love may still shine bright.

W. Shakespeare

VII
THE PASSIONATE SHEPHERD TO HIS LOVE

Come live with me and be my Love,
And we will all the pleasures prove
That hills and valleys, dale and field,
And all the craggy mountains yield.

There will we sit upon the rocks
And see the shepherds feed their flocks,
By shallow rivers, to whose falls
Melodious birds sing madrigals.

There will I make thee beds of roses
And a thousand fragrant posies,
A cap of flowers, and a kirtle
Embroider'd all with leaves of myrtle.

A gown made of the finest wool,
Which from our pretty lambs we pull,
Fair linéd slippers for the cold,
With buckles of the purest gold.

A belt of straw and ivy buds
With coral clasps and amber studs:
And if these pleasures may thee move,
Come live with me and be my Love.

Thy silver dishes for thy meat
As precious as the gods do eat,
Shall on an ivory table be
Prepared each day for thee and me.

The shepherd swains shall dance and sing
For thy delight each May-morning:
If these delights thy mind may move,
Then live with me and be my Love.

C. Marlowe

VIII
OMNIA VINCIT
[*Added 1890*]

Fain would I change that note
To which fond Love hath charm'd me
Long long to sing by rote,
Fancying that that harm'd me:
Yet when this thought doth come
'Love is the perfect sum
    Of all delight,'
I have no other choice
Either for pen or voice
    To sing or write.

O Love! they wrong thee much
That say thy sweet is bitter,
When thy rich fruit is such
As nothing can be sweeter.
Fair house of joy and bliss,
Where truest pleasure is,
    I do adore thee:
I know thee what thou art,
I serve thee with my heart,
    And fall before thee!

Anon.

IX

A MADRIGAL

Crabbed Age and Youth
Cannot live together:
Youth is full of pleasance,
Age is full of care;
Youth like summer morn,
Age like winter weather,
Youth like summer brave,
Age like winter bare:
Youth is full of sport,
Age's breath is short,
Youth is nimble, Age is lame:
Youth is hot and bold,
Age is weak and cold,
Youth is wild, and Age is tame: –
Age, I do abhor thee,
Youth, I do adore thee;
O! my Love, my Love is young!
Age, I do defy thee –
O sweet shepherd, hie thee,
For methinks thou stay'st too long.

W. Shakespeare

X

Under the greenwood tree,
Who loves to lie with me,
And turn his merry note
Unto the sweet bird's throat –
Come hither, come hither, come hither!
                    Here shall he see
                    No enemy
But winter and rough weather.

Who doth ambition shun
And loves to live i' the sun,
Seeking the food he eats
And pleased with what he gets –
Come hither, come hither, come hither!
                    Here shall he see
                    No enemy
But winter and rough weather.

W. Shakespeare

XI

It was a lover and his lass
    With a hey and a ho, and a hey nonino!
That o'er the green corn-field did pass
In the spring time, the only pretty ring time,
When birds do sing hey ding a ding:
    Sweet lovers love the Spring.

Between the acres of the rye
These pretty country folks would lie:
This carol they began that hour,
How that life was but a flower:

And therefore take the present time
   With a hey and a ho and a hey nonino!
For love is crownéd with the prime
In spring time, the only pretty ring time,
When birds do sing hey ding a ding:
   Sweet lovers love the Spring.

W. Shakespeare

XII
PRESENT IN ABSENCE

Absence, hear thou this protestation
    Against thy strength,
    Distance, and length;
Do what thou canst for alteration:
   For hearts of truest mettle
Absence doth join, and Time doth settle.

Who loves a mistress of such quality,
    His mind hath found
    Affection's ground
Beyond time, place, and mortality.
   To hearts that cannot vary
Absence is present, Time doth tarry.

By absence this good means I gain,
    That I can catch her,
    Where none can match her,
In some close corner of my brain:
   There I embrace and kiss her;
And so I both enjoy and miss her.

J. Donne

XIII

VIA AMORIS

[*Added 1890*]

High-way, since you my chief Parnassus be,
And that my Muse, to some ears not unsweet,
Tempers her words to trampling horses' feet
More oft than to a chamber melody, –

Now, blesséd you bear onward blesséd me
To her, where I my heart, safe-left, shall meet;
My Muse and I must you of duty greet
With thanks and wishes, wishing thankfully;

Be you still fair, honour'd by public heed;
By no encroachment wrong'd, nor time forgot;
Nor blamed for blood, nor shamed for sinful deed;
And that you know I envy you no lot

Of highest wish, I wish you so much bliss, –
Hundreds of years you Stella's feet may kiss!

Sir P. Sidney

XIV

ABSENCE

Being your slave, what should I do but tend
Upon the hours and times of your desire?
I have no precious time at all to spend
Nor services to do, till you require:

Nor dare I chide the world-without-end-hour
Whilst I, my sovereign, watch the clock for you,
Nor think the bitterness of absence sour
When you have bid your servant once adieu:

Nor dare I question with my jealous thought
Where you may be, or your affairs suppose,
But like a sad slave, stay and think of nought
Save, where you are, how happy you make those; –

So true a fool is love, that in your will
Though you do anything, he thinks no ill.

W. Shakespeare

XV

How like a winter hath my absence been
From Thee, the pleasure of the fleeting year!
What freezings have I felt, what dark days seen,
What old December's bareness everywhere!

And yet this time removed was summer's time:
The teeming autumn, big with rich increase,
Bearing the wanton burden of the prime
Like widow'd wombs after their lords' decease:

Yet this abundant issue seem'd to me
But hope of orphans, and unfather'd fruit;
For summer and his pleasures wait on thee,
And, thou away, the very birds are mute;

Or if they sing, 'tis with so dull a cheer,
That leaves look pale, dreading the winter's near.

W. Shakespeare

XVI
A CONSOLATION

When in disgrace with fortune and men's eyes
I all alone beweep my outcast state,
And trouble deaf heaven with my bootless cries,
And look upon myself, and curse my fate;

Wishing me like to one more rich in hope,
Featured like him, like him with friends possest,
Desiring this man's art, and that man's scope,
With what I most enjoy contented least;

Yet in these thoughts myself almost despising,
Haply I think on Thee – and then my state,
Like to the lark at break of day arising
From sullen earth, sings hymns at heaven's gate;

For thy sweet love remember'd, such wealth brings
That then I scorn to change my state with kings.

W. Shakespeare

XVII
THE UNCHANGEABLE

O never say that I was false of heart,
Though absence seem'd my flame to qualify:
As easy might I from myself depart
As from my soul, which in thy breast doth lie;

That is my home of love; if I have ranged,
Like him that travels, I return again,
Just to the time, not with the time exchanged,
So that myself bring water for my stain.

Never believe, though in my nature reign'd
All frailties that besiege all kinds of blood,
That it could so preposterously be stain'd
To leave for nothing all thy sum of good:

For nothing this wide universe I call,
Save thou, my rose: in it thou art my all.

W. Shakespeare

XVIII

To me, fair Friend, you never can be old,
For as you were when first your eye I eyed
Such seems your beauty still. Three winters' cold
Have from the forests shook three summers' pride;

Three beauteous springs to yellow autumn turn'd
In process of the seasons have I seen,
Three April perfumes in three hot Junes burn'd,
Since first I saw you fresh, which yet are green.

Ah! yet doth beauty, like a dial-hand,
Steal from his figure, and no pace perceived;
So your sweet hue, which methinks still doth stand,
Hath motion, and mine eye may be deceived:

For fear of which, hear this, thou age unbred, –
Ere you were born, was beauty's summer dead.

W. Shakespeare

DIAPHENIA
[*Dropped 1891*]

Diaphenia like the daffadowndilly,
    White as the sun, fair as the lily,
Heigh ho, how I do love thee!
    I do love thee as my lambs
    Are belovéd of their dams;
How blest were I if thou would'st prove me.

Diaphenia like the spreading roses,
    That in thy sweets all sweets encloses,
Fair sweet, how I do love thee!
    I do love thee as each flower
    Loves the sun's life-giving power;
For dead, thy breath to life might move me.

Diaphenia like to all things blesséd
   When all thy praises are expresséd,
Dear joy, how I do love thee!
   As the birds do love the spring,
   Or the bees their careful king:
Then in requite, sweet virgin, love me!

                              H. Constable

XIX
ROSALINE

Like to the clear in highest sphere
Where all imperial glory shines,
For selfsame colour is her hair
Whether unfolded, or in twines:
   Heigh ho, fair Rosaline!
Her eyes are sapphires set in snow,
Resembling heaven by every wink;
The Gods do fear whenas they glow,
And I do tremble when I think
   Heigh ho, would she were mine!

Her cheeks are like the blushing cloud
That beautifies Aurora's face,
Or like the silver crimson shroud
That Phoebus' smiling looks doth grace;
   Heigh ho, fair Rosaline!
Her lips are like two budded roses
Whom ranks of lilies neighbour nigh,
Within which bounds she balm encloses
Apt to entice a deity:
   Heigh ho, would she were mine!

Her neck is like a stately tower
Where Love himself imprison'd lies,
To watch for glances every hour
From her divine and sacred eyes:
   Heigh ho, for Rosaline!
Her paps are centres of delight,
Her breasts are orbs of heavenly frame,
Where Nature moulds the dew of light
To feed perfection with the same:
   Heigh ho, would she were mine!

With orient pearl, with ruby red,
With marble white, with sapphire blue
Her body every way is fed,
Yet soft in touch and sweet in view:
   Heigh ho, fair Rosaline!
Nature herself her shape admires;
The Gods are wounded in her sight;
And Love forsakes his heavenly fires
And at her eyes his brand doth light:
   Heigh ho, would she were mine!

Then muse not, Nymphs, though I bemoan
The absence of fair Rosaline,
Since for a fair there's fairer none,
Nor for her virtues so divine:
   Heigh ho, fair Rosaline;
Heigh ho, my heart! would God that she were mine!

T. Lodge

XX
COLIN

Beauty sat bathing by a spring
    Where fairest shades did hide her;
The winds blew calm, the birds did sing,
    The cool streams ran beside her.
My wanton thoughts enticed mine eye
    To see what was forbidden:
But better memory said, fie!
    So vain desire was chidden: –
        Hey nonny nonny O!
        Hey nonny nonny!

Into a slumber then I fell,
    When fond imagination
Seeméd to see, but could not tell
    Her feature or her fashion.
But ev'n as babes in dreams do smile,
    And sometimes fall a-weeping,
So I awaked, as wise this while
    As when I fell a-sleeping: –
        Hey nonny nonny O!
        Hey nonny nonny!

The Shepherd Tonie

XXI
A PICTURE
[*Added 1890*]

Sweet Love, if thou wilt gain a monarch's glory,
Subdue her heart, who makes me glad and sorry:
    Out of thy golden quiver
    Take thou thy strongest arrow
    That will through bone and marrow,
And me and thee of grief and fear deliver: –
But come behind, for if she look upon thee,
Alas! poor Love! then thou art woe-begone thee!

Anon.

XXII
A SONG FOR MUSIC
[Added 1883]

Weep you no more, sad fountains: –
    What need you flow so fast?
Look how the snowy mountains
    Heaven's sun doth gently waste!
      But my Sun's heavenly eyes
        View not your weeping,
        That now lies sleeping
    Softly, now softly lies,
        Sleeping.

Sleep is a reconciling,
    A rest that peace begets: –
Doth not the sun rise smiling,
    When fair at even he sets?
        – Rest you, then, rest, sad eyes!
        Melt not in weeping!
        While She lies sleeping
    Softly, now softly lies,
        Sleeping!

                    Anon.

XXIII
TO HIS LOVE

Shall I compare thee to a summer's day?
Thou art more lovely and more temperate:
Rough winds do shake the darling buds of May,
And summer's lease hath all too short a date:

Sometime too hot the eye of heaven shines,
And often is his gold complexion dimm'd:
And every fair from fair sometime declines,
By chance, or nature's changing course, untrimm'd.

But thy eternal summer shall not fade
Nor lose possession of that fair thou owest;
Nor shall Death brag thou wanderest in his shade,
When in eternal lines to time thou growest: –

So long as men can breathe, or eyes can see,
So long lives this, and this gives life to thee.

W. Shakespeare

XXIV
TO HIS LOVE

When in the chronicle of wasted time
I see descriptions of the fairest wights,
And beauty making beautiful old rhyme
In praise of ladies dead, and lovely knights;

Then in the blazon of sweet beauty's best
Of hand, of foot, of lip, of eye, of brow,
I see their antique pen would have exprest
Ev'n such a beauty as you master now.

So all their praises are but prophecies
Of this our time, all, you prefiguring;
And for they look'd but with divining eyes,
They had not skill enough your worth to sing:

For we, which now behold these present days,
Have eyes to wonder, but lack tongues to praise.

W. Shakespeare

XXV
BASIA
[Added 1890]

Turn back, you wanton flyer,
And answer my desire
    With mutual greeting.
Yet bend a little nearer, –
True beauty still shines clearer
    In closer meeting!
Hearts with hearts delighted
Should strive to be united,
Each other's arms with arms enchaining, –
    Hearts with a thought,
Rosy lips with a kiss still entertaining.

What harvest half so sweet is
As still to reap the kisses
    Grown ripe in sowing?
And straight to be receiver
Of that which thou art giver,
    Rich in bestowing?
There is no strict observing
Of times' or seasons' swerving,
There is ever one fresh spring abiding;
    Then what we sow with our lips
Let us reap, love's gains dividing.

T. Campion

XXVI
ADVICE TO A GIRL
[Added 1891]

Never love unless you can
Bear with all the faults of man!
Men sometimes will jealous be
Though but little cause they see,

And hang the head as discontent,
And speak what straight they will repent.

Men, that but one Saint adore,
Make a show of love to more;
Beauty must be scorn'd in none,
Though but truly served in one:
For what is courtship but disguise?
True hearts may have dissembling eyes.

Men, when their affairs require,
Must awhile themselves retire;
Sometimes hunt, and sometimes hawk,
And not ever sit and talk: —
If these and such-like you can bear,
Then like, and love, and never fear!

T. Campion

XXVII
LOVE'S PERJURIES

On a day, alack the day!
Love, whose month is ever May,
Spied a blossom passing fair
Playing in the wanton air:
Through the velvet leaves the wind,
All unseen, 'gan passage find:
That the lover, sick to death,
Wish'd himself the heaven's breath.
Air, quoth he, thy cheeks may blow;
Air, would I might triumph so!
But, alack, my hand is sworn
Ne'er to pluck thee from thy thorn:
Vow, alack, for youth unmeet;
Youth so apt to pluck a sweet.

Do not call it sin in me
That I am forsworn for thee:
Thou for whom Jove would swear
Juno but an Ethiope were,
And deny himself for Jove,
Turning mortal for thy love.

W. Shakespeare

XXVIII
A SUPPLICATION

Forget not yet the tried intent
Of such a truth as I have meant;
My great travail so gladly spent,
   Forget not yet!

Forget not yet when first began
The weary life ye know, since whan
The suit, the service none tell can;
   Forget not yet!

Forget not yet the great assays,
The cruel wrong, the scornful ways,
The painful patience in delays,
   Forget not yet!

Forget not! O, forget not this,
How long ago hath been, and is
The mind that never meant amiss –
   Forget not yet!

Forget not then thine own approved
The which so long hath thee so loved,
Whose steadfast faith yet never moved –
   Forget not this!

Sir T. Wyat

XXIX
TO AURORA

O if thou knew'st how thou thyself dost harm,
And dost prejudge thy bliss, and spoil my rest;
Then thou would'st melt the ice out of thy breast
And thy relenting heart would kindly warm.

O if thy pride did not our joys controul,
What world of loving wonders should'st thou see!
For if I saw thee once transform'd in me,
Then in thy bosom I would pour my soul;

Then all my thoughts should in thy visage shine,
And if that aught mischanced thou should'st not moan
Nor bear the burthen of thy griefs alone;
No, I would have my share in what were thine:

And whilst we thus should make our sorrows one,
This happy harmony would make them none.

W. Alexander, Earl of Sterline

XXX
IN LACRIMAS
[*Added 1891*]

I saw my Lady weep,
And Sorrow proud to be advancéd so
In those fair eyes where all perfections keep.
Her face was full of woe,
But such a woe (believe me) as wins more hearts
Than Mirth can do with her enticing parts.

Sorrow was there made fair,
And Passion, wise; Tears, a delightful thing;
Silence, beyond all speech, a wisdom rare:
She made her sighs to sing,
And all things with so sweet a sadness move
As made my heart at once both grieve and love.

O fairer than aught else
The world can show, leave off in time to grieve!
Enough, enough: your joyful look excels:
    Tears kill the heart, believe.
O strive not to be excellent in woe,
Which only breeds your beauty's overthrow.

                                      Anon.

XXXI
TRUE LOVE

Let me not to the marriage of true minds
Admit impediments. Love is not love
Which alters when it alteration finds,
Or bends with the remover to remove: –

O no! it is an ever-fixéd mark
That looks on tempests, and is never shaken;
It is the star to every wandering bark,
Whose worth's unknown, although his height be taken.

Love's not Time's fool, though rosy lips and cheeks
Within his bending sickle's compass come;
Love alters not with his brief hours and weeks,
But bears it out ev'n to the edge of doom: –

If this be error, and upon me proved,
I never writ, nor no man ever loved.

                                  W. Shakespeare

XXXII
A DITTY

My true-love hath my heart, and I have his,
By just exchange one for another given:
I hold his dear, and mine he cannot miss,
There never was a better bargain driven:
   My true-love hath my heart, and I have his.

His heart in me keeps him and me in one,
My heart in him his thoughts and senses guides:
He loves my heart, for once it was his own,
I cherish his because in me it bides:
   My true-love hath my heart, and I have his.

Sir P. Sidney

XXXIII
LOVE'S INSIGHT
[*Added 1890*]

Though others may Her brow adore
Yet more must I, that therein see far more
Than any other's eyes have power to see:
     She is to me
More than to any others she can be!
I can discern more secret notes
That in the margin of her cheeks Love quotes,
Than any else besides have art to read:
     No looks proceed
From those fair eyes but to me wonder breed.

Anon.

XXXIV
LOVE'S OMNIPRESENCE

Were I as base as is the lowly plain,
And you, my Love, as high as heaven above,
Yet should the thoughts of me your humble swain
Ascend to heaven, in honour of my Love.

Were I as high as heaven above the plain,
And you, my Love, as humble and as low
As are the deepest bottoms of the main,
Whereso'er you were, with you my love should go.

Were you the earth, dear Love, and I the skies,
My love should shine on you like to the sun,
And look upon you with ten thousand eyes
Till heaven wax'd blind, and till the world were done.

Whereso'er I am, below, or else above you,
Whereso'er you are, my heart shall truly love you.

J. Sylvester

XXXV
CARPE DIEM

O Mistress mine, where are you roaming?
O stay and hear! your true-love's coming
      That can sing both high and low;
Trip no further, pretty sweeting,
Journeys end in lovers meeting –
      Every wise man's son doth know.

What is love? 'tis not hereafter;
Present mirth hath present laughter;
      What's to come is still unsure:
In delay there lies no plenty, –
Then come kiss me, Sweet-and-twenty,
      Youth's a stuff will not endure.

W. Shakespeare

XXXVI
AN HONEST AUTOLYCUS
[*Added 1890*]

Fine knacks for ladies, cheap, choice, brave, and new,
   Good penny-worths, – but money cannot move:
I keep a fair but for the Fair to view;
   A beggar may be liberal of love.
Though all my wares be trash, the heart is true –
           The heart is true.

Great gifts are guiles and look for gifts again;
   My trifles come as treasures from my mind;
It is a precious jewel to be plain;
   Sometimes in shell the orient'st pearls we find: –
Of others take a sheaf, of me a grain!
           Of me a grain!

Anon.

XXXVII
WINTER

When icicles hang by the wall
   And Dick the shepherd blows his nail,
And Tom bears logs into the hall,
   And milk comes frozen home in pail;
When blood is nipt, and ways be foul,
Then nightly sings the staring owl
         Tu-whit!
To-who! A merry note!
While greasy Joan doth keel the pot.

When all about the wind doth blow,
   And coughing drowns the parson's saw,
And birds sit brooding in the snow,
   And Marian's nose looks red and raw;

When roasted crabs hiss in the bowl –
Then nightly sings the staring owl
        Tu-whit!
To-who! A merry note!
While greasy Joan doth keel the pot.

W. Shakespeare

XXXVIII

That time of year thou may'st in me behold
When yellow leaves, or none, or few, do hang
Upon those boughs which shake against the cold,
Bare ruin'd choirs, where late the sweet birds sang:

In me thou see'st the twilight of such day
As after sunset fadeth in the west,
Which by and by black night doth take away,
Death's second self, that seals up all in rest:

In me thou see'st the glowing of such fire,
That on the ashes of his youth doth lie
As the death-bed whereon it must expire,
Consumed with that which it was nourish'd by:

– This thou perceiv'st, which makes thy love more strong,
To love that well which thou must leave ere long.

W. Shakespeare

XXXIX
MEMORY

When to the sessions of sweet silent thought
I summon up remembrance of things past,
I sigh the lack of many a thing I sought,
And with old woes new wail my dear time's waste;

Then can I drown an eye, unused to flow,
For precious friends hid in death's dateless night,
And weep afresh love's long-since-cancell'd woe,
And moan the expense of many a vanish'd sight.

Then can I grieve at grievances foregone,
And heavily from woe to woe tell o'er
The sad account of fore-bemoanèd moan,
Which I new pay as if not paid before:

– But if the while I think on thee, dear Friend,
All losses are restored, and sorrows end.

W. Shakespeare

XL
SLEEP
[*Added 1883*]

Come, Sleep: O Sleep! the certain knot of peace,
The baiting-place of wit, the balm of woe,
The poor man's wealth, the prisoner's release,
Th' indifferent judge between the high and low;

With shield of proof shield me from out the prease
Of those fierce darts Despair at me doth throw:
O make in me those civil wars to cease;
I will good tribute pay, if thou do so.

Take thou of me smooth pillows, sweetest bed,
A chamber deaf of noise and blind of light,
A rosy garland and a weary head:
And if these things, as being thine in right,

Move not thy heavy grace, thou shalt in me,
Livelier than elsewhere, Stella's image see.

Sir P. Sidney

XLI
REVOLUTIONS

Like as the waves make towards the pebbled shore
So do our minutes hasten to their end;
Each changing place with that which goes before,
In sequent toil all forwards do contend.

Nativity, once in the main of light,
Crawls to maturity, wherewith being crown'd,
Crooked eclipses 'gainst his glory fight,
And Time that gave, doth now his gift confound.

Time doth transfix the flourish set on youth,
And delves the parallels in beauty's brow;
Feeds on the rarities of nature's truth,
And nothing stands but for his scythe to mow: –

And yet, to times in hope, my verse shall stand
Praising Thy worth, despite his cruel hand.

W. Shakespeare

XLII

Farewell! thou art too dear for my possessing,
And like enough thou know'st thy estimate:
The charter of thy worth gives thee releasing;
My bonds in thee are all determinate.

For how do I hold thee but by thy granting?
And for that riches where is my deserving?
The cause of this fair gift in me is wanting,
And so my patent back again is swerving.

Thyself thou gav'st, thy own worth then not knowing,
Or me, to whom thou gav'st it, else mistaking;
So thy great gift, upon misprision growing,
Comes home again, on better judgment making.

Thus have I had thee as a dream doth flatter;
In sleep, a king; but waking, no such matter.

W. Shakespeare

XLIII
THE LIFE WITHOUT PASSION

They that have power to hurt, and will do none,
That do not do the thing they most do show,
Who, moving others, are themselves as stone,
Unmovéd, cold, and to temptation slow, –

They rightly do inherit heaven's graces,
And husband nature's riches from expense;
They are the lords and owners of their faces,
Others, but stewards of their excellence.

The summer's flower is to the summer sweet,
Though to itself it only live and die;
But if that flower with base infection meet,
The basest weed outbraves his dignity:

For sweetest things turn sourest by their deeds;
Lilies that fester smell far worse than weeds.

W. Shakespeare

XLIV
THE LOVER'S APPEAL

And wilt thou leave me thus?
Say nay! say nay! for shame,
To save thee from the blame
Of all my grief and grame.
And wilt thou leave me thus?
Say nay! say nay!

And wilt thou leave me thus,
That hath loved thee so long
In wealth and woe among:
And is thy heart so strong
As for to leave me thus?
Say nay! say nay!

And wilt thou leave me thus,
That hath given thee my heart
Never for to depart
Neither for pain nor smart:
And wilt thou leave me thus?
Say nay! say nay!

And wilt thou leave me thus,
And have no more pity
Of him that loveth thee?
Alas! thy cruelty!
And wilt thou leave me thus?
Say nay! say nay!

Sir T. Wyat

XLV
THE NIGHTINGALE

As it fell upon a day
In the merry month of May,
Sitting in a pleasant shade
Which a grove of myrtles made,

Beasts did leap and birds did sing,
Trees did grow and plants did spring;
Every thing did banish moan
Save the Nightingale alone.
She, poor bird, as all forlorn,
Lean'd her breast up-till a thorn,
And there sung the dolefull'st ditty
That to hear it was great pity.
Fie, fie, fie, now would she cry;
Teru, teru, by and by:
That to hear her so complain
Scarce I could from tears refrain;
For her griefs so lively shown
Made me think upon mine own.
– Ah, thought I, thou mourn'st in vain,
None takes pity on thy pain:
Senseless trees, they cannot hear thee,
Ruthless beasts, they will not cheer thee;
King Pandion, he is dead,
All thy friends are lapp'd in lead:
All thy fellow birds do sing
Careless of thy sorrowing:
Even so, poor bird, like thee
None alive will pity me.

R. Barnefield

XLVI

Care-charmer Sleep, son of the sable Night,
Brother to Death, in silent darkness born,
Relieve my languish, and restore the light;
With dark forgetting of my care return.

And let the day be time enough to mourn
The shipwreck of my ill-adventured youth:
Let waking eyes suffice to wail their scorn,
Without the torment of the night's untruth.

Cease, dreams, the images of day-desires,
To model forth the passions of the morrow;
Never let rising Sun approve you liars,
To add more grief to aggravate my sorrow:

Still let me sleep, embracing clouds in vain,
And never wake to feel the day's disdain.

S. Daniel

XLVII
[Added 1890]

The nightingale, as soon as April bringeth
   Unto her rested sense a perfect waking,
While late-bare earth, proud of new clothing, springeth,
   Sings out her woes, a thorn her song-book making;
      And mournfully bewailing,
      Her throat in tunes expresseth
      What grief her breast oppresseth
For Tereus' force on her chaste will prevailing.

O Philomela fair, O take some gladness,
That here is juster cause of plaintful sadness:
      Thine earth now springs, mine fadeth;
Thy thorn without, my thorn my heart invadeth.

Alas, she hath no other cause of anguish
   But Tereus' love, on her by strong hand wroken,
Wherein she suffering, all her spirits languish,
   Full womanlike complains her will was broken.
      But I, who, daily craving,
      Cannot have to content me,
      Have more cause to lament me,
Since wanting is more woe than too much having.

O Philomela fair, O take some gladness
That here is juster cause of plaintful sadness:
    Thine earth now springs, mine fadeth;
Thy thorn without, my thorn my heart invadeth.

Sir P. Sidney

XLVIII
FRUSTRA

Take, O take those lips away
That so sweetly were forsworn,
And those eyes, the break of day,
Lights that do mislead the morn:
But my kisses bring again,
    Bring again –
Seals of love, but seal'd in vain,
    Seal'd in vain!

W. Shakespeare

XLIX
LOVE'S FAREWELL

Since there's no help, come let us kiss and part, –
Nay I have done, you get no more of me;
And I am glad, yea, glad with all my heart,
That thus so cleanly I myself can free;

Shake hands for ever, cancel all our vows,
And when we meet at any time again,
Be it not seen in either of our brows
That we one jot of former love retain.

Now at the last gasp of love's latest breath,
When his pulse failing, passion speechless lies,
When faith is kneeling by his bed of death,
And innocence is closing up his eyes,

– Now if thou would'st, when all have given him over,
From death to life thou might'st him yet recover!

M. Drayton

L

IN IMAGINE PERTRANSIT HOMO
[*Added 1890*]

Follow thy fair sun, unhappy shadow!
  Though thou be black as night
  And she made all of light,
Yet follow thy fair sun, unhappy shadow!

Follow her, whose light thy light depriveth!
  Though here thou liv'st disgraced,
  And she in heaven is placed,
Yet follow her whose light the world reviveth!

Follow those pure beams, whose beauty burneth,
  That so have scorchéd thee
  As thou still black must be
Till her kind beams thy black to brightness turneth.

Follow her, while yet her glory shineth!
  There comes a luckless night
  That will dim all her light;
– And this the black unhappy shade divineth.

Follow still, since so thy fates ordainéd!
  The sun must have his shade,
  Till both at once do fade, –
The sun still proved, the shadow still disdainéd.

T. Campion

LI
BLIND LOVE

O me! what eyes hath Love put in my head
Which have no correspondence with true sight:
Or if they have, where is my judgment fled
That censures falsely what they see aright?

If that be fair whereon my false eyes dote,
What means the world to say it is not so?
If it be not, then love doth well denote
Love's eye is not so true as all men's: No,

How can it? O how can love's eye be true,
That is so vex'd with watching and with tears?
No marvel then though I mistake my view:
The sun itself sees not till heaven clears.

O cunning Love! with tears thou keep'st me blind,
Lest eyes well-seeing thy foul faults should find!

W. Shakespeare

LII
[*Added 1890*]

Sleep, angry beauty, sleep and fear not me!
    For who a sleeping lion dares provoke?
It shall suffice me here to sit and see
    Those lips shut up that never kindly spoke:
What sight can more content a lover's mind
Than beauty seeming harmless, if not kind?

My words have charm'd her, for secure she sleeps,
    Though guilty much of wrong done to my love;
And in her slumber, see! she close-eyed weeps:
    Dreams often more than waking passions move.
Plead, Sleep, my cause, and make her soft like thee:
That she in peace may wake and pity me.

T. Campion

LIII

THE UNFAITHFUL SHEPHERDESS

While that the sun with his beams hot
Scorchéd the fruits in vale and mountain,
Philon the shepherd, late forgot,
Sitting beside a crystal fountain,
   In shadow of a green oak tree
   Upon his pipe this song play'd he:
Adieu, Love, adieu, Love, untrue Love,
Untrue Love, untrue Love, adieu, Love;
Your mind is light, soon lost for new love.

So long as I was in your sight
I was your heart, your soul, and treasure;
And evermore you sobb'd and sigh'd
Burning in flames beyond all measure:
   – Three days endured your love to me,
   And it was lost in other three!
Adieu, Love, adieu, Love, untrue Love,
Untrue Love, untrue Love, adieu, Love;
Your mind is light, soon lost for new love.

Another Shepherd you did see
To whom your heart was soon enchainéd;
Full soon your love was leapt from me,
Full soon my place he had obtainéd.
   Soon came a third, your love to win,
   And we were out and he was in.
Adieu, Love, adieu, Love, untrue Love,
Untrue Love, untrue Love, adieu, Love;
Your mind is light, soon lost for new love.

Sure you have made me passing glad
That you your mind so soon removéd,
Before that I the leisure had
To choose you for my best belovéd:
   For all your love was past and done
   Two days before it was begun: –
Adieu, Love, adieu, Love, untrue Love,
Untrue Love, untrue Love, adieu, Love;
Your mind is light, soon lost for new love.

Anon.

LIV
ADVICE TO A LOVER
[*Added 1890*]

The sea hath many thousand sands,
The sun hath motes as many;
The sky is full of stars, and Love
As full of woes as any:
Believe me, that do know the elf,
And make no trial by thyself!

It is in truth a pretty toy
For babes to play withal: –
But O! the honeys of our youth
Are oft our age's gall!
Self-proof in time will make thee know
He was a prophet told thee so;

A prophet that, Cassandra-like,
Tells truth without belief;
For headstrong Youth will run his race,
Although his goal be grief: –
Love's Martyr, when his heat is past,
Proves Care's Confessor at the last.

Anon.

A RENUNCIATION
[*Dropped 1891*]

If women could be fair, and yet not fond,
Or that their love were firm, not fickle still,
I would not marvel that they make men bond
By service long to purchase their good will;
But when I see how frail those creatures are,
I muse that men forget themselves so far.

To mark the choice they make, and how they change,
How oft from Phoebus they do flee to Pan;
Unsettled still, like haggards wild they range,
These gentle birds that fly from man to man;
Who would not scorn and shake them from the fist,
And let them fly, fair fools, which way they list?

Yet for disport we fawn and flatter both,
To pass the time when nothing else can please,
And train them to our lure with subtle oath,
Till, weary of their wiles, ourselves we ease;
And then we say when we their fancy try,
To play with fools, O what a fool was I!

E. Vere, Earl of Oxford

LV
A RENUNCIATION
[*Added 1891*]

Thou art not fair, for all thy red and white,
   For all those rosy ornaments in thee, –
Thou art not sweet, though made of mere delight,
   Nor fair, nor sweet – unless thou pity me!
I will not soothe thy fancies; thou shalt prove
That beauty is no beauty without love.

– Yet love not me, nor seek not to allure
  My thoughts with beauty, were it more divine:
Thy smiles and kisses I cannot endure,
  I'll not be wrapp'd up in those arms of thine:
– Now show it, if thou be a woman right –
Embrace and kiss and love me in despite!

T. Campion

LVI

Blow, blow, thou winter wind,
Thou art not so unkind
As man's ingratitude;
Thy tooth is not so keen
Because thou art not seen,
Although thy breath be rude.
Heigh ho! sing heigh ho! unto the green holly:
Most friendship is feigning, most loving mere folly:
Then, heigh ho! the holly!
This life is most jolly.

Freeze, freeze, thou bitter sky,
Thou dost not bite so nigh
As benefits forgot:
Though thou the waters warp,
Thy sting is not so sharp
As friend remember'd not.
Heigh ho! sing heigh ho! unto the green holly:
Most friendship is feigning, most loving mere folly:
Then, heigh ho! the holly!
This life is most jolly.

W. Shakespeare

LVII
A SWEET LULLABY
[*Added 1891*]

Come little babe, come silly soul,
Thy father's shame, thy mother's grief,
Born as I doubt to all our dole,
And to thy self unhappy chief:
     Sing Lullaby and lap it warm,
     Poor soul that thinks no creature harm.

Thou little think'st and less dost know,
The cause of this thy mother's moan,
Thou want'st the wit to wail her woe,
And I myself am all alone:
     Why dost thou weep? why dost thou wail?
     And knowest not yet what thou dost ail.

Come little wretch, ah silly heart,
Mine only joy, what can I more?
If there be any wrong thy smart
That may the destinies implore:
     'Twas I, I say, against my will,
     I wail the time, but be thou still.

And dost thou smile, oh thy sweet face!
Would God Himself He might thee see,
No doubt thou would'st soon purchase grace,
I know right well, for thee and me:
     But come to mother, babe, and play,
     For father false is fled away.

Sweet boy, if it by fortune chance,
Thy father home again to send,
If death do strike me with his lance,
Yet mayst thou me to him commend:
     If any ask thy mother's name,
     Tell how by love she purchased blame.

Then will his gentle heart soon yield,
I know him of a noble mind,
Although a Lion in the field,
A Lamb in town thou shalt him find:
    Ask blessing, babe, be not afraid,
    His sugar'd words hath me betray'd.

Then mayst thou joy and be right glad,
Although in woe I seem to moan,
Thy father is no rascal lad,
A noble youth of blood and bone:
    His glancing looks, if he once smile,
    Right honest women may beguile.

Come, little boy, and rock asleep,
Sing lullaby and be thou still,
I that can do nought else but weep,
Will sit by thee and wail my fill:
    God bless my babe, and lullaby
    From this thy father's quality!

Anon.

LVIII
[*Added 1890*]

With how sad steps, O Moon, thou climb'st the skies!
How silently, and with how wan a face!
What, may it be that e'en in heavenly place
That busy archer his sharp arrows tries!

Sure, if that long-with-love-acquainted eyes
Can judge of love, thou feel'st a lover's case,
I read it in thy looks; thy languish'd grace,
To me, that feel the like, thy state descries.

Then, e'en of fellowship, O Moon, tell me,
Is constant love deem'd there but want of wit?
Are beauties there as proud as here they be?
Do they above love to be loved, and yet

Those lovers scorn whom that love doth possess?
Do they call virtue, there, ungratefulness?

Sir P. Sidney

LIX

O CRUDELIS AMOR
[*Added 1890*]

When thou must home to shades of underground,
And there arrived, a new admired guest,
The beauteous spirits do engirt thee round,
White Iopé, blithe Helen, and the rest,
To hear the stories of thy finish'd love
From that smooth tongue whose music hell can move;

Then wilt thou speak of banqueting delights,
Of masques and revels which sweet youth did make,
Of tourneys and great challenges of Knights,
And all these triumphs for thy beauty's sake:
When thou hast told these honours done to thee,
Then tell, O tell, how thou didst murder me!

T. Campion

LX

SEPHESTIA'S SONG TO HER CHILD
[*Added 1891*]

Weep not, my wanton, smile upon my knee;
When thou art old there's grief enough for thee.
  Mother's wag, pretty boy,
  Father's sorrow, father's joy;
  When thy father first did see
  Such a boy by him and me,
  He was glad, I was woe,
  Fortune changéd made him so,
  When he left his pretty boy
  Last his sorrow, first his joy.

Weep not, my wanton, smile upon my knee,
When thou art old there's grief enough for thee.
  Streaming tears that never stint,
  Like pearl drops from a flint,
  Fell by course from his eyes,
  That one another's place supplies;
  Thus he grieved in every part,
  Tears of blood fell from his heart,
  When he left his pretty boy,
  Father's sorrow, father's joy.

Weep not, my wanton, smile upon my knee,
When thou art old, there's grief enough for thee.
  The wanton smiled, father wept,
  Mother cried, baby leapt;
  More he crow'd, more we cried,
  Nature could not sorrow hide:
  He must go, he must kiss
  Child and mother, baby bless,
  For he left his pretty boy,
  Father's sorrow, father's joy.
Weep not, my wanton, smile upon my knee,
When thou art old, there's grief enough for thee.

R. Greene

LXI
A LAMENT

My thoughts hold mortal strife;
I do detest my life,
And with lamenting cries
Peace to my soul to bring
Oft call that prince which here doth monarchize:
– But he, grim grinning King,
Who caitiffs scorns, and doth the blest surprize,
Late having deck'd with beauty's rose his tomb,
Disdains to crop a weed, and will not come.

W. Drummond

LXII
DIRGE OF LOVE

Come away, come away, Death,
And in sad cypres let me be laid;
Fly away, fly away, breath;
I am slain by a fair cruel maid.
My shroud of white, stuck all with yew,
    O prepare it!
My part of death, no one so true
    Did share it.

Not a flower, not a flower sweet
On my black coffin let there be strown;
Not a friend, not a friend greet
My poor corpse, where my bones shall be thrown:
A thousand thousand sighs to save,
    Lay me, O where
Sad true lover never find my grave,
    To weep there.

W. Shakespeare

LXIII
TO HIS LUTE

My lute, be as thou wert when thou didst grow
With thy green mother in some shady grove,
When immelodious winds but made thee move,
And birds their ramage did on thee bestow.

Since that dear Voice which did thy sounds approve,
Which wont in such harmonious strains to flow,
Is reft from Earth to tune those spheres above,
What art thou but a harbinger of woe?

Thy pleasing notes be pleasing notes no more,
But orphans' wailings to the fainting ear;
Each stroke a sigh, each sound draws forth a tear;
For which be silent as in woods before:

Or if that any hand to touch thee deign,
Like widow'd turtle, still her loss complain.

W. Drummond

LXIV
FIDELE

Fear no more the heat o' the sun
    Nor the furious winter's rages;
Thou thy worldly task hast done,
    Home art gone and ta'en thy wages:
Golden lads and girls all must,
As chimney-sweepers, come to dust.

Fear no more the frown o' the great,
    Thou art past the tyrant's stroke;
Care no more to clothe and eat;
    To thee the reed is as the oak:
The sceptre, learning, physic, must
All follow this, and come to dust.

Fear no more the lightning-flash
    Nor the all-dreaded thunder-stone;
Fear not slander, censure rash;
    Thou hast finish'd joy and moan:
All lovers young, all lovers must
Consign to thee, and come to dust.

               W. Shakespeare

LXV
A SEA DIRGE

Full fathom five thy father lies:
    Of his bones are coral made;
Those are pearls that were his eyes:
    Nothing of him that doth fade,
But doth suffer a sea-change
Into something rich and strange.
Sea-nymphs hourly ring his knell:
    Hark! now I hear them, –
        Ding, dong, bell.

               W. Shakespeare

LXVI
A LAND DIRGE

Call for the robin-redbreast and the wren,
Since o'er shady groves they hover
And with leaves and flowers do cover
The friendless bodies of unburied men.
Call unto his funeral dole
The ant, the field-mouse, and the mole

To rear him hillocks that shall keep him warm
And (when gay tombs are robb'd) sustain no harm;
But keep the wolf far thence, that's foe to men,
For with his nails he'll dig them up again.

J. Webster

LXVII
POST MORTEM

If Thou survive my well-contented day
When that churl Death my bones with dust shall cover,
And shalt by fortune once more re-survey
These poor rude lines of thy deceaséd lover;

Compare them with the bettering of the time,
And though they be outstripp'd by every pen,
Reserve them for my love, not for their rhyme
Exceeded by the height of happier men.

O then vouchsafe me but this loving thought –
'Had my friend's Muse grown with this growing age,
A dearer birth than this his love had brought,
To march in ranks of better equipage:

But since he died, and poets better prove,
Theirs for their style I'll read, his for his love.'

W. Shakespeare

LXVIII
THE TRIUMPH OF DEATH

No longer mourn for me when I am dead
Than you shall hear the surly sullen bell
Give warning to the world, that I am fled
From this vile world, with vilest worms to dwell;

Nay, if you read this line, remember not
The hand that writ it; for I love you so,
That I in your sweet thoughts would be forgot
If thinking on me then should make you woe.

O if, I say, you look upon this verse
When I perhaps compounded am with clay,
Do not so much as my poor name rehearse,
But let your love even with my life decay;

Lest the wise world should look into your moan,
And mock you with me after I am gone.

W. Shakespeare

LXIX
YOUNG LOVE

Tell me where is Fancy bred,
Or in the heart, or in the head?
How begot, how nourishéd?
      Reply, reply.

It is engender'd in the eyes;
With gazing fed; and Fancy dies
In the cradle where it lies:
Let us all ring Fancy's knell;
I'll begin it, – Ding, dong, bell.
      – Ding, dong, bell.

W. Shakespeare

LXX
A DILEMMA
[*Added 1890*]

Lady, when I behold the roses sprouting
    Which clad in damask mantles deck the arbours,
        And then behold your lips where sweet love harbours,
My eyes present me with a double doubting:
For viewing both alike, hardly my mind supposes
Whether the roses be your lips, or your lips the roses.

Anon.

LXXI
ROSALYND'S MADRIGAL
[*Added 1891*]

Love in my bosom, like a bee,
            Doth suck his sweet;
Now with his wings he plays with me,
            Now with his feet.
    Within mine eyes he makes his nest,
    His bed amidst my tender breast;
    My kisses are his daily feast,
    And yet he robs me of my rest:
            Ah! wanton, will ye?

And if I sleep, then percheth he
            With pretty flight,
And makes his pillow of my knee
            The livelong night.
    Strike I my lute, he tunes the string;
    He music plays if so I sing;
    He lends me every lovely thing,
    Yet cruel he my heart doth sting:
            Whist, wanton, will ye?

Else I with roses every day
            Will whip you hence,
And bind you, when you long to play,
            For your offence;

I'll shut my eyes to keep you in;
I'll make you fast it for your sin;
I'll count your power not worth a pin;
– Alas! what hereby shall I win,
   If he gainsay me?

What if I beat the wanton boy
   With many a rod?
He will repay me with annoy,
   Because a god.
Then sit thou safely on my knee,
And let thy bower my bosom be;
Lurk in mine eyes, I like of thee,
O Cupid! so thou pity me,
   Spare not, but play thee!

       T. Lodge

LXXII
CUPID AND CAMPASPE

Cupid and my Campaspé play'd
At cards for kisses; Cupid paid:
He stakes his quiver, bow, and arrows,
His mother's doves, and team of sparrows;
Loses them too; then down he throws
The coral of his lip, the rose
Growing on's cheek (but none knows how);
With these, the crystal of his brow,
And then the dimple on his chin;
All these did my Campaspé win:
And last he set her both his eyes –
She won, and Cupid blind did rise.
  O Love! has she done this to thee?
  What shall, alas! become of me?

       J. Lylye

LXXIII

Pack, clouds, away, and welcome day,
   With night we banish sorrow;
Sweet air blow soft, mount larks aloft
   To give my Love good-morrow!
Wings from the wind to please her mind
   Notes from the lark I'll borrow;
Bird, prune thy wing, nightingale sing,
   To give my Love good-morrow;
      To give my Love good-morrow
      Notes from them both I'll borrow.

Wake from thy nest, Robin-red-breast,
    Sing, birds, in every furrow;
And from each hill, let music shrill
    Give my fair Love good-morrow!
Blackbird and thrush in every bush,
    Stare, linnet, and cock-sparrow!
You pretty elves, amongst yourselves
    Sing my fair Love good-morrow;
      To give my Love good-morrow
      Sing, birds, in every furrow!

T. Heywood

LXXIV
PROTHALAMION

Calm was the day, and through the trembling air
Sweet-breathing Zephyrus did softly play –
A gentle spirit, that lightly did delay
Hot Titan's beams, which then did glister fair;
When I, (whom sullen care,
Through discontent of my long fruitless stay
In princes' court, and expectation vain
Of idle hopes, which still do fly away

Like empty shadows, did afflict my brain)
Walk'd forth to ease my pain
Along the shore of silver-streaming Thames;
Whose rutty bank, the which his river hems,
Was painted all with variable flowers,
And all the meads adorn'd with dainty gems
Fit to deck maidens' bowers,
And crown their paramours
Against the bridal day, which is not long:
    Sweet Thames! run softly, till I end my song.

There in a meadow by the river's side
A flock of nymphs I chancéd to espy,
All lovely daughters of the flood thereby,
With goodly greenish locks all loose untied
As each had been a bride;
And each one had a little wicker basket
Made of fine twigs, entrailéd curiously,
In which they gather'd flowers to fill their flasket,
And with fine fingers cropt full feateously
The tender stalks on high.
Of every sort which in that meadow grew
They gather'd some; the violet, pallid blue,
The little daisy that at evening closes,
The virgin lily and the primrose true,
With store of vermeil roses,
To deck their bridegrooms' posies
Against the bridal day, which was not long:
    Sweet Thames! run softly, till I end my song.

With that I saw two Swans of goodly hue
Come softly swimming down along the Lee;
Two fairer birds I yet did never see;
The snow which doth the top of Pindus strow
Did never whiter show,
Nor Jove himself, when he a swan would be
For love of Leda, whiter did appear;
Yet Leda was (they say) as white as he,

Yet not so white as these, nor nothing near;
So purely white they were
That even the gentle stream, the which them bare,
Seem'd foul to them, and bade his billows spare
To wet their silken feathers, lest they might
Soil their fair plumes with water not so fair,
And mar their beauties bright
That shone as Heaven's light
Against their bridal day, which was not long:
    Sweet Thames! run softly, till I end my song.

Eftsoons the nymphs, which now had flowers their fill,
Ran all in haste to see that silver brood
As they came floating on the crystal flood;
Whom when they saw, they stood amazéd still
Their wondering eyes to fill;
Them seem'd they never saw a sight so fair
Of fowls, so lovely, that they sure did deem
Them heavenly born, or to be that same pair
Which through the sky draw Venus' silver team;
For sure they did not seem
To be begot of any earthly seed,
But rather Angels, or of Angels' breed;
Yet were they bred of summer's heat, they say,
In sweetest season, when each flower and weed
The earth did fresh array;
So fresh they seem'd as day,
Ev'n as their bridal day, which was not long:
    Sweet Thames! run softly, till I end my song.

Then forth they all out of their baskets drew
Great store of flowers, the honour of the field,
That to the sense did fragrant odours yield,
All which upon those goodly birds they threw
And all the waves did strew,
That like old Peneus' waters they did seem
When down along by pleasant Tempe's shore
Scatter'd with flowers, through Thessaly they stream,

That they appear, through lilies' plenteous store,
Like a bride's chamber-floor.
Two of those nymphs meanwhile two garlands bound
Of freshest flowers which in that mead they found,
The which presenting all in trim array,
Their snowy foreheads therewithal they crown'd;
Whilst one did sing this lay
Prepared against that day,
Against their bridal day, which was not long:
   Sweet Thames! run softly, till I end my song.

'Ye gentle birds! the world's fair ornament,
And Heaven's glory, whom this happy hour
Doth lead unto your lovers' blissful bower,
Joy may you have, and gentle heart's content
Of your love's couplement;
And let fair Venus, that is queen of love,
With her heart-quelling son upon you smile,
Whose smile, they say, hath virtue to remove
All love's dislike, and friendship's faulty guile
For ever to assoil.
Let endless peace your steadfast hearts accord,
And blessèd plenty wait upon your board;
And let your bed with pleasures chaste abound,
That fruitful issue may to you afford
Which may your foes confound,
And make your joys redound
Upon your bridal day, which is not long:
   Sweet Thames! run softly, till I end my song.'

So ended she; and all the rest around
To her redoubled that her undersong,
Which said their bridal day should not be long:
And gentle Echo from the neighbour ground
Their accents did resound.
So forth those joyous birds did pass along
Adown the Lee that to them murmur'd low,
As he would speak but that he lack'd a tongue;

Yet did by signs his glad affection show,
Making his stream run slow.
And all the fowl which in his flood did dwell
'Gan flock about these twain, that did excel
The rest, so far as Cynthia doth shend
The lesser stars. So they, enrangéd well,
Did on those two attend,
And their best service lend
Against their wedding day, which was not long:
   Sweet Thames! run softly, till I end my song.

At length they all to merry London came,
To merry London, my most kindly nurse,
That to me gave this life's first native source,
Though from another place I take my name,
An house of ancient fame:
There when they came whereas those bricky towers
The which on Thames' broad agéd back do ride,
Where now the studious lawyers have their bowers,
There whilome wont the Templar-knights to bide,
Till they decay'd through pride;
Next whereunto there stands a stately place,
Where oft I gainéd gifts and goodly grace
Of that great lord, which therein wont to dwell,
Whose want too well now feels my friendless case;
But ah! here fits not well
Old woes, but joys to tell
Against the bridal day, which is not long:
   Sweet Thames! run softly, till I end my song.

Yet therein now doth lodge a noble peer,
Great England's glory and the world's wide wonder,
Whose dreadful name late through all Spain did thunder,
And Hercules' two pillars standing near
Did make to quake and fear:
Fair branch of honour, flower of chivalry!
That fillest England with thy triumphs' fame
Joy have thou of thy noble victory,

And endless happiness of thine own name
That promiseth the same;
That through thy prowess and victorious arms
Thy country may be freed from foreign harms,
And great Elisa's glorious name may ring
Through all the world, fill'd with thy wide alarms,
Which some brave Muse may sing
To ages following,
Upon the bridal day, which is not long:
   Sweet Thames! run softly, till I end my song.

From those high towers this noble lord issúing
Like radiant Hesper, when his golden hair
In th' ocean billows he hath bathéd fair,
Descended to the river's open viewing
With a great train ensuing.
Above the rest were goodly to be seen
Two gentle knights of lovely face and feature,
Beseeming well the bower of any queen,
With gifts of wit and ornaments of nature,
Fit for so goodly stature,
That like the twins of Jove they seem'd in sight
Which deck the baldric of the Heavens bright;
They two, forth pacing to the river's side,
Received those two fair brides, their love's delight;
Which, at th' appointed tide,
Each one did make his bride
Against their bridal day, which is not long:
   Sweet Thames! run softly, till I end my song.

E. Spenser

LXXV
THE HAPPY HEART

Art thou poor, yet hast thou golden slumbers?
      O sweet content!
Art thou rich, yet is thy mind perplex'd?
      O punishment!
Dost thou laugh to see how fools are vex'd
To add to golden numbers, golden numbers?
O sweet content! O sweet, O sweet content!
  Work apace, apace, apace, apace;
  Honest labour bears a lovely face;
Then hey nonny nonny, hey nonny nonny!

Canst drink the waters of the crispéd spring?
      O sweet content!
Swimm'st thou in wealth, yet sink'st in thine own tears?
      O punishment!
Then he that patiently want's burden bears
No burden bears, but is a king, a king!
O sweet content! O sweet, O sweet content!
  Work apace, apace, apace, apace;
  Honest labour bears a lovely face;
Then hey nonny nonny, hey nonny nonny!

T. Dekker

LXXVI
SIC TRANSIT
[*Added 1890*]

Come, cheerful day, part of my life to me;
  For while thou view'st me with thy fading light
Part of my life doth still depart with thee,
  And I still onward haste to my last night:
Time's fatal wings do ever forward fly —
So every day we live a day we die.

But O ye nights, ordain'd for barren rest,
   How are my days deprived of life in you
When heavy sleep my soul hath dispossest,
   By feignéd death life sweetly to renew!
Part of my life, in that, you life deny:
So every day we live, a day we die.

                  T. Campion

LXXVII

This Life, which seems so fair,
Is like a bubble blown up in the air
By sporting children's breath,
Who chase it everywhere
And strive who can most motion it bequeath.
And though it sometimes seem of its own might
Like to an eye of gold to be fix'd there,
And firm to hover in that empty height,
That only is because it is so light.
– But in that pomp it doth not long appear;
For when 'tis most admired, in a thought,
Because it erst was nought, it turns to nought.

                  W. Drummond

LXXVIII
SOUL AND BODY

Poor Soul, the centre of my sinful earth,
[Foil'd by] those rebel powers that thee array,
Why doth thou pine within, and suffer dearth,
Painting thy outward walls so costly gay?

Why so large cost, having so short a lease,
Dost thou upon thy fading mansion spend?
Shall worms, inheritors of this excess,
Eat up thy charge? is this thy body's end?

Then, Soul, live thou upon thy servant's loss,
And let that pine to aggravate thy store;
Buy terms divine in selling hours of dross;
Within be fed, without be rich no more: –

So shalt thou feed on death, that feeds on men,
And death once dead, there's no more dying then.

W. Shakespeare

LIFE
[*Dropped 1890*]

The World's a bubble, and the Life of Man
        Less than a span:
In his conception wretched, from the womb
        So to the tomb;
Curst from his cradle, and brought up to years
        With cares and fears.
Who then to frail mortality shall trust,
But limns on water, or but writes in dust.

Yet whilst with sorrow here we live opprest,
        What life is best?
Courts are but only superficial schools
        To dandle fools:
The rural parts are turn'd into a den
        Of savage men:
And where's a city from foul vice so free,
But may be term'd the worst of all the three?

Domestic cares afflict the husband's bed,
        Or pains his head:
Those that live single, take it for a curse,
        Or do things worse:
Some would have children: those that have them,
          moan
        Or wish them gone:
What is it, then, to have, or have no wife,
But single thraldom, or a double strife?

Our own affections still at home to please
            Is a disease:
To cross the seas to any foreign soil,
            Peril and toil:
Wars with their noise affright us; when they cease,
            We are worse in peace; –
What then remains, but that we still should cry
For being born, or, being born, to die?

Lord Bacon

LXXIX
[*Added 1890*]

The man of life upright,
    Whose guiltless heart is free
From all dishonest deeds,
    Or thought of vanity;

The man whose silent days
    In harmless joys are spent,
Whom hopes cannot delude
    Nor sorrow discontent:

That man needs neither towers
    Nor armour for defence,
Nor secret vaults to fly
    From thunder's violence:

He only can behold
    With unaffrighted eyes
The horrors of the deep
    And terrors of the skies.

Thus scorning all the cares
 That fate or fortune brings,
He makes the heaven his book,
 His wisdom heavenly things;

Good thoughts his only friends,
 His wealth a well-spent age,
The earth his sober inn
 And quiet pilgrimage.

T. Campion

LXXX
THE LESSONS OF NATURE

Of this fair volume which we World do name
If we the sheets and leaves could turn with care,
Of Him who it corrects, and did it frame,
We clear might read the art and wisdom rare:

Find out His power which wildest powers doth tame,
His providence extending everywhere,
His justice which proud rebels doth not spare,
In every page, no period of the same.

But silly we, like foolish children, rest
Well pleased with colour'd vellum, leaves of gold,
Fair dangling ribbands, leaving what is best,
On the great Writer's sense ne'er taking hold;

Or if by chance we stay our minds on aught,
It is some picture on the margin wrought.

W. Drummond

LXXXI

Doth then the world go thus, doth all thus move?
Is this the justice which on earth we find?
Is this that firm decree which all doth bind?
Are these your influences, Powers above?

Those souls which vice's moody mists most blind,
Blind Fortune, blindly, most their friend doth prove;
And they who thee, poor idol Virtue! love,
Ply like a feather toss'd by storm and wind.

Ah! if a Providence doth sway this all
Why should best minds groan under most distress?
Or why should pride humility make thrall,
And injuries the innocent oppress?

Heavens! hinder, stop this fate; or grant a time
When good may have, as well as bad, their prime!

W. Drummond

LXXXII
THE WORLD'S WAY

Tired with all these, for restful death I cry –
As, to behold desert a beggar born,
And needy nothing trimm'd in jollity,
And purest faith unhappily forsworn,

And gilded honour shamefully misplaced,
And maiden virtue rudely strumpeted,
And right perfection wrongfully disgraced,
And strength by limping sway disabled,

And art made tongue-tied by authority,
And folly, doctor-like, controlling skill,
And simple truth miscall'd simplicity,
And captive Good attending captain Ill: –

– Tired with all these, from these would I be gone,
Save that, to die, I leave my Love alone.

W. Shakespeare

LXXXIII
A WISH
[*Added 1890*]

Happy were he could finish forth his fate
In some unhaunted desert, where, obscure
From all society, from love and hate
Of worldly folk, there should he sleep secure;

Then wake again, and yield God ever praise;
Content with hip, with haws, and brambleberry;
In contemplation passing still his days,
And change of holy thoughts to make him merry:

Who, when he dies, his tomb might be the bush
Where harmless robin resteth with the thrush:
              – Happy were he!

R. Devereux, Earl of Essex

LXXXIV
SAINT JOHN BAPTIST

The last and greatest Herald of Heaven's King
Girt with rough skins, hies to the deserts wild,
Among that savage brood the woods forth bring,
Which he more harmless found than man, and mild.

His food was locusts, and what there doth spring,
With honey that from virgin hives distill'd;
Parch'd body, hollow eyes, some uncouth thing
Made him appear, long since from earth exiled.

There burst he forth: All ye whose hopes rely
On God, with me amidst these deserts mourn,
Repent, repent, and from old errors turn!
– Who listen'd to his voice, obey'd his cry?

Only the echoes, which he made relent,
Rung from their flinty caves, Repent! Repent!

W. Drummond

LXXXV
ODE ON THE MORNING OF CHRIST'S NATIVITY

This is the month, and this the happy morn
Wherein the Son of Heaven's Eternal King
Of wedded maid and virgin mother born,
Our great redemption from above did bring;
For so the holy sages once did sing
That He our deadly forfeit should release,
And with His Father work us a perpetual peace.

That glorious Form, that Light unsufferable,
And that far-beaming blaze of Majesty
Wherewith He wont at Heaven's high council-table
To sit the midst of Trinal Unity,
He laid aside; and, here with us to be,
Forsook the courts of everlasting day,
And chose with us a darksome house of mortal clay.

Say, heavenly Muse, shall not thy sacred vein
Afford a present to the Infant God?
Hast thou no verse, no hymn, or solemn strain
To welcome Him to this His new abode,
Now while the heaven, by the sun's team untrod,
Hath took no print of the approaching light,
And all the spangled host keep watch in squadrons bright?

See how from far, upon the eastern road,
The star-led wizards haste with odours sweet:
O run, prevent them with thy humble ode
And lay it lowly at His blessed feet;

Have thou the honour first thy Lord to greet,
And join thy voice unto the Angel quire
From out His secret altar touch'd with hallow'd fire.

THE HYMN

It was the winter wild
While the heaven-born Child
All meanly wrapt in the rude manger lies;
Nature in awe to Him
Had doff'd her gaudy trim,
With her great Master so to sympathize:
It was no season then for her
To wanton with the sun, her lusty paramour.

Only with speeches fair
She woos the gentle air
To hide her guilty front with innocent snow;
And on her naked shame,
Pollute with sinful blame,
The saintly veil of maiden white to throw;
Confounded, that her Maker's eyes
Should look so near upon her foul deformities.

But He, her fears to cease,
Sent down the meek-eyed Peace;
She, crown'd with olive green, came softly sliding
Down through the turning sphere,
His ready harbinger,
With turtle wing the amorous clouds dividing;
And waving wide her myrtle wand,
She strikes a universal peace through sea and land.

No war, or battle's sound
Was heard the world around:
The idle spear and shield were high uphung;
The hookéd chariot stood
Unstain'd with hostile blood;

The trumpet spake not to the arméd throng;
And kings sat still with awful eye,
As if they surely knew their sovran Lord was by.

But peaceful was the night
Wherein the Prince of Light
His reign of peace upon the earth began:
The winds, with wonder whist,
Smoothly the waters kist
Whispering new joys to the mild oceán –
Who now hath quite forgot to rave,
While birds of calm sit brooding on the charméd wave.

The stars, with deep amaze,
Stand fix'd in steadfast gaze,
Bending one way their precious influence;
And will not take their flight
For all the morning light,
Or Lucifer that often warn'd them thence;
But in their glimmering orbs did glow
Until their Lord Himself bespake, and bid them go.

And though the shady gloom
Had given day her room,
The sun himself withheld his wonted speed,
And hid his head for shame,
As his inferior flame
The new-enlighten'd world no more should need;
He saw a greater Sun appear
Than his bright throne, or burning axletree could bear.

The shepherds on the lawn
Or ere the point of dawn
Sate simply chatting in a rustic row;
Full little thought they than
That the mighty Pan
Was kindly come to live with them below;
Perhaps their loves, or else their sheep
Was all that did their silly thoughts so busy keep: –

When such music sweet
Their hearts and ears did greet
As never was by mortal finger strook –
Divinely-warbled voice
Answering the stringéd noise
As all their souls in blissful rapture took:
The air, such pleasure loth to lose,
With thousand echoes still prolongs each heavenly close.

Nature, that heard such sound
Beneath the hollow round
Of Cynthia's seat the airy region thrilling,
Now was almost won
To think her part was done,
And that her reign had here its last fulfilling;
She knew such harmony alone
Could hold all Heaven and Earth in happier union.

At last surrounds their sight
A globe of circular light
That with long beams the shamefaced night array'd;
The helméd Cherubim
And sworded Seraphim
Are seen in glittering ranks with wings display'd,
Harping in loud and solemn quire
With unexpressive notes, to Heaven's new-born Heir.

Such music (as 'tis said)
Before was never made
But when of old the Sons of Morning sung,
While the Creator great
His constellations set
And the well-balanced world on hinges hung;
And cast the dark foundations deep,
And bid the weltering waves their oozy channel keep.

Ring out, ye crystal spheres!
Once bless our human ears,
If ye have power to touch our senses so;

And let your silver chime
Move in melodious time;
And let the bass of heaven's deep organ blow;
And with your ninefold harmony
Make up full consort to the angelic symphony.

For if such holy song
Enwrap our fancy long,
Time will run back, and fetch the age of gold;
And speckled Vanity
Will sicken soon and die,
And leprous Sin will melt from earthly mould;
And Hell itself will pass away,
And leave her dolorous mansions to the peering day.

Yea, Truth and Justice then
Will down return to men,
Orb'd in a rainbow; and, like glories wearing,
Mercy will sit between
Throned in celestial sheen,
With radiant feet the tissued clouds down steering;
And Heaven, as at some festival,
Will open wide the gates of her high palace-hall.

But wisest Fate says No;
This must not yet be so;
The Babe yet lies in smiling infancy
That on the bitter cross
Must redeem our loss;
So both Himself and us to glorify:
Yet first, to those ychain'd in sleep
The wakeful trump of doom must thunder through the deep;

With such a horrid clang
As on Mount Sinai rang
While the red fire and smouldering clouds outbrake:
The aged Earth aghast
With terror of that blast
Shall from the surface to the centre shake,

When, at the world's last sessión,
The dreadful Judge in middle air shall spread His throne.

And then at last our bliss
Full and perfect is,
But now begins; for from this happy day
The old Dragon under ground,
In straiter limits bound,
Not half so far casts his usurpéd sway;
And, wroth to see his kingdom fail,
Swinges the scaly horror of his folded tail.

The Oracles are dumb;
No voice or hideous hum
Runs through the archéd roof in words deceiving.
Apollo from his shrine
Can no more divine,
With hollow shriek the steep of Delphos leaving:
No nightly trance or breathéd spell
Inspires the pale-eyed priest from the prophetic cell.

The lonely mountains o'er
And the resounding shore
A voice of weeping heard, and loud lament;
From haunted spring and dale
Edged with poplar pale
The parting Genius is with sighing sent;
With flower-inwoven tresses torn
The Nymphs in twilight shade of tangled thickets mourn.

In consecrated earth
And on the holy hearth
The Lars and Lemurés moan with midnight plaint;
In urns, and altars round
A drear and dying sound
Affrights the Flamens at their service quaint;
And the chill marble seems to sweat,
While each peculiar Power foregoes his wonted seat.

Peor and Baalim
Forsake their temples dim,
With that twice-batter'd god of Palestine;
And moonéd Ashtaroth
Heaven's queen and mother both,
Now sits not girt with tapers' holy shine;
The Lybic Hammon shrinks his horn:
In vain the Tyrian maids their wounded Thammuz mourn.

And sullen Moloch, fled,
Hath left in shadows dread
His burning idol all of blackest hue;
In vain with cymbals' ring
They call the grisly king,
In dismal dance about the furnace blue;
The brutish gods of Nile as fast,
Isis, and Orus, and the dog Anubis, haste.

Nor is Osiris seen
In Memphian grove, or green,
Trampling the unshower'd grass with lowings loud:
Nor can he be at rest
Within his sacred chest;
Nought but profoundest Hell can be his shroud;
In vain with timbrell'd anthems dark
The sable-stoléd sorcerers bear his worshipt ark.

He feels from Juda's land
The dreaded Infant's hand;
The rays of Bethlehem blind his dusky eyn;
Nor all the gods beside
Longer dare abide,
Not Typhon huge ending in snaky twine:
Our Babe, to show His Godhead true,
Can in His swaddling bands control the damnéd crew.

So, when the sun in bed
Curtain'd with cloudy red
Pillows his chin upon an orient wave,

The flocking shadows pale
Troop to the infernal jail,
Each fetter'd ghost slips to his several grave;
And the yellow-skirted fays
Fly after the night-steeds, leaving their moon-loved maze.

But see! the Virgin blest
Hath laid her Babe to rest;
Time is, our tedious song should here have ending:
Heaven's youngest-teeméd star
Hath fix'd her polish'd car,
Her sleeping Lord with hand-maid lamp attending:
And all about the courtly stable
Bright-harness'd Angels sit in order serviceable.

J. Milton

LXXXVI

SONG FOR ST. CECILIA'S DAY, 1687

From Harmony, from heavenly Harmony
   This universal frame began:
  When Nature underneath a heap
     Of jarring atoms lay
   And could not heave her head,
The tuneful voice was heard from high,
     Arise, ye more than dead!
Then cold and hot and moist and dry
In order to their stations leap,
     And Music's power obey.
From harmony, from heavenly harmony
     This universal frame began:
     From harmony to harmony
Through all the compass of the notes it ran,
The diapason closing full in Man.

What passion cannot Music raise and quell?
     When Jubal struck the chorded shell

His listening brethren stood around,
And, wondering, on their faces fell
To worship that celestial sound.
Less than a god they thought there could not dwell
    Within the hollow of that shell
    That spoke so sweetly and so well.
What passion cannot Music raise and quell?

    The trumpet's loud clangor
      Excites us to arms,
    With shrill notes of anger
      And mortal alarms.
    The double double double beat
      Of the thundering drum
      Cries 'Hark! the foes come;
Charge, charge, 'tis too late to retreat!'

    The soft complaining flute
      In dying notes discovers
    The woes of hopeless lovers,
Whose dirge is whisper'd by the warbling lute.

    Sharp violins proclaim
Their jealous pangs and desperation,
Fury, frantic indignation,
Depth of pains, and height of passion
    For the fair disdainful dame.

But oh! what art can teach,
What human voice can reach
    The sacred organ's praise?
Notes inspiring holy love,
Notes that wing their heavenly ways
    To mend the choirs above.

Orpheus could lead the savage race,
And trees unrooted left their place
    Sequacious of the lyre:
But bright Cecilia raised the wonder higher:

When to her Organ vocal breath was given
An Angel heard, and straight appear'd–
    Mistaking Earth for Heaven.

Grand Chorus

As from the power of sacred lays
    The spheres began to move,
And sung the great Creator's praise
    To all the blest above;
So when the last and dreadful hour
This crumbling pageant shall devour,
The trumpet shall be heard on high,
The dead shall live, the living die,
And Music shall untune the sky.

J. Dryden

LXXXVII
ON THE LATE MASSACRE IN PIEMONT

Avenge, O Lord! Thy slaughter'd saints, whose bones
Lie scatter'd on the Alpine mountains cold;
Even them who kept Thy truth so pure of old
When all our fathers worshipt stocks and stones,

Forget not: In Thy book record their groans
Who were Thy sheep, and in their ancient fold
Slain by the bloody Piemontese, that roll'd
Mother with infant down the rocks. Their moans

The vales redoubled to the hills, and they
To Heaven. Their martyr'd blood and ashes sow
O'er all the Italian fields, where still doth sway

The triple Tyrant: that from these may grow
A hundred-fold, who, having learnt Thy way,
Early may fly the Babylonian woe.

J. Milton

HORATIAN ODE UPON CROMWELL'S RETURN FROM IRELAND

The forward youth that would appear,
Must now forsake his Muses dear,
    Nor in the shadows sing
    His numbers languishing.

'Tis time to leave the books in dust,
And oil the unuséd armour's rust,
    Removing from the wall
    The corslet of the hall.

So restless Cromwell could not cease
In the inglorious arts of peace,
    But through adventurous war
    Urgéd his active star:

And like the three-fork'd lightning, first
Breaking the clouds where it was nurst,
    Did thorough his own Side
    His fiery way divide:

For 'tis all one to courage high,
The emulous, or enemy;
    And with such, to enclose
    Is more than to oppose;

Then burning through the air he went
And palaces and temples rent;
    And Caesar's head at last
    Did through his laurels blast.

'Tis madness to resist or blame
The face of angry heaven's flame;
   And if we would speak true,
    Much to the Man is due

Who, from his private gardens, where
He lived reservéd and austere,
    (As if his highest plot
    To plant the bergamot,)

Could by industrious valour climb
To ruin the great work of time,
    And cast the Kingdoms old
    Into another mould;

Though Justice against Fate complain,
And plead the ancient Rights in vain –
    But those do hold or break
    As men are strong or weak;

Nature, that hateth emptiness,
Allows of penetration less,
    And therefore must make room
    Where greater spirits come.

What field of all the civil war
Where his were not the deepest scar?
    And Hampton shows what part
    He had of wiser art,

Where, twining subtle fears with hope,
He wove a net of such a scope
    That Charles himself might chase
    To Carisbrook's narrow case,

That thence the Royal actor borne
The tragic scaffold might adorn:
    While round the arméd bands
    Did clap their bloody hands.

He nothing common did or mean
Upon that memorable scene,
    But with his keener eye
    The axe's edge did try;

Nor call'd the Gods, with vulgar spite,
To vindicate his helpless right;
    But bow'd his comely head
    Down, as upon a bed.

– This was that memorable hour
Which first assured the forcéd power:
    So when they did design
    The Capitol's first line,

A Bleeding Head, where they begun,
Did fright the architects to run;
    And yet in that the State
    Foresaw its happy fate!

And now the Irish are ashamed
To see themselves in one year tamed:
    So much one man can do
    That does both act and know.

They can affirm his praises best,
And have, though overcome, confest
    How good he is, how just
    And fit for highest trust.

Nor yet grown stiffer with command,
But still in the Republic's hand –
    How fit he is to sway
    That can so well obey!

He to the Commons' feet presents
A Kingdom for his first year's rents,
    And (what he may) forbears
    His fame, to make it theirs:

And has his sword and spoils ungirt
To lay them at the Public's skirt.
    So when the falcon high
    Falls heavy from the sky,

She, having kill'd, no more doth search
But on the next green bough to perch,
    Where, when he first does lure,
    The falconer has her sure.

– What may not then our Isle presume
While victory his crest does plume?
    What may not others fear
    If thus he crowns each year?

As Caesar he, ere long, to Gaul,
To Italy an Hannibal,
    And to all States not free
    Shall climacteric be.

The Pict no shelter now shall find
Within his parti-colour'd mind,
    But from this valour sad
    Shrink underneath the plaid –

Happy, if in the tufted brake
The English hunter him mistake,
    Nor lay his hounds in near
    The Caledonian deer.

But Thou, the War's and Fortune's son,
March indefatigably on;
    And for the last effect
    Still keep the sword erect:

Besides the force it has to fright
The spirits of the shady night,
    The same arts that did gain
    A power, must it maintain.

A. Marvell

LXXXIX
LYCIDAS
Elegy on a Friend drowned in the Irish Channel 1637

Yet once more, O ye laurels, and once more
Ye myrtles brown, with ivy never sere,
I come to pluck your berries harsh and crude,
And with forced fingers rude
Shatter your leaves before the mellowing year.
Bitter constraint and sad occasion dear
Compels me to disturb your season due:
For Lycidas is dead, dead ere his prime,
Young Lycidas, and hath not left his peer.
Who would not sing for Lycidas? he knew
Himself to sing, and build the lofty rhyme.
He must not float upon his watery bier
Unwept, and welter to the parching wind,
Without the meed of some melodious tear.

    Begin then, Sisters of the sacred well
That from beneath the seat of Jove doth spring;
Begin, and somewhat loudly sweep the string.
Hence with denial vain and coy excuse:
So may some gentle Muse
With lucky words favour my destined urn;
And as he passes, turn
And bid fair peace be to my sable shroud.

    For we were nursed upon the self-same hill,
Fed the same flock by fountain, shade, and rill:
Together both, ere the high lawns appear'd
Under the opening eyelids of the Morn,
We drove a-field, and both together heard
What time the gray-fly winds her sultry horn,
Battening our flocks with the fresh dews of night,
Oft till the star that rose at evening bright
Toward heaven's descent had sloped his westering wheel.
Meanwhile the rural ditties were not mute,
Temper'd to the oaten flute,

Rough Satyrs danced, and Fauns with cloven heel
From the glad sound would not be absent long;
And old Damoetas loved to hear our song.

　　But, oh! the heavy change, now thou art gone,
Now thou art gone, and never must return!
Thee, Shepherd, thee the woods and desert caves
With wild thyme and the gadding vine o'ergrown,
And all their echoes, mourn:
The willows and the hazel copses green
Shall now no more be seen
Fanning their joyous leaves to thy soft lays: –
As killing as the canker to the rose,
Or taint-worm to the weanling herds that graze,
Or frost to flowers, that their gay wardrobe wear
When first the white-thorn blows;
Such, Lycidas, thy loss to shepherd's ear.

　　Where were ye, Nymphs, when the remorseless deep
Closed o'er the head of your loved Lycidas?
For neither were ye playing on the steep
Where your old bards, the famous Druids, lie,
Nor on the shaggy top of Mona high,
Nor yet where Deva spreads her wizard stream:
Ay me! I fondly dream –
Had ye been there . . . For what could that have done?
What could the Muse herself that Orpheus bore,
The Muse herself, for her enchanting son,
Whom universal nature did lament,
When by the rout that made the hideous roar
His gory visage down the stream was sent,
Down the swift Hebrus to the Lesbian shore?

　　Alas! what boots it with uncessant care
To tend the homely, slighted, shepherd's trade
And strictly meditate the thankless Muse?
Were it not better done, as others use,
To sport with Amaryllis in the shade,
Or with the tangles of Neaera's hair?
Fame is the spur that the clear spirit doth raise

(That last infirmity of noble mind)
To scorn delights, and live laborious days;
But the fair guerdon when we hope to find,
And think to burst out into sudden blaze,
Comes the blind Fury with the abhorréd shears
And slits the thin-spun life. 'But not the praise'
Phoebus replied, and touch'd my trembling ears;
'Fame is no plant that grows on mortal soil,
Nor in the glistering foil
Set off to the world, nor in broad rumour lies:
But lives and spreads aloft by those pure eyes
And perfect witness of all-judging Jove;
As he pronounces lastly on each deed,
Of so much fame in heaven expect thy meed.'

   O fountain Arethuse, and thou honour'd flood
Smooth-sliding Mincius, crown'd with vocal reeds,
That strain I heard was of a higher mood.
But now my oat proceeds,
And listens to the herald of the sea
That came in Neptune's plea;
He ask'd the waves, and ask'd the felon winds,
What hard mishap hath doom'd this gentle swain?
And question'd every gust of rugged wings
That blows from off each beakéd promontory:
They knew not of his story;
And sage Hippotadés their answer brings,
That not a blast was from his dungeon stray'd;
The air was calm, and on the level brine
Sleek Panopé with all her sisters play'd.
It was that fatal and perfidious bark
Built in the eclipse, and rigg'd with curses dark,
That sunk so low that sacred head of thine.

   Next Camus, reverend sire, went footing slow,
His mantle hairy, and his bonnet sedge
Inwrought with figures dim, and on the edge
Like to that sanguine flower inscribed with woe:
'Ah! who hath reft,' quoth he, 'my dearest pledge!'

Last came, and last did go
The Pilot of the Galilean lake;
Two massy keys he bore of metals twain
(The golden opes, the iron shuts amain);
He shook his mitred locks, and stern bespake:
'How well could I have spared for thee, young swain,
Enow of such, as for their bellies' sake
Creep and intrude and climb into the fold!
Of other care they little reckoning make
Than how to scramble at the shearers' feast,
And shove away the worthy bidden guest.
Blind mouths! that scarce themselves know how to hold
A sheep-hook, or have learn'd aught else the least
That to the faithful herdman's art belongs!
What recks it them? What need they? They are sped;
And when they list, their lean and flashy songs
Grate on their scrannel pipes of wretched straw;
The hungry sheep look up, and are not fed,
But swoln with wind and the rank mist they draw
Rot inwardly, and foul contagion spread:
Besides what the grim wolf with privy paw
Daily devours apace, and nothing said:
– But that two-handed engine at the door
Stands ready to smite once, and smite no more.'

Return, Alphéus; the dread voice is past
That shrunk thy streams; return, Sicilian Muse,
And call the vales, and bid them hither cast
Their bells and flowerets of a thousand hues.
Ye valleys low, where the mild whispers use
Of shades, and wanton winds, and gushing brooks
On whose fresh lap the swart star sparely looks;
Throw hither all your quaint enamell'd eyes
That on the green turf suck the honey'd showers
And purple all the ground with vernal flowers.
Bring the rathe primrose that forsaken dies,
The tufted crow-toe, and pale jessamine,

The white pink, and the pansy freak'd with jet,
The glowing violet,
The musk-rose, and the well-attired woodbine,
With cowslips wan that hang the pensive head,
And every flower that sad embroidery wears:
Bid amarantus all his beauty shed,
And daffadillies fill their cups with tears
To strew the laureat hearse where Lycid lies.
For so to interpose a little ease,
Let our frail thoughts dally with false surmise: –
Ay me! whilst thee the shores and sounding seas
Wash far away, – where'er thy bones are hurl'd,
Whether beyond the stormy Hebrides
Where thou perhaps, under the whelming tide,
Visitest the bottom of the monstrous world;
Or whether thou, to our moist vows denied,
Sleep'st by the fable of Bellerus old,
Where the great Vision of the guarded mount
Looks toward Namancos and Bayona's hold,
– Look homeward, Angel, now, and melt with ruth:
– And, O ye dolphins, waft the hapless youth!

    Weep no more, woeful shepherds, weep no more,
For Lycidas, your sorrow, is not dead,
Sunk though he be beneath the watery floor:
So sinks the day-star in the ocean-bed,
And yet anon repairs his drooping head
And tricks his beams, and with new-spangled ore
Flames in the forehead of the morning sky:
So Lycidas sunk low, but mounted high
Through the dear might of Him that walk'd the waves;
Where, other groves and other streams along,
With nectar pure his oozy locks he laves,
And hears the unexpressive nuptial song
In the blest kingdoms meek of joy and love.
There entertain him all the Saints above
In solemn troops, and sweet societies,

That sing, and singing, in their glory move,
And wipe the tears for ever from his eyes.
Now, Lycidas, the shepherds weep no more;
Henceforth thou art the Genius of the shore
In thy large recompense, and shalt be good
To all that wander in that perilous flood.

  Thus sang the uncouth swain to the oaks and rills,
While the still morn went out with sandals gray;
He touch'd the tender stops of various quills,
With eager thought warbling his Doric lay:
And now the sun had stretch'd out all the hills,
And now was dropt into the western bay:
At last he rose, and twitch'd his mantle blue:
To-morrow to fresh woods, and pastures new.

J. Milton

XC
ON THE TOMBS IN WESTMINSTER ABBEY

Mortality, behold and fear
What a change of flesh is here!
Think how many royal bones
Sleep within these heaps of stones;
Here they lie, had realms and lands,
Who now want strength to stir their hands,
Where from their pulpits seal'd with dust
They preach, 'In greatness is no trust.'
Here's an acre sown indeed
With the richest royallest seed
That the earth did e'er suck in
Since the first man died for sin:
Here the bones of birth have cried
'Though gods they were, as men they died!'

Here are sands, ignoble things,
Dropt from the ruin'd sides of kings:
Here's a world of pomp and state
Buried in dust, once dead by fate.

F. Beaumont

XCI
THE LAST CONQUEROR

Victorious men of earth, no more
   Proclaim how wide your empires are;
Though you bind-in every shore
   And your triumphs reach as far
      As night or day,
   Yet you, proud monarchs, must obey
And mingle with forgotten ashes, when
Death calls ye to the crowd of common men.

Devouring Famine, Plague, and War
   Each able to undo mankind,
Death's servile emissaries are;
   Nor to these alone confined,
      He hath at will
   More quaint and subtle ways to kill;
A smile or kiss, as he will use the art,
Shall have the cunning skill to break a heart.

J. Shirley

XCII
DEATH THE LEVELLER

The glories of our blood and state
     Are shadows, not substantial things;
There is no armour against fate;
     Death lays his icy hand on kings:
     Sceptre and Crown

          Must tumble down,
And in the dust be equal made
With the poor crooked scythe and spade.

Some men with swords may reap the field,
        And plant fresh laurels where they kill:
But their strong nerves at last must yield;
        They tame but one another still:
           Early or late
           They stoop to fate,
And must give up their murmuring breath
When they, pale captives, creep to death.

The garlands wither on your brow;
        Then boast no more your mighty deeds;
Upon Death's purple altar now
        See where the victor-victim bleeds:
           Your heads must come
           To the cold tomb;
Only the actions of the just
Smell sweet, and blossom in their dust.

                    J. Shirley

XCIII

WHEN THE ASSAULT WAS INTENDED TO THE CITY

Captain, or Colonel, or Knight in Arms,
Whose chance on these defenceless doors may seize,
If deed of honour did thee ever please,
Guard them, and him within protect from harms.

He can requite thee; for he knows the charms
That call fame on such gentle acts as these,
And he can spread thy name o'er lands and seas,
Whatever clime the sun's bright circle warms.

Lift not thy spear against the Muses' bower:
The great Emathian conqueror bid spare
The house of Pindarus, when temple and tower

Went to the ground: and the repeated air
Of sad Electra's poet had the power
To save the Athenian walls from ruin bare.

J. Milton

XCIV
ON HIS BLINDNESS

When I consider how my light is spent
Ere half my days, in this dark world and wide,
And that one talent which is death to hide
Lodged with me useless, though my soul more bent

To serve therewith my Maker, and present
My true account, lest He returning chide, –
Doth God exact day-labour, light denied?
I fondly ask: – But Patience, to prevent

That murmur, soon replies; God doth not need
Either man's work, or His own gifts: who best
Bear His mild yoke, they serve Him best: His state

Is kingly; thousands at His bidding speed
And post o'er land and ocean without rest: –
They also serve who only stand and wait.

J. Milton

XCV
CHARACTER OF A HAPPY LIFE

How happy is he born and taught
That serveth not another's will;
Whose armour is his honest thought
And simple truth his utmost skill!

Whose passions not his masters are,
Whose soul is still prepared for death,
Untied unto the world by care
Of public fame, or private breath;

Who envies none that chance doth raise
Nor vice; Who never understood
How deepest wounds are given by praise;
Nor rules of state, but rules of good:

Who hath his life from rumours freed,
Whose conscience is his strong retreat;
Whose state can neither flatterers feed,
Nor ruin make oppressors great;

Who God doth late and early pray
More of His grace than gifts to lend;
And entertains the harmless day
With a religious book or friend,

– This man is freed from servile bands
Of hope to rise, or fear to fall;
Lord of himself, though not of lands;
And having nothing, yet hath all.

Sir H. Wotton

XCVI
THE NOBLE NATURE

It is not growing like a tree
In bulk, doth make Man better be;
Or standing long an oak, three hundred year,
To fall a log at last, dry, bald, and sere:
A lily of a day
Is fairer far in May,
Although it fall and die that night –
It was the plant and flower of Light.
In small proportions we just beauties see;
And in short measures life may perfect be.

B. Jonson

XCVII
THE GIFTS OF GOD

When God at first made Man,
Having a glass of blessings standing by;
Let us (said He) pour on him all we can:
Let the world's riches, which dispersèd lie,
    Contract into a span.

So strength first made a way;
Then beauty flow'd, then wisdom, honour, pleasure:
When almost all was out, God make a stay,
Perceiving that alone, of all His treasure,
    Rest in the bottom lay.

For if I should (said He)
Bestow this jewel also on My creature,
He would adore My gifts instead of Me,
And rest in Nature, not the God of Nature,
    So both should losers be.

Yet let him keep the rest,
But keep them with repining restlessness:
Let him be rich and weary, that at least,
If goodness lead him not, yet weariness
    May toss him to My breast.

G. Herbert

XCVIII
THE RETREAT

Happy those early days, when I
Shined in my Angel-infancy!
Before I understood this place
Appointed for my second race,
Or taught my soul to fancy aught
But a white, celestial thought;
When yet I had not walk'd above
A mile or two from my first Love,
And looking back, at that short space
Could see a glimpse of His bright face;
When on some gilded cloud or flower
My gazing soul would dwell an hour,
And in those weaker glories spy
Some shadows of eternity;
Before I taught my tongue to wound
My conscience with a sinful sound,
Or had the black art to dispense
A several sin to every sense,
But felt through all this fleshly dress
Bright shoots of everlastingness.

O how I long to travel back,
And tread again that ancient track!
That I might once more reach that plain
Where first I left my glorious train;
From whence th' enlighten'd spirit sees
That shady City of palm trees!
But ah! my soul with too much stay
Is drunk, and staggers in the way:—
Some men a forward motion love,
But I by backward steps would move;
And when this dust falls to the urn,
In that state I came, return.

H. Vaughan

XCIX
TO MR. LAWRENCE

Lawrence, of virtuous father virtuous son,
Now that the fields are dank and ways are mire,
Where shall we sometimes meet, and by the fire
Help waste a sullen day, what may be won

From the hard season gaining? Time will run
On smoother, till Favonius re-inspire
The frozen earth, and clothe in fresh attire
The lily and rose, that neither sow'd nor spun.

What neat repast shall feast us, light and choice,
Of Attic taste, with wine, whence we may rise
To hear the lute well touch'd, or artful voice

Warble immortal notes and Tuscan air?
He who of those delights can judge, and spare
To interpose them oft, is not unwise.

J. Milton

C ·
TO CYRIACK SKINNER

Cyriack, whose grandsire, on the royal bench
Of British Themis, with no mean applause
Pronounced, and in his volumes taught, our laws,
Which others at their bar so often wrench;

To-day deep thoughts resolve with me to drench
In mirth, that after no repenting draws;
Let Euclid rest, and Archimedes pause,
And what the Swede intend, and what the French.

To measure life learn thou betimes, and know
Toward solid good what leads the nearest way;
For other things mild Heaven a time ordains,
And disapproves that care, though wise in show,
That with superfluous burden loads the day,
And, when God sends a cheerful hour, refrains.

J. Milton

CI
A HYMN IN PRAISE OF NEPTUNE
[*Added 1890*]

Of Neptune's empire let us sing,
At whose command the waves obey;
To whom the rivers tribute pay,
Down the high mountains sliding;
To whom the scaly nation yields
Homage for the crystal fields
          Wherein they dwell;
And every sea-god pays a gem
Yearly out of his watery cell,
To deck great Neptune's diadem.

The Tritons dancing in a ring,
Before his palace gates do make
The water with their echoes quake,
Like the great thunder sounding:
The sea-nymphs chaunt their accents shrill,
And the Syrens taught to kill
          With their sweet voice,
Make every echoing rock reply,
Unto their gentle murmuring noise,
The praise of Neptune's empery.

T. Campion

CII
HYMN TO DIANA

Queen and Huntress, chaste and fair,
    Now the sun is laid to sleep,
Seated in thy silver chair
      State in wonted manner keep:
        Hesperus entreats thy light,
        Goddess excellently bright.

Earth, let not thy envious shade
    Dare itself to interpose;
Cynthia's shining orb was made
      Heaven to clear when day did close:
        Bless us then with wishéd sight,
        Goddess excellently bright.

Lay thy bow of pearl apart
    And thy crystal-shining quiver;
Give unto the flying hart
      Space to breathe, how short soever:
        Thou that mak'st a day of night,
        Goddess excellently bright!

B. Jonson

CIII
WISHES FOR THE SUPPOSED MISTRESS

Whoe'er she be,
That not impossible She
That shall command my heart and me;

Where'er she lie,
Lock'd up from mortal eye
In shady leaves of destiny:

Till that ripe birth
Of studied Fate stand forth,
And teach her fair steps tread our earth;

Till that divine
Idea take a shrine
Of crystal flesh, through which to shine:

– Meet you her, my Wishes,
Bespeak her to my blisses,
And be ye call'd, my absent kisses.

I wish her beauty
That owes not all its duty
To gaudy tire, or glist'ring shoe-tie:

Something more than
Taffata or tissue can,
Or rampant feather, or rich fan.

A face that's best
By its own beauty drest,
And can alone commend the rest:

A face made up
Out of no other shop
Than what Nature's white hand sets ope.

Sidneian showers
Of sweet discourse, whose powers
Can crown old Winter's head with flowers.

Whate'er delight
Can make day's forehead bright
Or give down to the wings of night.

Soft silken hours,
Open suns, shady bowers;
'Bove all, nothing within that lowers.

Days, that need borrow
No part of their good morrow
From a fore-spent night of sorrow:

Days, that in spite
Of darkness, by the light
Of a clear mind are day all night.

Life, that dares send
A challenge to his end,
And when it comes, say, 'Welcome, friend.'

I wish her store
Of worth may leave her poor
Of wishes; and I wish – no more.

– Now, if Time knows
That Her, whose radiant brows
Weave them a garland of my vows;

Her that dares be
What these lines wish to see:
I seek no further, it is She.

'Tis She, and here
Lo! I unclothe and clear
My wishes' cloudy character.

Such worth as this is
Shall fix my flying wishes,
And determine them to kisses.

Let her full glory,
My fancies, fly before ye;
Be ye my fictions: – but her story.

R. Crashaw

CIV
THE GREAT ADVENTURER

Over the mountains
And over the waves,
Under the fountains
And under the graves;

Under floods that are deepest,
Which Neptune obey;
Over rocks that are steepest
Love will find out the way.

Where there is no place
For the glow-worm to lie;
Where there is no space
For receipt of a fly;
Where the midge dares not venture
Lest herself fast she lay;
If love come, he will enter
And soon find out his way.

You may esteem him
A child for his might;
Or you may deem him
A coward from his flight;
But if she whom love doth honour
Be conceal'd from the day,
Set a thousand guards upon her,
Love will find out the way.

Some think to lose him
By having him confined;
And some do suppose him,
Poor thing, to be blind;
But if ne'er so close ye wall him,
Do the best that you may,
Blind love, if so ye call him,
Will find out his way.

You may train the eagle
To stoop to your fist;
Or you may inveigle
The phoenix of the east;

The lioness, ye may move her
To give o'er her prey;
But you'll ne'er stop a lover:
He will find out his way.

Anon.

CV
THE PICTURE OF LITTLE T.C. IN A PROSPECT OF FLOWERS
[*Added 1891*]

See with what simplicity
This nymph begins her golden days!
In the green grass she loves to lie,
And there with her fair aspect tames
The wilder flowers, and gives them names:
But only with the roses plays,
                    And them does tell
What colours best become them, and what smell.

Who can foretell for what high cause
This darling of the Gods was born?
Yet this is she whose chaster laws
The wanton Love shall one day fear,
And, under her command severe,
See his bow broke, and ensigns torn.
                    Happy who can
Appease this virtuous enemy of man!

O then let me in time compound
And parley with those conquering eyes,
Ere they have tried their force to wound;
Ere with their glancing wheels they drive
In triumph over hearts that strive,
And them that yield but more despise:
                    Let me be laid,
Where I may see the glories from some shade.

Mean time, whilst every verdant thing
Itself does at thy beauty charm,
Reform the errors of the Spring;
Make that the tulips may have share
Of sweetness, seeing they are fair,
And roses of their thorns disarm,
               But most procure
That violets may a longer age endure.

But O young beauty of the woods,
Whom Nature courts with fruits and flowers,
Gather the flowers, but spare the buds;
Lest FLORA, angry at thy crime
To kill her infants in their prime,
Should quickly make th' example yours;
               And ere we see –
Nip in the blossom – all our hopes and thee.

A. Marvell

CVI
CHILD AND MAIDEN

Ah, Chloris! could I now but sit
   As unconcern'd as when
Your infant beauty could beget
   No happiness or pain!
When I the dawn used to admire,
   And praised the coming day,
I little thought the rising fire
   Would take my rest away.

Your charms in harmless childhood lay
   Like metals in a mine;
Age from no face takes more away
   Than youth conceal'd in thine.

But as your charms insensibly
    To their perfection prest,
So love as unperceived did fly,
    And center'd in my breast.

My passion with your beauty grew,
    While Cupid at my heart,
Still as his mother favour'd you,
    Threw a new flaming dart:
    Each gloried in their wanton part;
        To make a lover, he
    Employ'd the utmost of his art –
        To make a beauty, she.

Sir C. Sedley

CVII
CONSTANCY
[*Added 1891*]

I cannot change, as others do,
    Though you unjustly scorn,
Since that poor swain that sighs for you,
    For you alone was born;
No, Phyllis, no, your heart to move
    A surer way I'll try, –
And to revenge my slighted love,
    Will still love on, and die.

When, kill'd with grief, Amintas lies,
    And you to mind shall call
The sighs that now unpitied rise,
    The tears that vainly fall,
That welcome hour that ends his smart
    Will then begin your pain,
For such a faithful tender heart
    Can never break in vain.

J. Wilmot, Earl of Rochester

CVIII
COUNSEL TO GIRLS

Gather ye rose-buds while ye may,
    Old Time is still a-flying:
And this same flower that smiles to-day,
    To-morrow will be dying.

The glorious Lamp of Heaven, the Sun,
    The higher he's a-getting
The sooner will his race be run,
    And nearer he's to setting.

That age is best which is the first,
    When youth and blood are warmer;
But being spent, the worse, and worst
    Times, still succeed the former.

Then be not coy, but use your time;
    And while ye may, go marry:
For having lost but once your prime,
    You may for ever tarry.

R. Herrick

CIX
TO LUCASTA, ON GOING TO THE WARS

Tell me not, Sweet, I am unkind
    That from the nunnery
Of thy chaste breast and quiet mind,
    To war and arms I fly.

True, a new mistress now I chase,
    The first foe in the field;
And with a stronger faith embrace
    A sword, a horse, a shield.

Yet this inconstancy is such
   As you too shall adore;
I could not love thee, Dear, so much,
   Loved I not Honour more.

Colonel Lovelace

CX
ELIZABETH OF BOHEMIA

You meaner beauties of the night,
   That poorly satisfy our eyes
More by your number than your light,
   You common people of the skies,
What are you, when the Moon shall rise?

You curious chanters of the wood
   That warble forth dame Nature's lays,
Thinking your passions understood
   By your weak accents; what's your praise
When Philomel her voice doth raise?

You violets that first appear,
   By your pure purple mantles known
Like the proud virgins of the year,
   As if the spring were all your own, –
What are you, when the Rose is blown?

So when my Mistress shall be seen
   In form and beauty of her mind,
By virtue first, then choice, a Queen,
   Tell me, if she were not design'd
Th' eclipse and glory of her kind?

Sir H. Wotton

CXI
TO THE LADY MARGARET LEY

Daughter to that good Earl, once President
Of England's Council and her Treasury,
Who lived in both, unstain'd with gold or fee,
And left them both, more in himself content,

Till the sad breaking of that Parliament
Broke him, as that dishonest victory
At Chaeroneia, fatal to liberty,
Kill'd with report that old man eloquent; –

Though later born than to have known the days
Wherein your father flourish'd, yet by you,
Madam, methinks I see him living yet;

So well your words his noble virtues praise,
That all both judge you to relate them true,
And to possess them, honour'd Margaret.

J. Milton

THE PURSUIT OF THE IDEAL
[*Dropped 1891. Title changed to* The Loveliness of Love
from the third issue, November 1861]

It is not Beauty I demand,
A crystal brow, the moon's despair,
Nor the snow's daughter, a white hand,
Nor mermaid's yellow pride of hair:

Tell me not of your starry eyes,
Your lips that seem on roses fed,
Your breasts, where Cupid tumbling lies
Nor sleeps for kissing of his bed:–

A bloomy pair of vermeil cheeks
Like Hebe's in her ruddiest hours,
A breath that softer music speaks
Than summer winds a-wooing flowers,

These are but gauds: nay what are lips?
Coral beneath the ocean-stream,
Whose brink when your adventurer slips
Full oft he perisheth on them.

And what are cheeks, but ensigns oft
That wave hot youth to fields of blood?
Did Helen's breast, though ne'er so soft,
Do Greece or Ilium any good?

Eyes can with baleful ardour burn;
Poison can breath, that erst perfumed;
There's many a white hand holds an urn
With lovers' hearts to dust consumed.

For crystal brows there's nought within;
They are but empty cells for pride;
He who the Syren's hair would win
Is mostly strangled in the tide.

Give me, instead of Beauty's bust,
A tender heart, a loyal mind
Which with temptation I would trust,
Yet never link'd with error find, –

One in whose gentle bosom I
Could pour my secret heart of woes,
Like the care-burthen'd honey-fly
That hides his murmurs in the rose, –

My earthly Comforter! whose love
So indefeasible might be
That, when my spirit wonn'd above,
Hers could not stay, for sympathy.

Anon.

CXII
THE TRUE BEAUTY

He that loves a rosy cheek
  Or a coral lip admires,
Or from star-like eyes doth seek
  Fuel to maintain his fires;
As old Time makes these decay,
So his flames must waste away.

But a smooth and steadfast mind,
  Gentle thoughts, and calm desires,
Hearts with equal love combined,
  Kindle never-dying fires: –
Where these are not, I despise
Lovely cheeks or lips or eyes.

T. Carew

CXIII
TO DIANEME

Sweet, be not proud of those two eyes
Which starlike sparkle in their skies;
Nor be you proud, that you can see
All hearts your captives; yours yet free:
Be you not proud of that rich hair
Which wantons with the lovesick air;
Whenas that ruby which you wear,
Sunk from the tip of your soft ear,
Will last to be a precious stone
When all your world of beauty's gone.

R. Herrick

CXIV

[Added 1890]

Love in thy youth, fair Maid, be wise;
    Old Time will make thee colder,
And though each morning new arise
    Yet we each day grow older.
Thou as Heaven art fair and young,
    Thine eyes like twin stars shining;
But ere another day be sprung
    All these will be declining.
Then winter comes with all his fears,
    And all thy sweets shall borrow;
Too late then wilt thou shower thy tears, –
    And I too late shall sorrow!

Anon.

CXV

    Go, lovely Rose!
Tell her, that wastes her time and me,
    That now she knows,
When I resemble her to thee,
How sweet and fair she seems to be.

    Tell her that's young
And shuns to have her graces spied,
    That hadst thou sprung
In deserts, where no men abide,
Thou must have uncommended died.

    Small is the worth
Of beauty from the light retired:
    Bid her come forth,
Suffer herself to be desired,
And not blush so to be admired.

Then die! that she
The common fate of all things rare
May read in thee:
How small a part of time they share
That are so wondrous sweet and fair!

E. Waller

CXVI
TO CELIA

Drink to me only with thine eyes,
    And I will pledge with mine;
Or leave a kiss but in the cup
    And I'll not look for wine.
The thirst that from the soul doth rise
    Doth ask a drink divine;
But might I of Jove's nectar sup,
    I would not change for thine.

I sent thee late a rosy wreath,
    Not so much honouring thee
As giving it a hope that there
    It could not wither'd be;
But thou thereon didst only breathe
    And sent'st it back to me;
Since when it grows, and smells, I swear,
    Not of itself but thee!

B. Jonson

CXVII
CHERRY-RIPE

There is a garden in her face
    Where roses and white lilies blow;
A heavenly paradise is that place,
    Wherein all pleasant fruits do grow;
There cherries grow that none may buy,
Till Cherry-Ripe themselves do cry.

Those cherries fairly do enclose
   Of orient pearl, a double row,
Which when her lovely laughter shows,
   They look like rose-buds fill'd with snow:
Yet them no peer nor prince may buy,
Till Cherry-Ripe themselves do cry.

Her eyes like angels watch them still;
   Her brows like bended bows do stand,
Threat'ning with piercing frowns to kill
   All that approach with eye or hand
These sacred cherries to come nigh,
Till Cherry-Ripe themselves do cry!

Anon.

CXVIII
CORINNA'S MAYING
[*Added 1883*]

Get up, get up for shame! The blooming morn
Upon her wings presents the god unshorn.
   See how Aurora throws her fair
   Fresh-quilted colours through the air:
   Get up, sweet Slug-a-bed, and see
   The dew bespangling herb and tree.
Each flower has wept, and bow'd toward the east,
Above an hour since; yet you not drest,
   Nay! not so much as out of bed?
   When all the birds have matins said,
   And sung their thankful hymns: 'tis sin,
   Nay, profanation, to keep in, –
Whenas a thousand virgins on this day,
Spring, sooner than the lark, to fetch-in May.

Rise; and put on your foliage, and be seen
To come forth, like the Spring-time, fresh and green
    And sweet as Flora. Take no care
    For jewels for your gown, or hair:
    Fear not; the leaves will strew
    Gems in abundance upon you:
Besides, the childhood of the day has kept,
Against you come, some orient pearls unwept:
    Come, and receive them while the light
    Hangs on the dew-locks of the night:
    And Titan on the eastern hill
    Retires himself, or else stands still
Till you come forth. Wash, dress, be brief in praying:
Few beads are best, when once we go a Maying.

Come, my Corinna, come; and coming, mark
How each field turns a street; each street a park
    Made green, and trimm'd with trees: see how
    Devotion gives each house a bough
    Or branch: Each porch, each door, ere this,
    An ark, a tabernacle is,
Made up of white-thorn neatly interwove;
As if here were those cooler shades of love.
    Can such delights be in the street,
    And open fields, and we not see't?
    Come we'll abroad: and let's obey
    The proclamation made for May:
And sin no more, as we have done, by staying;
But, my Corinna, come, let's go a Maying.

There's not a budding boy, or girl, this day,
But is got up, and gone to bring in May.
    A deal of youth, ere this, is come
    Back, and with white-thorn laden home.
    Some have despatch'd their cakes and cream,
    Before that we have left to dream:

And some have wept, and woo'd, and plighted troth
And chose their priest, ere we can cast off sloth:
    Many a green-gown has been given;
    Many a kiss, both odd and even:
    Many a glance too has been sent
    From out the eye, Love's firmament:
Many a jest told of the keys betraying
This night, and locks pick'd: – Yet we're not a Maying.

– Come, let us go, while we are in our prime;
And take the harmless folly of the time!
    We shall grow old apace, and die
    Before we know our liberty.
    Our life is short; and our days run
    As fast away as does the sun: –
And as a vapour, or a drop of rain
Once lost, can ne'er be found again:
    So when or you or I are made
    A fable, song, or fleeting shade;
    All love, all liking, all delight
    Lies drown'd with us in endless night.
Then while time serves, and we are but decaying,
Come, my Corinna! come, let's go a Maying.

R. Herrick

CXIX
THE POETRY OF DRESS

I

    A sweet disorder in the dress
    Kindles in clothes a wantonness: –
    A lawn about the shoulders thrown
    Into a fine distraction, –
    An erring lace, which here and there
    Enthrals the crimson stomacher, –

A cuff neglectful, and thereby
Ribbands to flow confusedly, –
A winning wave, deserving note,
In the tempestuous petticoat, –
A careless shoe-string, in whose tie
I see a wild civility, –
Do more bewitch me, than when art
Is too precise in every part.

                  R. Herrick

CXX
2

Whenas in silks my Julia goes
Then, then (methinks) how sweetly flows
That liquefaction of her clothes.

Next, when I cast mine eyes and see
That brave vibration each way free;
O how that glittering taketh me!

                  R. Herrick

CXXI
3

My Love in her attire doth shew her wit,
    It doth so well become her:
For every season she hath dressings fit,
    For Winter, Spring, and Summer.
No beauty she doth miss
When all her robes are on:
But Beauty's self she is
When all her robes are gone.

                  Anon.

CXXII
ON A GIRDLE

That which her slender waist confined
Shall now my joyful temples bind:
No monarch but would give his crown
His arms might do what this has done.

It was my Heaven's extremest sphere,
The pale which held that lovely deer:
My joy, my grief, my hope, my love
Did all within this circle move.

A narrow compass! and yet there
Dwelt all that's good, and all that's fair:
Give me but what this ribband bound,
Take all the rest the Sun goes round.

E. Waller

CXXIII
A MYSTICAL ECSTASY
[Added 1883]

E'en like two little bank-dividing brooks,
    That wash the pebbles with their wanton streams,
And having ranged and search'd a thousand nooks,
    Meet both at length in silver-breasted Thames,
        Where in a greater current they conjoin:
So I my Best-Belovéd's am; so He is mine.

E'en so we met; and after long pursuit,
    E'en so we join'd; we both became entire;
No need for either to renew a suit,
    For I was flax and he was flames of fire:
        Our firm-united souls did more than twine;
So I my Best-Belovéd's am; so He is mine.

If all those glittering Monarchs that command
 The servile quarters of this earthly ball,
Should tender, in exchange, their shares of land,
 I would not change my fortunes for them all:
 Their wealth is but a counter to my coin:
The world's but theirs; but my Belovéd's mine.

        F. Quarles

CXXIV

TO ANTHEA WHO MAY COMMAND HIM ANY THING

Bid me to live, and I will live
 Thy Protestant to be:
Or bid me love, and I will give
 A loving heart to thee.

A heart as soft, a heart as kind,
 A heart as sound and free
As in the whole world thou canst find,
 That heart I'll give to thee.

Bid that heart stay, and it will stay,
 To honour thy decree:
Or bid it languish quite away,
 And 't shall do so for thee.

Bid me to weep, and I will weep
 While I have eyes to see:
And having none, yet I will keep
 A heart to weep for thee.

Bid me despair, and I'll despair,
 Under that cypress tree:
Or bid me die, and I will dare
 E'en Death, to die for thee.

Thou art my life, my love, my heart,
　The very eyes of me,
And hast command of every part,
　To live and die for thee.

R. Herrick

CXXV

Love not me for comely grace,
For my pleasing eye or face,
Nor for any outward part,
No, nor for my constant heart, –
　For those may fail, or turn to ill,
　　So thou and I shall sever:
Keep therefore a true woman's eye,
And love me still, but know not why –
　So hast thou the same reason still
　　To doat upon me ever!

Anon.

CXXVI

Not, Celia, that I juster am
　Or better than the rest;
For I would change each hour, like them
　Were not my heart at rest.

But I am tied to very thee
　By every thought I have;
Thy face I only care to see,
　Thy heart I only crave.

All that in woman is adored
　In thy dear self I find –
For the whole sex can but afford
　The handsome and the kind.

Why then should I seek further store,
    And still make love anew?
When change itself can give no more,
    'Tis easy to be true.

                            Sir C. Sedley

CXXVII
TO ALTHEA FROM PRISON

When Love with unconfinéd wings
    Hovers within my gates,
And my divine Althea brings
    To whisper at the grates;
When I lie tangled in her hair
    And fetter'd to her eye,
The Gods that wanton in the air
    Know no such liberty.

When flowing cups run swiftly round
    With no allaying Thames,
Our careless heads with roses bound,
    Our hearts with loyal flames;
When thirsty grief in wine we steep,
    When healths and draughts go free –
Fishes that tipple in the deep
    Know no such liberty.

When, (like committed linnets), I
    With shriller throat shall sing
The sweetness, mercy, majesty
    And glories of my King;
When I shall voice aloud how good
    He is, how great should be,
Enlargéd winds, that curl the flood,
    Know no such liberty.

Stone walls do not a prison make,
    Nor iron bars a cage;
Minds innocent and quiet take
    That for an hermitage;
If I have freedom in my love
    And in my soul am free,
Angels alone, that soar above,
    Enjoy such liberty.

Colonel Lovelace

CXXVIII

TO LUCASTA, GOING BEYOND THE SEAS

If to be absent were to be
    Away from thee;
  Or that when I am gone
  You or I were alone;
Then, my Lucasta, might I crave
Pity from blustering wind, or swallowing wave.

But I'll not sigh one blast or gale
    To swell my sail,
  Or pay a tear to 'suage
  The foaming blue-god's rage;
For whether he will let me pass
Or no, I'm still as happy as I was.

Though seas and land betwixt us both,
    Our faith and troth,
  Like separated souls,
  All time and space controls:
Above the highest sphere we meet
Unseen, unknown, and greet as Angels greet.

So then we do anticipate
    Our after-fate,
And are alive i' the skies,
    If thus our lips and eyes
Can speak like spirits unconfined
In Heaven, their earthy bodies left behind.

Colonel Lovelace

CXXIX
ENCOURAGEMENTS TO A LOVER

Why so pale and wan, fond lover?
        Prythee, why so pale?
Will, if looking well can't move her
        Looking ill prevail?
        Prythee, why so pale?

Why so dull and mute, young sinner?
        Prythee, why so mute?
Will, when speaking well can't win her,
        Saying nothing do't?
        Prythee, why so mute?

Quit, quit, for shame! this will not move,
        This cannot take her;
If of herself she will not love,
        Nothing can make her:
        The D—l take her!

Sir J. Suckling

CXXX
A SUPPLICATION

Awake, awake, my Lyre!
And tell thy silent master's humble tale
In sounds that may prevail;
Sounds that gentle thoughts inspire:
Though so exalted she
And I so lowly be
Tell her, such different notes make all thy harmony.

Hark, how the strings awake!
And, though the moving hand approach not near,
Themselves with awful fear
A kind of numerous trembling make.
Now all thy forces try;
Now all thy charms apply;
Revenge upon her ear the conquests of her eye.

Weak Lyre! thy virtue sure
Is useless here, since thou art only found
To cure, but not to wound,
And she to wound, but not to cure.
Too weak too wilt thou prove
My passion to remove;
Physic to other ills, thou'rt nourishment to Love.

Sleep, sleep again, my Lyre!
For thou canst never tell my humble tale
In sounds that will prevail,
Nor gentle thoughts in her inspire;
All thy vain mirth lay by,
Bid thy strings silent lie,
Sleep, sleep again, my Lyre, and let thy master die.

A. Cowley

CXXXI
THE MANLY HEART

Shall I, wasting in despair,
Die because a woman's fair?
Or make pale my cheeks with care
'Cause another's rosy are?
Be she fairer than the day
Or the flowery meads in May —
        If she think not well of me
        What care I how fair she be?

Shall my silly heart be pined
'Cause I see a woman kind;
Or a well disposéd nature
Joinéd with a lovely feature?
Be she meeker, kinder than
Turtle-dove or pelican,
        If she be not so to me
        What care I how kind she be?

Shall a woman's virtues move
Me to perish for her love?
Or her well-deservings known
Make me quite forget mine own?
Be she with that goodness blest
Which may merit name of Best;
        If she be not such to me,
        What care I how good she be?

'Cause her fortune seems too high,
Shall I play the fool and die?
She that bears a noble mind
If not outward helps she find,
Thinks what with them he would do
Who without them dares her woo;
        And unless that mind I see,
        What care I how great she be?

Great or good, or kind or fair,
I will ne'er the more despair;
If she love me, this believe,
I will die ere she shall grieve;
If she slight me when I woo,
I can scorn and let her go;
     For if she be not for me,
     What care I for whom she be?

                              G. Wither

CXXXII
MELANCHOLY

Hence, all you vain delights,
As short as are the nights
Wherein you spend your folly:
There's nought in this life sweet
If man were wise to see't,
But only melancholy,
O sweetest Melancholy!
Welcome, folded arms, and fixéd eyes,
A sigh that piercing mortifies,
A look that's fasten'd to the ground,
A tongue chain'd up without a sound!
Fountain-heads and pathless groves,
Places which pale passion loves!
Moonlight walks, when all the fowls
Are warmly housed save bats and owls!
A midnight bell, a parting groan!
These are the sounds we feed upon;
Then stretch our bones in a still gloomy valley;
Nothing's so dainty sweet as lovely melancholy.

                              J. Fletcher

TO A LOCK OF HAIR
[*Dropped 1890*]

Thy hue, dear pledge, is pure and bright
As in that well-remember'd night
When first thy mystic braid was wove,
And first my Agnes whisper'd love.

  Since then how often hast thou prest
The torrid zone of this wild breast,
Whose wrath and hate have sworn to dwell
With the first sin that peopled hell;
A breast whose blood's a troubled ocean,
Each throb the earthquake's wild commotion!
O if such clime thou canst endure
Yet keep thy hue unstain'd and pure,
What conquest o'er each erring thought
Of that fierce realm had Agnes wrought!
I had not wander'd far and wide
With such an angel for my guide;
Nor heaven nor earth could then reprove me
If she had lived, and lived to love me.

  Not then this world's wild joys had been
To me one savage hunting scene,
My sole delight the headlong race
And frantic hurry of the chase;
To start, pursue, and bring to bay,
Rush in, drag down, and rend my prey,
Then – from the carcass turn away!
Mine ireful mood had sweetness tamed,
And soothed each wound which pride inflamed: –
Yes, God and man might now approve me
If thou hadst lived, and lived to love me!

Sir W. Scott

CXXXIII
FORSAKEN

O waly waly up the bank,
   And waly waly down the brae,
And waly waly yon burn-side
   Where I and my Love wont to gae!
I leant my back unto an aik,
   I thought it was a trusty tree;
But first it bow'd, and syne it brak,
   Sae my true Love did lichtly me.

O waly waly, but love be bonny
   A little time while it is new;
But when 'tis auld, it waxeth cauld
   And fades awa' like morning dew.
O wherefore should I busk my head?
   Or wherefore should I kame my hair?
For my true Love has me forsook,
   And says he'll never loe me mair.

Now Arthur-seat sall be my bed;
   The sheets shall ne'er be prest by me:
Saint Anton's well sall be my drink,
   Since my true Love has forsaken me.
Marti'mas wind, when wilt thou blaw
   And shake the green leaves aff the tree?
O gentle Death, when wilt thou come?
   For of my life I am wearíe.

'Tis not the frost, that freezes fell,
   Nor blawing snaw's inclemencie;
'Tis not sic cauld that makes me cry,
   But my Love's heart grown cauld to me.
When we came in by Glasgow town
   We were a comely sight to see;
My Love was clad in the black velvét,
   And I myself in cramasie.

But had I wist, before I kist,
    That love had been sae ill to win;
I had lockt my heart in a case of gowd
    And pinn'd it with a siller pin.
And, O! if my young babe were born,
    And set upon the nurse's knee,
And I mysell were dead and gane,
    And the green grass growing over me!

Anon.

CXXXIV
[*Added 1890*]

Upon my lap my sovereign sits
And sucks upon my breast;
Meantime his love maintains my life
And gives my sense her rest.
        Sing lullaby, my little boy,
        Sing lullaby, mine only joy!

When thou hast taken thy repast,
Repose, my babe, on me;
So may thy mother and thy nurse
Thy cradle also be.
        Sing lullaby, my little boy,
        Sing lullaby, mine only joy!

I grieve that duty doth not work
All that my wishing would,
Because I would not be to thee
But in the best I should.
        Sing lullaby, my little boy,
        Sing lullaby, mine only joy!

Yet as I am, and as I may,
I must and will be thine,
Though all too little for thy self
Vouchsafing to be mine.
    Sing lullaby, my little boy,
    Sing lullaby, mine only joy!

Anon.

CXXXV
FAIR HELEN

I wish I were where Helen lies;
Night and day on me she cries;
O that I were where Helen lies
    On fair Kirconnell lea!

Curst be the heart that thought the thought,
And curst the hand that fired the shot,
When in my arms burd Helen dropt,
    And died to succour me!

O think na but my heart was sair
When my Love dropt down and spak nae mair!
I laid her down wi' meikle care
    On fair Kirconnell lea.

As I went down the water-side,
None but my foe to be my guide,
None but my foe to be my guide,
    On fair Kirconnell lea;

I lighted down my sword to draw,
I hackéd him in pieces sma',
I hackéd him in pieces sma',
    For her sake that died for me.

O Helen fair, beyond compare!
I'll make a garland of thy hair
Shall bind my heart for evermair
    Until the day I die.

O that I were where Helen lies!
Night and day on me she cries;
Out of my bed she bids me rise,
    Says, 'Haste and come to me!'

O Helen fair! O Helen chaste!
If I were with thee, I were blest,
Where thou lies low and takes thy rest
    On fair Kirconnell lea.

I wish my grave were growing green,
A winding-sheet drawn ower my een,
And I in Helen's arms lying,
    On fair Kirconnell lea.

I wish I were where Helen lies;
Night and day on me she cries;
And I am weary of the skies,
    Since my Love died for me.

Anon.

CXXXVI
THE TWA CORBIES

As I was walking all alane
I heard twa corbies making a mane;
The tane unto the t'other say,
'Where sall we gang and dine today?'

' – In behint yon auld fail dyke,
I wot there lies a new-slain Knight;
And naebody kens that he lies there,
But his hawk, his hound, and lady fair.

'His hound is to the hunting gane,
His hawk to fetch the wild-fowl hame,
His lady's ta'en another mate,
So we may mak our dinner sweet.

'Ye'll sit on his white hause-bane,
And I'll pick out his bonnie blue een;
Wi' ae lock o' his gowden hair
We'll theek our nest when it grows bare.

'Mony a one for him makes mane,
But nane sall ken where he is gane;
O'er his white banes, when they are bare,
The wind sall blaw for evermair.'

Anon.

CXXXVII
ON THE DEATH OF MR. WILLIAM HERVEY
[*Added 1891*]

It was a dismal and a fearful night, –
Scarce could the Morn drive on th' unwilling light,
When sleep, death's image, left my troubled breast,
    By something liker death possest.
My eyes with tears did uncommanded flow,
      And on my soul hung the dull weight
      Of some intolerable fate.
What bell was that? Ah me! Too much I know!

My sweet companion, and my gentle peer,
Why hast thou left me thus unkindly here,
Thy end for ever, and my life, to moan?
    O thou hast left me all alone!
Thy soul and body, when death's agony
      Besieged around thy noble heart,
      Did not with more reluctance part
Than I, my dearest friend, do part from thee.

Ye fields of Cambridge, our dear Cambridge, say,
Have ye not seen us, walking every day?
Was there a tree about which did not know
    The love betwixt us two?
Henceforth, ye gentle trees, for ever fade,
    Or your sad branches thicker join,
    And into darksome shades combine,
Dark as the grave wherein my friend is laid.

Large was his soul; as large a soul as e'er
Submitted to inform a body here;
High as the place 'twas shortly in Heaven to have,
    But low and humble as his grave;
So high that all the virtues there did come
    As to the chiefest seat
    Conspicuous, and great;
So low that for me too it made a room.

Knowledge he only sought, and so soon caught,
As if for him knowledge had rather sought;
Nor did more learning ever crowded lie
    In such a short mortality.
Whene'er the skilful youth discoursed or writ,
    Still did the notions throng
    About his eloquent tongue;
Nor could his ink flow faster than his wit.

His mirth was the pure spirits of various wit,
Yet never did his God or friends forget.
And when deep talk and wisdom came in view,
    Retired, and gave to them their due.
For the rich help of books he always took,
    Though his own searching mind before
    Was so with notions written o'er,
As if wise Nature had made that her book.

With as much zeal, devotion, piety,
He always lived, as other saints do die.
Still with his soul severe account he kept,
      Weeping all debts out ere he slept.
Then down in peace and innocence he lay,
      Like the sun's laborious light,
      Which still in water sets at night,
Unsullied with his journey of the day.

A. Cowley

CXXXVIII
FRIENDS IN PARADISE
[Added 1890]

They are all gone into the world of light!
    And I alone sit lingering here;
Their very memory is fair and bright,
      And my sad thoughts doth clear: –

It glows and glitters in my cloudy breast,
    Like stars upon some gloomy grove,
Or those faint beams in which this hill is drest,
      After the sun's remove.

I see them walking in an air of glory,
    Whose light doth trample on my days:
My days, which are at best but dull and hoary,
      Mere glimmering and decays.

O holy Hope! and high Humility,
    High as the heavens above!
These are your walks, and you have shew'd them me,
      To kindle my cold love.

Dear, beauteous Death! the jewel of the just
    Shining no where, but in the dark;
What mysteries do lie beyond thy dust,
      Could man outlook that mark!

He that hath found some fledged bird's nest, may know
    At first sight, if the bird be flown;
But what fair well or grove he sings in now,
     That is to him unknown.

And yet, as Angels in some brighter dreams
    Call to the soul, when man doth sleep;
So some strange thoughts transcend our wonted themes,
     And into glory peep.

                   H. Vaughan

CXXXIX
TO BLOSSOMS

Fair pledges of a fruitful tree,
    Why do ye fall so fast?
    Your date is not so past,
But you may stay yet here awhile
    To blush and gently smile,
     And go at last.

What, were ye born to be
    An hour or half's delight,
    And so to bid good-night?
'Twas pity Nature brought ye forth
    Merely to show your worth,
     And lose you quite.

But you are lovely leaves, where we
    May read how soon things have
    Their end, though ne'er so brave:
And after they have shown their pride
    Like you, awhile, they glide
     Into the grave.

                   R. Herrick

CXL
TO DAFFODILS

Fair Daffodils, we weep to see
    You haste away so soon:
As yet the early-rising Sun
    Has not attain'd his noon.
      Stay, stay,
    Until the hasting day
      Has run
    But to the even-song;
And, having pray'd together, we
    Will go with you along.

We have short time to stay, as you,
    We have as short a Spring;
As quick a growth to meet decay
    As you, or any thing.
      We die,
    As your hours do, and dry
      Away
    Like to the Summer's rain;
Or as the pearls of morning's dew
    Ne'er to be found again.

R. Herrick

CXLI
THE GIRL DESCRIBES HER FAWN
[*Added 1890*]

With sweetest milk and sugar first
I it at my own fingers nursed;
And as it grew, so every day
It wax'd more white and sweet than they –

It had so sweet a breath! and oft
I blush'd to see its foot more soft
And white, – shall I say, – than my hand?
Nay, any lady's of the land!

It is a wondrous thing how fleet
'Twas on those little silver feet:
With what a pretty skipping grace
It oft would challenge me the race: –
And when 't had left me far away
'Twould stay, and run again, and stay:
For it was nimbler much than hinds,
And trod as if on the four winds.

I have a garden of my own,
But so with roses overgrown
And lilies, that you would it guess
To be a little wilderness:
And all the spring-time of the year
It only lovéd to be there.
Among the beds of lilies I
Have sought it oft, where it should lie;
Yet could not, till itself would rise,
Find it, although before mine eyes: –
For in the flaxen lilies' shade
It like a bank of lilies laid.
Upon the roses it would feed,
Until its lips e'en seem'd to bleed:
And then to me 'twould boldly trip,
And print those roses on my lip.
But all its chief delight was still
On roses thus itself to fill,
And its pure virgin limbs to fold
In whitest sheets of lilies cold: –
Had it lived long, it would have been
Lilies without – roses within.

A. Marvell

CXLII
THOUGHTS IN A GARDEN

How vainly men themselves amaze
To win the palm, the oak, or bays,
And their uncessant labours see
Crown'd from some single herb or tree,
Whose short and narrow-vergéd shade
Does prudently their toils upbraid;
While all the flowers and trees do close
To weave the garlands of Repose.

Fair Quiet, have I found thee here,
And Innocence thy sister dear!
Mistaken long, I sought you then
In busy companies of men:
Your sacred plants, if here below,
Only among the plants will grow:
Society is all but rude
To this delicious solitude.

No white nor red was ever seen
So amorous as this lovely green.
Fond lovers, cruel as their flame,
Cut in these trees their mistress' name:
Little, alas, they know or heed
How far these beauties hers exceed!
Fair trees! wheres'e'er your barks I wound,
No name shall but your own be found.

When we have run our passions' heat
Love hither makes his best retreat:
The gods, who mortal beauty chase,
Still in a tree did end their race;
Apollo hunted Daphne so
Only that she might laurel grow;
And Pan did after Syrinx speed
Not as a nymph, but for a reed.

What wondrous life is this I lead!
Ripe apples drop about my head;
The luscious clusters of the vine
Upon my mouth do crush their wine;
The nectarine and curious peach
Into my hands themselves do reach;
Stumbling on melons, as I pass,
Ensnared with flowers, I fall on grass.

Meanwhile the mind from pleasure less
Withdraws into its happiness;
The mind, that ocean where each kind
Does straight its own resemblance find;
Yet it creates, transcending these,
Far other worlds, and other seas;
Annihilating all that's made
To a green thought in a green shade.

Here at the fountain's sliding foot
Or at some fruit-tree's mossy root,
Casting the body's vest aside
My soul into the boughs does glide;
There, like a bird, it sits and sings,
Then whets and claps its silver wings,
And, till prepared for longer flight,
Waves in its plumes the various light.

Such was that happy Garden-state
While man there walk'd without a mate:
After a place so pure and sweet,
What other help could yet be meet!
But 'twas beyond a mortal's share
To wander solitary there:
Two paradises 'twere in one,
To live in Paradise alone.

How well the skilful gardener drew
Of flowers and herbs this dial new!
Where, from above, the milder sun
Does through a fragrant zodiac run:

And, as it works, th' industrious bee
Computes its time as well as we.
How could such sweet and wholesome hours
Be reckon'd, but with herbs and flowers!

A. Marvell

CXLIII
FORTUNATI NIMIUM
[*Added 1891*]

Jack and Joan, they think no ill,
But loving live, and merry still;
Do their week-day's work, and pray
Devoutly on the holy-day:
Skip and trip it on the green,
And help to choose the Summer Queen;
Lash out at a country feast
Their silver penny with the best.

Well can they judge of nappy ale,
And tell at large a winter tale;
Climb up to the apple loft,
And turn the crabs till they be soft.
Tib is all the father's joy,
And little Tom the mother's boy: –
All their pleasure is, Content,
And care, to pay their yearly rent.

Joan can call by name her cows
And deck her windows with green boughs;
She can wreaths and tutties make,
And trim with plums a bridal cake.
Jack knows what brings gain or loss,
And his long flail can stoutly toss:
Makes the hedge which others break,
And ever thinks what he doth speak.

– Now, you courtly dames and knights,
That study only strange delights,
Though you scorn the homespun gray,
And revel in your rich array;
Though your tongues dissemble deep
And can your heads from danger keep;
Yet, for all your pomp and train,
Securer lives the silly swain!

                                        T. Campion

CXLIV

L'ALLEGRO

Hence, loathéd Melancholy,
   Of Cerberus and blackest Midnight born
In Stygian cave forlorn
   'Mongst horrid shapes, and shrieks, and sights unholy!
Find out some uncouth cell
   Where brooding Darkness spreads his jealous wings
And the night-raven sings;
   There under ebon shades, and low-brow'd rocks
As ragged as thy locks,
   In dark Cimmerian desert ever dwell.

      But come, thou Goddess fair and free,
         In heaven yclept Euphrosyne,
         And by men, heart-easing Mirth,
         Whom lovely Venus at a birth
         With two sister Graces more
         To ivy-crownéd Bacchus bore;
         Or whether (as some sager sing)
         The frolic wind that breathes the spring
         Zephyr, with Aurora playing,
         As he met her once a-Maying –

There on beds of violets blue
And fresh-blown roses wash'd in dew
Fill'd her with thee, a daughter fair,
So buxom, blithe, and debonair.

    Haste thee, Nymph, and bring with thee
Jest, and youthful jollity,
Quips, and cranks, and wanton wiles,
Nods, and becks, and wreathéd smiles
Such as hang on Hebe's cheek,
And love to live in dimple sleek;
Sport that wrinkled Care derides,
And Laughter holding both his sides: –
Come, and trip it as you go
On the light fantastic toe;
And in thy right hand lead with thee
The mountain-nymph, sweet Liberty;
And if I give thee honour due
Mirth, admit me of thy crew,
To live with her, and live with thee
In unreprovéd pleasures free;
To hear the lark begin his flight
And singing startle the dull night
From his watch-tower in the skies,
Till the dappled dawn doth rise;
Then to come, in spite of sorrow,
And at my window bid good-morrow
Through the sweetbriar, or the vine,
Or the twisted eglantine:
While the cock with lively din
Scatters the rear of darkness thin,
And to the stack, or the barn-door,
Stoutly struts his dames before:
Oft listening how the hounds and horn
Cheerly rouse the slumbering morn,
From the side of some hoar hill,
Through the high wood echoing shrill:

Sometime walking, not unseen,
By hedge-row elms, on hillocks green,
Right against the eastern gate
Where the great Sun begins his state
Robed in flames and amber light,
The clouds in thousand liveries dight;
While the ploughman, near at hand,
Whistles o'er the furrow'd land,
And the milkmaid singeth blithe,
And the mower whets his scythe,
And every shepherd tells his tale
Under the hawthorn in the dale.

    Straight mine eye hath caught new pleasures
Whilst the landscape round it measures;
Russet lawns, and fallows gray,
Where the nibbling flocks do stray;
Mountains, on whose barren breast
The labouring clouds do often rest;
Meadows trim with daisies pied,
Shallow brooks, and rivers wide;
Towers and battlements it sees
Bosom'd high in tufted trees,
Where perhaps some Beauty lies,
The Cynosure of neighbouring eyes.

    Hard by, a cottage chimney smokes
From betwixt two aged oaks,
Where Corydon and Thyrsis, met,
Are at their savoury dinner set
Of herbs, and other country messes
Which the neat-handed Phillis dresses;
And then in haste her bower she leaves
With Thestylis to bind the sheaves;
Or, if the earlier season lead,
To the tann'd haycock in the mead.

    Sometimes with secure delight
The upland hamlets will invite,
When the merry bells ring round,

And the jocund rebecks sound
To many a youth and many a maid,
Dancing in the chequer'd shade;
And young and old come forth to play
On a sun-shine holyday,
Till the live-long day-light fail:
Then to the spicy nut-brown ale,
With stories told of many a feat,
How Faery Mab the junkets eat:–
She was pinch'd, and pull'd, she said;
And he, by Friar's lantern led;
Tells how the drudging Goblin sweat
To earn his cream-bowl duly set,
When in one night, ere glimpse of morn,
His shadowy flail hath thresh'd the corn
That ten day-labourers could not end;
Then lies him down the lubber fiend,
And, stretch'd out all the chimney's length,
Basks at the fire his hairy strength;
And crop-full out of doors he flings,
Ere the first cock his matin rings.
     Thus done the tales, to bed they creep,
By whispering winds soon lull'd asleep.
     Tower'd cities please us then
And the busy hum of men,
Where throngs of knights and barons bold,
In weeds of peace, high triumphs hold,
With store of ladies, whose bright eyes
Rain influence, and judge the prize
Of wit or arms, while both contend
To win her grace, whom all commend.
There let Hymen oft appear
In saffron robe, with taper clear,
And pomp, and feast, and revelry,
With mask, and antique pageantry;
Such sights as youthful poets dream
On summer eves by haunted stream.

Then to the well-trod stage anon,
If Jonson's learned sock be on,
Or sweetest Shakespeare, Fancy's child,
Warble his native wood-notes wild.
        And ever against eating cares
Lap me in soft Lydian airs
Married to immortal verse,
Such as the meeting soul may pierce
In notes, with many a winding bout
Of linkéd sweetness long drawn out,
With wanton heed and giddy cunning,
The melting voice through mazes running,
Untwisting all the chains that tie
The hidden soul of harmony;
That Orpheus' self may heave his head
From golden slumber, on a bed
Of heap'd Elysian flowers, and hear
Such strains as would have won the ear
Of Pluto, to have quite set free
His half-regain'd Eurydice.
        These delights if thou canst give,
Mirth, with thee I mean to live.

J. Milton

CXLV

IL PENSEROSO

Hence, vain deluding Joys,
    The brood of Folly without father bred!
How little you bestead
    Or fill the fixéd mind with all your toys!
Dwell in some idle brain,

And fancies fond with gaudy shapes possess
As thick and numberless
    As the gay motes that people the sunbeams,
Or likest hovering dreams,
    The fickle pensioners of Morpheus' train.

    But hail, thou goddess sage and holy,
    Hail, divinest Melancholy!
    Whose saintly visage is too bright
    To hit the sense of human sight,
    And therefore to our weaker view
    O'erlaid with black, staid Wisdom's hue;
    Black, but such as in esteem
    Prince Memnon's sister might beseem,
    Or that starr'd Ethiop queen that strove
    To set her beauty's praise above
    The sea-nymphs, and their powers offended:
    Yet thou art higher far descended:
    Thee bright-hair'd Vesta, long of yore,
    To solitary Saturn bore;
    His daughter she; in Saturn's reign
    Such mixture was not held a stain:
    Oft in glimmering bowers and glades
    He met her, and in secret shades
    Of woody Ida's inmost grove,
    While yet there was no fear of Jove.
    Come, pensive Nun, devout and pure,
    Sober, steadfast, and demure,
    All in a robe of darkest grain
    Flowing with majestic train,
    And sable stole of Cipres lawn
    Over thy decent shoulders drawn:
    Come, but keep thy wonted state,
    With even step, and musing gait,
    And looks commercing with the skies,
    Thy rapt soul sitting in thine eyes:
    There, held in holy passion still,

Forget thyself to marble, till
With a sad leaden downward cast
Thou fix them on the earth as fast:
And join with thee calm Peace, and Quiet,
Spare Fast, that oft with gods doth diet,
And hears the Muses in a ring
Aye round about Jove's altar sing:
And add to these retired Leisure
That in trim gardens takes his pleasure: –
But first and chiefest, with thee bring
Him that yon soars on golden wing
Guiding the fiery-wheeléd throne,
The cherub Contemplatión;
And the mute Silence hist along,
'Less Philomel will deign a song
In her sweetest saddest plight
Smoothing the rugged brow of Night,
While Cynthia checks her dragon yoke
Gently o'er the accustom'd oak.
– Sweet bird, that shunn'st the noise of folly,
Most musical, most melancholy!
Thee, chauntress, oft, the woods among
I woo, to hear thy even-song;
And missing thee, I walk unseen
On the dry smooth-shaven green,
To behold the wandering Moon
Riding near her highest noon,
Like one that had been led astray
Through the heaven's wide pathless way,
And oft, as if her head she bow'd,
Stooping through a fleecy cloud.
   Oft, on a plat of rising ground
I hear the far-off Curfeu sound
Over some wide-water'd shore,
Swinging slow with sullen roar:
Or, if the air will not permit,
Some still removéd place will fit,

Where glowing embers through the room
Teach light to counterfeit a gloom;
Far from all resort of mirth,
Save the cricket on the hearth,
Or the bellman's drowsy charm
To bless the doors from nightly harm.
   Or let my lamp at midnight hour
Be seen in some high lonely tower,
Where I may oft out-watch the Bear
With thrice-great Hermes, or unsphere
The spirit of Plato, to unfold
What worlds or what vast regions hold
The immortal mind, that hath forsook
Her mansion in this fleshy nook:
And of those demons that are found
In fire, air, flood, or under ground,
Whose power hath a true consent
With planet, or with element.
Sometime let gorgeous Tragedy
In scepter'd pall come sweeping by,
Presenting Thebes, or Pelops' line,
Or the tale of Troy divine;
Or what (though rare) of later age
Ennobled hath the buskin'd stage.
   But, O sad Virgin, that thy power
Might raise Musaeus from his bower,
Or bid the soul of Orpheus sing
Such notes as, warbled to the string,
Drew iron tears down Pluto's cheek
And made Hell grant what Love did seek!
Or call up him that left half-told
The story of Cambuscan bold,
Of Camball, and of Algarsife,
And who had Canacé to wife
That own'd the virtuous ring and glass;
And of the wondrous horse of brass
On which the Tartar king did ride:

And if aught else great bards beside
In sage and solemn tunes have sung
Of turneys, and of trophies hung,
Of forests, and enchantments drear,
Where more is meant than meets the ear.

   Thus, Night, oft see me in thy pale career,
Till civil-suited Morn appear,
Not trick'd and frounced as she was wont
With the Attic Boy to hunt,
But kercheft in a comely cloud
While rocking winds are piping loud,
Or usher'd with a shower still,
When the gust hath blown his fill,
Ending on the rustling leaves
With minute drops from off the eaves.
And when the sun begins to fling
His flaring beams, me, goddess, bring
To archéd walks of twilight groves,
And shadows brown, that Sylvan loves,
Of pine, or monumental oak,
Where the rude axe, with heavéd stroke,
Was never heard the nymphs to daunt
Or fright them from their hallow'd haunt.
There in close covert by some brook
Where no profaner eye may look,
Hide me from day's garish eye,
While the bee with honey'd thigh
That at her flowery work doth sing,
And the waters murmuring,
With such consort as they keep
Entice the dewy-feather'd Sleep;
And let some strange mysterious dream
Wave at his wings in airy stream
Of lively portraiture display'd,
Softly on my eyelids laid:
And, as I wake, sweet music breathe
Above, about, or underneath,

Sent by some Spirit to mortals good,
Or the unseen Genius of the wood.
    But let my due feet never fail
To walk the studious cloister's pale,
And love the high-embowéd roof,
With antique pillars massy proof,
And storied windows richly dight
Casting a dim religious light.
There let the pealing organ blow
To the full-voiced quire below
In service high and anthems clear,
As may with sweetness, through mine ear,
Dissolve me into ecstasies,
And bring all Heaven before mine eyes.
   And may at last my weary age
Find out the peaceful hermitage,
The hairy gown and mossy cell
Where I may sit and rightly spell
Of every star that heaven doth shew,
And every herb that sips the dew;
Till old experience do attain
To something like prophetic strain.

   These pleasures, Melancholy, give,
And I with thee will choose to live.

J. Milton

CXLVI
SONG OF THE EMIGRANTS IN BERMUDA

Where the remote Bermudas ride
In the ocean's bosom unespied,
From a small boat that row'd along
The listening winds received this song.
   'What should we do but sing His praise

That led us through the watery maze
Where He the huge sea-monsters wracks,
That lift the deep upon their backs,
Unto an isle so long unknown,
And yet far kinder than our own?
He lands us on a grassy stage,
Safe from the storms, and prelate's rage;
He gave us this eternal Spring
Which here enamels everything,
And sends the fowls to us in care
On daily visits through the air.
He hangs in shades the orange bright
Like golden lamps in a green night,
And does in the pomegranates close
Jewels more rich than Ormus shows:
He makes the figs our mouths to meet
And throws the melons at our feet;
But apples plants of such a price,
No tree could ever bear them twice.
With cedars chosen by His hand
From Lebanon He stores the land;
And makes the hollow seas that roar
Proclaim the ambergris on shore.
He cast (of which we rather boast)
The Gospel's pearl upon our coast;
And in these rocks for us did frame
A temple where to sound His name.
Oh! let our voice His praise exalt
Till it arrive at Heaven's vault,
Which thence (perhaps) rebounding may
Echo beyond the Mexique bay!'
– Thus sung they in the English boat
A holy and a cheerful note:
And all the way, to guide their chime,
With falling oars they kept the time.

A. Marvell

CXLVII
AT A SOLEMN MUSIC

Blest pair of Sirens, pledges of Heaven's joy,
Sphere-born harmonious Sisters, Voice and Verse!
Wed your divine sounds, and mixt power employ,
Dead things with inbreathed sense able to pierce;
And to our high-raised phantasy present
That undisturbéd Song of pure concent
Aye sung before the sapphire-colour'd throne
      To Him that sits thereon,
With saintly shout and solemn jubilee;
Where the bright Seraphim in burning row
Their loud uplifted angel-trumpets blow;
And the Cherubic host in thousand quires
Touch their immortal harps of golden wires,
With those just Spirits that wear victorious palms,
      Hymns devout and holy psalms
      Singing everlastingly:
That we on Earth, with undiscording voice
May rightly answer that melodious noise;
As once we did, till disproportion'd sin
Jarr'd against nature's chime, and with harsh din
Broke the fair music that all creatures made
To their great Lord, whose love their motion sway'd
In perfect diapason, whilst they stood
In first obedience, and their state of good.
O may we soon again renew that Song,
And keep in tune with Heaven, till God ere long
To His celestial consort us unite,
To live with Him, and sing in endless morn of light!

         J. Milton

CXLVIII

NOX NOCTI INDICAT SCIENTIAM
[*Added 1891*]

When I survey the bright
    Celestial sphere:
So rich with jewels hung, that night
Doth like an Ethiop bride appear;

My soul her wings doth spread,
    And heaven-ward flies,
The Almighty's mysteries to read
In the large volumes of the skies.

For the bright firmament
    Shoots forth no flame
So silent, but is eloquent
In speaking the Creator's name.

No unregarded star
    Contracts its light
Into so small a character,
Removed far from our human sight,

But if we steadfast look,
    We shall discern
In it as in some holy book,
How man may heavenly knowledge learn.

It tells the Conqueror,
    That far-stretch'd power
Which his proud dangers traffic for,
Is but the triumph of an hour.

That from the farthest North
    Some nation may
Yet undiscover'd issue forth,
And o'er his new-got conquest sway.

Some nation yet shut in
With hills of ice,
May be let out to scourge his sin,
Till they shall equal him in vice.

And then they likewise shall
Their ruin have;
For as yourselves your Empires fall,
And every Kingdom hath a grave.

Thus those celestial fires,
Though seeming mute,
The fallacy of our desires
And all the pride of life, confute.

For they have watch'd since first
The world had birth:
And found sin in itself accursed,
And nothing permanent on earth.

W. Habington

CXLIX
HYMN TO DARKNESS
[*Added 1890*]

Hail thou most sacred venerable thing!
What Muse is worthy thee to sing?
Thee, from whose pregnant universal womb
All things, ev'n Light, thy rival, first did come.
What dares he not attempt that sings of thee,
Thou first and greatest mystery?
Who can the secrets of thy essence tell?
Thou, like the light of God, art inaccessible.

Before great Love this monument did raise
    This ample theatre of praise;
  Before the folding circles of the sky
  Were tuned by Him, Who is all harmony;
  Before the morning Stars their hymn began,
    Before the council held for man,
  Before the birth of either time or place,
Thou reign'st unquestion'd monarch in the empty space.

  Thy native lot thou didst to Light resign,
    But still half of the globe is thine.
  Here with a quiet, but yet awful hand,
  Like the best emperors thou dost command.
  To thee the stars above their brightness owe,
    And mortals their repose below:
  To thy protection fear and sorrow flee,
And those that weary are of light, find rest in thee.

J. Norris of Bemerton

CL

A VISION
[*Added 1883*]

I saw Eternity the other night,
Like a great ring of pure and endless light,
    All calm, as it was bright: –
And round beneath it, Time, in hours, days, years,
    Driven by the spheres,
Like a vast shadow moved; in which the World
    And all her train were hurl'd.

H. Vaughan

CLI

ALEXANDER'S FEAST, OR, THE POWER OF MUSIC

'Twas at the royal feast for Persia won
    By Philip's warlike son –
    Aloft in awful sate
    The godlike hero sate
    On his imperial throne;
    His valiant peers were placed around,
    Their brows with roses and with myrtles bound,
    (So should desert in arms be crown'd);
    The lovely Thais by his side
    Sate like a blooming Eastern bride
    In flower of youth and beauty's pride: –
    Happy, happy, happy pair!
    None but the brave
    None but the brave
    None but the brave deserves the fair!

  Timotheus placed on high
Amid the tuneful quire
With flying fingers touch'd the lyre:
The trembling notes ascend the sky
And heavenly joys inspire.
The song began from Jove
Who left his blissful seats above –
Such is the power of mighty love!
A dragon's fiery form belied the god;
Sublime on radiant spires he rode
When he to fair Olympia prest,
And while he sought her snowy breast,
Then round her slender waist he curl'd,
And stamp'd an image of himself, a sovereign of the world.
– The listening crowd admire the lofty sound;
A present deity! they shout around:
A present deity! the vaulted roofs rebound:
With ravish'd ears
The monarch hears,

Assumes the god;
Affects to nod
And seems to shake the spheres.

   The praise of Bacchus then the sweet musician sung,
Of Bacchus ever fair and ever young:
The jolly god in triumph comes;
Sound the trumpets, beat the drums!
Flush'd with a purple grace
He shows his honest face:
Now give the hautboys breath; he comes, he comes!
Bacchus, ever fair and young,
Drinking joys did first ordain;
Bacchus' blessings are a treasure,
Drinking is the soldier's pleasure:
Rich the treasure,
Sweet the pleasure,
Sweet is pleasure after pain.

   Soothed with the sound, the king grew vain;
Fought all his battles o'er again,
And thrice he routed all his foes, and thrice he slew the slain!
The master saw the madness rise,
His glowing cheeks, his ardent eyes;
And while he Heaven and Earth defied
Changed his hand and check'd his pride.
He chose a mournful Muse
Soft pity to infuse:
He sung Darius great and good,
By too severe a fate
Fallen, fallen, fallen, fallen,
Fallen from his high estate,
And weltering in his blood;
Deserted at his utmost need
By those his former bounty fed;
On the bare earth exposed he lies
With not a friend to close his eyes.
– With downcast looks the joyless victor sate,

Revolving in his alter'd soul
The various turns of Chance below;
And now and then a sigh he stole,
And tears began to flow.

The mighty master smiled to see
That love was in the next degree;
'Twas but a kindred sound to move,
For pity melts the mind to love.
Softly sweet, in Lydian measures
Soon he soothed his soul to pleasures.
War, he sung, is toil and trouble,
Honour but an empty bubble;
Never ending, still beginning,
Fighting still, and still destroying;
If the world be worth thy winning,
Think, O think, it worth enjoying:
Lovely Thais sits beside thee,
Take the good the gods provide thee!
– The many rend the skies with loud applause;
So Love was crown'd, but Music won the cause.
The prince, unable to conceal his pain,
Gazed on the fair
Who caused his care,
And sigh'd and look'd, sigh'd and look'd,
Sigh'd and look'd, and sigh'd again:
At length with love and wine at once opprest
The vanquish'd victor sunk upon her breast.

Now strike the golden lyre again:
A louder yet, and yet a louder strain!
Break his bands of sleep asunder
And rouse him like a rattling peal of thunder.
Hark, hark! the horrid sound
Has raised up his head:
As awaked from the dead
And amazed he stares around.
Revenge, revenge, Timotheus cries,

See the Furies arise!
See the snakes that they rear
How they hiss in their hair,
And the sparkles that flash from their eyes!
Behold a ghastly band,
Each a torch in his hand!
Those are Grecian ghosts, that in battle were slain
And unburied remain
Inglorious on the plain:
Give the vengeance due
To the valiant crew!
Behold how they toss their torches on high,
How they point to the Persian abodes
And glittering temples of their hostile gods.
– The princes applaud with a furious joy:
And the King seized a flambeau with zeal to destroy;
Thais led the way
To light him to his prey,
And like another Helen, fired another Troy!

  – Thus, long ago,
Ere heaving bellows learn'd to blow,
While organs yet were mute,
Timotheus, to his breathing flute
And sounding lyre
Could swell the soul to rage, or kindle soft desire.
At last divine Cecilia came,
Inventress of the vocal frame;
The sweet enthusiast from her sacred store
Enlarged the former narrow bounds,
And added length to solemn sounds,
With Nature's mother-wit, and arts unknown before.
– Let old Timotheus yield the prize
Or both divide the crown;
He raised a mortal to the skies;
She drew an angel down!

                                              J. Dryden

ODE ON THE PLEASURE ARISING FROM VICISSITUDE

Now the golden Morn aloft
   Waves her dew-bespangled wing,
With vermeil cheek and whisper soft
   She woos the tardy Spring:
Till April starts, and calls around
The sleeping fragrance from the ground,
And lightly o'er the living scene
Scatters his freshest, tenderest green.

New-born flocks, in rustic dance,
   Frisking ply their feeble feet;
Forgetful of their wintry trance
   The birds his presence greet:
But chief, the sky-lark warbles high
His trembling thrilling ecstasy;
And lessening from the dazzled sight,
Melts into air and liquid light.

Yesterday the sullen year
   Saw the snowy whirlwind fly;
Mute was the music of the air,
   The herd stood drooping by:
Their raptures now that wildly flow
No yesterday nor morrow know;
'Tis Man alone that joy descries
With forward and reverted eyes.

Smiles on past misfortune's brow
    Soft reflection's hand can trace,
And o'er the cheek of sorrow throw
    A melancholy grace;
While hope prolongs our happier hour,
Or deepest shades, that dimly lour
And blacken round our weary way,
Gilds with a gleam of distant day.

Still, where rosy pleasure leads,
    See a kindred grief pursue;
Behind the steps that misery treads
    Approaching comfort view:
The hues of bliss more brightly glow
Chastised by sabler tints of woe,
And blended form, with artful strife,
The strength and harmony of life.

See the wretch that long has tost
    On the thorny bed of pain,
At length repair his vigour lost
    And breathe and walk again:
The meanest floweret of the vale,
The simplest note that swells the gale,
The common sun, the air, the skies,
To him are opening Paradise.

T. Gray

CLIII

ODE TO SIMPLICITY
[*Added 1891*]

O Thou, by Nature taught
To breathe her genuine thought
In numbers warmly pure, and sweetly strong;

Who first, on mountains wild,
In Fancy, loveliest child,
Thy babe, or Pleasure's, nursed the powers of song!
Thou, who with hermit heart,
Disdain'st the wealth of art,
And gauds, and pageant weeds, and trailing pall,
But com'st, a decent maid
In Attic robe array'd,
O chaste, unboastful Nymph, to thee I call!

By all the honey'd store
On Hybla's thymy shore,
By all her blooms and mingled murmurs dear;
By her whose love-lorn woe
In evening musings slow
Soothed sweetly sad Electra's poet's ear:

By old Cephisus deep,
Who spread his wavy sweep
In warbled wanderings round thy green retreat;
On whose enamell'd side,
When holy Freedom died,
No equal haunt allured thy future feet: –

O sister meek of Truth,
To my admiring youth
Thy sober aid and native charms infuse!
The flowers that sweetest breathe,
Though Beauty cull'd the wreath,
Still ask thy hand to range their order'd hues.

While Rome could none esteem
But Virtue's patriot theme,
You loved her hills, and led her laureat band;
But stay'd to sing alone
To one distinguish'd throne;
And turn'd thy face, and fled her alter'd land.

No more, in hall or bower,
　The Passions own thy power;
Love, only Love, her forceless numbers mean:
　　For thou hast left her shrine;
　　Nor olive more, nor vine,
Shall gain thy feet to bless the servile scene.

　　Though taste, though genius, bless
　　To some divine excess,
Faints the cold work till thou inspire the whole;
　　What each, what all supply
　　May court, may charm our eye;
Thou, only thou, canst raise the meeting soul!

　　Of these let others ask
　　To aid some mighty task;
I only seek to find thy temperate vale;
　　Where oft my reed might sound
　　To maids and shepherds round,
And all thy sons, O Nature! learn my tale.

W. Collins

CLIV
SOLITUDE

Happy the man, whose wish and care
A few paternal acres bound,
Content to breathe his native air
　　　　In his own ground.

Whose herds with milk, whose fields with bread,
Whose flocks supply him with attire;
Whose trees in summer yield him shade,
　　　　In winter fire.

Blest, who can unconcern'dly find
Hours, days, and years, slide soft away
In health of body, peace of mind,
　　　　Quiet by day,

Sound sleep by night; study and ease
Together mixt, sweet recreation,
And innocence, which most does please
                With meditation.

Thus let me live, unseen, unknown;
Thus unlamented let me die;
Steal from the world, and not a stone
                Tell where I lie.

A. Pope

CLV
THE BLIND BOY

O say what is that thing call'd Light,
   Which I must ne'er enjoy;
What are the blessings of the sight,
   O tell your poor blind boy!

You talk of wondrous things you see,
   You say the sun shines bright;
I feel him warm, but how can he
   Or make it day or night?

My day or night myself I make .
   Whene'er I sleep or play;
And could I ever keep awake
   With me 'twere always day.

With heavy sighs I often hear
   You mourn my hapless woe;
But sure with patience I can bear
   A loss I ne'er can know.

Then let not what I cannot have
   My cheer of mind destroy:
Whilst thus I sing, I am a king,
   Although a poor blind boy.

C. Cibber

CLVI

ON A FAVOURITE CAT, DROWNED IN A TUB OF GOLD FISHES

'Twas on a lofty vase's side,
Where China's gayest art had dyed
The azure flowers that blow,
Demurest of the tabby kind
The pensive Selima, reclined,
Gazed on the lake below.

Her conscious tail her joy declared:
The fair round face, the snowy beard,
The velvet of her paws,
Her coat that with the tortoise vies,
Her ears of jet, and emerald eyes –
She saw, and purr'd applause.

Still had she gazed, but 'midst the tide
Two angel forms were seen to glide,
The Genii of the stream:
Their scaly armour's Tyrian hue
Through richest purple, to the view
Betray'd a golden gleam.

The hapless Nymph with wonder saw:
A whisker first, and then a claw
With many an ardent wish
She stretch'd, in vain, to reach the prize –
What female heart can gold despise?
What Cat's averse to fish?

Presumptuous maid! with looks intent
Again she stretch'd, again she bent,
Nor knew the gulf between –
Malignant Fate sat by and smiled –
The slippery verge her feet beguiled;
She tumbled headlong in!

Eight times emerging from the flood
She mew'd to every watery God
Some speedy aid to send: –
No Dolphin came, no Nereid stirr'd,
Nor cruel Tom nor Susan heard –
A favourite has no friend!

From hence, ye Beauties! undeceived
Know one false step is ne'er retrieved,
And be with caution bold:
Not all that tempts your wandering eyes
And heedless hearts, is lawful prize,
Nor all that glisters, gold!

T. Gray

CLVII
TO CHARLOTTE PULTENEY

Timely blossom, Infant fair,
Fondling of a happy pair,
Every morn and every night
Their solicitous delight,
Sleeping, waking, still at ease,
Pleasing, without skill to please;
Little gossip, blithe and hale,
Tattling many a broken tale,
Singing many a tuneless song,
Lavish of a heedless tongue;
Simple maiden, void of art,
Babbling out the very heart,
Yet abandon'd to thy will,
Yet imagining no ill,
Yet too innocent to blush;
Like the linnet in the bush
To the mother-linnet's note
Moduling her slender throat;

Chirping forth thy petty joys,
Wanton in the change of toys,
Like the linnet green, in May
Flitting to each bloomy spray;
Wearied then and glad of rest,
Like the linnet in the nest: –
This thy present happy lot
This, in time will be forgot:
Other pleasures, other cares,
Ever-busy Time prepares;
And thou shalt in thy daughter see,
This picture, once, resembled thee.

A. Philips

CLVIII
RULE BRITANNIA

When Britain first at Heaven's command
   Arose from out the azure main,
This was the charter of her land,
   And guardian angels sung the strain:
Rule, Britannia! Britannia rules the waves!
   Britons never shall be slaves.

The nations not so blest as thee
   Must in their turn to tyrants fall,
Whilst thou shalt flourish great and free
   The dread and envy of them all.

Still more majestic shalt thou rise,
   More dreadful from each foreign stroke;
As the loud blast that tears the skies
   Serve but to root thy native oak.

Thee haughty tyrants ne'er shall tame;
   All their attempts to bend thee down
Will but arouse thy generous flame,
   And work their woe and thy renown.

To thee belongs the rural reign;
    Thy cities shall with commerce shine;
All thine shall be the subject main,
    And every shore it circles thine!

The Muses, still with Freedom found,
    Shall to thy happy coast repair;
Blest Isle, with matchless beauty crown'd
    And manly hearts to guard the fair: −
Rule, Britannia! Britannia rules the waves!
    Britons never shall be slaves!

J. Thomson

CLIX

THE BARD
Pindaric Ode

'Ruin seize thee, ruthless King!
  Confusion on thy banners wait;
Tho' fann'd by Conquest's crimson wing
  They mock the air with idle state.
Helm, nor hauberk's twisted mail,
Nor e'en thy virtues, Tyrant, shall avail
To save thy secret soul from nightly fears,
From Cambria's curse, from Cambria's tears!'
− Such were the sounds that o'er the crested pride
  Of the first Edward scatter'd wild dismay,
As down the steep of Snowdon's shaggy side
  He wound with toilsome march his long array: −
Stout Glo'ster stood aghast in speechless trance;
'To arms!' cried Mortimer, and couch'd his quivering lance.

  On a rock, whose haughty brow
Frowns o'er old Conway's foaming flood,
  Robed in the sable garb of woe
With haggard eyes the Poet stood;

(Loose his beard and hoary hair
Stream'd like a meteor to the troubled air)
And with a master's hand and prophet's fire
Struck the deep sorrows of his lyre:
   'Hark, how each giant-oak and desert-cave
Sighs to the torrent's awful voice beneath!
O'er thee, oh King! their hundred arms they wave,
   Revenge on thee in hoarser murmurs breathe;
Vocal no more, since Cambria's fatal day,
To high-born Hoel's harp, or soft Llewellyn's lay.

   'Cold is Cadwallo's tongue,
     That hush'd the stormy main:
Brave Urien sleeps upon his craggy bed:
     Mountains, ye mourn in vain
     Modred, whose magic song
Made huge Plinlimmon bow his cloud-topt head.
   On dreary Arvon's shore they lie
Smear'd with gore and ghastly pale:
   Far, far aloof the affrighted ravens sail;
     The famish'd eagle screams, and passes by.
Dear lost companions of my tuneful art,
   Dear as the light that visits these sad eyes,
Dear as the ruddy drops that warm my heart,
   Ye died amidst your dying country's cries –
No more I weep; They do not sleep;
   On yonder cliffs, a griesly band,
I see them sit; They linger yet,
   Avengers of their native land:
With me in dreadful harmony they join,
And weave with bloody hands the tissue of thy line.

   'Weave the warp and weave the woof
     The winding sheet of Edward's race:
   Give ample room and verge enough
     The characters of hell to trace.
Mark the year, and mark the night,
When Severn shall re-echo with affright

The shrieks of death thro' Berkley's roof that ring,
Shrieks of an agonizing king!
　　She-wolf of France, with unrelenting fangs
That tear'st the bowels of thy mangled mate,
　　From thee be born, who o'er thy country hangs
The scourge of heaven! What terrors round him wait!
Amazement in his van, with flight combined,
And sorrow's faded form, and solitude behind.

'Mighty victor, mighty lord,
　　Low on his funeral couch he lies!
No pitying heart, no eye, afford
　　A tear to grace his obsequies.
Is the sable warrior fled?
Thy son is gone. He rests among the dead.
The swarm that in thy noon-tide beam were born?
– Gone to salute the rising morn.
Fair laughs the Morn, and soft the zephyr blows,
　　While proudly riding o'er the azure realm
In gallant trim the gilded vessel goes:
　　Youth on the prow, and Pleasure at the helm:
Regardless of the sweeping whirlwind's sway,
That hush'd in grim repose expects his evening prey.

'Fill high the sparkling bowl,
The rich repast prepare;
　　Reft of a crown, he yet may share the feast:
Close by the regal chair
　　Fell Thirst and Famine scowl
　　A baleful smile upon their baffled guest,
Heard ye the din of battle bray,
　　Lance to lance, and horse to horse?
　　Long years of havock urge their destined course,
And thro' the kindred squadrons mow their way.
　　Ye towers of Julius, London's lasting shame,
With many a foul and midnight murder fed,
　　Revere his consort's faith, his father's fame,
And spare the meek usurper's holy head!

Above, below, the rose of snow,
 Twined with her blushing foe, we spread:
The bristled boar in infant-gore
 Wallows beneath the thorny shade.
Now, brothers, bending o'er the accursèd loom,
Stamp we our vengeance deep, and ratify his doom.

'*Edward, lo! to sudden fate*
 (Weave we the woof; The thread is spun;)
Half of thy heart we consecrate.
 (The web is wove; The work is done.)
– Stay, oh stay! nor thus forlorn
Leave me unbless'd, unpitied, here to mourn:
In yon bright track that fires the western skies
They melt, they vanish from my eyes.
But oh! what solemn scenes on Snowdon's height
 Descending slow their glittering skirts unroll?
Visions of glory, spare my aching sight,
Ye unborn ages, crowd not on my soul!
No more our long-lost Arthur we bewail: –
All hail, ye genuine kings! Britannia's issue, hail!

 'Girt with many a baron bold
Sublime their starry fronts they rear;
 And gorgeous dames, and statesmen old
In bearded majesty, appear.
In the midst a form divine!
Her eye proclaims her of the Briton-line:
Her lion-port, her awe-commanding face
Attemper'd sweet to virgin-grace.
What strings symphonious tremble in the air,
 What strains of vocal transport round her play?
Hear from the grave, great Taliessin, hear;
 They breathe a soul to animate thy clay.
Bright Rapture calls, and soaring as she sings,
Waves in the eye of heaven her many-colour'd wings.

'The verse adorn again
    Fierce war, and faithful love,
And truth severe, by fairy fiction drest.
    In buskin'd measures move
Pale grief, and pleasing pain,
With horror, tyrant of the throbbing breast.
A voice as of the cherub-choir
    Gales from blooming Eden bear,
    And distant warblings lessen on my ear
That lost in long futurity expire.
Fond impious man, think'st thou yon sanguine cloud
    Raised by thy breath, has quench'd the orb of day?
To-morrow he repairs the golden flood
    And warms the nations with redoubled ray.
Enough for me: with joy I see
    The different doom our fates assign:
Be thine despair and sceptred care,
    To triumph and to die are mine.'
– He spoke, and headlong from the mountain's height
Deep in the roaring tide he plunged to endless night.

T. Gray

CLX
ODE WRITTEN IN 1746

How sleep the brave, who sink to rest
By all their country's wishes blest!
When Spring, with dewy fingers cold,
Returns to deck their hallow'd mould,
She there shall dress a sweeter sod
Than Fancy's feet have ever trod.

By fairy hands their knell is rung,
By forms unseen their dirge is sung:
There Honour comes, a pilgrim gray,
To bless the turf that wraps their clay;
And Freedom shall awhile repair
To dwell a weeping hermit there!

W. Collins

CLXI
LAMENT FOR CULLODEN

The lovely lass o' Inverness,
Nae joy nor pleasure can she see;
For e'en and morn she cries, Alas!
And aye the saut tear blins her ee:
Drumossie moor – Drumossie day –
A waefu' day it was to me!
For there I lost my father dear,
My father dear, and brethren three.

Their winding-sheet the bluidy clay,
Their graves are growing green to see:
And by them lies the dearest lad
That ever blest a woman's ee!
Now wae to thee, thou cruel lord,
A bluidy man I trow thou be;
For mony a heart thou hast made sair
That ne'er did wrang to thine or thee.

R. Burns

CLXII
LAMENT FOR EN

I've heard them lilting at our ewe-milking,
    Lasses a' lilting before dawn o' day;
But now they are moaning on ilka green loaning –
    The Flowers of the Forest are a' wede away.

At bughts, in the morning, nae blythe lads are scorning,
    Lasses are lonely and dowie and wae;
Nae daffin', nae gabbin', but sighing and sabbing,
    Ilk ane lifts her leglin and hies her away.
In har'st, at the shearing, nae youths now are jeering,
    Bandsters are lyart, and runkled, and gray;
At fair or at preaching, nae wooing, nae fleeching –
    The Flowers of the Forest are a' wede away.

At e'en, in the gloaming, nae younkers are roaming
    'Bout stacks wi' the lasses at bogle to play;
But ilk ane sits drearie, lamenting her dearie –
    The Flowers of the Forest are weded away.

Dool and wae for the order, sent our lads to the Border!
    The English, for ance, by guile wan the day;
The Flowers of the Forest, that fought aye the foremost,
    The prime of our land, are cauld in the clay.

We'll hear nae mair lilting at the ewe-milking;
    Women and bairns are heartless and wae;
Sighing and moaning on ilka green loaning –
    The Flowers of the Forest are a' wede away.

J. Elliott

CLXIII
THE BRAES OF YARROW

Thy braes were bonny, Yarrow stream,
When first on them I met my lover;
Thy braes how dreary, Yarrow stream,
When now thy waves his body cover!
For ever now, O Yarrow stream!
Thou art to me a stream of sorrow;
For never on thy banks shall I
Behold my Love, the flower of Yarrow!

He promised me a milk-white steed
To bear me to his father's bowers;
He promised me a little page
To squire me to his father's towers;
He promised me a wedding-ring, –
The wedding-day was fix'd to-morrow; –
Now he is wedded to his grave,
Alas, his watery grave, in Yarrow!

Sweet were his words when last we met;
My passion I as freely told him;
Clasp'd in his arms, I little thought
That I should never more behold him!
Scarce was he gone, I saw his ghost;
It vanish'd with a shriek of sorrow;
Thrice did the water-wraith ascend,
And gave a doleful groan thro' Yarrow.

His mother from the window look'd
With all the longing of a mother;
His little sister weeping walk'd
The green-wood path to meet her brother;
They sought him east, they sought him west,
They sought him all the forest thorough;
They only saw the cloud of night,
They only heard the roar of Yarrow.

No longer from thy window look –
Thou hast no son, thou tender mother!
No longer walk, thou lovely maid;
Alas, thou hast no more a brother!
No longer seek him east or west
And search no more the forest thorough;
For, wandering in the night so dark,
He fell a lifeless corpse in Yarrow.

The tear shall never leave my cheek,
No other youth shall be my marrow –
I'll seek thy body in the stream,
And then with thee I'll sleep in Yarrow.
– The tear did never leave her cheek,
No other youth became her marrow;
She found his body in the stream,
And now with him she sleeps in Yarrow.

J. Logan

CLXIV
WILLY DROWNED IN YARROW

Down in yon garden sweet and gay
  Where bonnie grows the lily,
I heard a fair maid sighing say,
  'My wish be wi' sweet Willie!

'Willie's rare, and Willie's fair,
  And Willie's wondrous bonny;
And Willie hecht to marry me
  Gin e'er he married ony.

'O gentle wind, that bloweth south
  From where my Love repaireth,
Convey a kiss frae his dear mouth
  And tell me how he fareth!

'O tell sweet Willie to come doun
  And hear the mavis singing,
And see the birds on ilka bush
  And leaves around them hinging.

'The lav'rock there, wi' her white breast
  And gentle throat sae narrow;
There's sport eneuch for gentlemen
  On Leader haughs and Yarrow.

'O Leader haughs are wide and braid
   And Yarrow haughs are bonny;
There Willie hecht to marry me
   If e'er he married ony.

'But Willie's gone, whom I thought on,
   And does not hear me weeping;
Draws many a tear frae true love's e'e
   When other maids are sleeping.

'Yestreen I made my bed fu' braid,
   The night I'll mak' it narrow,
For a' the live-lang winter night
   I lie twined o' my marrow.

'O came ye by yon water-side?
   Pou'd you the rose or lily?
Or came you by yon meadow green,
   Or saw you my sweet Willie?'

She sought him up, she sought him down,
   She sought him braid and narrow;
Syne, in the cleaving of a craig,
   She found him drown'd in Yarrow!

Anon.

CLXV
LOSS OF THE ROYAL GEORGE

Toll for the Brave!
The brave that are no more!
All sunk beneath the wave
Fast by their native shore!

Eight hundred of the brave
Whose courage well was tried,
Had made the vessel heel
And laid her on her side.

A land-breeze shook the shrouds
And she was overset;
Down went the Royal George,
With all her crew complete.

Toll for the brave!
Brave Kempenfelt is gone;
His last sea-fight is fought,
His work of glory done.

It was not in the battle;
No tempest gave the shock;
She sprang no fatal leak,
She ran upon no rock.

His sword was in its sheath,
His fingers held the pen,
When Kempenfelt went down
With twice four hundred men.

– Weigh the vessel up
Once dreaded by our foes!
And mingle with our cup
The tears that England owes.

Her timbers yet are sound,
And she may float again
Full charged with England's thunder,
And plough the distant main:

But Kempenfelt is gone,
His victories are o'er;
And he and his eight hundred
Shall plough the wave no more.

W. Cowper

CLXVI
BLACK-EYED SUSAN

All in the Downs the fleet was moor'd,
    The streamers waving in the wind,
When black-eyed Susan came aboard;
    'O! where shall I my true-love find?
Tell me, ye jovial sailors, tell me true
If my sweet William sails among the crew.'

William, who high upon the yard
    Rock'd with the billow to and fro,
Soon as her well-known voice he heard
    He sigh'd, and cast his eyes below:
The cord slides swiftly through his glowing hands,
And quick as lightning on the deck he stands.

So the sweet lark, high poised in air,
    Shuts close his pinions to his breast
If chance his mate's shrill call he hear,
    And drops at once into her nest: —
The noblest captain in the British fleet
Might envy William's lip those kisses sweet.

'O Susan, Susan, lovely dear,
    My vows shall ever true remain;
Let me kiss off that falling tear;
    We only part to meet again.
Change as ye list, ye winds; my heart shall be
The faithful compass that still points to thee.

'Believe not what the landmen say
    Who tempt with doubts thy constant mind;
They'll tell thee, sailors, when away,
    In every port a mistress find:
Yes, yes, believe them when they tell thee so,
For Thou art present wheresoe'er I go.

'If to fair India's coast we sail
  Thy eyes are seen in diamonds bright,
Thy breath is Afric's spicy gale,
  Thy skin is ivory so white.
Thus every beauteous object that I view
Wakes in my soul some charm of lovely Sue.

'Though battle call me from thy arms
  Let not my pretty Susan mourn;
Though cannons roar, yet safe from harms
  William shall to his Dear return.
Love turns aside the balls that round me fly,
Lest precious tears should drop from Susan's eye.'

The boatswain gave the dreadful word,
  The sails their swelling bosom spread;
No longer must she stay aboard;
  They kiss'd, she sigh'd, he hung his head.
Her lessening boat unwilling rows to land;
'Adieu!' she cries; and waved her lily hand.

J. Gay

CLXVII
SALLY IN OUR ALLEY

Of all the girls that are so smart
  There's none like pretty Sally;
She is the darling of my heart,
  And she lives in our alley.
There is no lady in the land
  Is half so sweet as Sally;
She is the darling of my heart,
  And she lives in our alley.

Her father he makes cabbage-nets
  And through the streets does cry 'em;
Her mother she sells laces long
  To such as please to buy 'em:

But sure such folks could ne'er beget
   So sweet a girl as Sally!
She is the darling of my heart,
    And she lives in our alley.

When she is by, I leave my work,
   I love her so sincerely;
My master comes like any Turk,
   And bangs me most severely –
But let him bang his bellyful,
   I'll bear it all for Sally;
She is the darling of my heart,
   And she lives in our alley.

Of all the days that's in the week
   I dearly love but one day –
And that's the day that comes betwixt
   A Saturday and Monday;
For then I'm drest all in my best
   To walk abroad with Sally;
She is the darling of my heart,
   And she lives in our alley.

My master carries me to church,
   And often am I blamed
Because I leave him in the lurch
   As soon as text is named;
I leave the church in sermon-time
   And slink away to Sally;
She is the darling of my heart,
   And she lives in our alley.

When Christmas comes about again
   O then I shall have money;
I'll hoard it up, and box it all,
   I'll give it to my honey:
I would it were ten thousand pound,
   I'd give it all to Sally;
She is the darling of my heart,
   And she lives in our alley.

My master and the neighbours all
    Make game of me and Sally,
And, but for her, I'd better be
    A slave and row a galley;
But when my seven long years are out
    O then I'll marry Sally, –
O then we'll wed, and then we'll bed . . .
    But not in our alley!

H. Carey

CLXVIII
A FAREWELL

Go fetch to me a pint o' wine,
    An' fill it in a silver tassie;
That I may drink before I go
    A service to my bonnie lassie:
The boat rocks at the pier o' Leith,
    Fu' loud the wind blaws frae the ferry,
The ship rides by the Berwick-law,
    And I maun leave my bonnie Mary.

The trumpets sound, the banners fly,
    The glittering spears are rankéd ready;
The shouts o' war are heard afar,
    The battle closes thick and bloody;
But it's not the roar o' sea or shore
    Wad make me langer wish to tarry;
Nor shout o' war that's heard afar –
    It's leaving thee, my bonnie Mary.

R. Burns

CLXIX

If doughty deeds my lady please
　　Right soon I'll mount my steed;
And strong his arm, and fast his seat
　　That bears frae me the meed.
I'll wear thy colours in my cap
　　Thy picture at my heart;
And he that bends not to thine eye
　　Shall rue it to his smart!
　　　　Then tell me how to woo thee, Love;
　　　　　　O tell me how to woo thee!
　　　　For thy dear sake, nae care I'll take
　　　　　　Tho' ne'er another trow me.

If gay attire delight thine eye
　　I'll dight me in array;
I'll tend thy chamber door all night,
　　And squire thee all the day.
If sweetest sounds can win thine ear,
　　These sounds I'll strive to catch;
Thy voice I'll steal to woo thysell,
　　That voice that nane can match.

But if fond love thy heart can gain,
　　I never broke a vow;
Nae maiden lays her skaith to me,
　　I never loved but you.
For you alone I ride the ring,
　　For you I wear the blue;
For you alone I strive to sing,
　　O tell me how to woo!
Then tell me how to woo thee, Love;
　　O tell me how to woo thee!
For thy dear sake, nae care I'll take,
　　Tho' ne'er another trow me.

R. Graham of Gartmore

CLXX
TO A YOUNG LADY

Sweet stream, that winds through yonder glade,
Apt emblem of a virtuous maid –
Silent and chaste she steals along,
Far from the world's gay busy throng:
With gentle yet prevailing force,
Intent upon her destined course;
Graceful and useful all she does.
Blessing and blest where'er she goes;
Pure-bosom'd as that watery glass
And Heaven reflected in her face.

W. Cowper

CLXXI
THE SLEEPING BEAUTY

Sleep on, and dream of Heaven awhile –
Tho' shut so close thy laughing eyes,
Thy rosy lips still wear a smile
And move, and breathe delicious sighs!

Ah, now soft blushes tinge her cheeks
And mantle o'er her neck of snow:
Ah, now she murmurs, now she speaks
What most I wish – and fear to know!

She starts, she trembles, and she weeps!
Her fair hands folded on her breast:
– And now, how like a saint she sleeps!
A seraph in the realms of rest!

Sleep on secure! Above controul
Thy thoughts belong to Heaven and thee:
And may the secret of thy soul
Remain within its sanctuary!

S. Rogers

CLXXII

For ever, Fortune, wilt thou prove
An unrelenting foe to Love,
And when we meet a mutual heart
Come in between, and bid us part?

Bid us sigh on from day to day,
And wish and wish the soul away;
Till youth and genial years are flown,
And all the life of life is gone?

But busy, busy, still art thou,
To bind the loveless joyless vow,
The heart from pleasure to delude,
To join the gentle to the rude.

For once, O Fortune, hear my prayer,
And I absolve thy future care;
All other blessings I resign,
Make but the dear Amanda mine.

J. Thomson

CLXXIII

The merchant, to secure his treasure,
Conveys it in a borrow'd name:
Euphelia serves to grace my measure,
But Cloe is my real flame.

My softest verse, my darling lyre
Upon Euphelia's toilet lay –
When Cloe noted her desire
That I should sing, that I should play.

My lyre I tune, my voice I raise,
But with my numbers mix my sighs;
And whilst I sing Euphelia's praise,
I fix my soul on Cloe's eyes.

Fair Cloe blush'd: Euphelia frown'd:
I sung, and gazed; I play'd, and trembled:
And Venus to the Loves around
Remark'd how ill we all dissembled.

M. Prior

CLXXIV
LOVE'S SECRET
[*Added 1890*]

Never seek to tell thy love,
    Love that never told can be;
For the gentle wind doth move
    Silently, invisibly.

I told my love, I told my love,
    I told her all my heart,
Trembling, cold, in ghastly fears: –
    Ah! she did depart.

Soon after she was gone from me
    A traveller came by,
Silently, invisibly:
    He took her with a sigh.

W. Blake

CLXXV

When lovely woman stoops to folly
And finds too late that men betray, –
What charm can soothe her melancholy,
What art can wash her guilt away?

The only art her guilt to cover,
   To hide her shame from every eye,
To give repentance to her lover
   And wring his bosom, is – to die.

O. Goldsmith

CLXXVI

Ye banks and braes o' bonnie Doon
   How can ye blume sae fair!
How can ye chant, ye little birds,
   And I sae fu' o' care! ·

Thou'll break my heart, thou bonnie bird
   That sings upon the bough;
Thou minds me o' the happy days
   When my fause Luve was true.

Thou'll break my heart, thou bonnie bird
   That sings beside thy mate;
For sae I sat, and sae I sang,
   And wist na o' my fate.

Aft hae I roved by bonnie Doon
   To see the woodbine twine,
And ilka bird sang o' its love;
   And sae did I o' mine.

Wi' lightsome heart I pu'd a rose,
   Frae aff its thorny tree;
And my fause luver staw the rose,
   But left the thorn wi' me.

R. Burns

CLXXVII
THE PROGRESS OF POESY
A Pindaric Ode

Awake, Aeolian lyre, awake,
And give to rapture all thy trembling strings.
From Helicon's harmonious springs
    A thousand rills their mazy progress take;
The laughing flowers that round them blow
Drink life and fragrance as they flow.
Now the rich stream of music winds along
Deep, majestic, smooth, and strong,
Thro' verdant vales, and Ceres' golden reign;
Now rolling down the steep amain
Headlong, impetuous, see it pour:
The rocks and nodding groves re-bellow to the roar.

Oh! Sovereign of the willing soul,
Parent of sweet and solemn-breathing airs,
Enchanting shell! the sullen Cares
    And frantic Passions hear thy soft controul,
On Thracia's hills the Lord of War
Has curb'd the fury of his car
And dropt his thirsty lance at thy command.
Perching on the sceptred hand
Of Jove, thy magic lulls the feather'd king
With ruffled plumes, and flagging wing:
Quench'd in dark clouds of slumber lie
The terror of his beak, and lightnings of his eye.

Thee the voice, the dance, obey
Temper'd to thy warbled lay.
O'er Idalia's velvet-green
The rosy-crownéd Loves are seen
On Cytherea's day;
With antic Sport, and blue-eyed Pleasures,
Frisking light in frolic measures;

Now pursuing, now retreating,
   Now in circling troops they meet:
To brisk notes in cadence beating
   Glance their many-twinkling feet.
Slow melting strains their Queen's approach declare:
   Where'er she turns, the Graces homage pay:
With arms sublime that float upon the air
   In gliding state she wins her easy way:
O'er her warm cheek and rising bosom move
The bloom of young Desire and purple light of Love.

   Man's feeble race what ills await!
Labour, and Penury, the racks of Pain,
Disease, and Sorrow's weeping train,
   And Death, sad refuge from the storms of fate!
The fond complaint, my song, disprove,
And justify the laws of Jove.
Say, has he given in vain the heavenly Muse?
Night, and all her sickly dews,
Her spectres wan, and birds of boding cry
He gives to range the dreary sky:
Till down the eastern cliffs afar
Hyperion's march they spy, and glittering shafts of war.

   In climes beyond the solar road
Where shaggy forms o'er ice-built mountains roam,
The Muse has broke the twilight gloom
   To cheer the shivering native's dull abode.
And oft, beneath the odorous shade
Of Chili's boundless forests laid,
She deigns to hear the savage youth repeat
In loose numbers wildly sweet
Their feather-cinctured chiefs, and dusky loves.
Her track, where'er the goddess roves,
Glory pursue, and generous Shame,
Th' unconquerable Mind, and Freedom's holy flame.

Woods, that wave o'er Delphi's steep,
Isles,.that crown th' Aegean deep,
Fields that cool Ilissus laves,
Or where Maeander's amber waves
In lingering labyrinths creep,
How do your tuneful echoes languish,
Mute, but to the voice of anguish!
Where each old poetic mountain
   Inspiration breathed around;
Every shade and hallow'd fountain
   Murmur'd deep a solemn sound:
Till the sad Nine, in Greece's evil hour
   Left their Parnassus for the Latian plains.
Alike they scorn the pomp of tyrant Power,
   And coward Vice, that revels in her chains.
When Latium had her lofty spirit lost,
They sought, oh Albion! next, thy sea-encircled coast.

   Far from the sun and summer-gale
In thy green lap was Nature's Darling laid,
What time, where lucid Avon stray'd,
   To him the mighty Mother did unveil
Her awful face: the dauntless child
Stretch'd forth his little arms, and smiled.
'This pencil take' (she said), 'whose colours clear
Richly paint the vernal year:
Thine, too, these golden keys, immortal Boy!
This can unlock the gates of joy;
Of horror that, and thrilling fears,
Or ope the sacred source of sympathetic tears.'

   Nor second He, that rode sublime
Upon the seraph-wings of Extasy
The secrets of the abyss to spy:
   He pass'd the flaming bounds of place and time:
The living Throne, the sapphire-blaze
Where angels tremble while they gaze,

He saw; but blasted with excess of light,
Closed his eyes in endless night.
Behold where Dryden's less presumptuous car
Wide o'er the fields of glory bear
Two coursers of ethereal race,
With necks in thunder clothed, and long-resounding pace.

Hark, his hands the lyre explore!
Bright-eyed Fancy, hovering o'er,
Scatters from her pictured urn
Thoughts that breathe, and words that burn.
But ah! 'tis heard no more –
Oh! lyre divine, what daring spirit
Wakes thee now? Tho' he inherit
Nor the pride, nor ample pinion,
    That the Theban eagle bear,
Sailing with supreme dominion
    Thro' the azure deep of air:
Yet oft before his infant eyes would run
    Such forms as glitter in the Muse's ray
With orient hues, unborrow'd of the sun:
    Yet shall he mount, and keep his distant way
Beyond the limits of a vulgar fate:
Beneath the Good how far – but far above the Great.

                                        T. Gray

                    CLXXVIII
                THE PASSIONS
                An Ode for Music

    When Music, heavenly maid, was young,
    While yet in early Greece she sung,
    The Passions oft, to hear her shell,
    Throng'd around her magic cell
    Exulting, trembling, raging, fainting,
    Possest beyond the Muse's painting;

By turns they felt the glowing mind
Disturb'd, delighted, raised, refined:
'Till once, 'tis said, when all were fired,
Fill'd with fury, rapt, inspired,
From the supporting myrtles round
They snatch'd her instruments of sound,
And, as they oft had heard apart
Sweet lessons of her forceful art,
Each (for Madness ruled the hour)
Would prove his own expressive power.

First Fear his hand, its skill to try,
   Amid the chords bewilder'd laid,
And back recoil'd, he knew not why,
   E'en at the sound himself had made.

Next Anger rush'd, his eyes on fire,
   In lightnings, own'd his secret stings;
In one rude clash he struck the lyre
   And swept with hurried hand the strings.

With woeful measures wan Despair,
   Low sullen sounds, his grief beguiled;
A solemn, strange, and mingled air,
   'Twas sad by fits, by starts 'twas wild.

But thou, O Hope, with eyes so fair,
   What was thy delighted measure?
Still it whisper'd promised pleasure
   And bade the lovely scenes at distance hail!
Still would her touch the strain prolong;
   And from the rocks, the woods, the vale
She call'd on Echo still through all the song;
   And, where her sweetest theme she chose,
   A soft responsive voice was heard at every close;
And Hope enchanted smiled, and waved her golden hair; –

And longer had she sung: – but with a frown
    Revenge impatient rose:
He threw his blood-stain'd sword in thunder down;
    And with a withering look
  The war-denouncing trumpet took
And blew a blast so loud and dread,
Were ne'er prophetic sounds so full of woe!
    And ever and anon he beat
    The doubling drum with furious heat;
And, though sometimes, each dreary pause between,
    Dejected Pity at his side
    Her soul-subduing voice applied,
  Yet still he kept his wild unalter'd mien,
While each strain'd ball of sight seem'd bursting from his head.

Thy numbers, Jealousy, to nought were fix'd:
  Sad proof of thy distressful state!
Of differing themes the veering song was mix'd;
  And now it courted Love, now raving call'd on Hate.

With eyes up-raised, as one inspired,
Pale Melancholy sat retired;
And from her wild sequester'd seat,
In notes by distance made more sweet,
Pour'd through the mellow horn her pensive soul:
    And dashing soft from rocks around
    Bubbling runnels join'd the sound;
Through glades and glooms the mingled measure stole,
  Or, o'er some haunted stream, with fond delay,
    Round an holy calm diffusing,
    Love of peace, and lonely musing,
  In hollow murmurs died away.

But O! how alter'd was its sprightlier tone
When Cheerfulness, a nymph of healthiest hue,
  Her bow across her shoulder flung,
  Her buskins gemm'd with morning dew,
Blew an inspiring air, that dale and thicket rung,

The hunter's call to Faun and Dryad known!
The oak-crown'd Sisters and their chaste-eyed Queen,
 Satyrs and Sylvan Boys, were seen
 Peeping from forth their alleys green:
Brown Exercise rejoiced to hear;
 And Sport leapt up, and seized his beechen spear.

Last came Joy's ecstatic trial:
He, with viny crown advancing,
 First to the lively pipe his hand addrest:
But soon he saw the brisk awakening viol
 Whose sweet entrancing voice he loved the best:
They would have thought who heard the strain
  They saw, in Tempe's vale, her native maids
  Amidst the festal-sounding shades
To some unwearied minstrel dancing;
While, as his flying fingers kiss'd the strings,
 Love framed with Mirth a gay fantastic round:
 Loose were her tresses seen, her zone unbound;
 And he, amidst his frolic play,
 As if he would the charming air repay,
Shook thousand odours from his dewy wings.

O Music! sphere-descended maid,
Friend of Pleasure, Wisdom's aid!
Why, goddess! why, to us denied,
Lay'st thou thy ancient lyre aside?
As in that loved Athenian bower
You learn'd an all-commanding power,
Thy mimic soul, O Nymph endear'd,
Can well recall what then it heard.
Where is thy native simple heart
Devote to Virtue, Fancy, Art?
Arise, as in that elder time,
Warm, energic, chaste, sublime!
Thy wonders, in that god-like age,
Fill thy recording Sister's page; –

'Tis said, and I believe the tale,
Thy humblest reed could more prevail,
Had more of strength, diviner rage,
Than all which charms this laggard age:
E'en all at once together found,
Cecilia's mingled world of sound: —
O bid our vain endeavours cease:
Revive the just designs of Greece:
Return in all thy simple state!
Confirm the tales her sons relate!

W. Collins

CLXXIX
THE SONG OF DAVID
[*Added 1883*]

He sang of God, the mighty source
Of all things, the stupendous force
   On which all strength depends:
From Whose right arm, beneath Whose eyes,
All period, power, and enterprise
   Commences, reigns, and ends.

The world, the clustering spheres He made,
The glorious light, the soothing shade,
   Dale, champaign, grove and hill:
The multitudinous abyss,
Where secrecy remains in bliss,
   And wisdom hides her skill.

Tell them, I AM, Jehovah said
To Moses: while Earth heard in dread,
   And, smitten to the heart,
At once, above, beneath, around,
All Nature, without voice or sound,
   Replied, 'O Lord, THOU ART.'

C. Smart

CLXXX
INFANT JOY
[*Added 1883*]

'I have no name;
I am but two days old.'
– What shall I call thee?
'I happy am;
Joy is my name.'
– Sweet joy befall thee!

Pretty joy!
Sweet joy, but two days old;
Sweet joy I call thee:
Thou dost smile:
I sing the while,
Sweet joy befall thee!

W. Blake

CLXXXI
A CRADLE SONG
[*Added 1890*]

Sleep, sleep, beauty bright,
Dreaming in the joys of night;
Sleep, sleep; in thy sleep
Little sorrows sit and weep.

Sweet babe, in thy face
Soft desires I can trace,
Secret joys and secret smiles,
Little pretty infant wiles.

As thy softest limbs I feel,
Smiles as of the morning steal
O'er thy cheek, and o'er thy breast
Where thy little heart doth rest.

Oh the cunning wiles that creep
In thy little heart asleep!
When thy little heart doth wake,
Then the dreadful light shall break.

W. Blake

CLXXXII
ODE ON THE SPRING

Lo! where the rosy-bosom'd Hours,
　Fair Venus' train, appear,
Disclose the long-expecting flowers
　And wake the purple year!
The Attic warbler pours her throat
Responsive to the cuckoo's note,
The untaught harmony of Spring:
While, whispering pleasure as they fly,
Cool Zephyrs thro' the clear blue sky
　Their gather'd fragrance fling.

Where'er the oak's thick branches stretch
　A broader, browner shade,
Where'er the rude and moss-grown beech
　O'er-canopies the glade,
Beside some water's rushy brink
With me the Muse shall sit, and think
(At ease reclined in rustic state)
How vain the ardour of the crowd,
How low, how little are the proud,
　How indigent the great!

Still is the toiling hand of Care;
   The panting herds repose:
Yet hark, how thro' the peopled air
   The busy murmur glows!
The insect-youth are on the wing,
Eager to taste the honied spring
And float amid the liquid noon:
Some lightly o'er the current skim,
Some show their gaily-gilded trim
   Quick-glancing to the sun.

To Contemplation's sober eye
   Such is the race of Man:
And they that creep, and they that fly
   Shall end where they began.
Alike the Busy and the Gay
But flutter thro' life's little day,
In Fortune's varying colours drest:
Brush'd by the hand of rough Mischance,
Or chill'd by Age, their airy dance
   They leave, in dust to rest.

Methinks I hear in accents low
   The sportive kind reply:
Poor moralist! and what art thou?
   A solitary fly!
Thy joys no glittering female meets,
No hive hast thou of hoarded sweets,
No painted plumage to display:
On hasty wings thy youth is flown;
Thy sun is set, thy spring is gone –
   We frolic while 'tis May.

T. Gray

CLXXXIII
THE POPLAR FIELD

The poplars are fell'd; farewell to the shade
And the whispering sound of the cool colonnade;
The winds play no longer and sing in the leaves,
Nor Ouse on his bosom their image receives.

Twelve years have elapsed since I first took a view
Of my favourite field, and the bank where they grew:
And now in the grass behold they are laid,
And the tree is my seat that once lent me a shade!

The blackbird has fled to another retreat
Where the hazels afford him a screen from the heat;
And the scene where his melody charm'd me before
Resounds with his sweet-flowing ditty no more.

My fugitive years are all hasting away,
And I must ere long lie as lowly as they,
With a turf on my breast and a stone at my head,
Ere another such grove shall arise in its stead.

The change both my heart and my fancy employs;
I reflect on the frailty of man and his joys:
Short-lived as we are, yet our pleasures, we see,
Have a still shorter date, and die sooner than we.

W. Cowper

CLXXXIV
TO A MOUSE
On turning her up in her nest, with the plough, November, 1785

Wee, sleekit, cow'rin', tim'rous beastie,
O what a panic's in thy breastie!
Thou need na start awa sae hasty,
Wi' bickering brattle!
I wad be laith to rin an' chase thee
Wi' murd'ring pattle!

I'm truly sorry man's dominion
Has broken Nature's social union,
An' justifies that ill opinion
Which makes thee startle
At me, thy poor earth-born companion,
An' fellow-mortal!

I doubt na, whiles, but thou may thieve;
What then? poor beastie, thou maun live!
A daimen-icker in a thrave
'S a sma' request:
I'll get a blessin' wi' the lave,
And never miss't!

Thy wee bit housie, too, in ruin!
Its silly wa's the win's are strewin:
And naething, now, to big a new ane,
O' foggage green!
An' bleak December's winds ensuin'
Baith snell an' keen!

Thou saw the fields laid bare an' waste
An' weary winter comin' fast,
An' cozie here, beneath the blast,
Thou thought to dwell,
Till, crash! the cruel coulter past
Out thro' thy cell.

That wee bit heap o' leaves an' stibble
Has cost thee mony a weary nibble!
Now thou's turn'd out, for a' thy trouble,
But house or hald,
To thole the winter's sleety dribble
An' cranreuch cauld!

But, Mousie, thou art no thy lane
In proving foresight may be vain:
The best laid schemes o' mice an' men
Gang aft a-gley,
An' lea'e us nought but grief an' pain,
For promised joy.

Still thou art blest, compared wi' me!
The present only toucheth thee:
But, Och! I backward cast my e'e
On prospects drear!
An' forward, tho' I canna see,
I guess an' fear!

R. Burns

CLXXXV

A WISH

Mine be a cot beside the hill;
A bee-hive's hum shall soothe my ear;
A willowy brook that turns a mill,
With many a fall shall linger near.

The swallow, oft, beneath my thatch
Shall twitter from her clay-built nest;
Oft shall the pilgrim lift the latch,
And share my meal, a welcome guest.

Around my ivied porch shall spring
Each fragrant flower that drinks the dew;
And Lucy, at her wheel, shall sing
In russet-gown and apron blue.

The village-church among the trees,
Where first our marriage-vows were given,
With merry peals shall swell the breeze
And point with taper spire to Heaven.

S. Rogers

CLXXXVI
ODE TO EVENING

If aught of oaten stop or pastoral song
May hope, O pensive Eve, to soothe thine ear
    Like thy own solemn springs,
    Thy springs, and dying gales;

O Nymph reserved, – while now the bright-hair'd sun
Sits in yon western tent, whose cloudy skirts,
    With brede ethereal wove,
    O'erhang his wavy bed;

Now air is hush'd, save where the weak-eyed bat
With short shrill shriek flits by on leathern wing,
    Or where the beetle winds
    His small but sullen horn,

As oft he rises midst the twilight path,
Against the pilgrim borne in heedless hum, –
    Now teach me, maid composed,
    To breathe some soften'd strain

Whose numbers, stealing through thy darkening vale,
May not unseemly with its stillness suit;
    As, musing slow, I hail
    Thy genial loved return.

For when thy folding-star arising shows
His paly circlet, at his warning lamp
    The fragrant Hours, and Elves
    Who slept in buds the day,

And many a Nymph who wreathes her brows with sedge
And sheds the freshening dew, and, lovelier still,
    The pensive Pleasures sweet,
    Prepare thy shadowy car.

Then let me rove some wild and heathy scene;
Or find some ruin midst its dreary dells,
    Whose walls more awful nod
    By thy religious gleams.

Or, if chill blustering winds or driving rain
Prevent my willing feet, be mine the hut
    That, from the mountain's side,
    Views wilds, and swelling floods,

And hamlets brown, and dim-discover'd spires;
And hears their simple bell; and marks o'er all
    Thy dewy fingers draw
    The gradual dusky veil.

While Spring shall pour his showers, as oft he wont,
And bathe thy breathing tresses, meekest Eve!
    While Summer loves to sport
    Beneath thy lingering light;

While sallow Autumn fills thy lap with leaves;
Or Winter, yelling through the troublous air,
    Affrights thy shrinking train
    And rudely rends thy robes;

So long, regardful of thy quiet rule,
Shall Fancy, Friendship, Science, smiling Peace,
    Thy gentlest influence own,
    And love thy favourite name!

W. Collins

CLXXXVII
ELEGY WRITTEN IN A COUNTRY CHURCHYARD

The curfew tolls the knell of parting day,
The lowing herd wind slowly o'er the lea,
The ploughman homeward plods his weary way,
And leaves the world to darkness and to me.

Now fades the glimmering landscape on the sight,
And all the air a solemn stillness holds,
Save where the beetle wheels his droning flight,
And drowsy tinklings lull the distant folds:

Save that from yonder ivy-mantled tower
The moping owl does to the moon complain
Of such as, wandering near her secret bower,
Molest her ancient solitary reign.

Beneath those rugged elms, that yew-tree's shade
Where heaves the turf in many a mouldering heap,
Each in his narrow cell for ever laid,
The rude forefathers of the hamlet sleep.

The breezy call of incense-breathing morn,
The swallow twittering from the straw-built shed,
The cock's shrill clarion, or the echoing horn,
No more shall rouse them from their lowly bed.

For them no more the blazing hearth shall burn
Or busy housewife ply her evening care:
No children run to lisp their sire's return,
Or climb his knees the envied kiss to share.

Oft did the harvest to their sickle yield,
Their furrow oft the stubborn glebe has broke;
How jocund did they drive their team afield!
How bow'd the woods beneath their sturdy stroke!

Let not ambition mock their useful toil,
Their homely joys, and destiny obscure;
Nor grandeur hear with a disdainful smile
The short and simple annals of the poor.

The boast of heraldry, the pomp of power,
And all that beauty, all that wealth e'er gave,
Awaits alike th' inevitable hour: –
The paths of glory lead but to the grave.

Nor you, ye proud, impute to these the fault
If memory o'er their tomb no trophies raise,
Where through the long-drawn aisle and fretted vault
The pealing anthem swells the note of praise.

Can storied urn or animated bust
Back to its mansion call the fleeting breath?
Can honour's voice provoke the silent dust,
Or flattery soothe the dull cold ear of death?

Perhaps in this neglected spot is laid
Some heart once pregnant with celestial fire;
Hands, that the rod of empire might have sway'd,
Or waked to extasy the living lyre:

But knowledge to their eyes her ample page
Rich with the spoils of time, did ne'er unroll;
Chill penury repress'd their noble rage,
And froze the genial current of the soul.

Full many a gem of purest ray serene
The dark unfathom'd caves of ocean bear:
Full many a flower is born to blush unseen,
And waste its sweetness on the desert air.

Some village-Hampden, that with dauntless breast
The little tyrant of his fields withstood,
Some mute inglorious Milton here may rest,
Some Cromwell, guiltless of his country's blood.

Th' applause of listening senates to command,
The threats of pain and ruin to despise,
To scatter plenty o'er a smiling land,
And read their history in a nation's eyes

Their lot forbad: nor circumscribed alone
Their growing virtues, but their crimes confined;
Forbad to wade thro' slaughter to a throne,
And shut the gates of mercy on mankind;

The struggling pangs of conscious truth to hide,
To quench the blushes of ingenuous shame,
Or heap the shrine of luxury and pride
With incense kindled at the Muse's flame.

Far from the madding crowd's ignoble strife
Their sober wishes never learn'd to stray;
Along the cool sequester'd vale of life
They kept the noiseless tenour of their way.

Yet e'en these bones from insult to protect
Some frail memorial still erected nigh,
With uncouth rhymes and shapeless sculpture deck'd,
Implores the passing tribute of a sigh.

Their name, their years, spelt by th' unletter'd Muse,
The place of fame and elegy supply:
And many a holy text around she strews,
That teach the rustic moralist to die.

For who, to dumb forgetfulness a prey,
This pleasing anxious being e'er resign'd,
Left the warm precincts of the cheerful day,
Nor cast one longing lingering look behind?

On some fond breast the parting soul relies,
Some pious drops the closing eye requires;
E'en from the tomb the voice of nature cries,
E'en in our ashes live their wonted fires.

For thee, who, mindful of th' unhonour'd dead,
Dost in these lines their artless tale relate;
If chance, by lonely contemplation led,
Some kindred spirit shall enquire thy fate, –

Haply some hoary-headed swain may say,
'Oft have we seen him at the peep of dawn
Brushing with hasty steps the dews away,
To meet the sun upon the upland lawn;

'There at the foot of yonder nodding beech
That wreathes its old fantastic roots so high,
His listless length at noon-tide would he stretch,
And pore upon the brook that babbles by.

'Hard by yon wood, now smiling as in scorn,
Muttering his wayward fancies he would rove;
Now drooping, woeful-wan, like one forlorn,
Or crazed with care, or cross'd in hopeless love.

'One morn I miss'd him on the custom'd hill,
Along the heath, and near his favourite tree;
Another came; nor yet beside the rill,
Nor up the lawn, nor at the wood was he;

'The next with dirges due in sad array
Slow through the church-way path we saw him borne, –
Approach and read (for thou canst read) the lay
Graved on the stone beneath yon aged thorn.'

THE EPITAPH

Here rests his head upon the lap of earth
A youth, to fortune and to fame unknown;
Fair science frown'd not on his humble birth
And melancholy mark'd him for her own.

Large was his bounty, and his soul sincere;
Heaven did a recompense as largely send:
He gave to misery (all he had) a tear,
He gain'd from Heaven ('twas all he wish'd) a friend.

No farther seek his merits to disclose,
Or draw his frailties from their dread abode,
(There they alike in trembling hope repose,)
The bosom of his Father and his God.

T. Gray

CLXXXVIII
MARY MORISON

O Mary, at thy window be,
It is the wish'd, the trysted hour!
Those smiles and glances let me see
That make the miser's treasure poor:
How blithely wad I bid the stoure,
A weary slave frae sun to sun,
Could I the rich reward secure,
The lovely Mary Morison.

Yestreen when to the trembling string
The dance gaed thro' the lighted ha',
To thee my fancy took its wing, –
I sat, but neither heard nor saw:
Tho' this was fair, and that was braw,
And yon the toast of a' the town,
I sigh'd, and said amang them a',
'Ye are na Mary Morison.'

O Mary, canst thou wreck his peace
Wha for thy sake wad gladly dee?
Or canst thou break that heart of his,
Whase only faut is loving thee?
If love for love thou wilt na gie,
At least be pity to me shown;
A thought ungentle canna be
The thought o' Mary Morison.

R. Burns

CLXXXIX
BONNIE LESLEY

O saw ye bonnie Lesley
   As she gaed o'er the border?
She's gane, like Alexander,
   To spread her conquests farther.

To see her is to love her,
   And love but her for ever;
For Nature made her what she is,
   And ne'er made sic anither!

Thou art a queen, Fair Lesley,
   Thy subjects we, before thee;
Thou art divine, Fair Lesley,
   The hearts o' men adore thee.

The Deil he could na scaith thee,
   Or aught that wad belang thee;
He'd look into thy bonnie face,
   And say 'I canna wrang thee!'

The Powers aboon will tent thee;
   Misfortune sha' na steer thee;
Thou'rt like themselves sae lovely
   That ill they'll ne'er let near thee.

Return again, Fair Lesley,
   Return to Caledonie!
That we may brag we hae a lass
   There's nane again sae bonnie.

R. Burns

CXC

O my Luve's like a red, red rose
   That's newly sprung in June:
O my Luve's like the melodie
   That's sweetly play'd in tune.

As fair art thou, my bonnie lass,
   So deep in luve am I:
And I will luve thee still, my dear,
   Till a' the seas gang dry:

Till a' the seas gang dry, my dear,
   And the rocks melt wi' the sun;
I will luve thee still, my dear,
   While the sands o' life shall run.

And fare thee weel, my only Luve!
   And fare thee weel awhile;
And I will come again, my Luve,
   Tho' it were ten thousand mile.

R. Burns

CXCI
HIGHLAND MARY

Ye banks and braes and streams around
   The castle o' Montgomery,
Green be your woods, and fair your flowers,
   Your waters never drumlie!
There simmer first unfauld her robes,
   And there the langest tarry;
For there I took the last fareweel
   O' my sweet Highland Mary.

How sweetly bloom'd the gay green birk,
   How rich the hawthorn's blossom,
As underneath their fragrant shade
   I clasp'd her to my bosom!

The golden hours on angel wings
   Flew o'er me and my dearie;
For dear to me as light and life
   Was my sweet Highland Mary.

Wi' mony a vow and lock'd embrace
   Our parting was fu' tender;
And pledging aft to meet again,
   We tore oursels asunder;
But, Oh! fell Death's untimely frost,
   That nipt my flower sae early!
Now green's the sod, and cauld's the clay,
   That wraps my Highland Mary!

O pale, pale now, those rosy lips,
   I aft hae kiss'd sae fondly;
And closed for aye the sparkling glance
   That dwelt on me sae kindly;
And mouldering now in silent dust
   That heart that lo'ed me dearly!
But still within my bosom's core
   Shall live my Highland Mary.

R. Burns

CXCII
AULD ROBIN GRAY

When the sheep are in the fauld, and the kye at hame,
And a' the world to rest are gane,
The waes o' my heart fa' in showers frae my e'e,
While my gudeman lies sound by me.

Young Jamie lo'ed me weel, and sought me for his bride;
But saving a croun he had naething else beside:
To make the croun a pund, young Jamie gaed to sea;
And the croun and the pund were baith for me.

He hadna been awa' a week but only twa,
When my father brak his arm, and the cow was stown awa;
My mother she fell sick, and my Jamie at the sea–
And auld Robin Gray came a-courtin' me.

My father couldna work, and my mother couldna spin;
I toil'd day and night, but their bread I couldna win;
Auld Rob maintain'd them baith, and wi' tears in his e'e
Said, Jennie, for their sakes, O, marry me!

My heart it said nay; I look'd for Jamie back;
But the wind it blew high, and the ship it was a wrack;
His ship it was a wrack – why didna Jamie dee?
Or why do I live to cry, Wae's me?

My father urgit sair: my mother didna speak;
But she look'd in my face till my heart was like to break:
They gi'ed him my hand, but my heart was at the sea;
Sae auld Robin Gray he was gudeman to me.

I hadna been a wife a week but only four,
When mournfu' as I sat on the stane at the door,
I saw my Jamie's wraith, for I couldna think it he
Till he said, I'm come hame to marry thee.

O sair, sair did we greet, and muckle did we say;
We took but ae kiss, and I bad him gang away;
I wish that I were dead, but I'm no like to dee;
And why was I born to say, Wae's me!

I gang like a ghaist, and I carena to spin;
I daurna think on Jamie, for that wad be a sin;
But I'll do my best a gude wife aye to be,
For auld Robin Gray he is kind unto me.

Lady A. Lindsay

CXCIII

DUNCAN GRAY

Duncan Gray cam here to woo,
 Ha, ha, the wooing o't;
On blythe Yule night when we were fou,
 Ha, ha, the wooing o't:
Maggie coost her head fu' high,
Look'd asklent and unco skeigh,
Gart poor Duncan stand abeigh;
 Ha, ha, the wooing o't!

Duncan fleech'd, and Duncan pray'd;
Meg was deaf as Ailsa Craig;
Duncan sigh'd baith out and in,
Grat his een baith bleer't and blin',
Spak o' lowpin ower a linn!

Time and chance are but a tide,
Slighted love is sair to bide;
Shall I, like a fool, quoth he,
For a haughty hizzie dee?
She may gae to – France for me!

How it comes let doctors tell,
Meg grew sick – as he grew well;
Something in her bosom wrings,
For relief a sigh she brings!
And O, her een, they spak sic things!

Duncan was a lad o' grace;
Maggie's was a piteous case;
Duncan couldna be her death,
Swelling pity smoor'd his wrath;
Now they're crouse and canty baith:
 Ha, ha, the wooing o't!

R. Burns

THE SAILOR'S WIFE

And are ye sure the news is true?
   And are ye sure he's weel?
Is this the time to think o' wark?
   Ye jades, lay by your wheel;
Is this the time to spin a thread,
   When Colin's at the door?
Reach down my cloak, I'll to the quay,
   And see him come ashore.
For there's nae luck about the house,
   There's nae luck at a';
There's little pleasure in the house
   When our gudeman's awa'.

And gie to me my bigonet,
   My bishop's satin gown;
For I maun tell the baillie's wife
   That Colin's in the town.
My Turkey slippers maun gae on,
   My stockins pearly blue;
It's a' to pleasure our gudeman,
   For he's baith leal and true.

Rise, lass, and mak a clean fireside,
   Put on the muckle pot;
Gie little Kate her button gown
   And Jock his Sunday coat;
And mak their shoon as black as slaes,
   Their hose as white as snaw;
It's a' to please my ain gudeman,
   For he's been long awa.

There's twa fat hens upo' the coop
   Been fed this month and mair;
Mak haste and thraw their necks about,
   That Colin weel may fare;

And spread the table neat and clean,
   Gar ilka thing look braw,
For wha can tell how Colin fared
   When he was far awa?

Sae true his heart, sae smooth his speech,
   His breath like caller air;
His very foot has music in't
   As he comes up the stair –
And will I see his face again?
   And will I hear him speak?
I'm downright dizzy wi' the thought,
   In troth I'm like to greet!

If Colin's weel, and weel content,
   I hae nae mair to crave:
And gin I live to keep him sae,
   I'm blest aboon the lave:
And will I see his face again,
   And will I hear him speak?
I'm downright dizzy wi' the thought,
   In troth I'm like to greet.
For there's nae luck about the house,
   There's nae luck at a';
There's little pleasure in the house
   When our gudeman's awa'.

W. J. Mickle

CXCV
ABSENCE
[*Added 1883*]

When I think on the happy days
   I spent wi' you, my dearie;
And now what lands between us lie,
   How can I be but eerie!

How slow ye move, ye heavy hours,
   As ye were wae and weary!
It was na sae ye glinted by
   When I was wi' my dearie.

Anon.

CXCVI
JEAN

Of a' the airts the wind can blaw
   I dearly like the West,
For there the bonnie lassie lives,
   The lassie I lo'e best:
There wild woods grow, and rivers row,
   And mony a hill between;
But day and night my fancy's flight
   Is ever wi' my Jean.

I see her in the dewy flowers,
   I see her sweet and fair:
I hear her in the tunefu' birds,
   I hear her charm the air:
There's not a bonnie flower that springs
   By fountain, shaw, or green,
There's not a bonnie bird that sings
   But minds me o' my Jean.

O blaw ye westlin winds, blaw saft
   Amang the leafy trees;
Wi' balmy gale, frae hill and dale
   Bring hame the laden bees;
And bring the lassie back to me
   That's aye sae neat and clean;
Ae smile o' her wad banish care,
   Sae charming is my Jean.

What sighs and vows amang the knowes
    Hae pass'd atween us twa!
How fond to meet, how wae to part
    That night she gaed awa!
The Powers aboon can only ken
    To whom the heart is seen,
That nane can be sae dear to me
    As my sweet lovely Jean!

R. Burns

CXCVII
JOHN ANDERSON

John Anderson my jo, John,
When we were first acquent
Your locks were like the raven,
Your bonnie brow was brent;
But now your brow is bald, John,
Your locks are like the snow;
But blessings on your frosty pow,
John Anderson my jo.

John Anderson my jo, John,
We clamb the hill thegither,
And mony a canty day, John,
We've had wi' ane anither:
Now we maun totter down, John,
But hand in hand we'll go,
And sleep thegither at the foot,
John Anderson my jo.

R. Burns

CXCVIII
THE LAND O' THE LEAL

I'm wearing awa', Jean,
Like snaw when its thaw, Jean,
I'm wearing awa'
   To the land o' the leal.
There's nae sorrow there, Jean,
There's neither cauld nor care, Jean,
The day is aye fair
   In the land o' the leal.

Ye were aye leal and true, Jean,
You task's ended noo, Jean,
And I'll welcome you
   To the land o' the leal.
Our bonnie bairn's there, Jean,
She was baith guid and fair, Jean;
O we grudged her right sair
   To the land o' the leal!

Then dry that tearfu' e'e, Jean,
My soul langs to be free, Jean,
And angels wait on me
   To the land o' the leal.
Now fare ye weel, my ain Jean,
This warld's care is vain, Jean;
We'll meet and aye be fain
   In the land o' the leal!

Lady Nairn

CXCIX
ODE ON A DISTANT PROSPECT OF ETON COLLEGE

Ye distant spires, ye antique towers
   That crown the watery glade,
Where grateful Science still adores
   Her Henry's holy shade;
And ye, that from the stately brow
Of Windsor's heights th' expanse below
Of grove, of lawn, of mead survey,
Whose turf, whose shade, whose flowers among
Wanders the hoary Thames along
   His silver-winding way:

Ah happy hills! ah pleasing shade!
   Ah fields beloved in vain!
Where once my careless childhood stray'd,
   A stranger yet to pain!
I feel the gales that from ye blow
A momentary bliss bestow,
As waving fresh their gladsome wing
My weary soul they seem to soothe,
And, redolent of joy and youth,
   To breathe a second spring.

Say, Father Thames, for thou hast seen
   Full many a sprightly race
Disporting on thy margent green
   The paths of pleasure trace;
Who foremost now delight to cleave
With pliant arm, thy glassy wave?
The captive linnet which enthral?
What idle progeny succeed
To chase the rolling circle's speed
   Or urge the flying ball?

While some on earnest business bent
   Their murmuring labours ply
'Gainst graver hours that bring constraint
   To sweeten liberty:

Some bold adventurers disdain
The limits of their little reign
And unknown regions dare descry:
Still as they run they look behind,
They hear a voice in every wind,
   And snatch a fearful joy.

Gay hope is theirs by fancy fed,
   Less pleasing when possest;
The tear forgot as soon as shed,
   The sunshine of the breast:
Theirs buxom health, of rosy hue,
Wild wit, invention ever new,
And lively cheer, of vigour born;
The thoughtless day, the easy night,
The spirits pure, the slumbers light
   That fly th' approach of morn.

Alas! regardless of their doom
   The little victims play;
No sense have they of ills to come
   Nor care beyond to-day:
Yet see how all around 'em wait
The ministers of human fate
And black Misfortune's baleful train!
Ah show them where in ambush stand
To seize their prey, the murderous band!
   Ah, tell them they are men!

These shall the fury Passions tear,
   The vultures of the mind,
Disdainful Anger, pallid Fear,
   And Shame that sculks behind;
Or pining Love shall waste their youth,
Or Jealousy with rankling tooth
That inly gnaws the secret heart,
And Envy wan, and faded Care,
Grim-visaged comfortless Despair,
   And Sorrow's piercing dart.

Ambition this shall tempt to rise,
   Then whirl the wretch from high
To bitter Scorn a sacrifice
   And grinning Infamy.
The stings of Falsehood those shall try
And hard Unkindness' alter'd eye,
That mocks the tear it forced to flow;
And keen Remorse with blood defiled,
And moody Madness laughing wild
   Amid severest woe.

Lo, in the vale of years beneath
   A griesly troop are seen,
The painful family of Death,
   More hideous than their queen:
This racks the joints, this fires the veins,
That every labouring sinew strains,
Those in the deeper vitals rage:
Lo! Poverty, to fill the band,
That numbs the soul with icy hand,
   And slow-consuming Age.

To each his sufferings: all are men,
   Condemn'd alike to groan;
The tender for another's pain,
   Th' unfeeling for his own.
Yet, ah! why should they know their fate,
Since sorrow never comes too late,
And happiness too swiftly flies?
Thought would destroy their paradise.
No more; – where ignorance is bliss,
   'Tis folly to be wise.

T. Gray

CC
THE SHRUBBERY
[Added 1883]

O happy shades! to me unblest!
   Friendly to peace, but not to me!
How ill the scene that offers rest,
   And heart that cannot rest, agree!

This glassy stream, that spreading pine,
   Those alders quivering to the breeze,
Might soothe a soul less hurt than mine,
   And please, if anything could please.

But fix'd unalterable Care
   Foregoes not what she feels within,
Shows the same sadness everywhere,
   And slights the season and the scene.

For all that pleased in wood or lawn
   While Peace possess'd these silent bowers,
Her animating smile withdrawn,
   Has lost its beauties and its powers.

The saint or moralist should tread
   This moss-grown alley, musing, slow,
They seek like me the secret shade,
   But not, like me, to nourish woe!

Me, fruitful scenes and prospects waste
   Alike admonish not to roam;
These tell me of enjoyments past,
   And those of sorrows yet to come.

W. Cowper

CCI

HYMN TO ADVERSITY

Daughter of Jove, relentless power,
    Thou tamer of the human breast,
Whose iron scourge and torturing hour
    The bad affright, afflict the best!
Bound in thy adamantine chain
The proud are taught to taste of pain,
And purple tyrants vainly groan
With pangs unfelt before, unpitied and alone.

When first thy Sire to send on earth
    Virtue, his darling child, design'd,
To thee he gave the heavenly birth
    And bade to form her infant mind.
Stern, rugged nurse; thy rigid lore
With patience many a year she bore;
What sorrow was, thou bad'st her know,
And from her own she learn'd to melt at others' woe.

Scared at thy frown terrific, fly
    Self-pleasing Folly's idle brood,
Wild Laughter, Noise, and thoughtless Joy,
    And leave us leisure to be good.
Light they disperse, and with them go
The summer friend, the flattering foe;
By vain Prosperity received,
To her they vow their truth, and are again believed.

Wisdom in sable garb array'd
    Immersed in rapturous thought profound,
And Melancholy, silent maid,
    With leaden eye, that loves the ground,
Still on thy solemn steps attend:
Warm Charity, the general friend,
With Justice, to herself severe,
And Pity dropping soft the sadly-pleasing tear.

Oh! gently on thy suppliant's head
　　Dread goddess, lay thy chastening hand!
Not in thy Gorgon terrors clad,
　　Nor circled with the vengeful band
(As by the impious thou art seen)
With thundering voice, and threatening mien,
With screaming Horror's funeral cry,
Despair, and fell Disease, and ghastly Poverty; –

Thy form benign, oh goddess, wear,
　　Thy milder influence impart,
Thy philosophic train be there
　　To soften, not to wound my heart.
The generous spark extinct revive,
Teach me to love and to forgive,
Exact my own defects to scan,
What others are to feel, and know myself a Man.

　　　　　　　　　　　　　　　T. Gray

CCII
THE SOLITUDE OF ALEXANDER SELKIRK

I am monarch of all I survey;
My right there is none to dispute;
From the centre all round to the sea
I am lord of the fowl and the brute.
O Solitude! where are the charms
That sages have seen in thy face?
Better dwell in the midst of alarms,
Than reign in this horrible place.

I am out of humanity's reach,
I must finish my journey alone,
Never hear the sweet music of speech;
I start at the sound of my own.
The beasts that roam over the plain
My form with indifference see;

They are so unacquainted with man,
Their tameness is shocking to me.

Society, Friendship, and Love
Divinely bestow'd upon man,
Oh, had I the wings of a dove
How soon would I taste you again!
My sorrows I then might assuage
In the ways of religion and truth,
Might learn from the wisdom of age,
And be cheer'd by the sallies of youth.

Ye winds that have made me your sport,
Convey to this desolate shore
Some cordial endearing report
Of a land I shall visit no more:
My friends, do they now and then send
A wish or a thought after me?
O tell me I yet have a friend,
Though a friend I am never to see.

How fleet is a glance of the mind!
Compared with the speed of its flight,
The tempest itself lags behind,
And the swift-wingéd arrows of light.
When I think of my own native land
In a moment I seem to be there;
But alas! recollection at hand
Soon hurries me back to despair.

But the sea-fowl is gone to her nest,
The beast is laid down in his lair;
Even here is a season of rest,
And I to my cabin repair.
There's mercy in every place,
And mercy, encouraging thought!
Gives even affliction a grace
And reconciles man to his lot.

W. Cowper

CCIII
TO MARY UNWIN

Mary! I want a lyre with other strings,
Such aid from Heaven as some have feign'd they drew,
An eloquence scarce given to mortals, new
And undebased by praise of meaner things,

That ere through age or woe I shed my wings
I may record thy worth with honour due,
In verse as musical as thou art true,
And that immortalizes whom it sings: –

But thou hast little need. There is a Book
By seraphs writ with beams of heavenly light,
On which the eyes of God not rarely look,

A chronicle of actions just and bright –
There all thy deeds, my faithful Mary, shine;
And since thou own'st that praise, I spare thee mine.

W. Cowper

CCIV
TO THE SAME

The twentieth year is well-nigh past
Since first our sky was overcast;
Ah would that this might be the last!
   My Mary!

Thy spirits have a fainter flow,
I see thee daily weaker grow –
'Twas my distress that brought thee low,
   My Mary!

Thy needles, once a shining store,
For my sake restless heretofore,
Now rust disused, and shine no more;
   My Mary!

For though thou gladly wouldst fulfil
The same kind office for me still,
Thy sight now seconds not thy will,
     My Mary!

But well thou play'st the housewife's part,
And all thy threads with magic art
Have wound themselves about this heart,
     My Mary!

Thy indistinct expressions seem
Like language utter'd in a dream;
Yet me they charm, whate'er the theme,
     My Mary!

Thy silver locks, once auburn bright,
Are still more lovely in my sight
Than golden beams of orient light,
     My Mary!

For could I view nor them nor thee,
What sight worth seeing could I see?
The sun would rise in vain for me,
     My Mary!

Partakers of thy sad decline
Thy hands their little force resign;
Yet, gently prest, press gently mine,
     My Mary!

Such feebleness of limbs thou prov'st
That now at every step thou mov'st
Upheld by two; yet still thou lov'st,
     My Mary!

And still to love, though prest with ill,
In wintry age to feel no chill,
With me is to be lovely still,
     My Mary!

But ah! by constant heed I know
How oft the sadness that I show
Transforms thy smiles to looks of woe,
    My Mary!

And should my future lot be cast
With much resemblance of the past,
Thy worn-out heart will break at last –
    My Mary!

                             W. Cowper

THE DYING MAN IN HIS GARDEN
[Dropped 1890]

Why, Damon, with the forward day
Dost thou thy little spot survey,
From tree to tree, with doubtful cheer,
Pursue the progress of the year,
What winds arise, what rains descend,
When thou before that year shalt end?

What do thy noontide walks avail,
To clear the leaf, and pick the snail,
Then wantonly to death decree
An insect usefuller than thee?
Thou and the worm are brother-kind,
As low, as earthy, and as blind.

Vain wretch! canst thou expect to see
The downy peach make court to thee?
Or that thy sense shall ever meet
The bean-flower's deep-embosom'd sweet
Exhaling with an evening blast?
Thy evenings then will all be past!

Thy narrow pride, thy fancied green
(For vanity's in little seen),
All must be left when Death appears,
In spite of wishes, groans, and tears;
Nor one of all thy plants that grow
But Rosemary will with thee go.

G. Sewell

CCV
THE CASTAWAY
[*Added 1883*]

Obscurest night involved the sky,
    The Atlantic billows roar'd,
When such a destined wretch as I,
    Wash'd headlong from on board,
Of friends, of hope, of all bereft,
His floating home for ever left.

No braver chief could Albion boast
    Than he with whom he went,
Nor ever ship left Albion's coast
    With warmer wishes sent.
He loved them both, but both in vain,
Nor him beheld, nor her again.

Not long beneath the whelming brine,
    Expert to swim, he lay;
Nor soon he felt his strength decline,
    Or courage die away;
But waged with death a lasting strife,
Supported by despair of life.

He shouted: nor his friends had fail'd
    To check the vessel's course,
But so the furious blast prevail'd,
    That, pitiless perforce,

They left their outcast mate behind,
And scudded still before the wind.

Some succour yet they could afford;
    And such as storms allow,
The cask, the coop, the floated cord,
    Delay'd not to bestow.
But he (they knew) nor ship nor shore,
Whate'er they gave, should visit more.

Nor, cruel as it seem'd, could he
    Their haste himself condemn,
Aware that flight, in such a sea,
    Alone could rescue them;
Yet bitter felt it still to die
Deserted, and his friends so nigh.

He long survives, who lives an hour
    In ocean, self-upheld;
And so long he, with unspent power,
    His destiny repell'd;
And ever, as the minutes flew,
Entreated help, or cried 'Adieu!'

At length, his transient respite past,
    His comrades, who before
Had heard his voice in every blast,
    Could catch the sound no more;
For then, by toil subdued, he drank
The stifling wave, and then he sank.

No poet wept him; but the page
    Of narrative sincere,
That tells his name, his worth, his age,
    Is wet with Anson's tear:
And tears by bards or heroes shed
Alike immortalize the dead.

I therefore purpose not, or dream,
    Descanting on his fate,
To give the melancholy theme
    A more enduring date:
But misery still delights to trace
Its semblance in another's case.

No voice divine the storm allay'd,
    No light propitious shone,
When, snatch'd from all effectual aid,
    We perish'd, each alone:
But I beneath a rougher sea,
And whelm'd in deeper gulfs than he.

W. Cowper

CCVI
TOMORROW

In the downhill of life, when I find I'm declining,
    May my fate no less fortunate be
Than a snug elbow-chair will afford for reclining,
    And a cot that o'erlooks the wide sea;
With an ambling pad-pony to pace o'er the lawn,
    While I carol away idle sorrow,
And blithe as the lark that each day hails the dawn
    Look forward with hope for Tomorrow.

With a porch at my door, both for shelter and shade too,
    As the sunshine or rain may prevail;
And a small spot of ground for the use of the spade too,
    With a barn for the use of the flail:
A cow for my dairy, a dog for my game,
    And a purse when a friend wants to borrow;
I'll envy no Nabob his riches or fame,
    Or what honours may wait him Tomorrow.

From the bleak northern blast may my cot be completely
   Secured by a neighbouring hill;
And at night may repose steal upon me more sweetly
   By the sound of a murmuring rill:
And while peace and plenty I find at my board,
   With a heart free from sickness and sorrow,
With my friends may I share what Today may afford,
   And let them spread the table Tomorrow.

And when I at last must throw off this frail cov'ring
   Which I've worn for three-score years and ten,
On the brink of the grave I'll not seek to keep hov'ring,
   Nor my thread wish to spin o'er again:
But my face in the glass I'll serenely survey,
   And with smiles count each wrinkle and furrow;
As this old worn-out stuff, which is threadbare Today,
   May become Everlasting Tomorrow.

J. Collins

CCVII

Life! I know not what thou art,
But know that thou and I must part;
And when, or how, or where we met
I own to me's a secret yet.

  Life! we've been long together
Through pleasant and through cloudy weather;
'Tis hard to part when friends are dear –
Perhaps 'twill cost a sigh, a tear;
– Then steal away, give little warning,
Choose thine own time;
Say not Good Night, – but in some brighter clime
  Bid me Good Morning.

A. L. Barbauld

CCVIII

TO THE MUSES

[*Added 1890*]

Whether on Ida's shady brow,
    Or in the chambers of the East,
The chambers of the sun, that now
    From ancient melody have ceased;

Whether in Heaven ye wander fair,
    Or the green corners of the earth,
Or the blue regions of the air,
    Where the melodious winds have birth;

Whether on crystal rocks ye rove
    Beneath the bosom of the sea,
Wandering in many a coral grove,–
    Fair Nine, forsaking Poetry;

How have you left the ancient love
    That bards of old enjoy'd in you!
The languid strings do scarcely move,
    The sound is forced, the notes are few.

W. Blake

CCIX
ODE ON THE POETS

Bards of Passion and of Mirth
Ye have left your souls on earth!
Have ye souls in heaven too,
Double-lived in regions new?
– Yes, and those of heavens commune
With the spheres of sun and moon;
With the noise of fountains wond'rous
And the parle of voices thund'rous;
With the whisper of heaven's trees
And one another, in soft ease
Seated on Elysian lawns
Browsed by none but Dian's fawns;
Underneath large blue-bells tented,
Where the daisies are rose-scented,
And the rose herself has got
Perfume which on earth is not;
Where the nightingale doth sing
Not a senseless, tranced thing,
But divine melodious truth;
Philosophic numbers smooth;
Tales and golden histories
Of heaven and its mysteries,

Thus ye live on high, and then
On the earth ye live again;
And the souls ye left behind you
Teach us, here, the way to find you,
Where your other souls are joying,
Never slumber'd never cloying.
Here, your earth-born souls still speak
To mortals, of their little week;
Of their sorrows and delights;
Of their passions and their spites;
Of their glory and their shame;
What doth strengthen and what maim: –

Thus ye teach us, every day,
Wisdom, though fled far away.

Bards of Passion and of Mirth
Ye have left your souls on earth!
Ye have souls in heaven too,
Double-lived in regions new!

J. Keats

CCX
ON FIRST LOOKING INTO CHAPMAN'S HOMER

Much have I travell'd in the realms of gold
And many goodly states and kingdoms seen;
Round many western islands have I been
Which bards in fealty to Apollo hold.

Oft of one wide expanse had I been told
That deep-brow'd Homer ruled as his demesne:
Yet did I never breathe its pure serene
Till I heard Chapman speak out loud and bold:

– Then felt I like some watcher of the skies
When a new planet swims into his ken;
Or like stout Cortez, when with eagle eyes

He stared at the Pacific – and all his men
Look'd at each other with a wild surmise –
Silent, upon a peak in Darien.

J. Keats

CCXI
LOVE

All thoughts, all passions, all delights,
Whatever stirs this mortal frame,
All are but ministers of Love,
And feed his sacred flame.

Oft in my waking dreams do I
Live o'er again that happy hour,
When mid-way on the mount I lay,
　　Bedside the ruin'd tower.

The moonshine stealing o'er the scene
Had blended with the lights of eve;
And she was there, my hope, my joy,
　　My own dear Genevieve!

She lean'd against the arméd man,
The statue of the arméd knight;
She stood and listen'd to my lay,
　　Amid the lingering light.

Few sorrows hath she of her own,
My hope! my joy! my Genevieve!
She loves me best, whene'er I sing
　　The songs that make her grieve.

I play'd a soft and doleful air,
I sang an old and moving story –
An old rude song, that suited well
　　That ruin wild and hoary.

She listen'd with a flitting blush,
With downcast eyes and modest grace;
For well she knew, I could not choose
　　But gaze upon her face.

I told her of the Knight that wore
Upon his shield a burning brand;
And that for ten long years he woo'd
　　The Lady of the Land.

I told her how he pined: and ah!
The deep, the low, the pleading tone
With which I sang another's love
　　Interpreted my own.

She listen'd with a flitting blush,
With downcast eyes, and modest grace;
And she forgave me, that I gazed
    Too fondly on her face!

But when I told the cruel scorn
That crazed that bold and lovely Knight,
And that he cross'd the mountain-woods,
    Nor rested day nor night;

That sometimes from the savage den,
And sometimes from the darksome shade,
And sometimes starting up at once
    In green and sunny glade, –

There came and look'd him in the face
An angel beautiful and bright;
And that he knew it was a Fiend,
    This miserable Knight!

And that unknowing what he did,
He leap'd amid a murderous band,
And saved from outrage worse than death
    The Lady of the Land; –

And how she wept, and clasp'd his knees;
And how she tended him in vain –
And ever strove to expiate
    The scorn that crazed his brain; –

And that she nursed him in a cave,
And how his madness went away,
When on the yellow forest-leaves
    A dying man he lay; –

His dying words – but when I reach'd
That tenderest strain of all the ditty,
My faltering voice and pausing harp
    Disturb'd her soul with pity!

All impulses of soul and sense
Had thrill'd my guileless Genevieve;
The music and the doleful tale,
    The rich and balmy eve;

And hopes, and fears that kindle hope,
An undistinguishable throng,
And gentle wishes long subdued,
    Subdued and cherish'd long!

She wept with pity and delight,
She blush'd with love, and virgin shame;
And like the murmur of a dream,
    I heard her breathe my name.

Her bosom heaved – she stepp'd aside,
As conscious of my look she stept –
Then suddenly, with timorous eye
    She fled to me and wept.

She half inclosed me with her arms,
She press'd me with a meek embrace;
And bending back her head, look'd up,
    And gazed upon my face.

'Twas partly love, and partly fear,
And partly 'twas a bashful art
That I might rather feel, than see,
    The swelling of her heart.

I calm'd her fears, and she was calm
And told her love with virgin pride;
And so I won my Genevieve,
    My bright and beauteous Bride.

S. T. Coleridge

CCXII
ALL FOR LOVE

O talk not to me of a name great in story;
The days of our youth are the days of our glory;
And the myrtle and ivy of sweet two-and-twenty
Are worth all your laurels, though ever so plenty.

What are garlands and crowns to the brow that is wrinkled?
'Tis but as a dead flower with May-dew be-sprinkled:
Then away with all such from the head that is hoary –
What care I for the wreaths that can only give glory?

Oh fame! – if I e'er took delight in thy praises,
'Twas less for the sake of thy high-sounding phrases,
Than to see the bright eyes of the dear one discover
She thought that I was not unworthy to love her.

There chiefly I sought thee, there only I found thee;
Her glance was the best of the rays that surround thee;
When it sparkled o'er aught that was bright in my story,
I knew it was love, and I felt it was glory.

Lord Byron

CCXIII
THE OUTLAW

O Brignall banks are wild and fair,
    And Greta woods are green,
And you may gather garlands there
    Would grace a summer-queen.
And as I rode by Dalton-Hall
    Beneath the turrets high,
A Maiden on the castle-wall
    Was singing merrily:
'O Brignall banks are fresh and fair,
    And Greta woods are green;
I'd rather rove with Edmund there
    Than reign our English queen.'

'If, Maiden, thou wouldst wend with me,
    To leave both tower and town,
Thou first must guess what life lead we
    That dwell by dale and down.
And if thou canst that riddle read,
    As read full well you may,
Then to the greenwood shalt thou speed
    As blithe as Queen of May.'
Yet sung she, 'Brignall banks are fair,
    And Greta woods are green;
I'd rather rove with Edmund there
    Than reign our English queen.

'I read you, by your bugle-horn
    And by your palfrey good,
I read you for a ranger sworn
    To keep the king's greenwood.'
'A Ranger, lady, winds his horn,
    And 'tis at peep of light;
His blast is heard at merry morn,
    And mine at dead of night.'
Yet sung she, 'Brignall banks are fair,
    And Greta woods are gay;
I would I were with Edmund there
    To reign his Queen of May!

'With burnish'd brand and musketoon
    So gallantly you come,
I read you for a bold Dragoon
    That lists the tuck of drum.'
'I list no more the tuck of drum,
    No more the trumpet hear;
But when the beetle sounds his hum
    My comrades take the spear.
And O! though Brignall banks be fair
    And Greta woods be gay,
Yet mickle must the maiden dare
    Would reign my Queen of May!

'Maiden! a nameless life I lead,
  A nameless death I'll die;
The fiend whose lantern lights the mead
  Were better mate than I!
And when I'm with my comrades met
  Beneath the greenwood bough, –
What once we were we all forget,
  Nor think what we are now.'

Chorus

'Yet Brignall banks are fresh and fair,
  And Greta woods are green,
And you may gather garlands there
  Would grace a summer-queen.'

                                    Sir W. Scott

CCXIV

There be none of Beauty's daughters
  With a magic like Thee;
And like music on the waters
  Is thy sweet voice to me:
When, as if its sounds were causing
The charmed ocean's pausing,
The waves lie still and gleaming,
And the lull'd winds seem dreaming:

And the midnight moon is weaving
  Her bright chain o'er the deep,
Whose breast is gently heaving
  As an infant's asleep:
So the spirit bows before thee
To listen and adore thee;
With a full but soft emotion,
Like the swell of Summer's ocean.

                                    Lord Byron

CCXV
THE INDIAN SERENADE

I arise from dreams of Thee
In the first sweet sleep of night,
When the winds are breathing low
And the stars are shining bright:
I arise from dreams of thee,
And a spirit in my feet
Hath led me – who knows how?
To thy chamber-window, Sweet!

The wandering airs they faint
On the dark, the silent stream –
The champak odours fail
Like sweet thoughts in a dream;
The nightingale's complaint
It dies upon her heart,
As I must die on thine
O belovéd as thou art!

Oh lift me from the grass!
I die, I faint, I fail!
Let thy love in kisses rain
On my lips and eyelids pale.
My cheek is cold and white, alas!
My heart beats loud and fast;
Oh! press it close to thine again
Where it will break at last.

P. B. Shelley

CCXVI

She walks in beauty, like the night
Of cloudless climes and starry skies,
And all that's best of dark and bright
Meet in her aspect and her eyes;
Thus mellow'd to that tender light
Which heaven to gaudy day denies.

One shade the more, one ray the less,
Had half impair'd the nameless grace
Which waves in every raven tress
Or softly lightens o'er her face,
Where thoughts serenely sweet express
How pure, how dear their dwelling-place.

And on that cheek and o'er that brow
So soft, so calm, yet eloquent,
The smiles that win, the tints that glow
But tell of days in goodness spent, –
A mind at peace with all below,
A heart whose love is innocent.

Lord Byron

CCXVII

She was a Phantom of delight
When first she gleam'd upon my sight;
A lovely Apparition, sent
To be a moment's ornament;
Her eyes as stars of twilight fair;
Like Twilight's, too, her dusky hair;
But all things else about her drawn
From May-time and the cheerful dawn;
A dancing shape, an image gay,
To haunt, to startle, and waylay.

I saw her upon nearer view,
A Spirit, yet a Woman too!
Her household motions light and free,
And steps of virgin-liberty;
A countenance in which did meet
Sweet records, promises as sweet;
A creature not too bright or good
For human nature's daily food,
For transient sorrows, simple wiles,
Praise, blame, love, kisses, tears, and smiles.

And now I see with eye serene
The very pulse of the machine;
A being breathing thoughtful breath,
A traveller between life and death:
The reason firm, the temperate will,
Endurance, foresight, strength, and skill;
A perfect Woman, nobly plann'd
To warn, to comfort, and command;
And yet a Spirit still, and bright
With something of an angel-light.

W. Wordsworth

CCXVIII

She is not fair to outward view
   As many maidens be;
Her loveliness I never knew
   Until she smiled on me.
O then I saw her eye was bright,
A well of love, a spring of light.

But now her looks are coy and cold,
   To mine they ne'er reply,
And yet I cease not to behold
   The love-light in her eye:
Her very frowns are fairer far
Than smiles of other maidens are.

H. Coleridge

CCXIX

I fear thy kisses, gentle maiden;
Thou needest not fear mine;
My spirit is too deeply laden
Ever to burthen thine.

I fear thy mien, thy tones, thy motion;
Thou needest not fear mine;
Innocent is the heart's devotion
With which I worship thine.

P. B. Shelley

CCXX

She dwelt among the untrodden ways
    Beside the springs of Dove;
A maid whom there were none to praise,
    And very few to love.

A violet by a mossy stone
    Half-hidden from the eye!
– Fair as a star, when only one
    Is shining in the sky.

She lived unknown, and few could know
    When Lucy ceased to be;
But she is in her grave, and, oh,
    The difference to me!

W. Wordsworth

CCXXI

I travell'd among unknown men
   In lands beyond the sea;
Nor, England! did I know till then
   What love I bore to thee.

'Tis past, that melancholy dream!
   Nor will I quit thy shore
A second time; for still I seem
   To love thee more and more.

Among thy mountains did I feel
   The joy of my desire;
And she I cherish'd turn'd her wheel
   Beside an English fire.

Thy mornings show'd, thy nights conceal'd
   The bowers where Lucy play'd;
And thine too is the last green field
   That Lucy's eyes survey'd.

W. Wordsworth

CCXXII
THE EDUCATION OF NATURE

Three years she grew in sun and shower;
Then Nature said, 'A lovelier flower
On earth was never sown:
This Child I to myself will take;
She shall be mine, and I will make
A lady of my own.

'Myself will to my darling be
Both law and impulse: and with me
The girl, in rock and plain,

In earth and heaven, in glade and bower,
Shall feel an overseeing power
To kindle or restrain.

'She shall be sportive as the fawn
That wild with glee across the lawn
Or up the mountain springs;
And her's shall be the breathing balm,
And her's the silence and the calm
Of mute insensate things.

'The floating clouds their state shall lend
To her; for her the willow bend;
Nor shall she fail to see
Ev'n in the motions of the storm
Grace that shall mould the maiden's form
By silent sympathy.

'The stars of midnight shall be dear
To her; and she shall lean her ear
In many a secret place
Where rivulets dance their wayward round,
And beauty born of murmuring sound
Shall pass into her face.

'And vital feelings of delight
Shall rear her form to stately height,
Her virgin bosom swell;
Such thoughts to Lucy I will give
While she and I together live
Here in this happy dell.'

Thus Nature spake – The work was done –
How soon my Lucy's race was run!
She died, and left to me
This heath, this calm and quiet scene;
The memory of what has been,
And never more will be.

                                        W. Wordsworth

CCXXIII

A slumber did my spirit seal;
  I had no human fears:
She seem'd a thing that could not feel
  The touch of earthly years.

No motion has she now, no force;
  She neither hears nor sees;
Roll'd round in earth's diurnal course
  With rocks, and stones, and trees.

W. Wordsworth

CCXXIV
A LOST LOVE

I meet thy pensive, moonlight face;
  Thy thrilling voice I hear;
And former hours and scenes retrace,
  Too fleeting, and too dear!

Then sighs and tears flow fast and free,
  Though none is nigh to share;
And life has nought beside for me
  So sweet as this despair.

There are crush'd hearts that will not break;
  And mine, methinks, is one;
Or thus I should not weep and wake,
  And thou to slumber gone.

I little thought it thus could be
  In days more sad and fair –
That earth could have a place for me,
  And thou no longer there.

Yet death cannot our hearts divide,
  Or make thee less my own:
'Twere sweeter sleeping at thy side
  Than watching here alone.

Yet never, never can we part,
   While Memory holds her reign:
Thine, thine is still this wither'd heart,
   Till we shall meet again.

                    H. F. Lyte

CCXXV
LORD ULLIN'S DAUGHTER

A Chieftain to the Highlands bound
Cries 'Boatman, do not tarry!
And I'll give thee a silver pound
To row us o'er the ferry!'

'Now who be ye, would cross Lochgyle,
This dark and stormy water?'
'O I'm the chief of Ulva's isle,
And this, Lord Ullin's daughter.

'And fast before her father's men
Three days we've fled together,
For should he find us in the glen,
My blood would stain the heather.

'His horsemen hard behind us ride –
Should they our steps discover,
Then who will cheer my bonny bride,
When they have slain her lover?'

Out spoke the hardy Highland wight,
'I'll go, my chief, I'm ready:
It is not for your silver bright,
But for your winsome lady: –

'And by my word! the bonny bird
In danger shall not tarry;
So though the waves are raging white
I'll row you o'er the ferry.'

By this the storm grew loud apace,
The water-wraith was shrieking;
And in the scowl of Heaven each face
Grew dark as they were speaking.

But still as wilder blew the wind,
And as the night grew drearer,
Adown the glen rode arméd men,
Their trampling sounded nearer.

'O haste thee, haste!' the lady cries,
'Though tempests round us gather;
I'll meet the raging of the skies,
But not an angry father.'

The boat has left a stormy land,
A stormy sea before her, –
When, oh! too strong for human hand
The tempest gather'd o'er her.

And still they row'd amidst the roar
Of waters fast prevailing:
Lord Ullin reach'd that fatal shore, –
His wrath was changed to wailing.

For, sore dismay'd, through storm and shade
His child he did discover; –
One lovely hand she stretch'd for aid,
And one was round her lover.

'Come back! come back!' he cried in grief
'Across this stormy water:
And I'll forgive your Highland chief,
My daughter! – Oh, my daughter!'

'Twas vain: the loud waves lash'd the shore,
Return or aid preventing:
The waters wild went o'er his child,
And he was left lamenting.

T. Campbell

LUCY GRAY
[*Added 1890*]

Oft I had heard of Lucy Gray:
And when I cross'd the wild,
I chanced to see at break of day
The solitary child.

No mate, no comrade Lucy knew;
She dwelt on a wide moor,
The sweetest thing that ever grew
Beside a human door!

You yet may spy the fawn at play,
The hare upon the green;
But the sweet face of Lucy Gray
Will never more be seen.

'To-night will be a stormy night –
You to the town must go;
And take a lantern, Child, to light
Your mother through the snow.'

'That, Father! will I gladly do:
'Tis scarcely afternoon –
The minster-clock has just struck two,
And yonder is the moon!'

At this the father raised his hook,
And snapp'd a faggot-band;
He plied his work; – and Lucy took
The lantern in her hand.

Not blither is the mountain roe:
With many a wanton stroke
Her feet disperse the powdery snow,
That rises up like smoke.

The storm came on before its time:
She wander'd up and down;
And many a hill did Lucy climb:
But never reach'd the town.

The wretched parents all that night
Went shouting far and wide;
But there was neither sound nor sight
To serve them for a guide.

At day-break on a hill they stood
That overlook'd the moor;
And thence they saw the bridge of wood
A furlong from their door.

They wept – and, turning homeward, cried
'In heaven we all shall meet!'
– When in the snow the mother spied
The print of Lucy's feet.

Then downwards from the steep hill's edge
They track'd the footmarks small;
And through the broken hawthorn hedge,
And by the long stone-wall:

And then an open field they cross'd:
The marks were still the same;
They track'd them on, nor ever lost;
And to the bridge they came:

They follow'd from the snowy bank
Those footmarks, one by one,
Into the middle of the plank;
And further there were none!

– Yet some maintain that to this day
She is a living child;
That you may see sweet Lucy Gray
Upon the lonesome wild.

O'er rough and smooth she trips along,
And never looks behind;
And sings a solitary song
That whistles in the wind.

W. Wordsworth

CCXXVII
JOCK OF HAZELDEAN

'Why weep ye by the tide, ladie?
  Why weep ye by the tide?
I'll wed ye to my youngest son,
  And ye sall be his bride:
And ye sall be his bride, ladie,
  Sae comely to be seen' –
But aye she loot the tears down fa'
  For Jock of Hazeldean.

'Now let this wilfu' grief be done,
  And dry that cheek so pale;
Young Frank is chief of Errington
  And lord of Langley-dale;
His step is first in peaceful ha',
  His sword in battle keen' –
But aye she loot the tears down fa'
  For Jock of Hazeldean.

'A chain of gold ye sall not lack,
  Nor braid to bind your hair,
Nor mettled hound, nor managed hawk,
  Nor palfrey fresh and fair;
And you the foremost o' them a'
  Shall ride our forest-queen' –
But aye she loot the tears down fa'
  For Jock of Hazeldean.

The kirk was deck'd at morning-tide,
　　The taper glimmer'd fair;
The priest and bridegroom wait the bride,
　　And dame and knight are there:
They sought her baith by bower and ha';
　　The ladie was not seen!
She's o'er the Border, and awa'
　　Wi' Jock of Hazeldean.

Sir W. Scott

FREEDOM AND LOVE
[*Dropped 1891*]

How delicious is the winning
Of a kiss at love's beginning,
When two mutual hearts are sighing
For the knot there's no untying!

Yet remember, 'midst your wooing,
Love has bliss, but Love has ruing;
Other smiles may make you fickle,
Tears for other charms may trickle.

Love he comes, and Love he tarries,
Just as fate or fancy carries;
Longest stays, when sorest chidden;
Laughs and flies, when press'd and bidden.

Bind the sea to slumber stilly,
Bind its odour to the lily,
Bind the aspen ne'er to quiver,
Then bind Love to last for ever.

Love's a fire that needs renewal
Of fresh beauty for its fuel:
Love's wing moults when caged and captured,
Only free, he soars enraptured.

Can you keep the bee from ranging
Or the ringdove's neck from changing?
No! nor fetter'd Love from dying
In the knot there's no untying.

T. Campbell

CCXXVIII
LOVE'S PHILOSOPHY

The fountains mingle with the river
And the rivers with the ocean,
The winds of heaven mix for ever
With a sweet emotion;
Nothing in the world is single,
All things by a law divine
In one another's being mingle –
Why not I with thine?

See the mountains kiss high heaven,
And the waves clasp one another;
No sister-flower would be forgiven
If it disdain'd its brother:
And the sunlight clasps the earth,
And the moonbeams kiss the sea –
What are all these kissings worth,
If thou kiss not me?

P. B. Shelley

CCXXIX
ECHOES

How sweet the answer Echo makes
To Music at night
When, roused by lute or horn, she wakes,
And far away o'er lawns and lakes
Goes answering light!

Yet Love hath echoes truer far
And far more sweet
Then e'er, beneath the moonlight's star,
Of horn or lute or soft guitar
The songs repeat.

'Tis when the sigh, – in youth sincere
And only then,
The sigh that's breathed for one to hear –
Is by that one, that only Dear
Breathed back again.

T. Moore

CCXXX
A SERENADE

Ah! County Guy, the hour is nigh,
   The sun has left the lea,
The orange-flower perfumes the bower,
   The breeze is on the sea.
The lark, his lay who thrill'd all day,
   Sits hush'd his partner nigh;
Breeze, bird, and flower confess the hour,
   But where is County Guy?

The village maid steals through the shade
   Her shepherd's suit to hear;
To Beauty shy, by lattice high,
   Sings high-born Cavalier.
The star of Love, all stars above,
   Now reigns o'er earth and sky,
And high and low the influence know –
   But where is County Guy?

Sir W. Scott

CCXXXI
TO THE EVENING STAR

Gem of the crimson-colour'd Even,
Companion of retiring day,
Why at the closing gates of heaven,
Beloved Star, dost thou delay?

So fair thy pensile beauty burns
When soft the tear of twilight flows;
So due thy plighted love returns
To chambers brighter than the rose;

To Peace, to Pleasure, and to Love
So kind a star thou seem'st to be,
Sure some enamour'd orb above
Descends and burns to meet with thee.

Thine is the breathing, blushing hour
When all unheavenly passions fly,
Chased by the soul-subduing power
Of Love's delicious witchery.

O! sacred to the fall of day
Queen of propitious stars, appear,
And early rise, and long delay,
When Caroline herself is here!

Shine on her chosen green resort
Whose trees the sunward summit crown,
And wanton flowers, that well may court
An angel's feet to tread them down: –

Shine on her sweetly scented road
Thou star of evening's purple dome,
That lead'st the nightingale abroad,
And guid'st the pilgrim to his home.

Shine where my charmer's sweeter breath
Embalms the soft exhaling dew,
Where dying winds a sigh bequeath
To kiss the cheek of rosy hue: –

Where, winnow'd by the gentle air,
Her silken tresses darkly flow
And fall upon her brow so fair,
Like shadows on the mountain snow.

Thus, ever thus, at day's decline
In converse sweet to wander far –
O bring with thee my Caroline,
And thou shalt be my Ruling Star!

T. Campbell

CCXXXII
TO THE NIGHT

Swiftly walk over the western wave,
                Spirit of Night!
Out of the misty eastern cave
Where, all the long and lone daylight,
Thou wovest dreams of joy and fear
Which make thee terrible and dear, –
                Swift be thy flight!

Wrap thy form in a mantle gray
                Star-inwrought;
Blind with thine hair the eyes of Day,
Kiss her until she be wearied out:
Then wander o'er city and sea and land,
Touching all with thine opiate wand –
                Come, long-sought!

When I arose and saw the dawn,
   I sigh'd for thee;
When light rode high, and the dew was gone,
And noon lay heavy on flower and tree,
And the weary Day turn'd to his rest
Lingering like an unloved guest,
   I sigh'd for thee.

Thy brother Death came, and cried
   Wouldst thou me?
Thy sweet child Sleep, the filmy-eyed,
Murmur'd like a noon-tide bee
Shall I nestle near thy side?
Wouldst thou me? – And I replied
   No, not thee!

Death will come when thou art dead,
   Soon, too soon –
Sleep will come when thou art fled;
Of neither would I ask the boon
I ask of thee, belovéd Night –
Swift be thine approaching flight,
   Come soon, soon!

        P. B. Shelley

CCXXXIII
TO A DISTANT FRIEND

Why art thou silent? Is thy love a plant
Of such weak fibre that the treacherous air
Of absence withers what was once so fair?
Is there no debt to pay, no boon to grant?

Yet have my thoughts for thee been vigilant,
Bound to thy service with unceasing care –
The mind's least generous wish a mendicant
For nought but what thy happiness could spare.

Speak! – though this soft warm heart, once free to hold
A thousand tender pleasures, thine and mine,
Be left more desolate, more dreary cold

Than a forsaken bird's-nest fill'd with snow
'Mid its own bush of leafless eglantine –
Speak, that my torturing doubts their end may know!

W. Wordsworth

CCXXXIV

When we two parted
In silence and tears,
Half broken-hearted,
To sever for years,
Pale grew thy cheek and cold,
Colder thy kiss;
Truly that hour foretold
Sorrow to this!

The dew of the morning
Sunk chill on my brow;
It felt like the warning
Of what I feel now.
Thy vows are all broken,
And light is thy fame:
I hear thy name spoken
And share in its shame.

They name thee before me,
A knell to mine ear;
A shudder comes o'er me –
Why wert thou so dear?
They know not I knew thee
Who knew thee too well:
Long, long shall I rue thee,
Too deeply to tell.

In secret we met:
In silence I grieve
That thy heart could forget,
Thy spirit deceive.
If I should meet thee
After long years,
How should I greet thee? –
With silence and tears.

Lord Byron

CCXXXV
HAPPY INSENSIBILITY

In a drear-nighted December,
Too happy, happy tree,
Thy branches ne'er remember
Their green felicity:
The north cannot undo them
With a sleety whistle through them
Nor frozen thawings glue them
From budding at the prime.

In a drear-nighted December,
Too happy, happy brook,
Thy bubblings ne'er remember
Apollo's summer look;
But with a sweet forgetting
They stay their crystal fretting,
Never, never petting
About the frozen time.

Ah! would 'twere so with many
A gentle girl and boy!
But were there ever any
Writhed not at passéd joy?

To know the change and feel it,
When there is none to heal it
Nor numbéd sense to steal it –
Was never said in rhyme.

J. Keats

CCXXXVI

Where shall the lover rest
  Whom the fates sever
From his true maiden's breast
  Parted for ever?
Where, through groves deep and high
  Sounds the far billow,
Where early violets die
  Under the willow.
    Eleu loro
  Soft shall be his pillow.

There through the summer day
  Cool streams are laving:
There, while the tempests sway,
  Scarce are boughs waving;
There thy rest shalt thou take,
  Parted for ever,
Never again to wake
  Never, O never!
    Eleu loro
  Never, O never!

Where shall the traitor rest,
  He, the deceiver,
Who could win maiden's breast,
    Ruin, and leave her?

In the lost battle,
　　Borne down by the flying,
Where mingles war's rattle
　　With groans of the dying;
　　　　Eleu loro
　　There shall he be lying.

Her wing shall the eagle flap
　　O'er the falsehearted;
His warm blood the wolf shall lap
　　Ere life be parted:
Shame and dishonour sit
　　By his grave ever;
　　　　Blessing shall hallow it
　　Never, O never!
　　　　Eleu loro
　　Never, O never!

Sir W. Scott

CCXXXVII
LA BELLE DAME SANS MERCI

'O what can ail thee, knight-at-arms,
　　Alone and palely loitering?
The sedge has wither'd from the lake,
　　And no birds sing.

'O what can ail thee, knight-at-arms!
　　So haggard and so woe-begone?
The squirrel's granary is full,
　　And the harvest's done.

'I see a lily on thy brow
　　With anguish moist and fever-dew,
And on thy cheeks a fading rose
　　Fast withereth too.'

'I met a lady in the meads,
    Full beautiful – a faery's child,
Her hair was long, her foot was light,
    And her eyes were wild.

'I made a garland for her head,
    And bracelets too, and fragrant zone;
She look'd at me as she did love,
    And made sweet moan.

'I set her on my pacing steed
    And nothing else saw all day long,
For sidelong would she bend, and sing
    A faery's song.

'She found me roots of relish sweet,
    And honey wild and manna-dew,
And sure in language strange she said
    "I love thee true."

'She took me to her elfin grot,
    And there she wept and sigh'd full sore;
And there I shut her wild wild eyes
    With kisses four.

'And there she lulléd me asleep,
    And there I dream'd – Ah! woe betide!
The latest dream I ever dream'd
    On the cold hill's side.

'I saw pale kings and princes too,
    Pale warriors, death-pale were they all:
They cried – "La belle Dame sans Merci
    Hath thee in thrall!"

'I saw their starved lips in the gloam
    With horrid warning gapéd wide,
And I awoke and found me here
    On the cold hill's side.

'And this is why I sojourn here
   Alone and palely loitering,
Though the sedge is wither'd from the lake,
   And no birds sing.'

J. Keats

CCXXXVIII
THE ROVER

A weary lot is thine, fair maid,
   A weary lot is thine!
To pull the thorn thy brow to braid,
   And press the rue for wine.
A lightsome eye, a soldier's mien,
   A feather of the blue,
A doublet of the Lincoln green –
   No more of me you knew
                     My Love!
No more of me you knew.

'This morn is merry June, I trow,
   The rose is budding fain;
But she shall bloom in winter snow
   Ere we two meet again.'
He turn'd his charger as he spake
   Upon the river shore,
He gave the bridle-reins a shake,
   Said 'Adieu for evermore
                     My Love!
And adieu for evermore.'

Sir W. Scott

CCXXXIX
THE FLIGHT OF LOVE

When the lamp is shatter'd
The light in the dust lies dead –
When the cloud is scatter'd,
The rainbow's glory is shed.
When the lute is broken,
Sweet tones are remember'd not;
When the lips have spoken,
Loved accents are soon forgot.

As music and splendour
Survive not the lamp and the lute,
The heart's echoes render
No song when the spirit is mute –
No song but sad dirges,
Like the wind through a ruin'd cell,
Or the mournful surges
That ring the dead seaman's knell.

When hearts have once mingled,
Love first leaves the well-built nest;
The weak one is singled
To endure what it once possesst.
O Love! who bewailest
The frailty of all things here,
Why choose you the frailest
For your cradle, your home, and your bier?

Its passions will rock thee
As the storms rock the ravens on high;
Bright reason will mock thee
Like the sun from a wintry sky.
From thy nest every rafter
Will rot, and thine eagle home
Leave thee naked to laughter,
When leaves fall and cold winds come.

P. B. Shelley

CCXL
THE MAID OF NEIDPATH

O lovers' eyes are sharp to see,
    And lovers' ears in hearing;
And love, in life's extremity,
    Can lend an hour of cheering.
Disease had been in Mary's bower
    And slow decay from mourning,
Though now she sits on Neidpath's tower
    To watch her Love's returning.

All sunk and dim her eyes so bright,
    Her form decay'd by pining,
Till through her wasted hand, at night,
    You saw the taper shining.
By fits a sultry hectic hue
    Across her cheek was flying;
By fits so ashy pale she grew
    Her maidens thought her dying.

Yet keenest powers to see and hear
    Seem'd in her frame residing;
Before the watch-dog prick'd his ear
    She heard her lover's riding;
Ere scarce a distant form was kenn'd
    She knew and waved to greet him,
And o'er the battlement did bend
    As on the wing to meet him.

He came – he pass'd – an heedless gaze
    As o'er some stranger glancing;
Her welcome, spoke in faltering phrase,
    Lost in his courser's prancing –
The castle-arch, whose hollow tone
    Returns each whisper spoken,
Could scarcely catch the feeble moan
    Which told her heart was broken.

Sir W. Scott

CCXLI

Earl March look'd on his dying child,
    And, smit with grief to view her –
The youth, he cried, whom I exiled
    Shall be restored to woo her.

She's at the window many an hour
    His coming to discover:
And he look'd up to Ellen's bower
    And she look'd on her lover –

But ah! so pale, he knew her not,
    Though her smile on him was dwelling –
And am I then forgot – forgot?
    It broke the heart of Ellen.

In vain he weeps, in vain he sighs,
    Her cheek is cold as ashes;
Nor love's own kiss shall wake those eyes
    To lift their silken lashes.

T. Campbell

CCXLII

Bright Star! would I were steadfast as thou art –
Not in lone splendour hung aloft the night,
And watching, with eternal lids apart,
Like Nature's patient sleepless Eremite,

The moving waters at their priestlike task
Of pure ablution round earth's human shores,
Or gazing on the new soft fallen mask
Of snow upon the mountains and the moors: –

No – yet still steadfast, still unchangeable,
Pillow'd upon my fair Love's ripening breast
To feel for ever its soft fall and swell,
Awake for ever in a sweet unrest;

Still, still to hear her tender-taken breath,
And so live ever, – or else swoon to death.

J. Keats

CCXLIII
THE TERROR OF DEATH

When I have fears that I may cease to be
Before my pen has glean'd my teeming brain,
Before high-pilèd books, in charact'ry
Hold like rich garners the full-ripen'd grain;

When I behold, upon the night's starr'd face,
Huge cloudy symbols of a high romance,
And think that I may never live to trace
Their shadows, with the magic hand of chance;

And when I feel, fair Creature of an hour!
That I shall never look upon thee more,
Never have relish in the faery power
Of unreflecting love – then on the shore

Of the wide world I stand alone, and think
Till Love and Fame to nothingness do sink.

J. Keats

CCXLIV
DESIDERIA

Surprized by joy – impatient as the wind –
I turn'd to share the transport – Oh! with whom
But Thee – deep buried in the silent tomb,
That spot which no vicissitude can find?

Love, faithful love recall'd thee to my mind –
But how could I forget thee? Through what power
Even for the least division of an hour
Have I been so beguiled as to be blind

To my most grievous loss! – That thought's return
Was the worst pang that sorrow ever bore
Save one, one only, when I stood forlorn,

Knowing my heart's best treasure was no more;
That neither present time, nor years unborn
Could to my sight that heavenly face restore.

W. Wordsworth

CCXLV

At the mid hour of night, when stars are weeping, I fly
To the lone vale we loved, when life shone warm in thine eye;
And I think oft, if spirits can steal from the regions of air
To revisit past scenes of delight, thou wilt come to me there
And tell me our love is remember'd, even in the sky!

Then I sing the wild song it once was rapture to hear
When our voices, commingling, breathed like one on the ear;
And as Echo far off through the vale my sad orison rolls,
I think, oh my Love! 'tis thy voice, from the Kingdom of Souls
Faintly answering still the notes that once were so dear.

T. Moore

CCXLVI
ELEGY ON THYRZA

And thou art dead, as young and fair
    As aught of mortal birth;
And forms so soft and charms so rare
    Too soon return'd to Earth!
Though Earth received them in her bed,
And o'er the spot the crowd may tread
    In carelessness or mirth,
There is an eye which could not brook
A moment on that grave to look.

I will not ask where thou liest low
    Nor gaze upon the spot;
There flowers or weeds at will may grow
    So I behold them not:
It is enough for me to prove
That what I loved, and long must love,
    Like common earth can rot;
To me there needs no stone to tell
'Tis Nothing that I loved so well.

Yet did I love thee to the last,
    As fervently as thou
Who didst not change through all the past
    And canst not alter now.
The love where Death has set his seal
Nor age can chill, nor rival steal,
    Nor falsehood disavow:
And, what were worse, thou canst not see
Or wrong, or change, or fault in me.

The better days of life were ours;
    The worst can be but mine:
The sun that cheers, the storm that lours,
    Shall never more be thine.
The silence of that dreamless sleep
I envy now too much to weep;
    Nor need I to repine
That all those charms have pass'd away
I might have watch'd through long decay.

The flower in ripen'd bloom unmatch'd
    Must fall the earliest prey;
Though by no hand untimely snatch'd,
    The leaves must drop away.
And yet it were a greater grief
To watch it withering, leaf by leaf,
    Than see it pluck'd today;
Since earthly eye but ill can bear
To trace the change to foul from fair.

I know not if I could have borne
   To see thy beauties fade;
The night that follow'd such a morn
   Had worn a deeper shade:
Thy day without a cloud hath past,
And thou wert lovely to the last,
   Extinguish'd, not decay'd;
As stars that shoot along the sky
Shine brightest as they fall from high.

As once I wept, if I could weep,
   My tears might well be shed
To think I was not near, to keep
   One vigil o'er thy bed:
To gaze, how fondly! on thy face,
To fold thee in a faint embrace,
   Uphold thy drooping head;
And show that love, however vain,
Nor thou nor I can feel again.

Yet how much less it were to gain,
   Though thou hast left me free,
The loveliest things that still remain
   Than thus remember thee!
The all of thine that cannot die
Through dark and dread Eternity
   Returns again to me,
And more thy buried love endears
Than aught except its living years.

Lord Byron

CCXLVII

One word is too often profaned
   For me to profane it,
One feeling too falsely disdain'd
   For thee to disdain it.
One hope is too like despair
   For prudence to smother,
And pity from thee more dear
   Than that from another.

I can give not what men call love;
   But wilt thou accept not
The worship the heart lifts above
   And the Heavens reject not:
The desire of the moth for the star,
   Of the night for the morrow,
The devotion to something afar
   From the sphere of our sorrow?

P. B. Shelley

CCXLVIII

GATHERING SONG OF DONALD THE BLACK

Pibroch of Donuil Dhu
   Pibroch of Donuil
Wake thy wild voice anew,
   Summon Clan Conuil.
Come away, come away,
   Hark to the summons!
Come in your war-array,
   Gentles and commons.

Come from deep glen, and
    From mountain so rocky;
The war-pipe and pennon
    Are at Inverlocky.
Come every hill-plaid, and
    True heart that wears one,
Come every steel blade, and
    Strong hand that bears one.

Leave untended the herd,
    The flock without shelter;
Leave the corpse uninterr'd,
    The bride at the altar;
Leave the deer, leave the steer,
    Leave nets and barges:
Come with your fighting gear,
    Broadswords and targes.

Come as the winds come, when
    Forests are rended,
Come as the waves come, when
    Navies are stranded:
Faster come, faster come,
    Faster and faster,
Chief, vassal, page and groom,
    Tenant and master.

Fast they come, fast they come;
    See how they gather!
Wide waves the eagle plume
    Blended with heather.
Cast your plaids, draw your blades,
    Forward each man set!
Pibroch of Donuil Dhu
    Knell for the onset!

Sir W. Scott

CCXLIX

A wet sheet and a flowing sea,
  A wind that follows fast
And fills the white and rustling sail
  And bends the gallant mast;
And bends the gallant mast, my boys,
  While like the eagle free
Away the good ship flies, and leaves
  Old England on the lee.

O for a soft and gentle wind!
  I heard a fair one cry;
But give to me the snoring breeze
  And white waves heaving high;
And white waves heaving high, my lads,
  The good ship tight and free –
The world of waters is our home,
  And merry men are we.

There's tempest in yon hornéd moon,
  And lightning in yon cloud;
But hark the music, mariners!
  The wind is piping loud;
The wind is piping loud, my boys,
  The lightning flashes free –
While the hollow oak our palace is,
  Our heritage the sea.

A. Cunningham

CCL

Ye Mariners of England
That guard our native seas!
Whose flag has braved, a thousand years,
The battle and the breeze!
Your glorious standard launch again
To match another foe:
And sweep through the deep,
While the stormy winds do blow;
While the battle rages loud and long
And the stormy winds do blow.

The spirits of your fathers
Shall start from every wave –
For the deck it was their field of fame,
And Ocean was their grave:
Where Blake and mighty Nelson fell
Your manly hearts shall glow,
As ye sweep through the deep,
While the stormy winds do blow;
While the battle rages loud and long
And the stormy winds do blow.

Britannia needs no bulwarks,
No towers along the steep;
Her march is o'er the mountain-waves,
Her home is on the deep.
With thunders from her native oak
She quells the floods below –
As they roar on the shore,
When the stormy winds do blow;
When the battle rages loud and long,
And the stormy winds do blow.

The meteor flag of England
Shall yet terrific burn;
Till danger's troubled night depart
And the star of peace return.

Then, then, ye ocean-warriors!
Our song and feast shall flow
To the fame of your name,
When the storm has ceased to blow;
When the fiery fight is heard no more,
And the storm has ceased to blow.

T. Campbell

CCLI
BATTLE OF THE BALTIC

Of Nelson and the North
Sing the glorious day's renown,
When to battle fierce came forth
All the might of Denmark's crown,
And her arms along the deep proudly shone;
By each gun the lighted brand
In a bold determined hand,
And the Prince of all the land
Led them on.

Like leviathans afloat
Lay their bulwarks on the brine;
While the sign of battle flew
On the lofty British line:
It was ten of April morn by the chime:
As they drifted on their path
There was silence deep as death;
And the boldest held his breath
For a time.

But the might of England flush'd
To anticipate the scene;
And her van the fleeter rush'd
O'er the deadly space between.

'Hearts of oak!' our captains cried, when each gun
From its adamantine lips
Spread a death-shade round the ships,
Like the hurricane eclipse
Of the sun.

Again! again! again!
And the havoc did not slack,
Till a feeble cheer the Dane
To our cheering sent us back: –
Their shots along the deep slowly boom: –
Then ceased – and all is wail,
As they strike the shatter'd sail;
Or in conflagration pale
Light the gloom.

Out spoke the victor then
As he hail'd them o'er the wave,
'Ye are brothers! ye are men!
And we conquer but to save: –
So peace instead of death let us bring:
But yield, proud foe, thy fleet
With the crews, at England's feet,
And make submission meet
To our King.'

Then Denmark bless'd our chief
That he gave her wounds repose;
And the sounds of joy and grief
From her people wildly rose,
As death withdrew his shades from the day:
While the sun look'd smiling bright
O'er a wide and woeful sight,
Where the fires of funeral light
Died away.

Now joy, old England, raise!
For the tidings of thy might,
By the festal cities' blaze,
Whilst the wine-cup shines in light;
And yet amidst that joy and uproar,
Let us think of them that sleep
Full many a fathom deep
By thy wild and stormy steep,
Elsinore!

Brave hearts! to Britain's pride
Once so faithful and so true,
On the deck of fame that died,
With the gallant good Riou:
Soft sigh the winds of Heaven o'er their grave!
While the billow mournful rolls
And the mermaid's song condoles
Singing glory to the souls
Of the brave!

T. Campbell

CCLII
ODE TO DUTY

Stern Daughter of the Voice of God!
O Duty! if that name thou love
Who art a light to guide, a rod
To check the erring, and reprove;
Thou who art victory and law
When empty terrors overawe;
From vain temptations dost set free,
And calm'st the weary strife of frail humanity!

There are who ask not if thine eye
Be on them; who, in love and truth
Where no misgiving is, rely
Upon the genial sense of youth:

Glad hearts! without reproach or blot,
Who do thy work, and know it not:
Oh! if through confidence misplaced
They fail, thy saving arms, dread Power! around them cast.

Serene will be our days and bright
And happy will our nature be
When love is an unerring light,
And joy its own security.
And they a blissful course may hold
Ev'n now, who, not unwisely bold,
Live in the spirit of this creed;
Yet seek thy firm support, according to their need.

I, loving freedom, and untried,
No sport of every random gust,
Yet being to myself a guide,
Too blindly have reposed my trust:
And oft, when in my heart was heard
Thy timely mandate, I deferr'd
The task, in smoother walks to stray;
But thee I now would serve more strictly, if I may.

Through no disturbance of my soul
Or strong compunction in me wrought,
I supplicate for thy controul,
But in the quietness of thought:
Me this uncharter'd freedom tires;
I feel the weight of chance-desires:
My hopes no more must change their name;
I long for a repose that ever is the same.

Stern Lawgiver! yet thou dost wear
The Godhead's most benignant grace;
Nor know we anything so fair
As is the smile upon thy face:
Flowers laugh before thee on their beds,
And fragrance in thy footing treads;
Thou dost preserve the Stars from wrong;
And the most ancient Heavens, through Thee, are fresh and strong.

To humbler functions, awful Power!
I call thee: I myself commend
Unto thy guidance from this hour;
Oh let my weakness have an end!
Give unto me, made lowly wise,
The spirit of self-sacrifice;
The confidence of reason give;
And in the light of truth thy Bondman let me live.

W. Wordsworth

CCLIII
ON THE CASTLE OF CHILLON

Eternal Spirit of the chainless Mind!
Brightest in dungeons, Liberty! thou art,
For there thy habitation is the heart –
The heart which love of Thee alone can bind;

And when thy sons to fetters are consign'd,
To fetters and the damp vault's dayless gloom,
Their country conquers with their martyrdom,
And Freedom's fame finds wings on every wind.

Chillon! thy prison is a holy place
And thy sad floor an altar, for 'twas trod,
Until his very steps have left a trace

Worn as if thy cold pavement were a sod,
By Bonnivard! May none those marks efface!
For they appeal from tyranny to God.

Lord Byron

CCLIV
ENGLAND AND SWITZERLAND, 1802

Two Voices are there; one is of the Sea,
One of the Mountains; each a mighty voice:
In both from age to age thou didst rejoice,
They were thy chosen music, Liberty!

There came a tyrant, and with holy glee
Thou fought'st against him, – but hast vainly striven:
Thou from thy Alpine holds at length art driven,
Where not a torrent murmurs heard by thee.

– Of one deep bliss thine ear hath been bereft;
Then cleave, O cleave to that which still is left –
For, high-soul'd Maid, what sorrow would it be

That Mountain floods should thunder as before,
And Ocean bellow from his rocky shore,
And neither awful Voice be heard by Thee!

W. Wordsworth

CCLV
ON THE EXTINCTION OF THE VENETIAN REPUBLIC

Once did She hold the gorgeous East in fee
And was the safeguard of the West; the worth
Of Venice did not fall below her birth,
Venice, the eldest child of Liberty.

She was a maiden city, bright and free;
No guile seduced, no force could violate;
And when she took unto herself a mate,
She must espouse the everlasting Sea.

And what if she had seen those glories fade,
Those titles vanish, and that strength decay, –
Yet shall some tribute of regret be paid

When her long life hath reach'd its final day:
Men are we, and must grieve when even the shade
Of that which once was great is pass'd away.

W. Wordsworth

CCLVI
LONDON, 1802

O Friend! I know not which way I must look
For comfort, being, as I am, opprest
To think that now our life is only drest
For show; mean handy-work of craftsman, cook,

Or groom! – We must run glittering like a brook
In the open sunshine, or we are unblest;
The wealthiest man among us is the best:
No grandeur now in nature or in book

Delights us. Rapine, avarice, expense,
This is idolatry; and these we adore:
Plain living and high thinking are no more:

The homely beauty of the good old cause
Is gone; our peace, our fearful innocence,
And pure religion breathing household laws.

W. Wordsworth

CCLVII
THE SAME

Milton! thou shouldst be living at this hour:
England hath need of thee: she is a fen
Of stagnant waters: altar, sword and pen,
Fireside, the heroic wealth of hall and bower,

Have forfeited their ancient English dower
Of inward happiness. We are selfish men:
Oh! raise us up, return to us again;
And give us manners, virtue, freedom, power.

Thy soul was like a Star, and dwelt apart:
Thou hadst a voice whose sound was like the sea,
Pure as the naked heavens, majestic, free;

So didst thou travel on life's common way
In cheerful godliness; and yet thy heart
The lowliest duties on herself did lay.

W. Wordsworth

CCLVIII

When I have borne in memory what has tamed
Great nations; how ennobling thoughts depart
When men change swords for ledgers, and desert
The student's bower for gold, – some fears unnamed

I had, my Country! – am I to be blamed?
Now, when I think of thee, and what thou art,
Verily, in the bottom of my heart
Of those unfilial fears I am ashamed.

For dearly must we prize thee; we who find
In thee a bulwark for the cause of men;
And I by my affection was beguiled:

What wonder if a Poet now and then,
Among the many movements of his mind,
Felt for thee as a lover or a child!

W. Wordsworth

CCLIX
HOHENLINDEN

On Linden, when the sun was low,
All bloodless lay the untrodden snow;
And dark as winter was the flow
    Of Iser, rolling rapidly.

But Linden saw another sight,
When the drum beat at dead of night
Commanding fires of death to light
    The darkness of her scenery.

By torch and trumpet fast array'd
Each horseman drew his battle-blade,
And furious every charger neigh'd
    To join the dreadful revelry.

Then shook the hills with thunder riven;
Then rush'd the steed, to battle driven;
And louder than the bolts of Heaven
    Far flash'd the red artillery.

But redder yet that light shall glow
On Linden's hills of stainéd snow;
And bloodier yet the torrent flow
    Of Iser, rolling rapidly.

'Tis morn; but scarce yon level sun
Can pierce the war-clouds rolling dun,
Where furious Frank and fiery Hun
    Shout in their sulphurous canopy.

The combat deepens. On, ye Brave
Who rush to glory, or the grave!
Wave, Munich! all thy banners wave,
    And charge with all thy chivalry!

Few, few shall part, where many meet!
The snow shall be their winding-sheet,
And every turf beneath their feet
    Shall be a soldier's sepulchre.

                    T. Campbell

CCLX
AFTER BLENHEIM

It was a summer evening,
    Old Kaspar's work was done,
And he before his cottage door
    Was sitting in the sun;
And by him sported on the green
His little grandchild Wilhelmine.

She saw her brother Peterkin
    Roll something large and round
Which he beside the rivulet
    In playing there had found;
He came to ask what he had found
That was so large and smooth and round.

Old Kaspar took it from the boy
    Who stood expectant by;
And then the old man shook his head,
    And with a natural sigh
''Tis some poor fellow's skull,' said he,
'Who fell in the great victory.

'I find them in the garden,
    For there's many here about;
And often when I go to plough
    The ploughshare turns them out.
For many thousand men,' said he,
'Were slain in that great victory.'

'Now tell us what 'twas all about,'
    Young Peterkin he cries;
And little Wilhelmine looks up
    With wonder-waiting eyes;
'Now tell us all about the war,
And what they fought each other for.'

'It was the English,' Kaspar cried,
    'Who put the French to rout;
But what they fought each other for
    I could not well make out.
But everybody said,' quoth he,
'That 'twas a famous victory.

'My father lived at Blenheim then,
    Yon little stream hard by;
They burnt his dwelling to the ground,
    And he was forced to fly:
So with his wife and child he fled,
Nor had he where to rest his head.

'With fire and sword the country round
    Was wasted far and wide
And many a childing mother then
    And newborn baby died:
But things like that, you know, must be
At every famous victory.

'They say it was a shocking sight
    After the field was won;
For many thousand bodies here
    Lay rotting in the sun:
But things like that, you know, must be
After a famous victory.

'Great praise the Duke of Marlbro' won
    And our good Prince Eugene;'
'Why 'twas a very wicked thing!'
    Said little Wilhelmine;
'Nay . . . nay . . . my little girl,' quoth he,
'It was a famous victory.

'And everybody praised the Duke
    Who this great fight did win.'
'But what good came of it at last?'
    Quoth little Peterkin: –
'Why that I cannot tell,' said he,
'But 'twas a famous victory.'

                                        R. Southey

CCLXI
PRO PATRIA MORI

When he who adores thee has left but the name
    Of his fault and his sorrows behind,
Oh! say wilt thou weep, when they darken the fame
    Of a life that for thee was resign'd!
Yes, weep, and however my foes may condemn,
    Thy tears shall efface their decree;
For, Heaven can witness, though guilty to them,
    I have been but too faithful to thee.

With thee were the dreams of my earliest love;
    Every thought of my reason was thine:
In my last humble prayer to the Spirit above
    Thy name shall be mingled with mine!
Oh! blest are the lovers and friends who shall live
    The days of thy glory to see;
But the next dearest blessing that Heaven can give
    Is the pride of thus dying for thee.

                                        T. Moore

CCLXII
THE BURIAL OF SIR JOHN MOORE AT CORUNNA

Not a drum was heard, not a funeral note,
    As his corpse to the rampart we hurried;
Not a soldier discharged his farewell shot
    O'er the grave where our hero we buried.

We buried him darkly at dead of night,
   The sods with our bayonets turning;
By the struggling moonbeam's misty light
   And the lantern dimly burning.

No useless coffin enclosed his breast,
   Not in sheet or in shroud we wound him;
But he lay like a warrior taking his rest,
   With his martial cloak around him.

Few and short were the prayers we said,
   And we spoke not a word of sorrow;
But we steadfastly gazed on the face that was dead,
   And we bitterly thought of the morrow.

We thought, as we hollow'd his narrow bed
   And smoothed down his lonely pillow,
That the foe and the stranger would tread o'er his head,
   And we far away on the billow!

Lightly they'll talk of the spirit that's gone
   And o'er his cold ashes upbraid him, –
But little he'll reck, if they let him sleep on
   In the grave where a Briton has laid him.

But half of our heavy task was done
   When the clock struck the hour for retiring:
And we heard the distant and random gun
   That the foe was sullenly firing.

Slowly and sadly we laid him down,
   From the field of his fame fresh and gory;
We carved not a line, and we raised not a stone,
   But we left him alone with his glory.

C. Wolfe

CCLXIII

SIMON LEE THE OLD HUNTSMAN

In the sweet shire of Cardigan,
Not far from pleasant Ivor Hall,
An old man dwells, a little man,—
'Tis said he once was tall.
Full five-and-thirty years he lived
A running huntsman merry;
And still the centre of his cheek
Is red as a ripe cherry.

No man like him the horn could sound,
And hill and valley rang with glee,
When Echo bandied, round and round,
The halloo of Simon Lee.
In those proud days he little cared
For husbandry or tillage;
To blither tasks did Simon rouse
The sleepers of the village.

He all the country could outrun,
Could leave both man and horse behind;
And often, ere the chase was done
He reel'd and was stone-blind.
And still there's something in the world
At which his heart rejoices;
For when the chiming hounds are out,
He dearly loves their voices.

But oh the heavy change! — bereft
Of health, strength, friends and kindred, see!
Old Simon to the world is left
In liveried poverty: —
His master's dead, and no one now
Dwells in the Hall of Ivor;
Men, dogs, and horses, all are dead;
He is the sole survivor.

And he is lean and he is sick,
His body, dwindled and awry,
Rests upon ankles swoln and thick;
His legs are thin and dry.
One prop he has, and only one, –
His wife, an aged woman,
Lives with him, near the waterfall,
Upon the village common.

Beside their moss-grown hut of clay,
Not twenty paces from the door,
A scrap of land they have, but they
Are poorest of the poor.
This scrap of land he from the heath
Enclosed when he was stronger;
But what to them avails the land
Which he can till no longer?

Oft, working by her husband's side,
Ruth does what Simon cannot do;
For she, with scanty cause for pride,
Is stouter of the two.
And, though you with your utmost skill
From labour could not wean them,
'Tis little, very little, all
That they can do between them.

Few months of life has he in store
As he to you will tell,
For still, the more he works, the more
Do his weak ankles swell.
My gentle Reader, I perceive
How patiently you've waited,
And now I fear that you expect
Some tale will be related.

O Reader! had you in your mind
Such stores as silent thought can bring,
O gentle Reader! you would find
A tale in every thing.
What more I have to say is short,
And you must kindly take it:
It is no tale; but, should you think,
Perhaps a tale you'll make it.

One summer-day I chanced to see
This old Man doing all he could
To unearth the root of an old tree,
A stump of rotten wood.
The mattock totter'd in his hand;
So vain was his endeavour
That at the root of the old tree
He might have work'd for ever.

'You're overtask'd, good Simon Lee,
Give me your tool,' to him I said;
And at the word right gladly he
Received my proffer'd aid.
I struck, and with a single blow
The tangled root I sever'd,
At which the poor old man so long
And vainly had endeavour'd.

The tears into his eyes were brought,
And thanks and praises seem'd to run
So fast out of his heart, I thought
They never would have done.
– I've heard of hearts unkind, kind deed
With coldness still returning;
Alas! the gratitude of men
Hath oftener left me mourning.

W. Wordsworth

THE OLD FAMILIAR FACES

I have had playmates, I have had companions,
In my days of childhood, in my joyful school-days;
All, all are gone, the old familiar faces.

I have been laughing, I have been carousing,
Drinking late, sitting late, with my bosom cronies;
All, all are gone, the old familiar faces.

I loved a Love once, fairest among women:
Closed are her doors on me, I must not see her –
All, all are gone, the old familiar faces.

I have a friend, a kinder friend has no man:
Like an ingrate, I left my friend abruptly;
Left him, to muse on the old familiar faces.

Ghost-like I paced round the haunts of my childhood,
Earth seem'd a desert I was bound to traverse,
Seeking to find the old familiar faces.

Friend of my bosom, thou more than a brother,
Why wert not thou born in my father's dwelling?
So might we talk of the old familiar faces,

How some they have died, and some they have left me,
And some are taken from me; all are departed;
All, all are gone, the old familiar faces.

C. Lamb

CCLXV
THE JOURNEY ONWARDS

As slow our ship her foamy track
    Against the wind was cleaving,
Her trembling pennant still look'd back
    To that dear isle 'twas leaving.
So loth we part from all we love,
    From all the links that bind us;
So turn our hearts, as on we rove,
    To those we've left behind us!

When, round the bowl, of vanish'd years
    We talk with joyous seeming –
With smiles that might as well be tears,
    So faint, so sad their beaming;
While memory brings us back again
    Each early tie that twined us,
Oh, sweet's the cup that circles then
    To those we've left behind us!

And when, in other climes, we meet
    Some isle or vale enchanting,
Where all looks flowery, wild, and sweet,
    And nought but love is wanting;
We think how great had been our bliss
    If Heaven had but assign'd us
To live and die in scenes like this,
    With some we've left behind us!

As travellers oft look back at eve
    When eastward darkly going,
To gaze upon that light they leave
    Still faint behind them glowing, –
So, when the close of pleasure's day
    To gloom hath near consign'd us,
We turn to catch one fading ray
    Of joy that's left behind us.

T. Moore

CCLXVI
YOUTH AND AGE

There's not a joy the world can give like that it takes away
When the glow of early thought declines in feeling's dull decay;
'Tis not on youth's smooth cheek the blush alone, which fades so fast,
But the tender bloom of heart is gone, ere youth itself be past.

Then the few whose spirits float above the wreck of happiness
Are driven o'er the shoals of guilt, or ocean of excess:
The magnet of their course is gone, or only points in vain
The shore to which their shiver'd sail shall never stretch again.

Then the mortal coldness of the soul like death itself comes down;
It cannot feel for others' woes, it dare not dream its own;
That heavy chill has frozen o'er the fountain of our tears,
And though the eye may sparkle still, 'tis where the ice appears.

Though wit may flash from fluent lips, and mirth distract the breast,
Through midnight hours that yield no more their former hope of rest;
'Tis but as ivy-leaves around the ruin'd turret wreathe,
All green and wildly fresh without, but worn and gray beneath.

Oh could I feel as I have felt, or be what I have been,
Or weep as I could once have wept o'er many a vanish'd scene, –
As springs in deserts found seem sweet, all brackish though they be,
So midst the wither'd waste of life, those tears would flow to me!

Lord Byron

CCLXVII
A LESSON

There is a Flower, the lesser Celandine,
That shrinks like many more from cold and rain,
And the first moment that the sun may shine,
Bright as the sun himself, 'tis out again!

When hailstones have been falling, swarm on swarm,
Or blasts the green field and the trees distrest,
Oft have I seen it muffled up from harm
In close self-shelter, like a thing at rest.

But lately, one rough day, this Flower I past,
And recognized it, though an alter'd form,
Now standing forth an offering to the blast,
And buffeted at will by rain and storm.

I stopp'd and said, with inly-mutter'd voice,
'It doth not love the shower, nor seek the cold;
This neither is its courage nor its choice,
But its necessity in being old.

'The sunshine may not cheer it, nor the dew;
It cannot help itself in its decay;
Stiff in its members, wither'd, changed of hue,' –
And, in my spleen, I smiled that it was gray.

To be a prodigal's favourite – then, worse truth,
A miser's pensioner – behold our lot!
O Man! that from thy fair and shining youth
Age might but take the things Youth needed not!

                                        W. Wordsworth

CCLXVIII
PAST AND PRESENT

I remember, I remember
The house where I was born,
The little window where the sun
Came peeping in at morn;
He never came a wink too soon
Nor brought too long a day;
But now, I often wish the night
Had borne my breath away.

I remember, I remember
The roses, red and white,
The violets, and the lily-cups –
Those flowers made of light!
The lilacs where the robin built,
And where my brother set
The laburnum on his birth-day, –
The tree is living yet!

I remember, I remember
Where I was used to swing,
And thought the air must rush as fresh
To swallows on the wing;
My spirit flew in feathers then
That is so heavy now,
And summer pools could hardly cool
The fever on my brow.

I remember, I remember
The fir trees dark and high;
I used to think their slender tops
Were close against the sky:
It was a childish ignorance,
But now 'tis little joy
To know I'm farther off from Heaven
Than when I was a boy.

T. Hood

CCLXIX
THE LIGHT OF OTHER DAYS

Oft in the stilly night
  Ere slumber's chain has bound me,
Fond Memory brings the light
  Of other days around me:
    The smiles, the tears
    Of boyhood's years,
  The words of love then spoken;

The eyes that shone,
   Now dimm'd and gone,
The cheerful hearts now broken!
Thus in the stilly night
   Ere slumber's chain has bound me,
Sad Memory brings the light
   Of other days around me.

When I remember all
   The friends so link'd together
I've seen around me fall
   Like leaves in wintry weather,
      I feel like one
      Who treads alone
   Some banquet-hall deserted,
      Whose lights are fled
      Whose garlands dead,
   And all but he departed!
Thus in the stilly night
   Ere slumber's chain has bound me,
Sad memory brings the light
   Of other days around me.

                              T. Moore

INVOCATION
[*Dropped 1890*]

Rarely, rarely, comest thou,
   Spirit of Delight!
Wherefore hast thou left me now
   Many a day and night?
Many a weary night and day
'Tis since thou art fled away.

How shall ever one like me
   Win thee back again?
With the joyous and the free
   Thou wilt scoff at pain.
Spirit false! thou hast forgot
All but those who need thee not.

As a lizard with the shade
   Of a trembling leaf,
Thou with sorrow art dismay'd;
   Even the sighs of grief
Reproach thee, that thou art not near,
And reproach thou wilt not hear.

Let me set my mournful ditty
   To a merry measure; –
Thou wilt never come for pity,
   Thou wilt come for pleasure; –
Pity then will cut away
Those cruel wings, and thou wilt stay.

I love all that thou lovest,
   Spirit of Delight!
The fresh Earth in new leaves drest
   And the starry night;
Autumn evening, and the morn
When the golden mists are born.

I love snow and all the forms
   Of the radiant frost;
I love waves, and winds, and storms,
   Everything almost
Which is Nature's, and may be
Untainted by man's misery.

I love tranquil solitude,
   And such society
As is quiet, wise, and good;
   Between thee and me
What diff'rence? but thou dost possess
The things I seek, not love them less.

I love Love – though he has wings,
    And like light can flee,
But above all other things,
    Spirit, I love thee –
Thou art love and life! O come!
Make once more my heart thy home!

P. B. Shelley

STANZAS WRITTEN IN DEJECTION NEAR NAPLES

The sun is warm, the sky is clear,
The waves are dancing fast and bright,
Blue isles and snowy mountains wear
The purple noon's transparent might:
The breath of the moist earth is light
Around its unexpanded buds;
Like many a voice of one delight –
The winds', the birds', the ocean-floods' –
The city's voice itself is soft like Solitude's.

I see the deep's untrampled floor
With green and purple sea-weeds strown;
I see the waves upon the shore
Like light dissolved in star-showers thrown:
I sit upon the sands alone;
The lightning of the noon-tide ocean
Is flashing round me, and a tone
Arises from its measured motion –
How sweet! did any heart now share in my emotion.

Alas! I have nor hope nor health,
Nor peace within nor calm around,
Nor that content, surpassing wealth,
The sage in meditation found,

And walk'd with inward glory crown'd –
Nor fame, nor power, nor love, nor leisure;
Others I see whom these surround –
Smiling they live, and call life pleasure;
To me that cup has been dealt in another measure.

Yet now despair itself is mild
Even as the winds and water are;
I could lie down like a tired child,
And weep away the life of care
Which I have borne, and yet must bear, –
Till death like sleep might steal on me,
And I might feel in the warm air
My cheek grow cold, and hear the sea
Breathe o'er my dying brain its last monotony.

P. B. Shelley

CCLXXI
THE SCHOLAR

My days among the Dead are past;
Around me I behold,
Where'er these casual eyes are cast,
The mighty minds of old:
My never-failing friends are they,
With whom I converse day by day.

With them I take delight in weal
And seek relief in woe;
And while I understand and feel
How much to them I owe,
My cheeks have often been bedew'd
With tears of thoughtful gratitude.

My thoughts are with the Dead; with them
I live in long-past years,
Their virtues love, their faults condemn,
Partake their hopes and fears,

And from their lessons seek and find
Instruction with an humble mind.

My hopes are with the Dead; anon
My place with them will be,
And I with them shall travel on
Through all Futurity;
Yet leaving here a name, I trust,
That will not perish in the dust.

R. Southey

CCLXXII
THE MERMAID TAVERN

Souls of Poets dead and gone,
What Elysium have ye known,
Happy field or mossy cavern,
Choicer than the Mermaid Tavern?
Have ye tippled drink more fine
Than mine host's Canary wine?
Or are fruits of Paradise
Sweeter than those dainty pies
Of venison? O generous food!
Drest as though bold Robin Hood
Would, with his Maid Marian,
Sup and bowse from horn and can.

 I have heard that on a day
Mine host's sign-board flew away
Nobody knew whither, till
An astrologer's old quill
To a sheepskin gave the story,
Said he saw you in your glory,
Underneath a new-old sign
Sipping beverage divine,
And pledging with contented smack
The Mermaid in the Zodiac.

Souls of Poets dead and gone,
What Elysium have ye known,
Happy field or mossy cavern,
Choicer than the Mermaid Tavern?

J. Keats

CCLXXIII
THE PRIDE OF YOUTH

Proud Maisie is in the wood,
   Walking so early;
Sweet Robin sits on the bush,
   Singing so rarely.

'Tell me, thou bonny bird,
   When shall I marry me?'
– 'When six braw gentlemen
   Kirkward shall carry ye.'

'Who makes the bridal bed,
   Birdie say truly?'
– 'The gray-headed sexton
   That delves the grave duly.

'The glowworm o'er grave and stone
   Shall light thee steady;
The owl from the steeple sing
   Welcome, proud lady.'

Sir W. Scott

CCLXXIV
THE BRIDGE OF SIGHS

One more Unfortunate
Weary of breath
Rashly importunate,
Gone to her death!

Take her up tenderly,
Lift her with care;
Fashion'd so slenderly,
Young, and so fair!

Look at her garments
Clinging like cerements;
Whilst the wave constantly
Drips from her clothing;
Take her up instantly,
Loving, not loathing.

Touch her not scornfully,
Think of her mournfully,
Gently and humanly;
Not of the stains of her —
All that remains of her
Now is pure womanly.

Make no deep scrutiny
Into her mutiny
Rash and undutiful:
Past all dishonour,
Death has left on her
Only the beautiful.

Still, for all slips of hers,
One of Eve's family —
Wipe those poor lips of hers
Oozing so clammily.

Loop up her tresses
Escaped from the comb,
Her fair auburn tresses;
Whilst wonderment guesses
Where was her home?

Who was her father?
Who was her mother?
Had she a sister?

Had she a brother?
Or was there a dearer one
Still, and a nearer one
Yet, than all other?

Alas! for the rarity
Of Christian charity
Under the sun!
Oh! it was pitiful!
Near a whole city full,
Home she had none.

Sisterly, brotherly,
Fatherly, motherly
Feelings had changed:
Love, by harsh evidence,
Thrown from its eminence;
Even God's providence
Seeming estranged.

Where the lamps quiver
So far in the river,
With many a light
From window and casement,
From garret to basement,
She stood with amazement,
Houseless by night.

The bleak wind of March
Made her tremble and shiver
But not the dark arch,
Or the black flowing river:
Mad from life's history,
Glad to death's mystery
Swift to be hurl'd –
Any where, any where
Out of the world!

In she plunged boldly,
No matter how coldly

The rough river ran, –
Over the brink of it,
Picture it – think of it,
Dissolute Man!
Lave in it, drink of it,
Then, if you can!

Take her up tenderly,
Lift her with care;
Fashion'd so slenderly,
Young, and so fair!

Ere her limbs frigidly
Stiffen too rigidly,
Decently, kindly,
Smooth and compose them,
And her eyes, close them,
Staring so blindly!

Dreadfully staring
Thro' muddy impurity,
As when with the daring
Last look of despairing
Fix'd on futurity.

Perishing gloomily,
Spurr'd by contumely,
Cold inhumanity,
Burning insanity,
Into her rest.
– Cross her hands humbly
As if praying dumbly,
Over her breast!

Owning her weakness
Her evil behaviour,
And leaving, with meekness,
Her sins to her Saviour.

T. Hood

CCLXXV
ELEGY

Oh snatch'd away in beauty's bloom!
On thee shall press no ponderous tomb;
But on thy turf shall roses rear
Their leaves, the earliest of the year,
And the wild cypress wave in tender gloom:

And oft by yon blue gushing stream
Shall Sorrow lean her drooping head,
And feed deep thought with many a dream,
And lingering pause and lightly tread;
Fond wretch! as if her step disturb'd the dead!

Away! we know that tears are vain,
That Death nor heeds nor hears distress:
Will this unteach us to complain?
Or make one mourner weep the less?
And thou, who tell'st me to forget,
Thy looks are wan, thine eyes are wet.

Lord Byron

CCLXXVI
HESTER

When maidens such as Hester die
Their place ye may not well supply,
Though ye among a thousand try
      With vain endeavour.
A month or more hath she been dead,
Yet cannot I by force be led
To think upon the wormy bed
      And her together.

A springy motion in her gait,
A rising step, did indicate
Of pride and joy no common rate
      That flush'd her spirit:
I know not by what name beside
I shall it call: if 'twas not pride,
It was a joy to that allied
      She did inherit.

Her parents held the Quaker rule,
Which doth the human feeling cool;
But she was train'd in Nature's school,
      Nature had blest her.
A waking eye, a prying mind,
A heart that stirs, is hard to bind;
A hawk's keen sight ye cannot blind,
      Ye could not Hester.

My sprightly neighbour! gone before
To that unknown and silent shore,
Shall we not meet, as heretofore
      Some summer morning—
When from thy cheerful eyes a ray
Hath struck a bliss upon the day,
A bliss that would not go away,
      A sweet fore-warning?

C. Lamb

CCLXXVII
TO MARY
[Added 1883]

If I had thought thou couldst have died,
 I might not weep for thee;
But I forgot, when by thy side,
 That thou couldst mortal be:
It never through my mind had past
 The time would e'er be o'er,
And I on thee should look my last,
 And thou shouldst smile no more!

And still upon that face I look,
 And think 'twill smile again;
And still the thought I will not brook
 That I must look in vain!
But when I speak – thou dost not say
 What thou ne'er left'st unsaid;
And now I feel, as well I may,
 Sweet Mary! thou art dead!

If thou wouldst stay, e'en as thou art,
 All cold and all serene –
I still might press thy silent heart,
 And where thy smiles have been.
While e'en thy chill, bleak corse I have,
 Thou seemest still mine own;
But there I lay thee in thy grave –
 And I am now alone!

I do not think, where'er thou art,
 Thou hast forgotten me;
And I, perhaps, may soothe this heart,
 In thinking too of thee:
Yet there was round thee such a dawn
 Of light ne'er seen before,
As fancy never could have drawn,
 And never can restore!

C. Wolfe

CORONACH

He is gone on the mountain,
   He is lost to the forest,
Like a summer-dried fountain,
   When our need was the sorest.
The font reappearing
   From the raindrops shall borrow,
But to us comes no cheering,
   To Duncan no morrow!

The hand of the reaper
   Takes the ears that are hoary,
But the voice of the weeper
   Wails manhood in glory.
The autumn winds rushing
   Waft the leaves that are searest,
But our flower was in flushing
   When blighting was nearest.

Fleet foot on the correi,
   Sage counsel in cumber,
Red hand in the foray,
   How sound is thy slumber!
Like the dew on the mountain,
   Like the foam on the river,
Like the bubble on the fountain,
   Thou art gone; and for ever!

Sir W. Scott

THE DEATH BED

We watch'd her breathing thro' the night,
   Her breathing soft and low,
As in her breast the wave of life
   Kept heaving to and fro.

So silently we seem'd to speak,
    So slowly moved about,
As we had lent her half our powers
    To eke her living out.

Our very hopes belied our fears,
    Our fears our hopes belied –
We thought her dying when she slept,
    And sleeping when she died.

For when the morn came dim and sad
    And chill with early showers,
Her quiet eyelids closed – she had
    Another morn than ours.

                                        T. Hood

CCLXXX
AGNES
[*Added 1890*]

I saw her in childhood –
    A bright, gentle thing,
Like the dawn of the morn,
    Or the dews of the spring:
The daisies and hare-bells
    Her playmates all day;
Herself as light-hearted
    And artless as they.

I saw her again –
    A fair girl of eighteen,
Fresh glittering with graces
    Of mind and of mien.
Her speech was all music;
    Like moonlight she shone;
The envy of many,
    The glory of one.

Years, years fleeted over –
   I stood at her foot:
The bud had grown blossom,
   The blossom was fruit.
A dignified mother,
   Her infant she bore;
And look'd, I thought, fairer
   Than ever before.

I saw her once more –
   'Twas the day that she died;
Heaven's light was around her,
   And God at her side;
No wants to distress her,
   No fears to appal –
O then, I felt, then
   She was fairest of all!

H. F. Lyte

CCLXXXI
ROSABELLE

O listen, listen, ladies gay!
   No haughty feat of arms I tell;
Soft is the note, and sad the lay
   That mourns the lovely Rosabelle.

'Moor, moor the barge, ye gallant crew!
   And, gentle ladye, deign to stay!
Rest thee in Castle Ravensheuch,
   Nor tempt the stormy firth to-day.

'The blackening wave is edged with white;
   To inch and rock the sea-mews fly;
The fishers have heard the Water-Sprite,
   Whose screams forebode that wreck is nigh.

'Last night the gifted Seer did view
   A wet shroud swathed round ladye gay;
Then stay thee, Fair, in Ravensheuch;
   Why cross the gloomy firth to-day?'

''Tis not because Lord Lindesay's heir
   To-night at Roslin leads the ball,
But that my ladye-mother there
   Sits lonely in her castle-hall.

''Tis not because the ring they ride,
   And Lindesay at the ring rides well,
But that my sire the wine will chide
   If 'tis not fill'd by Rosabelle.'

– O'er Roslin all that dreary night
   A wondrous blaze was seen to gleam;
'Twas broader than the watch-fire's light,
   And redder than the bright moonbeam.

It glared on Roslin's castled rock,
   It ruddied all the copse-wood glen;
'Twas seen from Dryden's groves of oak,
   And seen from cavern'd Hawthornden.

Seem'd all on fire that chapel proud
   Where Roslin's chiefs uncoffin'd lie,
Each Baron, for a sable shroud,
   Sheathed in his iron panoply.

Seem'd all on fire within, around,
   Deep sacristy and altar's pale;
Shone every pillar foliage-bound,
   And glimmer'd all the dead men's mail.

Blazed battlement and pinnet high,
   Blazed every rose-carved buttress fair –
So still they blaze, when fate is nigh
   The lordly line of high Saint Clair.

There are twenty of Roslin's barons bold –
  Lie buried within that proud chapelle;
Each one the holy vault doth hold –
  But the sea holds lovely Rosabelle.

And each Saint Clair was buried there,
  With candle, with book, and with knell;
But the sea-caves rung, and the wild winds sung
  The dirge of lovely Rosabelle.

Sir W. Scott

CCLXXXII

ON AN INFANT DYING AS SOON AS BORN

I saw wherein the shroud did lurk
A curious frame of Nature's work;
A flow'ret crushéd in the bud,
A nameless piece of Babyhood,
Was in her cradle-coffin lying;
Extinct, with scarce the sense of dying:
So soon to exchange the imprisoning womb
For darker closets of the tomb!
She did but ope an eye, and put
A clear beam forth, then straight up shut
For the long dark: ne'er more to see
Through glasses of mortality.
Riddle of destiny, who can show
What thy short visit meant, or know
What thy errand here below?
Shall we say, that Nature blind
Check'd her hand, and changed her mind
Just when she had exactly wrought
A finish'd pattern without fault?
Could she flag, or could she tire,
Or lack'd she the Promethean fire

(With her nine moons' long workings sicken'd)
That should thy little limbs have quicken'd?
Limbs so firm, they seem'd to assure
Life of health, and days mature:
Woman's self in miniature!
Limbs so fair, they might supply
(Themselves now but cold imagery)
The sculptor to make Beauty by.
Or did the stern-eyed Fate descry
That babe or mother, one must die;
So in mercy left the stock
And cut the branch; to save the shock
Of young years widow'd, and the pain
When Single State comes back again
To the lone man who, reft of wife,
Thenceforward drags a maiméd life?
The economy of Heaven is dark,
And wisest clerks have miss'd the mark
Why human buds, like this, should fall,
More brief than fly ephemeral
That has his day; while shrivell'd crones
Stiffen with age to stocks and stones;
And crabbéd use the conscience sears
In sinners of an hundred years.
– Mother's prattle, mother's kiss,
Baby fond, thou ne'er wilt miss:
Rites, which custom does impose,
Silver bells, and baby clothes;
Coral redder than those lips
Which pale death did late eclipse;
Music framed for infants' glee,
Whistle never tuned for thee;
Though thou want'st not, thou shalt have them,
Loving hearts were they which gave them.
Let not one be missing; nurse,
See them laid upon the hearse
Of infant slain by doom perverse.

Why should kings and nobles have
Pictured trophies to their grave,
And we, churls, to thee deny
Thy pretty toys with thee to lie –
A more harmless vanity?

                                        C. Lamb

CCLXXXIII
IN MEMORIAM
[*Added 1891*]

A child's a plaything for an hour;
    Its pretty tricks we try
For that or for a longer space,–
    Then tire, and lay it by.

But I knew one that to itself
    All seasons could control;
That would have mock'd the sense of pain
    Out of a grievéd soul.

Thou straggler into loving arms,
    Young climber up of knees,
When I forget thy thousand ways
    Then life and all shall cease!

                                        M. Lamb

CCLXXXIV
THE AFFLICTION OF MARGARET

Where art thou, my beloved Son,
Where art thou, worse to me than dead?
Oh find me, prosperous or undone!
Or if the grave be now thy bed,

Why am I ignorant of the same
That I may rest; and neither blame
Nor sorrow may attend thy name?

Seven years, alas! to have received
No tidings of an only child –
To have despair'd, have hoped, believed,
And been for ever more beguiled, –
Sometimes with thoughts of very bliss!
I catch at them, and then I miss;
Was ever darkness like to this?

He was among the prime in worth,
An object beauteous to behold;
Well born, well bred; I sent him forth
Ingenuous, innocent, and bold:
If things ensued that wanted grace
As hath been said, they were not base;
And never blush was on my face.

Ah! little doth the young-one dream
When full of play and childish cares,
What power is in his wildest scream
Heard by his mother unawares!
He knows it not, he cannot guess;
Years to a mother bring distress;
But do not make her love the less.

Neglect me! no, I suffer'd long
From that ill thought; and being blind
Said 'Pride shall help me in my wrong:
Kind mother have I been, as kind
As ever breathed:' and that is true;
I've wet my path with tears like dew,
Weeping for him when no one knew.

My Son, if thou be humbled, poor,
Hopeless of honour and of gain,
Oh! do not dread thy mother's door;
Think not of me with grief and pain:

I now can see with better eyes;
And worldly grandeur I despise
And fortune with her gifts and lies.

Alas! the fowls of heaven have wings,
And blasts of heaven will aid their flight;
They mount – how short a voyage brings
The wanderers back to their delight!
Chains tie us down by land and sea;
And wishes, vain as mine, may be
All that is left to comfort thee.

Perhaps some dungeon hears thee groan
Maim'd, mangled by inhuman men;
Or thou upon a desert thrown
Inheritest the lion's den;
Or hast been summon'd to the deep
Thou, thou, and all thy mates to keep
An incommunicable sleep.

I look for ghosts: but none will force
Their way to me; 'tis falsely said
That there was ever intercourse
Between the living and the dead;
For surely then I should have sight
Of him I wait for day and night
With love and longings infinite.

My apprehensions come in crowds;
I dread the rustling of the grass;
The very shadows of the clouds
Have power to shake me as they pass:
I question things, and do not find
One that will answer to my mind;
And all the world appears unkind.

Beyond participation lie
My troubles, and beyond relief:
If any chance to heave a sigh
They pity me, and not my grief.

Then come to me, my Son, or send
Some tidings that my woes may end!
I have no other earthly friend.

W. Wordsworth

CCLXXXV
HUNTING SONG

Waken, lords and ladies gay,
On the mountain dawns the day;
All the jolly chase is here
With hawk and horse and hunting-spear;
Hounds are in their couples yelling,
Hawks are whistling, horns are knelling,
Merrily merrily mingle they,
'Waken, lords and ladies gay.'

Waken, lords and ladies gay,
The mist has left the mountain gray,
Springlets in the dawn are steaming,
Diamonds on the brake are gleaming;
And foresters have busy been
To track the buck in thicket green;
Now we come to chant our lay
'Waken, lords and ladies gay.'

Waken, lords and ladies gay,
To the greenwood haste away;
We can show you where he lies,
Fleet of foot and tall of size;
We can show the marks he made
When 'gainst the oak his antlers fray'd;
You shall see him brought to bay;
'Waken, lords and ladies gay.'

Louder, louder chant the lay
Waken, lords and ladies gay!
Tell them youth and mirth and glee
Run a course as well as we;
Time, stern huntsman! who can baulk,
Stanch as hound and fleet as hawk;
Think of this, and rise with day,
Gentle lords and ladies gay!

Sir W. Scott

CCLXXXVI
TO THE SKYLARK

Ethereal minstrel! pilgrim of the sky!
Dost thou despise the earth where cares abound?
Or while the wings aspire, are heart and eye
Both with thy nest upon the dewy ground?
Thy nest which thou canst drop into at will,
Those quivering wings composed, that music still!

To the last point of vision, and beyond
Mount, daring warbler! – that love-prompted strain
– 'Twixt thee and thine a never-failing bond –
Thrills not the less the bosom of the plain:
Yet might'st thou seem, proud privilege! to sing
All independent of the leafy Spring.

Leave to the nightingale her shady wood;
A privacy of glorious light is thine,
Whence thou dost pour upon the world a flood
Of harmony, with instinct more divine;
Type of the wise, who soar, but never roam –
True to the kindred points of Heaven and Home.

W. Wordsworth

TO A SKYLARK

Hail to thee, blithe Spirit!
    Bird thou never wert,
That from heaven, or near it
    Pourest thy full heart
In profuse strains of unpremeditated art.

Higher still and higher
    From the earth thou springest,
Like a cloud of fire,
    The blue deep thou wingest,
And singing still dost soar, and soaring ever singest.

In the golden lightning
    Of the sunken sun
O'er which clouds are brightening,
    Thou dost float and run,
Like an unbodied joy whose race is just begun.

The pale purple even
    Melts around thy flight;
Like a star of heaven
    In the broad daylight
Thou art unseen, but yet I hear thy shrill delight:

Keen as are the arrows
    Of that silver sphere,
Whose intense lamp narrows
    In the white dawn clear
Until we hardly see, we feel that it is there.

All the earth and air
    With thy voice is loud,
As, when night is bare,
    From one lonely cloud
The moon rains out her beams, and heaven is overflow'd.

What thou art we know not;
    What is most like thee?
From rainbow clouds there flow not
    Drops so bright to see
As from thy presence showers a rain of melody; –

Like a poet hidden
    In the light of thought,
Singing hymns unbidden,
    Till the world is wrought
To sympathy with hopes and fears it heeded not:

Like a high-born maiden
    In a palace tower,
Soothing her love-laden
    Soul in secret hour
With music sweet as love, which overflows her bower:

Like a glow-worm golden
    In a dell of dew,
Scattering unbeholden
    Its aerial hue
Among the flowers and grass, which screen it from the view:

Like a rose embower'd
    In its own green leaves,
By warm winds deflower'd,
    Till the scent it gives
Makes faint with too much sweet these heavy-wingéd thieves.

Sound of vernal showers
    On the twinkling grass,
Rain-awaken'd flowers,
    All that ever was
Joyous, and clear, and fresh, thy music doth surpass.

Teach us, sprite or bird,
    What sweet thoughts are thine:
I have never heard
    Praise of love or wine
That panted forth a flood of rapture so divine.

Chorus hymeneal
  Or triumphal chaunt
Match'd with thine, would be all
  But an empty vaunt —
A thing wherein we feel there is some hidden want.

What objects are the fountains
  Of thy happy strain?
What fields, or waves, or mountains?
  What shapes of sky or plain?
What love of thine own kind? what ignorance of pain?

With thy clear keen joyance
  Languor cannot be:
Shadow of annoyance
  Never came near thee:
Thou lovest; but ne'er knew love's sad satiety.

Waking or asleep
  Thou of death must deem
Things more true and deep
  Than we mortals dream,
Or how could thy notes flow in such a crystal stream?

We look before and after,
  And pine for what is not:
Our sincerest laughter
  With some pain is fraught;
Our sweetest songs are those that tell of saddest thought.

Yet if we could scorn
  Hate, and pride, and fear;
If we were things born
  Not to shed a tear,
I know not how thy joy we ever should come near.

Better than all measures
  Of delightful sound,
Better than all treasures
  That in books are found,
Thy skill to poet were, thou scorner of the ground!

Teach me half the gladness
    That thy brain must know,
Such harmonious madness
    From my lips would flow,
The world should listen then, as I am listening now!

                                        P. B. Shelley

THE GREEN LINNET

Beneath these fruit-tree boughs that shed
Their snow-white blossoms on my head,
With brightest sunshine round me spread
    Of Spring's unclouded weather,
In this sequester'd nook how sweet
To sit upon my orchard-seat!
And flowers and birds once more to greet,
    My last year's friends together.

One have I mark'd, the happiest guest
In all this covert of the blest:
Hail to Thee, far above the rest
    In joy of voice and pinion!
Thou, Linnet! in thy green array
Presiding Spirit here to-day
Dost lead the revels of the May;
    And this is thy dominion.

While birds, and butterflies and flowers,
Make all one band of paramours,
Thou, ranging up and down the bowers,
    Art sole in thy employment;
A Life, a Presence like the air,
Scattering thy gladness without care,
Too blest with any one to pair;
    Thyself thy own enjoyment.

Amid yon tuft of hazel trees
That twinkle to the gusty breeze,
Behold him perch'd in ecstasies
Yet seeming still to hover;
There! where the flutter of his wings
Upon his back and body flings
Shadows and sunny glimmerings,
That cover him all over.

My dazzled sight he oft deceives –
A brother of the dancing leaves;
Then flits, and from the cottage-eaves
Pours forth his song in gushes;
As if by that exulting strain
He mock'd and treated with disdain
The voiceless Form he chose to feign,
While fluttering in the bushes.

W. Wordsworth

CCLXXXIX
TO THE CUCKOO

O blithe new-comer! I have heard,
I hear thee and rejoice:
O Cuckoo! shall I call thee Bird,
Or but a wandering Voice?

While I am lying on the grass
Thy twofold shout I hear;
From hill to hill it seems to pass,
At once far off and near.

Though babbling only to the vale
Of sunshine and of flowers,
Thou bringest unto me a tale
Of visionary hours.

Thrice welcome, darling of the Spring!
Even yet thou art to me
No bird, but an invisible thing,
A voice, a mystery;

The same whom in my school-boy days
I listen'd to; that Cry
Which made me look a thousand ways
In bush, and tree, and sky.

To seek thee did I often rove
Through woods and on the green;
And thou wert still a hope, a love;
Still long'd for, never seen!

And I can listen to thee yet;
Can lie upon the plain
And listen, till I do beget
That golden time again.

O blessèd Bird! the earth we pace
Again appears to be
An unsubstantial, faery place,
That is fit home for Thee!

W. Wordsworth

CCXC
ODE TO A NIGHTINGALE

My heart aches, and a drowsy numbness pains
  My sense, as though of hemlock I had drunk,
Or emptied some dull opiate to the drains
  One minute past, and Lethe-wards had sunk:

'Tis not through envy of thy happy lot,
    But being too happy in thine happiness, –
        That thou, light-wingéd Dryad of the trees,
            In some melodious plot
    Of beechen green, and shadows numberless,
      Singest of summer in full-throated ease.

O, for a draught of vintage! that hath been
    Cool'd a long age in the deep-delvéd earth,
Tasting of Flora and the country green,
    Dance, and Provençal song, and sunburnt mirth!
O for a beaker full of the warm South,
    Full of the true, the blushful Hippocrene,
        With beaded bubbles winking at the brim,
            And purple-stainéd mouth;
That I might drink, and leave the world unseen,
    And with thee fade away into the forest dim:

Fade far away, dissolve, and quite forget
    What thou among the leaves hast never known,
The weariness, the fever, and the fret
    Here, where men sit and hear each other groan;
Where palsy shakes a few, sad, last gray hairs,
    Where youth grows pale, and spectre-thin, and dies;
        Where but to think is to be full of sorrow
            And leaden-eyed despairs;
    Where Beauty cannot keep her lustrous eyes,
      Or new Love pine at them beyond to-morrow.

Away! away! for I will fly to thee,
    Not charioted by Bacchus and his pards,
But on the viewless wings of Poesy,
    Though the dull brain perplexes and retards:
Already with thee! tender is the night,
    And haply the Queen-Moon is on her throne,
        Cluster'd around by all her starry Fays;
            But here there is no light,
    Save what from heaven is with the breezes blown
      Through verdurous glooms and winding mossy ways.

I cannot see what flowers are at my feet,
    Nor what soft incense hangs upon the boughs,
But, in embalméd darkness, guess each sweet
    Wherewith the seasonable month endows
The grass, the thicket, and the fruit-tree wild;
    White hawthorn, and the pastoral eglantine;
        Fast fading violets cover'd up in leaves;
                And mid-May's eldest child,
    The coming musk-rose, full of dewy wine,
        The murmurous haunt of flies on summer eves.

Darkling I listen; and for many a time
    I have been half in love with easeful Death,
Call'd him soft names in many a muséd rhyme,
    To take into the air my quiet breath;
Now more than ever seems it rich to die,
    To cease upon the midnight with no pain,
        While thou art pouring forth thy soul abroad
                In such an ecstasy!
    Still wouldst thou sing, and I have ears in vain –
        To thy high requiem become a sod.

Thou wast not born for death, immortal Bird!
    No hungry generations tread thee down;
The voice I hear this passing night was heard
    In ancient days by emperor and clown:
Perhaps the self-same song that found a path
    Through the sad heart of Ruth, when, sick for home,
        She stood in tears amid the alien corn;
                The same that oft-times hath
    Charm'd magic casements, opening on the foam
        Of perilous seas, in faery lands forlorn.

Forlorn! the very word is like a bell
    To toll me back from thee to my sole self!
Adieu! the fancy cannot cheat so well
    As she is famed to do, deceiving elf.

Adieu! adieu! thy plaintive anthem fades
  Past the near meadows, over the still stream,
    Up the hill-side; and now 'tis buried deep
      In the next valley-glades:
  Was it a vision, or a waking dream?
    Fled is that music: – Do I wake or sleep?

J. Keats

CCXCI
UPON WESTMINSTER BRIDGE, SEPT. 3, 1802

Earth has not anything to show more fair:
Dull would he be of soul who could pass by
A sight so touching in its majesty:
This City now doth like a garment wear

The beauty of the morning: silent, bare,
Ships, towers, domes, theatres, and temples lie
Open unto the fields, and to the sky,–
All bright and glittering in the smokeless air.

Never did sun more beautifully steep
In his first splendour valley, rock, or hill;
Ne'er saw I, never felt, a calm so deep!

The river glideth at its own sweet will:
Dear God! the very houses seem asleep;
And all that mighty heart is lying still!

W. Wordsworth

CCXCII
[*Added 1890*]

To one who has been long in city pent,
 'Tis very sweet to look into the fair
 And open face of heaven, – to breathe a prayer
Full in the smile of the blue firmament.

Who is more happy, when, with heart's content,
Fatigued he sinks into some pleasant lair
Of wavy grass, and reads a debonair
And gentle tale of love and languishment?

Returning home at evening, with an ear
Catching the notes of Philomel,—an eye
Watching the sailing cloudlet's bright career,

He mourns that day so soon has glided by:
E'en like the passage of an angel's tear
That falls through the clear ether silently.

J. Keats

CCXCIII
OZYMANDIAS OF EGYPT

I met a traveller from an antique land
Who said: Two vast and trunkless legs of stone
Stand in the desert. Near them on the sand,
Half sunk, a shatter'd visage lies, whose frown
And wrinkled lip and sneer of cold command
Tell that its sculptor well those passions read
Which yet survive, stamp'd on these lifeless things,
The hand that mock'd them and the heart that fed;
And on the pedestal these words appear:
'My name is Ozymandias, king of kings:
Look on my works, ye Mighty, and despair!'
Nothing beside remains. Round the decay
Of that colossal wreck, boundless and bare,
The lone and level sands stretch far away.

P. B. Shelley

COMPOSED AT NEIDPATH CASTLE, THE PROPERTY OF LORD QUEENSBERRY, 1803

Degenerate Douglas! oh, the unworthy lord!
Whom mere despite of heart could so far please
And love of havoc, (for which such disease
Fame taxes him,) that he could send forth word

To level with the dust a noble horde,
A brotherhood of venerable trees,
Leaving an ancient dome, and towers like these,
Beggar'd and outraged!–Many hearts deplored

The fate of those old trees; and oft with pain
The traveller at this day will stop and gaze
On wrongs, which Nature scarcely seems to heed:

For shelter'd places, bosoms, nooks, and bays,
And the pure mountains, and the gentle Tweed,
And the green silent pastures, yet remain.

W. Wordsworth

THE BEECH TREE'S PETITION
[*Added 1891*]

O leave this barren spot to me!
Spare, woodman, spare the beechen tree!
Though bush or floweret never grow
My dark unwarming shade below;
Nor summer bud perfume the dew
Of rosy blush, or yellow hue;
Nor fruits of autumn, blossom-born,
My green and glossy leaves adorn;
Nor murmuring tribes from me derive
Th' ambrosial amber of the hive;

Yet leave this barren spot to me:
Spare, woodman, spare the beechen tree!

Thrice twenty summers I have seen
The sky grow bright, the forest green;
And many a wintry wind have stood
In bloomless, fruitless solitude,
Since childhood in my pleasant bower
First spent its sweet and sportive hour;
Since youthful lovers in my shade
Their vows of truth and rapture made,
And on my trunk's surviving frame
Carved many a long-forgotten name.
Oh! by the sighs of gentle sound,
First breathed upon this sacred ground;
By all that Love has whisper'd here,
Or Beauty heard with ravish'd ear;
As Love's own altar honour me:
Spare, woodman, spare the beechen tree!

T. Campbell

CCXCVI
ADMONITION TO A TRAVELLER

Yes, there is holy pleasure in thine eye!
– The lovely Cottage in the guardian nook
Hath stirr'd thee deeply; with its own dear brook,
Its own small pasture, almost its own sky!

But covet not the abode; forbear to sigh
As many do, repining while they look;
Intruders – who would tear from Nature's book
This precious leaf with harsh impiety.

– Think what the home must be if it were thine,
Even thine, though few thy wants! – Roof, window, door,
The very flowers are sacred to the Poor,

The roses to the porch which they entwine:
Yea, all that now enchants thee, from the day
On which it should be touch'd, would melt away!

W. Wordsworth

CCXCVII
TO THE HIGHLAND GIRL OF INVERSNEYDE

Sweet Highland Girl, a very shower
Of beauty is thy earthly dower!
Twice seven consenting years have shed
Their utmost bounty on thy head:
And these gray rocks, that household lawn,
Those trees – a veil just half withdrawn,
This fall of water that doth make
A murmur near the silent lake,
This little bay, a quiet road
That holds in shelter thy abode;
In truth together ye do seem
Like something fashion'd in a dream;
Such forms as from their covert peep
When earthly cares are laid asleep!
But O fair Creature! in the light
Of common day, so heavenly bright,
I bless Thee, Vision as thou art,
I bless thee with a human heart:
God shield thee to thy latest years!
Thee neither know I nor thy peers:
And yet my eyes are fill'd with tears.

With earnest feeling I shall pray
For thee when I am far away;
For never saw I mien or face
In which more plainly I could trace
Benignity and home-bred sense
Ripening in perfect innocence.

Here scatter'd, like a random seed,
Remote from men, Thou dost not need
The embarrass'd look of shy distress,
And maidenly shamefacédness:
Thou wear'st upon thy forehead clear
The freedom of a Mountaineer:
A face with gladness overspread;
Soft smiles, by human kindness bred;
And seemliness complete, that sways
Thy courtesies, about thee plays;
With no restraint, but such as springs
From quick and eager visitings
Of thoughts that lie beyond the reach
Of thy few words of English speech:
A bondage sweetly brook'd, a strife
That gives thy gestures grace and life!
So have I, not unmoved in mind,
Seen birds of tempest-loving kind –
Thus beating up against the wind.

What hand but would a garland cull
For thee who art so beautiful?
O happy pleasure! here to dwell
Beside thee in some heathy dell;
Adopt your homely ways, and dress,
A shepherd, thou a shepherdess!
But I could frame a wish for thee
More like a grave reality:
Thou art to me but as a wave
Of the wild sea: and I would have
Some claim upon thee, if I could,
Though but of common neighbourhood.
What joy to hear thee, and to see!
Thy elder brother I would be,
Thy father – anything to thee.

Now thanks to Heaven! that of its grace
Hath led me to this lonely place:
Joy have I had; and going hence
I bear away my recompence.
In spots like these it is we prize
Our Memory, feel that she hath eyes:
Then why should I be loth to stir?
I feel this place was made for her;
To give new pleasure like the past,
Continued long as life shall last.
Nor am I loth, though pleased at heart,
Sweet Highland Girl! from thee to part;
For I, methinks, till I grow old
As fair before me shall behold
As I do now, the cabin small,
The lake, the bay, the waterfall;
And Thee, the Spirit of them all!

W. Wordsworth

CCXCVIII
THE REAPER

Behold her, single in the field,
Yon solitary Highland Lass!
Reaping and singing by herself;
Stop here, or gently pass!
Alone she cuts and binds the grain,
And sings a melancholy strain;
O listen! for the vale profound
Is overflowing with the sound.

No nightingale did ever chaunt
More welcome notes to weary bands
Of travellers in some shady haunt,
Among Arabian sands:

A voice so thrilling ne'er was heard
In spring-time from the cuckoo-bird,
Breaking the silence of the seas
Among the farthest Hebrides.

Will no one tell me what she sings?
Perhaps the plaintive numbers flow
For old, unhappy, far-off things,
And battles long ago:
Or is it some more humble lay,
Familiar matter of to-day?
Some natural sorrow, loss, or pain,
That has been, and may be again!

Whate'er the theme, the maiden sang
As if her song could have no ending;
I saw her singing at her work,
And o'er the sickle bending; —
I listen'd, motionless and still;
And, as I mounted up the hill,
The music in my heart I bore
Long after it was heard no more.

W. Wordsworth

CCXCIX

THE REVERIE OF POOR SUSAN

At the corner of Wood Street, when daylight appears,
Hangs a Thrush that sings loud, it has sung for three years:
Poor Susan has pass'd by the spot, and has heard
In the silence of morning the song of the bird.

'Tis a note of enchantment; what ails her? She sees
A mountain ascending, a vision of trees;
Bright volumes of vapour through Lothbury glide,
And a river flows on through the vale of Cheapside.

Green pastures she views in the midst of the dale
Down which she so often has tripp'd with her pail;
And a single small cottage, a nest like a dove's,
The one only dwelling on earth that she loves.

She looks, and her heart is in heaven: but they fade,
The mist and the river, the hill and the shade;
The stream will not flow, and the hill will not rise,
And the colours have all pass'd away from her eyes!

W. Wordsworth

CCC
TO A LADY, WITH A GUITAR

Ariel to Miranda: – Take
This slave of music, for the sake
Of him, who is the slave of thee;
And teach it all the harmony
In which thou canst, and only thou,
Make the delighted spirit glow,
Till joy denies itself again
And, too intense, is turn'd to pain.
For by permission and command
Of thine own Prince Ferdinand,
Poor Ariel sends this silent token
Of more than ever can be spoken;
Your guardian spirit, Ariel, who
From life to life must still pursue
Your happiness, for thus alone
Can Ariel ever find his own.
From Prospero's enchanted cell,
As the mighty verses tell,
To the throne of Naples he
Lit you o'er the trackless sea,

Flitting on, your prow before,
Like a living meteor.
When you die, the silent Moon
In her interlunar swoon
Is not sadder in her cell
Than deserted Ariel: –
When you live again on earth,
Like an unseen Star of birth
Ariel guides you o'er the sea
Of life from your nativity: –
Many changes have been run
Since Ferdinand and you begun
Your course of love, and Ariel still
Has track'd your steps and served your will.
Now in humbler, happier lot,
This is all remember'd not;
And now, alas! the poor Sprite is
Imprison'd for some fault of his
In a body like a grave –
From you he only dares to crave,
For his service and his sorrow
A smile to-day, a song to-morrow.

The artist who this idol wrought
To echo all harmonious thought,
Fell'd a tree, while on the steep
The woods were in their winter sleep,
Rock'd in that repose divine
On the wind-swept Apennine;
And dreaming, some of Autumn past,
And some of Spring approaching fast,
And some of April buds and showers,
And some of songs in July bowers,
And all of love: And so this tree, –
Oh that such our death may be! –
Died in sleep, and felt no pain,
To live in happier form again:

From which, beneath heaven's fairest star,
The artist wrought this loved Guitar;
And taught it justly to reply
To all who question skilfully
In language gentle as thine own;
Whispering in enamour'd tone
Sweet oracles of woods and dells,
And summer winds in sylvan cells:
– For it had learnt all harmonies
Of the plains and of the skies,
Of the forests and the mountains,
And the many-voicéd fountains;
The clearest echoes of the hills,
The softest notes of falling rills,
The melodies of birds and bees,
The murmuring of summer seas,
And pattering rain, and breathing dew,
And airs of evening; and it knew
That seldom-heard mysterious sound
Which, driven on its diurnal round,
As it floats through boundless day,
Our world enkindles on its way:
– All this it knows, but will not tell
To those who cannot question well
The Spirit that inhabits it;
It talks according to the wit
Of its companions; and no more
Is heard than has been felt before
By those who tempt it to betray
These secrets of an elder day.
But, sweetly as its answers will
Flatter hands of perfect skill,
It keeps its highest holiest tone
For our beloved Friend alone.

P. B. Shelley

CCCI
THE DAFFODILS

I wander'd lonely as a cloud
That floats on high o'er vales and hills,
When all at once I saw a crowd,
A host of golden daffodils,
Beside the lake, beneath the trees,
Fluttering and dancing in the breeze.

Continuous as the stars that shine
And twinkle on the milky way,
They stretch'd in never-ending line
Along the margin of a bay:
Ten thousand saw I at a glance
Tossing their heads in sprightly dance.

The waves beside them danced, but they
Out-did the sparkling waves in glee: –
A Poet could not but be gay
In such a jocund company!
I gazed – and gazed – but little thought
What wealth the show to me had brought;

For oft, when on my couch I lie
In vacant or in pensive mood,
They flash upon that inward eye
Which is the bliss of solitude;
And then my heart with pleasure fills,
And dances with the daffodils.

                                        W. Wordsworth

CCCII
TO THE DAISY

With little here to do or see
Of things that in the great world be,
Sweet Daisy! oft I talk to thee
      For thou art worthy,
Thou unassuming Common-place
Of Nature, with that homely face,
And yet with something of a grace
      Which Love makes for thee!

Oft on the dappled turf at ease
I sit and play with similes,
Loose types of things through all degrees,
      Thoughts of thy raising;
And many a fond and idle name
I give to thee, for praise or blame
As is the humour of the game,
      While I am gazing.

A nun demure, of lowly port;
Or sprightly maiden, of Love's court,
In thy simplicity the sport
      Of all temptations;
A queen in crown of rubies drest;
A starveling in a scanty vest;
Are all, as seems to suit thee best,
      Thy appellations.

A little Cyclops, with one eye
Staring to threaten and defy,
That thought comes next – and instantly
      The freak is over,
The shape will vanish, and behold!
A silver shield with boss of gold
That spreads itself, some faery bold
      In fight to cover.

I see thee glittering from afar –
And then thou art a pretty star,
Not quite so fair as many are
      In heaven above thee!
Yet like a star, with glittering crest,
Self-poised in air thou seem'st to rest; –
May peace come never to his nest
      Who shall reprove thee!

Sweet Flower! for by that name at last
When all my reveries are past
I call thee, and to that cleave fast,
      Sweet silent Creature!
That breath'st with me in sun and air,
Do thou, as thou art wont, repair
My heart with gladness, and a share
      Of thy meek nature!

              W. Wordsworth

CCCIII
ODE TO AUTUMN

Season of mists and mellow fruitfulness,
Close bosom-friend of the maturing sun;
Conspiring with him how to load and bless
With fruit the vines that round the thatch-eaves run;
To bend with apples the moss'd cottage-trees,
And fill all fruit with ripeness to the core;
To swell the gourd, and plump the hazel shells
With a sweet kernel; to set budding more,
And still more, later flowers for the bees,
Until they think warm days will never cease;
For Summer has o'erbrimm'd their clammy cells.

Who hath not seen thee oft amid thy store?
Sometimes whoever seeks abroad may find
Thee sitting careless on a granary floor,
Thy hair soft-lifted by the winnowing wind;

Or on a half-reap'd furrow sound asleep,
Drowsed with the fume of poppies, while thy hook
Spares the next swath and all its twinéd flowers:
And sometimes like a gleaner thou dost keep
Steady thy laden head across a brook;
Or by a cyder-press, with patient look,
Thou watchest the last oozings, hours by hours.

Where are the songs of Spring? Ay, where are they?
Think not of them, thou hast thy music too, –
While barréd clouds bloom the soft-dying day
And touch the stubble-plains with rosy hue;
Then in a wailful choir the small gnats mourn
Among the river-sallows, borne aloft
Or sinking as the light wind lives or dies;
And full-grown lambs loud bleat from hilly bourn;
Hedge-crickets sing; and now with treble soft
The red-breast whistles from a garden-croft;
And gathering swallows twitter in the skies.

J. Keats

CCCIV
ODE TO WINTER
Germany, December, 1800

When first the fiery-mantled Sun
His heavenly race began to run,
Round the earth and ocean blue
His children four the Seasons flew.
   First, in green apparel dancing,
The young Spring smiled with angel-grace;
   Rosy Summer next advancing,
Rush'd into her sire's embrace –
Her bright-hair'd sire, who bade her keep
   For ever nearest to his smiles,
On Calpe's olive-shaded steep
   Or India's citron-cover'd isles:

More remote, and buxom-brown,
   The Queen of vintage bow'd before his throne;
A rich pomegranate gemm'd her crown,
   A ripe sheaf bound her zone.

But howling Winter fled afar
To hills that prop the polar star;
And loves on deer-borne car to ride
With barren darkness by his side,
Round the shore where loud Lofoden
   Whirls to death the roaring whale,
Round the hall where Runic Odin
   Howls his war-song to the gale;
Save when adown the ravaged globe
   He travels on his native storm,
Deflowering Nature's grassy robe
   And trampling on her faded form: –
Till light's returning Lord assume
   The shaft that drives him to his polar field,
Of power to pierce his raven plume
   And crystal-cover'd shield.

Oh, sire of storms! whose savage ear
The Lapland drum delights to hear,
When Frenzy with her blood-shot eye
Implores thy dreadful deity –
Archangel! Power of desolation!
   Fast descending as thou art,
Say, hath mortal invocation
   Spells to touch thy stony heart?
Then, sullen Winter! hear my prayer,
And gently rule the ruin'd year;
Nor chill the wanderer's bosom bare
Nor freeze the wretch's falling tear:
To shuddering Want's unmantled bed
   Thy horror-breathing agues cease to lend,
And gently on the orphan head
   Of Innocence descend.

But chiefly spare, O king of clouds!
The sailor on his airy shrouds,
When wrecks and beacons strew the steep,
And spectres walk along the deep.
Milder yet thy snowy breezes
    Pour on yonder tented shores,
Where the Rhine's broad billow freezes,
    Or the dark-brown Danube roars.
Oh, winds of Winter! list ye there
    To many a deep and dying groan?
Or start, ye demons of the midnight air,
    At shrieks and thunders louder than your own?
Alas! ev'n your unhallow'd breath
    May spare the victim fallen low;
But Man will ask no truce to death, –
    No bounds to human woe.

T. Campbell

CCCV
YARROW UNVISITED, 1803

From Stirling Castle we had seen
The mazy Forth unravell'd,
Had trod the banks of Clyde and Tay
And with the Tweed had travell'd;
And when we came to Clovenford,
Then said my 'winsome Marrow,'
'Whate'er betide, we'll turn aside,
And see the Braes of Yarrow.'

'Let Yarrow folk, frae Selkirk town,
Who have been buying, selling,
Go back to Yarrow, 'tis their own,
Each maiden to her dwelling!

On Yarrow's banks let herons feed,
Hares couch, and rabbits burrow;
But we will downward with the Tweed,
Nor turn aside to Yarrow.

'There's Gala Water, Leader Haughs,
Both lying right before us;
And Dryburgh, where with chiming Tweed
The lintwhites sing in chorus;
There's pleasant Tiviot-dale, a land
Made blithe with plough and harrow:
Why throw away a needful day
To go in search of Yarrow?

'What's Yarrow but a river bare
That glides the dark hills under?
There are a thousand such elsewhere
As worthy of your wonder.'
—Strange words they seem'd of slight and scorn;
My True-love sigh'd for sorrow,
And look'd me in the face, to think
I thus could speak of Yarrow!

'O green,' said I, 'are Yarrow's holms,
And sweet is Yarrow flowing!
Fair hangs the apple frae the rock,
But we will leave it growing.
O'er hilly path and open strath
We'll wander Scotland thorough;
But, though so near, we will not turn
Into the dale of Yarrow.

'Let beeves and home-bred kine partake
The sweets of Burn-mill meadow;
The swan on still Saint Mary's Lake
Float double, swan and shadow!
We will not see them; will not go
To-day, nor yet to-morrow;
Enough if in our hearts we know
There's such a place as Yarrow.

'Be Yarrow stream unseen, unknown!
It must, or we shall rue it:
We have a vision of our own,
Ah! why should we undo it?
The treasured dreams of times long past,
We'll keep them, winsome Marrow!
For when we're there, although 'tis fair,
'Twill be another Yarrow!

'If Care with freezing years should come
And wandering seem but folly,–
Should we be loth to stir from home,
And yet be melancholy;
Should life be dull, and spirits low,
'Twill soothe us in our sorrow
That earth has something yet to show,
The bonny holms of Yarrow!'

W. Wordsworth

CCCVI
YARROW VISITED
September, 1814

And is this – Yarrow? – This the stream
Of which my fancy cherish'd
So faithfully, a waking dream,
An image that hath perish'd?
O that some minstrel's harp were near
To utter notes of gladness
And chase this silence from the air,
That fills my heart with sadness!

Yet why? – a silvery current flows
With uncontroll'd meanderings;
Nor have these eyes by greener hills
Been soothed, in all my wanderings.

And, through her depths, Saint Mary's Lake
Is visibly delighted;
For not a feature of those hills
Is in the mirror slighted.

A blue sky bends o'er Yarrow Vale,
Save where that pearly whiteness
Is round the rising sun diffused,
A tender hazy brightness;
Mild dawn of promise! that excludes
All profitless dejection;
Though not unwilling here to admit
A pensive recollection.

Where was it that the famous Flower
Of Yarrow Vale lay bleeding?
His bed perchance was yon smooth mound
On which the herd is feeding:
And haply from this crystal pool,
Now peaceful as the morning,
The Water-wraith ascended thrice,
And gave his doleful warning.

Delicious is the lay that sings
The haunts of happy lovers,
The path that leads them to the grove,
The leafy grove that covers:
And pity sanctifies the verse
That paints, by strength of sorrow,
The unconquerable strength of love;
Bear witness, rueful Yarrow!

But thou that didst appear so fair
To fond imagination,
Dost rival in the light of day
Her delicate creation:

Meek loveliness is round thee spread,
A softness still and holy:
The grace of forest charms decay'd,
And pastoral melancholy.

That region left, the vale unfolds
Rich groves of lofty stature,
With Yarrow winding through the pomp
Of cultivated nature;
And rising from those lofty groves
Behold a ruin hoary,
The shatter'd front of Newark's towers,
Renown'd in Border story.

Fair scenes for childhood's opening bloom,
For sportive youth to stray in,
For manhood to enjoy his strength,
And age to wear away in!
Yon cottage seems a bower of bliss,
A covert for protection
Of tender thoughts that nestle there –
The brood of chaste affection.

How sweet on this autumnal day
The wild-wood fruits to gather,
And on my True-love's forehead plant
A crest of blooming heather!
And what if I enwreathed my own?
'Twere no offence to reason;
The sober hills thus deck their brows
To meet the wintry season.

I see – but not by sight alone,
Loved Yarrow, have I won thee;
A ray of Fancy still survives –
Her sunshine plays upon thee!

Thy ever-youthful waters keep
A course of lively pleasure;
And gladsome notes my lips can breathe
Accordant to the measure.

The vapours linger round the heights,
They melt, and soon must vanish;
One hour is theirs, nor more is mine –
Sad thought! which I would banish,
But that I know, where'er I go,
Thy genuine image, Yarrow!
Will dwell with me, to heighten joy,
And cheer my mind in sorrow.

W. Wordsworth

CCCVII
THE INVITATION

Best and brightest, come away, –
Fairer far than this fair Day,
Which, like thee, to those in sorrow
Comes to bid a sweet good-morrow
To the rough year just awake
In its cradle on the brake.
The brightest hour of unborn Spring
Through the winter wandering,
Found, it seems, the halcyon morn
To hoar February born;
Bending from heaven, in azure mirth,
It kiss'd the forehead of the earth,
And smiled upon the silent sea,
And bade the frozen streams be free,
And waked to music all their fountains,
And breathed upon the frozen mountains,

And like a prophetess of May
Strew'd flowers upon the barren way,
Making the wintry world appear
Like one on whom thou smilest, dear.

   Away, away, from men and towns,
To the wild wood and the downs –
To the silent wilderness
Where the soul need not repress
Its music, lest it should not find
An echo in another's mind,
While the touch of Nature's art
Harmonizes heart to heart.

   Radiant Sister of the Day
Awake! arise! and come away!
To the wild woods and the plains,
To the pools where winter rains
Image all their roof of leaves,
Where the pine its garland weaves
Of sapless green, and ivy dun,
Round stems that never kiss the sun;
Where the lawns and pastures be
And the sandhills of the sea;
Where the melting hoar-frost wets
The daisy-star that never sets,
And wind-flowers and violets
Which yet join not scent to hue
Crown the pale year weak and new;
When the night is left behind
In the deep east, dim and blind,
And the blue noon is over us,
And the multitudinous
Billows murmur at our feet,
Where the earth and ocean meet,
And all things seem only one
In the universal Sun.

                        P. B. Shelley

CCCVIII
THE RECOLLECTION

Now the last day of many days
All beautiful and bright as thou,
The loveliest and the last, is dead:
Rise, Memory, and write its praise!
Up – to thy wonted work! come, trace
The epitaph of glory fled,
For now the earth has changed its face,
A frown is on the heaven's brow.

We wander'd to the Pine Forest
   That skirts the Ocean's foam;
The lightest wind was in its nest,
   The tempest in its home.
The whispering waves were half asleep,
   The clouds were gone to play,
And on the bosom of the deep
   The smile of heaven lay;
It seem'd as if the hour were one
   Sent from beyond the skies
Which scatter'd from above the sun
   A light of Paradise!

We paused amid the pines that stood
   The giants of the waste,
Tortured by storms to shapes as rude
   As serpents interlaced, –
And soothed by every azure breath
   That under heaven is blown,
To harmonies and hues beneath,
   As tender as its own:
Now all the tree-tops lay asleep
   Like green waves on the sea,
As still as in the silent deep
   The ocean-woods may be.

How calm it was! – The silence there
   By such a chain was bound,
That even the busy woodpecker
   Made stiller with her sound
The inviolable quietness;
   The breath of peace we drew
With its soft motion made not less
   The calm that round us grew.
There seem'd, from the remotest seat
   Of the white mountain waste
To the soft flower beneath our feet,
   A magic circle traced, –
A spirit interfused around,
   A thrilling silent life;
To momentary peace it bound
   Our mortal nature's strife; –
And still I felt the centre of
   The magic circle there
Was one fair form that fill'd with love
   The lifeless atmosphere.

We paused beside the pools that lie
   Under the forest bough;
Each seem'd as 'twere a little sky
   Gulf'd in a world below;
A firmament of purple light
   Which in the dark earth lay,
More boundless than the depth of night
   And purer than the day –
In which the lovely forests grew
   As in the upper air,
More perfect both in shape and hue
   Than any spreading there.
There lay the glade and neighbouring lawn,
   And through the dark-green wood
The white sun twinkling like the dawn
   Out of a speckled cloud.

Sweet views which in our world above
    Can never well be seen
Were imaged in the water's love
    Of that fair forest green:
And all was interfused beneath
    With an Elysian glow,
An atmosphere without a breath,
    A softer day below.
Like one beloved, the scene had lent
    To the dark water's breast
Its every leaf and lineament
    With more than truth exprest;
Until an envious wind crept by,
    Like an unwelcome thought
Which from the mind's too faithful eye
    Blots one dear image out.
– Though thou art ever fair and kind,
    The forests ever green,
Less oft is peace in Shelley's mind
    Than calm in waters seen!

P. B. Shelley

CCCIX
BY THE SEA

It is a beauteous evening, calm and free;
The holy time is quiet as a Nun
Breathless with adoration; the broad sun
Is sinking down in its tranquillity;

The gentleness of heaven is on the Sea:
Listen! the mighty Being is awake,
And doth with his eternal motion make
A sound like thunder – everlastingly.

Dear child! dear girl! that walkest with me here,
If thou appear untouch'd by solemn thought
Thy nature is not therefore less divine:

Thou liest in Abraham's bosom all the year,
And worshipp'st at the Temple's inner shrine,
God being with thee when we know it not.

W. Wordsworth

CCCX
SONG TO THE EVENING STAR

Star that bringest home the bee,
And sett'st the weary labourer free!
If any star shed peace, 'tis Thou
    That send'st it from above,
Appearing when Heaven's breath and brow
    Are sweet as hers we love.

Come to the luxuriant skies,
Whilst the landscape's odours rise,
Whilst far-off lowing herds are heard
    And songs when toil is done,
From cottages whose smoke unstirr'd
    Curls yellow in the sun.

Star of love's soft interviews,
Parted lovers on thee muse;
Their remembrancer in Heaven
    Of thrilling vows thou art,
Too delicious to be riven
    By absence from the heart.

T. Campbell

CCCXI
DATUR HORA QUIETI

The sun upon the lake is low,
    The wild birds hush their song,
The hills have evening's deepest glow,
    Yet Leonard tarries long.
Now all whom varied toil and care
    From home and love divide,
In the calm sunset may repair
    Each to the loved one's side.

The noble dame, on turret high,
    Who waits her gallant knight,
Looks to the western beam to spy
    The flash of armour bright.
The village maid, with hand on brow
    The level ray to shade,
Upon the footpath watches now
    For Colin's darkening plaid.

Now to their mates the wild swans row,
    By day they swam apart,
And to the thicket wanders slow
    The hind beside the hart.
The woodlark at his partner's side
    Twitters his closing song –
All meet whom day and care divide,
    But Leonard tarries long!

Sir W. Scott

CCCXII
TO THE MOON

Art thou pale for weariness
Of climbing heaven, and gazing on the earth,
Wandering companionless
Among the stars that have a different birth, –
And ever-changing, like a joyless eye
That finds no object worth its constancy?

P. B. Shelley

[*Dropped 1890*]

A widow bird sate mourning for her Love
    Upon a wintry bough;
The frozen wind crept on above,
    The freezing stream below.

There was no leaf upon the forest bare,
    No flower upon the ground,
And little motion in the air
    Except the mill-wheel's sound.

P. B. Shelley

CCCXIII
TO SLEEP

A flock of sheep that leisurely pass by
One after one; the sound of rain, and bees
Murmuring; the fall of rivers, winds and seas,
Smooth fields, white sheets of water, and pure sky;

I've thought of all by turns, and yet do lie
Sleepless; and soon the small birds' melodies
Must hear, first utter'd from my orchard trees,
And the first cuckoo's melancholy cry.

Even thus last night, and two nights more I lay,
    And could not win thee, Sleep! by any stealth:
So do not let me wear to-night away:

Without Thee what is all the morning's wealth?
    Come, blessèd barrier between day and day,
    Dear mother of fresh thoughts and joyous health!

W. Wordsworth

CCCXIV
THE SOLDIER'S DREAM

Our bugles sang truce, for the night-cloud had lower'd,
    And the sentinel stars set their watch in the sky;
And thousands had sunk on the ground overpower'd,
    The weary to sleep, and the wounded to die.

When reposing that night on my pallet of straw
    By the wolf-scaring faggot that guarded the slain,
At the dead of the night a sweet Vision I saw;
    And thrice ere the morning I dreamt it again.

Methought from the battle-field's dreadful array
    Far, far, I had roam'd on a desolate track:
'Twas Autumn, – and sunshine arose on the way
    To the home of my fathers, that welcomed me back.

I flew to the pleasant fields traversed so oft
    In life's morning march, when my bosom was young;
I heard my own mountain-goats bleating aloft,
    And knew the sweet strain that the corn-reapers sung.

Then pledged we the wine-cup, and fondly I swore
    From my home and my weeping friends never to part;
My little ones kiss'd me a thousand times o'er,
    And my wife sobb'd aloud in her fulness of heart.

'Stay – stay with us! – rest! – thou art weary and worn! –
    And fain was their war-broken soldier to stay; –
But sorrow return'd with the dawning of morn,
    And the voice in my dreaming ear melted away.

T. Campbell

CCCXV

A DREAM OF THE UNKNOWN

I dream'd that as I wander'd by the way
    Bare Winter suddenly was changed to Spring,
And gentle odours led my steps astray,
    Mix'd with a sound of waters murmuring
Along a shelving bank of turf, which lay
    Under a copse, and hardly dared to fling
Its green arms round the bosom of the stream,
But kiss'd it and then fled, as Thou mightest in dream.

There grew pied wind-flowers and violets,
    Daisies, those pearl'd Arcturi of the earth,
The constellated flower that never sets;
    Faint oxlips; tender blue-bells, at whose birth
The sod scarce heaved; and that tall flower that wets
    Its mother's face with heaven-collected tears,
When the low wind, its playmate's voice, it hears.

And in the warm hedge grew lush eglantine,
    Green cow-bind and the moonlight-colour'd May,
And cherry-blossoms, and white cups, whose wine
    Was the bright dew yet drain'd not by the day;
And wild roses, and ivy serpentine
    With its dark buds and leaves, wandering astray;
And flowers azure, black, and streak'd with gold,
Fairer than any waken'd eyes behold.

And nearer to the river's trembling edge
   There grew broad flag-flowers, purple prank'd with white,
And starry river-buds among the sedge,
   And floating water-lilies, broad and bright,
Which lit the oak that overhung the hedge
   With moonlight beams of their own watery light;
And bulrushes, and reeds of such deep green
As soothed the dazzled eye with sober sheen.

Methought that of these visionary flowers
   I made a nosegay, bound in such a way
That the same hues, which in their natural bowers
   Were mingled or opposed, the like array
Kept these imprison'd children of the Hours
   Within my hand, – and then, elate and gay,
I hasten'd to the spot whence I had come
That I might there present it – O! to Whom?

P. B. Shelley

CCCXVI

KUBLA KHAN

[*Added 1891*]

In Xanadu did Kubla Khan
A stately pleasure-dome decree:
Where Alph, the sacred river, ran
Through caverns measureless to man
   Down to a sunless sea.
So twice five miles of fertile ground
With walls and towers were girdled round:
And there were gardens bright with sinuous rills
Where blossom'd many an incense-bearing tree;
And here were forests ancient as the hills,
Enfolding sunny spots of greenery.

But oh! that deep romantic chasm which slanted
Down the green hill athwart a cedarn cover!
A savage place! as holy and enchanted
As e'er beneath a waning moon was haunted
By woman wailing for her demon-lover!
And from this chasm, with ceaseless turmoil seething,
As if this earth in fast thick pants were breathing,
A mighty fountain momently was forced:
Amid whose swift half-intermitted burst
Huge fragments vaulted like rebounding hail,
Or chaffy grain beneath the thresher's flail:
And mid these dancing rocks at once and ever
It flung up momently the sacred river.
Five miles meandering with a mazy motion
Through wood and dale the sacred river ran,
Then reach'd the caverns measureless to man,
And sank in tumult to a lifeless ocean:
And 'mid this tumult Kubla heard from far
Ancestral voices prophesying war!

    The shadow of the dome of pleasure
     Floated midway on the waves;
     Where was heard the mingled measure
     From the fountain and the caves.
It was a miracle of rare device,
A sunny pleasure-dome with caves of ice!
    A damsel with a dulcimer
    In a vision once I saw:
    It was an Abyssinian maid,
    And on her dulcimer she play'd,
    Singing of Mount Abora.
    Could I revive within me
    Her symphony and song,
To such a deep delight 'twould win me
That with music loud and long,
I would build that dome in air,
That sunny dome! those caves of ice!

And all who heard should see them there,
And all should cry, Beware! Beware!
His flashing eyes, his floating hair!
Weave a circle round him thrice,
And close your eyes with holy dread,
For he on honey-dew hath fed,
And drunk the milk of Paradise.

S. T. Coleridge

CCCXVII

THE INNER VISION

Most sweet it is with unuplifted eyes
To pace the ground, if path be there or none,
While a fair region round the traveller lies
Which he forbears again to look upon;

Pleased rather with some soft ideal scene,
The work of Fancy, or some happy tone
Of meditation, slipping in between
The beauty coming and the beauty gone.

– If Thought and Love desert us, from that day
Let us break off all commerce with the Muse:
With Thought and Love companions of our way –

Whate'er the senses take or may refuse, –
The Mind's internal heaven shall shed her dews
Of inspiration on the humblest lay.

W. Wordsworth

CCCXVIII

THE REALM OF FANCY

Ever let the Fancy roam;
Pleasure never is at home:
At a touch sweet Pleasure melteth,
Like to bubbles when rain pelteth;

Then let wingéd Fancy wander
Through the thought still spread beyond her:
Open wide the mind's cage-door,
She'll dart forth, and cloudward soar.
O sweet Fancy! let her loose;
Summer's joys are spoilt by use,
And the enjoying of the Spring
Fades as does its blossoming;
Autumn's red-lipp'd fruitage too,
Blushing through the mist and dew,
Cloys with tasting: What do then?
Sit thee by the ingle, when
The sear faggot blazes bright,
Spirit of a winter's night;
When the soundless earth is muffled,
And the cakéd snow is shuffled
From the ploughboy's heavy shoon;
When the Night doth meet the Noon
In a dark conspiracy
To banish Even from her sky.
Sit thee there, and send abroad,
With a mind self-overaw'd,
Fancy, high commission'd: – send her!
She has vassals to attend her:
She will bring, in spite of frost,
Beauties that the earth hath lost;
She will bring thee, all together,
All delights of summer weather;
All the buds and bells of May,
From dewy sward or thorny spray;
All the heapéd Autumn's wealth,
With a still, mysterious stealth:
She will mix these pleasures up
Like three fit wines in a cup,
And thou shalt quaff it: – thou shalt hear
Distant harvest-carols clear;
Rustle of the reapéd corn;

Sweet birds antheming the morn:
And, in the same moment – hark!
'Tis the early April lark,
Or the rooks, with busy caw,
Foraging for sticks and straw.
Thou shalt, at one glance, behold
The daisy and the marigold;
White-plumed lilies, and the first
Hedge-grown primrose that hath burst;
Shaded hyacinth, alway
Sapphire queen of the mid-May;
And every leaf, and every flower
Pearléd with the self-same shower.
Thou shalt see the field-mouse peep
Meagre from its celléd sleep;
And the snake all winter-thin
Cast on sunny bank its skin;
Freckled nest-eggs thou shalt see
Hatching in the hawthorn-tree,
When the hen-bird's wing doth rest
Quiet on her mossy nest;
Then the hurry and alarm
When the bee-hive casts its swarm;
Acorns ripe down-pattering,
While the autumn breezes sing.

Oh, sweet Fancy! let her loose;
Everything is spoilt by use:
Where's the cheek that doth not fade,
Too much gazed at? Where's the maid
Whose lip mature is ever new?
Where's the eye, however blue,
Doth not weary? Where's the face
One would meet in every place?
Where's the voice, however soft,
One would hear so very oft?

At a touch sweet Pleasure melteth
Like to bubbles when rain pelteth.
Let then wingéd Fancy find
Thee a mistress to thy mind:
Dulcet-eyed as Ceres' daughter,
Ere the God of Torment taught her
How to frown and how to chide;
With a waist and with a side
White as Hebe's, when her zone
Slipt its golden clasp, and down
Fell her kirtle to her feet,
While she held the goblet sweet,
And Jove grew languid. – Break the mesh
Of the Fancy's silken leash;
Quickly break her prison-string,
And such joys as these she'll bring.
– Let the wingéd Fancy roam,
Pleasure never is at home.

J. Keats

HYMN TO THE SPIRIT OF NATURE
[*Dropped 1890*]

Life of Life! Thy lips enkindle
  With their love the breath between them;
And thy smiles before they dwindle
  Make the cold air fire; then screen them
In those locks, where whoso gazes
Faints, entangled in their mazes.

Child of Light! Thy limbs are burning
  Through the veil which seems to hide them,
As the radiant lines of morning
  Through thin clouds, ere they divide them;
And this atmosphere divinest
Shrouds thee wheresoe'er thou shinest.

Fair are others: none beholds Thee;
   But thy voice sounds low and tender
Like the fairest, for it folds thee
   From the sight, that liquid splendour;
And all feel, yet see thee never, –
As I feel now, lost for ever!

Lamp of Earth! where'er thou movest
   Its dim shapes are clad with brightness,
And the souls of whom thou lovest
   Walk upon the winds with lightness
Till they fail, as I am failing,
Dizzy, lost, yet unbewailing!

                            P. B. Shelley

CCCXIX
WRITTEN IN EARLY SPRING

I heard a thousand blended notes
While in a grove I sate reclined,
In that sweet mood when pleasant thoughts
Bring sad thoughts to the mind.

To her fair works did Nature link
The human soul that through me ran;
And much it grieved my heart to think
What Man has made of Man.

Through primrose tufts, in that sweet bower,
The periwinkle trail'd its wreaths;
And 'tis my faith that every flower
Enjoys the air it breathes.

The birds around me hopp'd and play'd,
Their thoughts I cannot measure, –
But the least motion which they made
It seem'd a thrill of pleasure.

The budding twigs spread out their fan
To catch the breezy air;
And I must think, do all I can,
That there was pleasure there.

If this belief from heaven be sent,
If such be Nature's holy plan,
Have I not reason to lament
What Man has made of Man?

W. Wordsworth

CCCXX
RUTH: OR THE INFLUENCES OF NATURE

When Ruth was left half desolate
Her father took another mate;
And Ruth, not seven years old,
A slighted child, at her own will
Went wandering over dale and hill,
In thoughtless freedom, bold.

And she had made a pipe of straw,
And music from that pipe could draw
Like sounds of winds and floods;
Had built a bower upon the green,
As if she from her birth had been
An infant of the woods.

Beneath her father's roof, alone
She seem'd to live; her thoughts her own;
Herself her own delight:
Pleased with herself, nor sad nor gay;
And passing thus the live-long day,
She grew to woman's height.

There came a youth from Georgia's shore –
A military casque he wore
With splendid feathers drest;
He brought them from the Cherokees;
The feathers nodded in the breeze
And made a gallant crest.

From Indian blood you deem him sprung:
But no! he spake the English tongue
And bore a soldier's name;
And, when America was free
From battle and from jeopardy,
He 'cross the ocean came.

With hues of genius on his cheek,
In finest tones the youth could speak:
– While he was yet a boy
The moon, the glory of the sun,
And streams that murmur as they run
Had been his dearest joy.

He was a lovely youth! I guess
The panther in the wilderness
Was not so fair as he;
And when he chose to sport and play,
No dolphin ever was so gay
Upon the tropic sea.

Among the Indians he had fought;
And with him many tales he brought
Of pleasure and of fear;
Such tales as, told to any maid
By such a youth, in the green shade,
Were perilous to hear.

He told of girls, a happy rout!
Who quit their fold with dance and shout,
Their pleasant Indian town,

To gather strawberries all day long;
Returning with a choral song
When daylight is gone down.

He spake of plants that hourly change
Their blossoms, through a boundless range
Of intermingling hues;
With budding, fading, faded flowers,
They stand the wonder of the bowers
From morn to evening dews.

He told of the magnolia, spread
High as a cloud, high over head!
The cypress and her spire;
– Of flowers that with one scarlet gleam
Cover a hundred leagues, and seem
To set the hills on fire.

The youth of green savannahs spake,
And many an endless, endless lake
With all its fairy crowds
Of islands, that together lie
As quietly as spots of sky
Among the evening clouds.

'How pleasant,' then he said, 'it were
A fisher or a hunter there,
In sunshine or in shade
To wander with an easy mind,
And build a household fire, and find
A home in every glade!

'What days and what bright years! Ah me!
Our life were life indeed, with thee
So pass'd in quiet bliss;
And all the while,' said he, 'to know
That we were in a world of woe,
On such an earth as this!'

And then he sometimes interwove
Fond thoughts about a father's love,
'For there,' said he, 'are spun
Around the heart such tender ties,
That our own children to our eyes
Are dearer than the sun.

'Sweet Ruth! and could you go with me
My helpmate in the woods to be,
Our shed at night to rear;
Or run, my own adopted bride,
A sylvan huntress at my side,
And drive the flying deer!

'Beloved Ruth!' – No more he said.
The wakeful Ruth at midnight shed
A solitary tear:
She thought again – and did agree
With him to sail across the sea,
And drive the flying deer.

'And now, as fitting is and right,
We in the church our faith will plight,
A husband and a wife.'
Even so they did; and I may say
That to sweet Ruth that happy day
Was more than human life.

Through dream and vision did she sink,
Delighted all the while to think
That, on those lonesome floods
And green savannahs, she should share
His board with lawful joy, and bear
His name in the wild woods.

But, as you have before been told,
This Stripling, sportive, gay, and bold,
And with his dancing crest

So beautiful, through savage lands
Had roam'd about, with vagrant bands
Of Indians in the West.

The wind, the tempest roaring high,
The tumult of a tropic sky
Might well be dangerous food
For him, a youth to whom was given
So much of earth – so much of heaven,
And such impetuous blood.

Whatever in those climes he found
Irregular in sight or sound
Did to his mind impart
A kindred impulse, seem'd allied
To his own powers, and justified
The workings of his heart.

Nor less, to feed voluptuous thought,
The beauteous forms of Nature wrought, –
Fair trees and gorgeous flowers;
The breezes their own languor lent;
The stars had feelings, which they sent
Into those favour'd bowers.

Yet, in his worst pursuits, I ween
That sometimes there did intervene
Pure hopes of high intent:
For passions link'd to forms so fair
And stately, needs must have their share
Of noble sentiment.

But ill he lived, much evil saw,
With men to whom no better law
Nor better life was known;
Deliberately and undeceived
Those wild men's vices he received,
And gave them back his own.

His genius and his moral frame
Were thus impair'd, and he became
The slave of low desires:
A man who without self-control
Would seek what the degraded soul
Unworthily admires.

And yet he with no feign'd delight
Had woo'd the maiden, day and night
Had loved her, night and morn:
What could he less than love a maid
Whose heart with so much nature play'd –
So kind and so forlorn?

Sometimes most earnestly he said,
'O Ruth! I have been worse than dead;
False thoughts, thoughts bold and vain
Encompass'd me on every side
When I, in confidence and pride,
Had cross'd the Atlantic main.

'Before me shone a glorious world
Fresh as a banner bright, unfurl'd
To music suddenly:
I look'd upon those hills and plains,
And seem'd as if let loose from chains
To live at liberty!

'No more of this – for now, by thee,
Dear Ruth! more happily set free,
With nobler zeal I burn;
My soul from darkness is released
Like the whole sky when to the east
The morning doth return.'

Full soon that better mind was gone;
No hope, no wish remain'd, not one, –
They stirr'd him now no more;

New objects did new pleasure give,
And once again he wish'd to live
As lawless as before.

Meanwhile, as thus with him it fared,
They for the voyage were prepared,
And went to the sea-shore:
But, when they thither came, the youth
Deserted his poor bride, and Ruth
Could never find him more.

God help thee, Ruth! – Such pains she had
That she in half a year was mad
And in a prison housed;
And there, with many a doleful song
Made of wild words, her cup of wrong
She fearfully caroused.

Yet sometimes milder hours she knew,
Nor wanted sun, nor rain, nor dew,
Nor pastimes of the May,
– They all were with her in her cell;
And a clear brook with cheerful knell
Did o'er the pebbles play.

When Ruth three seasons thus had lain,
There came a respite to her pain;
She from her prison fled;
But of the Vagrant none took thought;
And where it liked her best she sought
Her shelter and her bread.

Among the fields she breathed again:
The master-current of her brain
Ran permanent and free;
And, coming to the banks of Tone,
There did she rest; and dwell alone
Under the greenwood tree.

The engines of her pain, the tools
That shaped her sorrow, rocks and pools,
And airs that gently stir
The vernal leaves – she loved them still,
Nor ever tax'd them with the ill
Which had been done to her.

A barn her Winter bed supplies;
But, till the warmth of Summer skies
And Summer days is gone,
(And all do in this tale agree)
She sleeps beneath the greenwood tree,
And other home hath none.

An innocent life, yet far astray!
And Ruth will, long before her day,
Be broken down and old.
Sore aches she needs must have! but less
Of mind, than body's wretchedness,
From damp, and rain, and cold.

If she is prest by want of food
She from her dwelling in the wood
Repairs to a road-side;
And there she begs at one steep place,
Where up and down with easy pace
The horsemen-travellers ride.

That oaten pipe of hers is mute
Or thrown away: but with a flute
Her loneliness she cheers;
This flute, made of a hemlock stalk,
At evening in his homeward walk
The Quantock woodman hears.

I, too, have pass'd her on the hills
Setting her little water-mills
By spouts and fountains wild –

Such small machinery as she turn'd
Ere she had wept, ere she had mourn'd, –
A young and happy child!

Farewell! and when thy days are told,
Ill-fated Ruth! in hallow'd mould
Thy corpse shall buried be;
For thee a funeral bell shall ring,
And all the congregation sing
A Christian psalm for thee.

W. Wordsworth

CCCXXI
WRITTEN AMONG THE EUGANEAN HILLS

Many a green isle needs must be
In the deep wide sea of Misery,
Or the mariner, worn and wan,
Never thus could voyage on
Day and night, and night and day,
Drifting on his dreary way,
With the solid darkness black
Closing round his vessel's track;
Whilst above, the sunless sky
Big with clouds, hangs heavily,
And behind the tempest fleet
Hurries on with lightning feet,
Riving sail, and cord, and plank,
Till the ship has almost drank
Death from the o'er-brimming deep;
And sinks down, down, like that sleep
When the dreamer seems to be
Weltering through eternity;
And the dim low line before
Of a dark and distant shore

Still recedes, as ever still
Longing with divided will,
But no power to seek or shun,
He is ever drifted on
O'er the unreposing wave,
To the haven of the grave.

Ah, many flowering islands lie
In the waters of wide Agony:
To such a one this morn was led
My bark, by soft winds piloted.
– 'Mid the mountains Euganean
I stood listening to the paean
With which the legion'd rooks did hail
The Sun's uprise majestical:
Gathering round with wings all hoar,
Through the dewy mist they soar
Like gray shades, till the eastern heaven
Bursts; and then, – as clouds of even
Fleck'd with fire and azure, lie
In the unfathomable sky, –
So their plumes of purple grain
Starr'd with drops of golden rain
Gleam above the sunlight woods,
As in silent multitudes
On the morning's fitful gale
Through the broken mist they sail;
And the vapours cloven and gleaming
Follow down the dark steep streaming,
Till all is bright, and clear, and still
Round the solitary hill.

Beneath is spread like a green sea
The waveless plain of Lombardy,
Bounded by the vaporous air,
Islanded by cities fair;
Underneath Day's azure eyes,
Ocean's nursling, Venice lies, –

A peopled labyrinth of walls,
Amphitrite's destined halls,
Which her hoary sire now paves
With his blue and beaming waves.
Lo! the sun upsprings behind,
Broad, red, radiant, half-reclined
On the level quivering line
Of the waters crystalline;
And before that chasm of light,
As within a furnace bright,
Column, tower, and dome, and spire,
Shine like obelisks of fire,
Pointing with inconstant motion
From the altar of dark ocean
To the sapphire-tinted skies;
As the flames of sacrifice
From the marble shrines did rise
As to pierce the dome of gold
Where Apollo spoke of old.

　　Sun-girt City! thou hast been
Ocean's child, and then his queen;
Now is come a darker day,
And thou soon must be his prey,
If the power that raised thee here
Hallow so thy watery bier.
A less drear ruin then than now,
With thy conquest-branded brow
Stooping to the slave of slaves
From thy throne among the waves
Wilt thou be, – when the sea-mew
Flies, as once before it flew,
O'er thine isles depopulate,
And all is in its ancient state,
Save where many a palace-gate
With green sea-flowers overgrown
Like a rock of ocean's own,

Topples o'er the abandon'd sea
As the tides change sullenly.
The fisher on his watery way
Wandering at the close of day,
Will spread his sail and seize his oar
Till he pass the gloomy shore,
Lest thy dead should, from their sleep,
Bursting o'er the starlight deep,
Lead a rapid masque of death
O'er the waters of his path.

Noon descends around me now:
'Tis the noon of autumn's glow,
When a soft and purple mist
Like a vaporous amethyst,
Or an air-dissolvéd star
Mingling light and fragrance, far
From the curved horizon's bound
To the point of heaven's profound,
Fills the overflowing sky;
And the plains that silent lie
Underneath; the leaves unsodden
Where the infant Frost has trodden
With his morning-wingéd feet
Whose bright print is gleaming yet;
And the red and golden vines
Piercing with their trellised lines
The rough, dark-skirted wilderness;
The dun and bladed grass no less,
Pointing from this hoary tower
In the windless air; the flower
Glimmering at my feet; the line
Of the olive-sandall'd Apennine
In the south dimly islanded;
And the Alps, whose snows are spread
High between the clouds and sun;
And of living things each one;

And my spirit, which so long
Darken'd this swift stream of song, –
Interpenetrated lie
By the glory of the sky;
Be it love, light, harmony,
Odour, or the soul of all
Which from heaven like dew doth fall,
Or the mind which feeds this verse,
Peopling the lone universe.

   Noon descends, and after noon
Autumn's evening meets me soon,
Leading the infantine moon
And that one star, which to her
Almost seems to minister
Half the crimson light she brings
From the sunset's radiant springs:
And the soft dreams of the morn
(Which like wingéd winds had borne
To that silent isle, which lies
'Mid remember'd agonies,
The frail bark of this lone being),
Pass, to other sufferers fleeing,
And its ancient pilot, Pain,
Sits beside the helm again.

   Other flowering isles must be
In the sea of Life and Agony:
Other spirits float and flee
O'er that gulf: Ev'n now, perhaps,
On some rock the wild wave wraps,
With folded wings they waiting sit
For my bark, to pilot it
To some calm and blooming cove;
Where for me, and those I love,
May a windless bower be built,
Far from passion, pain, and guilt,

In a dell 'mid lawny hills
Which the wild sea-murmur fills,
And soft sunshine, and the sound
Of old forests echoing round,
And the light and smell divine
Of all flowers that breathe and shine,
– We may live so happy there,
That the Spirits of the Air
Envying us, may ev'n entice
To our healing paradise
The polluting multitude:
But their rage would be subdued
By that clime divine and calm,
And the winds whose wings rain balm
On the uplifted soul, and leaves
Under which the bright sea heaves;
While each breathless interval
In their whisperings musical
The inspired soul supplies
With its own deep melodies;
And the Love which heals all strife
Circling, like the breath of life,
All things in that sweet abode
With its own mild brotherhood: –
They, not it, would change; and soon
Every sprite beneath the moon
Would repent its envy vain,
And the Earth grow young again.

P. B. Shelley

CCCXXII
ODE TO THE WEST WIND

O wild West Wind, thou breath of Autumn's being,
Thou, from whose unseen presence the leaves dead
Are driven, like ghosts from an enchanter fleeing,

Yellow, and black, and pale, and hectic red,
Pestilence-stricken multitudes! O thou
Who chariotest to their dark wintry bed
The wingéd seeds, where they lie cold and low,
Each like a corpse within its grave, until
Thine azure sister of the Spring shall blow
Her clarion o'er the dreaming earth, and fill
(Driving sweet buds like flocks to feed in air)
With living hues and odours plain and hill:
Wild Spirit, which art moving everywhere;
Destroyer and Preserver; Hear, oh hear!

  Thou on whose stream, 'mid the steep sky's commotion,
Loose clouds like earth's decaying leaves are shed,
Shook from the tangled boughs of heaven and ocean,
Angels of rain and lightning! there are spread
On the blue surface of thine airy surge,
Like the bright hair uplifted from the head
Of some fierce Maenad, ev'n from the dim verge
Of the horizon to the zenith's height –
The locks of the approaching storm. Thou dirge
Of the dying year, to which this closing night
Will be the dome of a vast sepulchre,
Vaulted with all thy congregated might
Of vapours, from whose solid atmosphere
Black rain, and fire, and hail, will burst: Oh hear!

  Thou who didst waken from his summer-dreams
The blue Mediterranean, where he lay,
Lull'd by the coil of his crystalline streams,
Beside a pumice isle in Baiae's bay,
And saw in sleep old palaces and towers
Quivering within the wave's intenser day,
All overgrown with azure moss, and flowers
So sweet, the sense faints picturing them! Thou
For whose path the Atlantic's level powers
Cleave themselves into chasms, while far below

The sea-blooms and the oozy woods which wear
The sapless foliage of the ocean, know
Thy voice, and suddenly grow gray with fear
And tremble and despoil themselves: Oh hear!

If I were a dead leaf thou mightest bear;
If I were a swift cloud to fly with thee;
A wave to pant beneath thy power, and share
The impulse of thy strength, only less free
Than Thou, O uncontrollable! If even
I were as in my boyhood, and could be
The comrade of thy wanderings over heaven,
As then, when to outstrip thy skiey speed
Scarce seem'd a vision, – I would ne'er have striven
As thus with thee in prayer in my sore need.
Oh! lift me as a wave, a leaf, a cloud!
I fall upon the thorns of life! I bleed!
A heavy weight of hours has chain'd and bow'd
One too like thee – tameless, and swift, and proud.

Make me thy lyre, ev'n as the forest is:
What if my leaves are falling like its own!
The tumult of thy mighty harmonies
Will take from both a deep autumnal tone,
Sweet though in sadness. Be thou, Spirit fierce,
My spirit! be thou me, impetuous one!
Drive my dead thoughts over the universe,
Like wither'd leaves, to quicken a new birth;
And, by the incantation of this verse,
Scatter, as from an unextinguish'd hearth
Ashes and sparks, my words among mankind!
Be through my lips to unawaken'd earth
The trumpet of a prophecy! O Wind,
If Winter comes, can Spring be far behind?

P. B. Shelley

NATURE AND THE POET

Suggested by a Picture of Peele Castle in a Storm, painted by Sir George Beaumont

I was thy neighbour once, thou rugged Pile!
Four summer weeks I dwelt in sight of thee:
I saw thee every day; and all the while
Thy Form was sleeping on a glassy sea.

So pure the sky, so quiet was the air!
So like, so very like, was day to day!
Whene'er I look'd, thy image still was there;
It trembled, but it never pass'd away.

How perfect was the calm! It seem'd no sleep,
No mood, which season takes away, or brings:
I could have fancied that the mighty Deep
Was even the gentlest of all gentle things.

Ah! then – if mine had been the painter's hand
To express what then I saw; and add the gleam,
The light that never was on sea or land,
The consecration, and the Poet's dream, –

I would have planted thee, thou hoary pile,
Amid a world how different from this!
Beside a sea that could not cease to smile;
On tranquil land, beneath a sky of bliss.

Thou shouldst have seem'd a treasure-house divine
Of peaceful years; a chronicle of heaven; –
Of all the sunbeams that did ever shine
The very sweetest had to thee been given.

A picture had it been of lasting ease,
Elysian quiet, without toil or strife;
No motion but the moving tide; a breeze;
Or merely silent Nature's breathing life.

Such, in the fond illusion of my heart,
Such picture would I at that time have made;
And seen the soul of truth in every part,
A steadfast peace that might not be betray'd.

So once it would have been, — 'tis so no more;
I have submitted to a new control:
A power is gone, which nothing can restore;
A deep distress hath humanized my soul.

Not for a moment could I now behold
A smiling sea, and be what I have been:
The feeling of my loss will ne'er be old;
This, which I know, I speak with mind serene.

Then, Beaumont, Friend! who would have been the friend
If he had lived, of Him whom I deplore,
This work of thine I blame not, but commend;
This sea in anger, and that dismal shore.

O 'tis a passionate work! — yet wise and well,
Well chosen is the spirit that is here;
That hulk which labours in the deadly swell,
This rueful sky, this pageantry of fear!

And this huge Castle, standing here sublime,
I love to see the look with which it braves,
— Cased in the unfeeling armour of old time —
The lightning, the fierce wind, and trampling waves.

— Farewell, farewell the heart that lives alone,
Housed in a dream, at distance from the Kind!
Such happiness, wherever it be known,
Is to be pitied; for 'tis surely blind.

But welcome fortitude, and patient cheer,
And frequent sights of what is to be borne!
Such sights, or worse, as are before me here: —
Not without hope we suffer and we mourn.

W. Wordsworth

CCCXXIV
THE POET'S DREAM

On a Poet's lips I slept
Dreaming like a love-adept
In the sound his breathing kept;
Nor seeks nor finds he mortal blisses,
But feeds on the aërial kisses
Of shapes that haunt Thought's wildernesses.
He will watch from dawn to gloom
The lake-reflected sun illume
The yellow bees in the ivy-bloom,
   Nor heed nor see what things they be –
But from these create he can
Forms more real than living Man,
   Nurslings of Immortality!

P. B. Shelley

CCCXXV
GLEN-ALMAIN, THE NARROW GLEN
[*Added 1890*]

In this still place, remote from men,
Sleeps Ossian, in the Narrow Glen;
In this still place, where murmurs on
But one meet streamlet, only one:
He sang of battles, and the breath
Of stormy war, and violent death;
And should, methinks, when all was past,
Have rightfully been laid at last
Where rocks were rudely heap'd, and rent
As by a spirit turbulent;
Where sights were rough, and sounds were wild,
And everything unreconciled;

In some complaining, dim retreat,
For fear and melancholy meet;
But this is calm; there cannot be
A more entire tranquillity.

Does then the Bard sleep here indeed?
Or is it but a groundless creed?
What matters it? – I blame them not
Whose fancy in this lonely spot
Was moved; and in such way express'd
Their notion of its perfect rest.
A convent, even a hermit's cell,
Would break the silence of this Dell:
It is not quiet, is not ease;
But something deeper far than these:
The separation that is here
Is of the grave; and of austere
Yet happy feelings of the dead:
And, therefore, was it rightly said
That Ossian, last of all his race!
Lies buried in this lonely place.

W. Wordsworth

CCCXXVI

The World is too much with us; late and soon,
Getting and spending, we lay waste our powers;
Little we see in Nature that is ours;
We have given our hearts away, a sordid boon!

This Sea that bares her bosom to the moon,
The winds that will be howling at all hours
And are up-gather'd now like sleeping flowers,
For this, for every thing, we are out of tune;

It moves us not. – Great God! I'd rather be
A Pagan suckled in a creed outworn, –
So might I, standing on this pleasant lea,

Have glimpses that would make me less forlorn;
Have sight of Proteus rising from the sea;
Or hear old Triton blow his wreathéd horn.

W. Wordsworth

CCCXXVII
WITHIN KING'S COLLEGE CHAPEL, CAMBRIDGE

Tax not the royal Saint with vain expense,
With ill-match'd aims the Architect who plann'd
(Albeit labouring for a scanty band
Of white-robed Scholars only) this immense

And glorious work of fine intelligence!
– Give all thou canst; high Heaven rejects the lore
Of nicely-calculated less or more: –
So deem'd the man who fashion'd for the sense

These lofty pillars, spread that branching roof
Self-poised, and scoop'd into ten thousand cells
Where light and shade repose, where music dwells

Lingering – and wandering on as loth to die;
Like thoughts whose very sweetness yieldeth proof
That they were born for immortality.

W. Wordsworth

ODE ON A GRECIAN URN
[*Added 1890*]

Thou still unravish'd bride of quietness,
   Thou foster-child of silence and slow time,
Sylvan historian, who canst thus express
   A flowery tale more sweetly than our rhyme:
What leaf-fringed legend haunts about thy shape
   Of deities or mortals, or of both,
     In Tempé or the dales of Arcady?
What men or gods are these? What maidens loth?
   What mad pursuit? What struggle to escape?
     What pipes and timbrels? What wild ecstasy?

Heard melodies are sweet, but those unheard
   Are sweeter; therefore, ye soft pipes, play on;
Not to the sensual ear, but, more endear'd,
   Pipe to the spirit ditties of no tone:
Fair youth, beneath the trees, thou canst not leave
   Thy song, nor ever can those trees be bare;
     Bold Lover, never, never canst thou kiss,
Though winning near the goal – yet, do not grieve;
   She cannot fade, though thou hast not thy bliss,
     For ever wilt thou love, and she be fair!

Ah, happy, happy boughs! that cannot shed
   Your leaves, nor ever bid the Spring adieu;
And, happy melodist, unweariéd,
   For ever piping songs for ever new;
More happy love! more happy, happy love!
   For ever warm and still to be enjoy'd,
     For ever panting, and for ever young;
All breathing human passion far above,
   That leaves a heart high-sorrowful and cloy'd,
     A burning forehead, and a parching tongue.

Who are these coming to the sacrifice?
  To what green altar, O mysterious priest,
Lead'st thou that heifer lowing at the skies,
  And all her silken flanks with garlands drest?
What little town by river or sea shore,
  Or mountain-built with peaceful citadel,
    Is emptied of this folk, this pious morn?
And, little town, thy streets for evermore
  Will silent be; and not a soul to tell
    Why thou art desolate, can e'er return.

O Attic shape! Fair attitude! with brede
  Of marble men and maidens overwrought,
With forest branches and the trodden weed;
  Thou, silent form, dost tease us out of thought
As doth eternity: Cold Pastoral!
  When old age shall this generation waste,
    Thou shalt remain, in midst of other woe
Than ours, a friend to man, to whom thou say'st,
  'Beauty is truth, truth beauty,' – that is all
    Ye know on earth, and all ye need to know.

J. Keats

CCCXXIX
YOUTH AND AGE

Verse, a breeze 'mid blossoms straying,
Where Hope clung feeding, like a bee –
Both were mine! Life went a-maying
        With Nature, Hope, and Poesy,
            When I was young!
When I was young? – Ah, woful when!
Ah! for the change 'twixt Now and Then!
This breathing house not built with hands,
This body that does me grievous wrong,
O'er aery cliffs and glittering sands
How lightly then it flash'd along:

Like those trim skiffs, unknown of yore,
On winding lakes and rivers wide,
That ask no aid of sail or oar,
That fear no spite of wind or tide!
Nought cared this body for wind or weather
When Youth and I lived in't together.

Flowers are lovely; Love is flower-like;
Friendship is a sheltering tree;
O! the joys, that came down shower-like,
Of Friendship, Love, and Liberty,
        Ere I was old!
Ere I was old? Ah woful Ere,
Which tells me, Youth's no longer here!
O Youth! for years so many and sweet,
'Tis known that Thou and I were one,
I'll think it but a fond conceit –
It cannot be, that Thou art gone!
Thy vesper-bell hath not yet toll'd: –
And thou wert aye a masker bold!
What strange disguise hast now put on
To make believe that Thou art gone?
I see these locks in silvery slips,
This drooping gait, this alter'd size:
But Springtide blossoms on thy lips,
And tears take sunshine from thine eyes!
Life is but Thought: so think I will
That Youth and I are house-mates still.

Dew-drops are the gems of morning,
But the tears of mournful eve!
Where no hope is, life's a warning
That only serves to make us grieve
        When we are old:
– That only serves to make us grieve
With oft and tedious taking-leave,

Like some poor nigh-related guest
That may not rudely be dismist,
Yet hath out-stay'd his welcome while,
And tells the jest without the smile.

S. T. Coleridge

CCCXXX
THE TWO APRIL MORNINGS

We walk'd along, while bright and red
Uprose the morning sun;
And Matthew stopp'd, he look'd, and said
'The will of God be done!'

A village schoolmaster was he,
With hair of glittering gray;
As blithe a man as you could see
On a spring holiday.

And on that morning, through the grass
And by the steaming rills
We travell'd merrily, to pass
A day among the hills.

'Our work,' said I, 'was well begun;
Then, from thy breast what thought,
Beneath so beautiful a sun,
So sad a sigh has brought?'

A second time did Matthew stop;
And fixing still his eye
Upon the eastern mountain-top,
To me he made reply:

'Yon cloud with that long purple cleft
Brings fresh into my mind
A day like this, which I have left
Full thirty years behind.

'And just above yon slope of corn
Such colours, and no other,
Were in the sky that April morn,
Of this the very brother.

'With rod and line I sued the sport
Which that sweet season gave,
And to the church-yard come, stopp'd short
Beside my daughter's grave.

'Nine summers had she scarcely seen,
The pride of all the vale;
And then she sang, – she would have been
A very nightingale.

'Six feet in earth my Emma lay;
And yet I loved her more –
For so it seem'd, – than till that day
I e'er had loved before.

'And turning from her grave, I met,
Beside the churchyard yew,
A blooming Girl, whose hair was wet
With points of morning dew.

'A basket on her head she bare;
Her brow was smooth and white:
To see a child so very fair,
It was a pure delight!

'No fountain from its rocky cave
E'er tripp'd with foot so free;
She seem'd as happy as a wave
That dances on the sea.

'There came from me a sigh of pain
Which I could ill confine;
I look'd at her, and look'd again:
And did not wish her mine!'

– Matthew is in his grave, yet now
Methinks I see him stand
As at that moment, with a bough
Of wilding in his hand.

W. Wordsworth

CCCXXXI
THE FOUNTAIN
A Conversation

We talk'd with open heart, and tongue
Affectionate and true,
A pair of friends, though I was young,
And Matthew seventy-two.

We lay beneath a spreading oak,
Beside a mossy seat;
And from the turf a fountain broke
And gurgled at our feet.

'Now, Matthew!' said I, 'let us match
This water's pleasant tune
With some old border-song, or catch
That suits a summer's noon;

'Or of the church-clock and the chimes
Sing here beneath the shade
That half-mad thing of witty rhymes
Which you last April made!'

In silence Matthew lay, and eyed
The spring beneath the tree;
And thus the dear old man replied,
The gray-hair'd man of glee:

'No check, no stay, this Streamlet fears,
How merrily it goes!
'Twill murmur on a thousand years
And flow as now it flows.

'And here, on this delightful day,
I cannot choose but think
How oft, a vigorous man, I lay
Beside this fountain's brink.

'My eyes are dim with childish tears,
My heart is idly stirr'd,
For the same sound is in my ears
Which in those days I heard.

'Thus fares it still in our decay:
And yet the wiser mind
Mourns less for what Age takes away,
Than what it leaves behind.

'The blackbird amid leafy trees,
The lark above the hill,
Let loose their carols when they please,
Are quiet when they will.

'With Nature never do they wage
A foolish strife; they see
A happy youth, and their old age
Is beautiful and free:

'But we are press'd by heavy laws;
And often, glad no more,
We wear a face of joy, because
We have been glad of yore.

'If there be one who need bemoan
His kindred laid in earth,
The household hearts that were his own, –
It is the man of mirth.

'My days, my friend, are almost gone,
My life has been approved,
And many love me; but by none
Am I enough beloved.'

'Now both himself and me he wrongs,
The man who thus complains!
I live and sing my idle songs
Upon these happy plains:

'And Matthew, for thy children dead
I'll be a son to thee!'
At this he grasp'd my hand and said,
'Alas! that cannot be.'

– We rose up from the fountain-side;
And down the smooth descent
Of the green sheep-track did we glide;
And through the wood we went;

And ere we came to Leonard's rock
He sang those witty rhymes
About the crazy old church-clock,
And the bewilder'd chimes.

W. Wordsworth

CCCXXXII
THE RIVER OF LIFE

The more we live, more brief appear
    Our life's succeeding stages:
A day to childhood seems a year,
    And years like passing ages.

The gladsome current of our youth,
    Ere passion yet disorders,
Steals lingering like a river smooth
    Along its grassy borders.

But as the care-worn cheek grows wan,
　　And sorrow's shafts fly thicker,
Ye Stars, that measure life to man,
　　Why seem your courses quicker?

When joys have lost their bloom and breath
　　And life itself is vapid,
Why, as we reach the Falls of Death,
　　Feel we its tide more rapid?

It may be strange – yet who would change
　　Time's course to slower speeding,
When one by one our friends have gone
　　And left our bosoms bleeding?

Heaven gives our years of fading strength
　　Indemnifying fleetness;
And those of youth, a seeming length,
　　Proportion'd to their sweetness.

T. Campbell

THE HUMAN SEASONS

Four Seasons fill the measure of the year;
There are four seasons in the mind of man:
He has his lusty Spring, when fancy clear
Takes in all beauty with an easy span:

He has his Summer, when luxuriously
Spring's honey'd cud of youthful thought he loves
To ruminate, and by such dreaming high
Is nearest unto heaven: quiet coves

His soul has in its Autumn, when his wings
He furleth close; contented so to look
On mists in idleness – to let fair things
Pass by unheeded as a threshold brook.

He has his Winter too of pale misfeature,
Or else he would forego his mortal nature.

J. Keats

CCCXXXIV
A DIRGE
[*Added 1891*]

Rough wind, that moanest loud
    Grief too sad for song;
Wild wind, when sullen cloud
    Knells all the night long;
Sad storm whose tears are vain,
Bare woods whose branches stain,
Deep caves and dreary main, –
    Wail for the worlds' wrong!

P. B. Shelley

CCCXXXV
THRENOS

O World! O Life! O Time!
On whose last steps I climb,
    Trembling at that where I had stood before;
When will return the glory of your prime?
        No more–Oh, never more!

Out of the day and night
A joy has taken flight:
  Fresh spring, and summer, and winter hoar
Move my faint heart with grief, but with delight
    No more – Oh, never more!

P. B. Shelley

CCCXXXVI
THE TROSACHS
[*Added 1883*]

There's not a nook within this solemn Pass,
But were an apt confessional for One
Taught by his summer spent, his autumn gone,
That Life is but a tale of morning grass

Wither'd at eve. From scenes of art which chase
That thought away, turn, and with watchful eyes
Feed it 'mid Nature's old felicities,
Rocks, rivers, and smooth lakes more clear than glass

Untouch'd, unbreathed upon: – Thrice happy quest,
If from a golden perch of aspen spray
(October's workmanship to rival May),

The pensive warbler of the ruddy breast
That moral sweeten by a heaven-taught lay,
Lulling the year, with all its cares, to rest!

W. Wordsworth

CCCXXXVII

My heart leaps up when I behold
  A rainbow in the sky:
So was it when my life began,
So is it now I am a man,
So be it when I shall grow old
    Or let me die!
The Child is father of the Man:
And I could wish my days to be
Bound each to each by natural piety.

                W. Wordsworth

CCCXXXVIII

ODE ON INTIMATIONS OF IMMORTALITY FROM RECOLLECTIONS OF EARLY CHILDHOOD

There was a time when meadow, grove, and stream,
The earth, and every common sight
    To me did seem
    Apparell'd in celestial light,
The glory and the freshness of a dream.
It is not now as it hath been of yore; –
    Turn whereso e'er I may,
    By night or day,
The things which I have seen I now can see no more.

    The rainbow comes and goes,
    And lovely is the rose;
    The moon doth with delight
Look round her when the heavens are bare;
    Waters on a starry night
    Are beautiful and fair;
The sunshine is a glorious birth;
But yet I know, where'er I go,
That there hath past away a glory from the earth.

Now, while the birds thus sing a joyous song,
    And while the young lambs bound
        As to the tabor's sound,
To me alone there came a thought of grief:
A timely utterance gave that thought relief,
        And I again am strong.
The cataracts blow their trumpets from the steep; –
No more shall grief of mine the season wrong:
I hear the echoes through the mountains throng,
The winds come to me from the fields of sleep,
        And all the earth is gay;
            Land and sea
    Give themselves up to jollity,
        And with the heart of May
    Doth every beast keep holiday; –
            Thou child of joy
Shout round me, let me hear thy shouts, thou happy Shepherd-boy!

Ye blessèd Creatures, I have heard the call
    Ye to each other make; I see
The heavens laugh with you in your jubilee;
    My heart is at your festival,
        My head hath its coronal,
The fulness of your bliss, I feel – I feel it all.
        Oh evil day! if I were sullen
        While Earth herself is adorning
            This sweet May-morning;
        And the children are culling
            On every side
        In a thousand valleys far and wide,
        Fresh flowers; while the sun shines warm
And the babe leaps up on his mother's arm: –
        I hear, I hear, with joy I hear!
        – But there's a tree, of many, one,
A single field which I have look'd upon,
Both of them speak of something that is gone:
            The pansy at my feet

Doth the same tale repeat:
Whither is fled the visionary gleam?
Where is it now, the glory and the dream?

Our birth is but a sleep and a forgetting;
The Soul that rises with us, our life's Star,
Hath had elsewhere its setting
And cometh from afar;
Not in entire forgetfulness,
And not in utter nakedness,
But trailing clouds of glory do we come
From God, who is our home:
Heaven lies about us in our infancy!
Shades of the prison-house begin to close
Upon the growing Boy,
But he beholds the light, and whence it flows,
He sees it in his joy;
The Youth, who daily farther from the east
Must travel, still is Nature's priest,
And by the vision splendid
Is on his way attended;
At length the Man perceives it die away,
And fade into the light of common day.

Earth fills her lap with pleasures of her own;
Yearnings she hath in her own natural kind,
And, even with something of a mother's mind
And no unworthy aim,
The homely nurse doth all she can
To make her foster-child, her inmate, Man,
Forget the glories he hath known,
And that imperial palace whence he came.

Behold the Child among his new-born blisses,
A six years' darling of a pigmy size!
See, where 'mid work of his own hand he lies,
Fretted by sallies of his mother's kisses,
With light upon him from his father's eyes!

See, at his feet, some little plan or chart,
Some fragment from his dream of human life,
Shaped by himself with newly-learnéd art;
        A wedding or a festival,
        A mourning or a funeral;
            And this hath now his heart,
        And unto this he frames his song:
            Then will he fit his tongue
To dialogues of business, love, or strife;
        But it will not be long
        Ere this be thrown aside,
        And with new joy and pride
The little actor cons another part;
Filling from time to time his 'humorous stage'
With all the Persons, down to palsied Age,
That life brings with her in her equipage;
        As if his whole vocation
        Were endless imitation.

Thou, whose exterior semblance doth belie
        Thy soul's immensity;
Thou best philosopher, who yet dost keep
Thy heritage, thou eye among the blind,
That, deaf and silent, read'st the eternal deep,
Haunted for ever by the eternal Mind, –
        Mighty Prophet! Seer blest!
        On whom those truths do rest
Which we are toiling all our lives to find,
In darkness lost, the darkness of the grave;
Thou, over whom thy Immortality
Broods like the day, a master o'er a slave,
A Presence which is not to be put by;
Thou little child, yet glorious in the might
Of heaven-born freedom on thy being's height,
Why with such earnest pains dost thou provoke
The years to bring the inevitable yoke,

Thus blindly with thy blessedness at strife?
Full soon thy soul shall have her earthly freight,
And custom lie upon thee with a weight
Heavy as frost, and deep almost as life!

       O joy! that in our embers
       Is something that doth live,
       That Nature yet remembers
       What was so fugitive!
The thought of our past years in me doth breed
Perpetual benediction: not indeed
For that which is most worthy to be blest,
Delight and liberty, the simple creed
Of Childhood, whether busy or at rest,
With new-fledged hope still fluttering in his breast: –
       – Not for these I raise
       The song of thanks and praise;
     But for those obstinate questionings
     Of sense and outward things,
     Fallings from us, vanishings;
     Blank misgivings of a creature
Moving about in worlds not realized,
High instincts, before which our mortal nature
Did tremble like a guilty thing surprized:
     But for those first affections,
     Those shadowy recollections,
       Which, be they what they may,
Are yet the fountain-light of all our day,
Are yet a master-light of all our seeing;
       Uphold us, cherish, and have power to make
Our noisy years seem moments in the being
Of the eternal Silence: truths that wake,
         To perish never;
Which neither listlessness, nor mad endeavour,
        Nor man nor boy
Nor all that is at enmity with joy,
Can utterly abolish or destroy!

Hence, in a season of calm weather
        Though inland far we be,
Our souls have sight of that immortal sea
            Which brought us hither;
        Can in a moment travel thither –
And see the children sport upon the shore,
And hear the mighty waters rolling evermore.

Then, sing ye birds, sing, sing a joyous song!
            And let the young lambs bound
            As to the tabor's sound!
    We, in thought, will join your throng
            Ye that pipe and ye that play,
            Ye that through your hearts to-day
            Feel the gladness of the May!
What though the radiance which was once so bright
Be now for ever taken from my sight,
        Though nothing can bring back the hour
Of splendour in the grass, of glory in the flower;
            We will grieve not, rather find
            Strength in what remains behind;
            In the primal sympathy
            Which having been must ever be;
            In the soothing thoughts that spring
            Out of human suffering;
            In the faith that looks through death,
In years that bring the philosophic mind.

And O, ye Fountains, Meadows, Hills, and Groves,
Forbode not any severing of our loves!
Yet in my heart of hearts I feel your might;
I only have relinquish'd one delight
To live beneath your more habitual sway:
I love the brooks which down their channels fret
Even more than when I tripp'd lightly as they;
The innocent brightness of a new-born day
                Is lovely yet;
The clouds that gather round the setting sun

Do take a sober colouring from an eye
That hath kept watch o'er man's mortality;
Another race hath been, and other palms are won.
Thanks to the human heart by which we live,
Thanks to its tenderness, its joys, and fears,
To me the meanest flower that blows can give
Thoughts that do often lie too deep for tears.

W. Wordsworth

CCCXXXIX

Music, when soft voices die,
Vibrates in the memory –
Odours, when sweet violets sicken,
Live within the sense they quicken.

Rose leaves, when the rose is dead,
Are heap'd for the beloved's bed;
And so thy thoughts, when Thou art gone,
Love itself shall slumber on.

P. B. Shelley

End of the Golden Treasury

NOTES

[by Palgrave]
(1861–1891)

Summary of Book First

The Elizabethan Poetry, as it is rather vaguely termed, forms the substance of this Book, which contains pieces from Wyat under Henry VIII to Shakespeare midway through the reign of James I, and Drummond who carried on the early manner to a still later period. There is here a wide range of style; – from simplicity expressed in a language hardly yet broken-in to verse,–through the pastoral fancies and Italian conceits of the strictly Elizabethan time, – to the passionate reality of Shakespeare: yet a general uniformity of tone prevails. Few readers can fail to observe the natural sweetness of the verse, the single-hearted straightforwardness of the thoughts: – nor less, the limitation of subject to the many phases of one passion, which then characterized our lyrical poetry, – unless when, as in especial with Shakespeare, the 'purple light of Love' is tempered by a spirit of sterner reflection. For the didactic verse of the century, although lyrical in form, yet very rarely rises to the pervading emotion, the golden cadence, proper to the lyric.

It should be observed that this and the following Summaries apply in the main to the Collection here presented, in which (besides its restriction to Lyrical Poetry) a strictly representative or historical Anthology has not been aimed at. Great excellence, in human art as in human character, has from the beginning of things been even more uniform than mediocrity, by virtue of the closeness of its approach to Nature: – and so far as the standard of Excellence kept in view has been attained in this volume, a comparative absence of extreme or temporary phases in style, a similarity of tone and manner, will be found throughout: – something neither modern nor ancient, but true and speaking to the heart of man alike throughout all ages.

III   *whist*: hushed, quieted.

IV   *Rouse Memnon's mother*: Awaken the Dawn from the dark Earth and the clouds where she is resting. This is one of that limited class of early mythes which may be reasonably interpreted as representations of natural phenomena. Aurora in the old mythology is mother of Memnon (the East), and wife of Tithonus (the appearances of Earth and Sky during the last hours of Night). She leaves him every morning in renewed youth, to prepare the way for Phoebus (the Sun), whilst Tithonus remains in perpetual old age and grayness.

l. 27 *by Peneus' stream*: Phoebus loved the Nymph Daphne whom he met by the river Peneus in the vale of Tempe. l. 31 *Amphion's lyre*: He was said to have built the walls of Thebes to the sound of his music. l. 39 *Night like a drunkard reels*: Compare Romeo and Juliet, Act II, Scene 3: 'The grey-eyed morn smiles,' &c. – It should be added that three lines, which appeared hopelessly misprinted, have been omitted in this Poem.

VI   *Time's chest*: in which he is figuratively supposed to lay up past treasures. So in Troilus, Act III, Scene 3, 'Time hath a wallet at his back' &c. In the *Arcadia, chest* is used to signify *tomb*.

VII   A fine example of the high wrought and conventional Elizabethan Pastoralism, which it would be unreasonable to criticize on the ground of the unshepherdlike or unreal character of some images suggested. Stanza 6 was perhaps inserted by Izaak Walton.

VIII   This beautiful lyric is one of several recovered from the very rare Elizabethan Song-books, for the publication of which our thanks are due to Mr. A. H. Bullen (1887, 1888).

XII   One stanza has been here omitted, in accordance with the principle noticed in the Preface. Similar omissions occur in a few other poems. The more serious abbreviation by which it has been attempted to bring Crashaw's 'Wishes' and Shelley's 'Euganean Hills,' with one or two more, within the scheme of this selection, is commended with much diffidence to the judgment of readers acquainted with the original pieces.

XIII   Sidney's poetry is singularly unequal; his short life, his frequent absorption in public employment, hindered doubtless the development of his genius. His great contemporary fame, second only, it appears, to Spenser's, has been hence obscured. At times he is heavy and even prosaic; his simplicity is rude and bare; his verse unmelodious. These, however, are the 'defects of his merits.' In a certain depth and chivalry of feeling,–in the rare and noble quality of disinterestedness (to put it in one word), – he has no superior, hardly perhaps an equal, amongst our Poets; and after or beside Shakespeare's Sonnets, his *Astrophel and Stella*, in the Editor's judgment, offers the most intense and powerful picture of the passion of love in the whole range of our poetry. – *Hundreds of years*: 'The very rapture of love,' says Mr. Ruskin; 'A lover like this does not believe his mistress can grow old or die.'

XIX   Readers who have visited Italy will be reminded of more than one picture by this gorgeous Vision of Beauty, equally sublime and pure in its Paradisaical naturalness. Lodge wrote it on a voyage to 'the Islands of Terceras and the Canaries;' and he seems to have caught, in those southern seas, no small portion of the qualities which marked the almost contemporary Art of Venice, – the glory and the glow of Veronese, Titian, or Tintoret. – From the same romance is No. LXXI: a charming picture in the purest style of the later Italian Renaissance.

The clear (l. 1) is the crystalline or outermost heaven of the old cosmography. *For a fair there's fairer none*: If you desire a Beauty, there is none more beautiful than Rosaline.

XXII   Another gracious lyric from an Elizabethan Song-book, first reprinted (it is believed) in Mr. W. J. Linton's 'Rare Poems,' in 1883.

XXIII   *that fair thou owest*: that beauty thou ownest.

XXV   From one of the three Song-books of T. Campion, who appears to have been author of the words which he set to music. His merit as a lyrical poet (recognized in his own time, but since then forgotten) has been again brought to light by Mr. Bullen's taste and research: *swerving* (st. 2) is his conjecture for *changing* in the text of 1601.

XXXI   *the star ... Whose worth's unknown, although his height be taken*: apparently, Whose stellar influence is uncalcu-
            lated, although his angular altitude from the plane of
            the astrolabe or artifical horizon used by astrologers
            has been determined.

XXXII   This lovely song appears, as here given, in Puttenham's
            'Arte of English Poesie,' 1589. A longer and inferior
            form was published in the 'Arcadia' of 1590; but Putten-
            ham's prefatory words clearly assign his version to
            Sidney's own authorship.

XXXVII   *keel*: keep cooler by stirring round.

XXXIX   *expense*: loss.

XL   *prease*: press.

XLI   *Nativity, once in the main of light*: when a star has risen
            and entered on the full stream of light: – another of the
            astrological phrases no longer familiar.

            Crooked eclipses: as coming athwart the Sun's apparent
            course.

            Wordsworth, thinking probably of the 'Venus' and the
            'Lucrece,' said finely of Shakespeare: 'Shakespeare *could*
            not have written an Epic; he would have died of
            plethora of thought.' This prodigality of nature is exem-
            plified equally in his Sonnets. The copious selection
            here given (which from the wealth of the material,
            required greater consideration than any other portion
            of the Editor's task), – contains many that will not be
            fully felt and understood without some earnestness of
            thought on the reader's part. But he is not likely to
            regret the labour.

XLII   *upon misprision growing*: either, granted in error, or, on
            the growth of contempt.

XLIII   With the tone of this Sonnet compare Hamlet's 'Give
            me that man That is not passion's slave' &c. Shake-
            speare's writings show the deepest sensitiveness to
            passion: – hence the attraction he felt in the contrast-
            ing effects of apathy.

XLIV   *grame*: sorrow. Renaissance influences long impeded the
            return of English poets to the charming realism of this
            and a few other poems by Wyat.

XLV   Pandion in the ancient fable was father to Philomela.

XLVII   In the old legend it is now Philomela, now Procne (the swallow) who suffers violence from Tereus. This song has a fascination in the calm intensity of passion; that 'sad earnestness and vivid exactness' which Cardinal Newman ascribes to the master-pieces of ancient poetry.

L   *proved*: approved.

LI   *censures*: judges.

LII   Exquisite in its equably-balanced metrical flow.

LIII   Judging by its style, this beautiful example of old simplicity and feeling may, perhaps, be referred to the earlier years of Elizabeth. *Late* forgot: lately.

LVII   Printed in a little Anthology by Nicholas Breton, 1597. It is, however, a stronger and finer piece of work than any known to be his. – St. 1 *silly*: simple; *dole*: grief; *chief*: chiefly. St. 3 *If there be . . .*: obscure: Perhaps, if there be any who speak harshly of thee, thy pain may plead for pity from Fate.
         This poem, with LX and CXLIII are each graceful variations of a long popular theme.

LVIII   *That busy archer*: Cupid. *Descries*: used actively; *points out*. – 'The last line of this poem is a little obscured by transposition. He means, *Do they call ungratefulness there a virtue?*' (C. Lamb).

LIX   *White Iopé*: suggested, Mr. Bullen notes, by a Passage in Propertius (iii, 20) describing Spirits in the lower world:
         Vobiscum est Iope, vobiscum candida Tyro.

LXII   *cypres* or cyprus, – used by the old writers for *crape*: whether from the French *crespe* or from the Island whence it was imported. Its accidental similarity in spelling to *cypress* has, here and in Milton's Penseroso, probably confused readers.

LXIII   *ramage*: confused noise.

LXVI   'I never saw anything like this funeral dirge,' says Charles Lamb, 'except the ditty which reminds Ferdinand of his drowned father in the Tempest. As that is of the water, watery; so this is of the earth, earthy. Both have that intenseness of feeling, which seems to resolve itself into the element which it contemplates.'

LXX   Paraphrased from an Italian madrigal.
                   . . . Non so conoscer poi
                   Se voi le rose, o sian le rose in voi.
LXXII   *crystal*: fairness.
LXXIII   *stare*: starling.
LXXIV   This 'Spousal Verse' was written in honour of the
               Ladies Elizabeth and Katherine Somerset. Nowhere
               has Spenser more emphatically displayed himself as the
               very poet of Beauty: The Renaissance impulse in Eng-
               land is here seen at its highest and purest.
                   The genius of Spenser, like Chaucer's, does itself justice
               only in poems of some length. Hence it is impossible to
               represent it in this volume by other pieces of equal
               merit, but of impracticable dimensions. And the same
               applies to such poems as the *Lover's Lament* or the
               Ancient Mariner.
                   entrailed: twisted. *Feateously*: elegantly.
                   shend: shame.
                   a noble peer: Robert Devereux, second Lord Essex, then
               at the height of his brief triumph after taking Cadiz:
               hence the allusion following to the Pillars of Hercules,
               placed near Gades by ancient legend.
                   Elisa: Elizabeth.
                   twins of Jove: the stars Castor and Pollux: *baldric*, belt;
               the zodiac.
LXXIX   This lyric may with very high probability be assigned
               to Campion, in whose first Book of Airs it appeared
               (1601). The evidence sometimes quoted ascribing it to
               Lord Bacon appears to be valueless.

Summary of Book Second

This division, embracing generally the latter eighty years of the Seventeenth
century, contains the close of our Early poetical style and the commencement
of the Modern. In Dryden we see the first master of the new: in Milton,
whose genius dominates here as Shakespeare's in the former book, – the
crown and consummation of the early period. Their splendid Odes are far
in advance of any prior attempts, Spenser's excepted: they exhibit that
wider and grander range which years and experience and the struggles of

the time conferred on Poetry. Our Muses now give expression to political feeling, to religious thought, to a high philosophic statesmanship in writers such as Marvell, Herbert, and Wotton: whilst in Marvell and Milton, again, we find noble attempts, hitherto rare in our literature, at pure description of nature, destined in our own age to be continued and equalled. Meanwhile the poetry of simple passion, although before 1600 often deformed by verbal fancies and conceits of thought, and afterwards by levity and an artificial tone, - produced in Herrick and Waller some charming pieces of more finished art than the Elizabethan: until in the courtly compliments of Sedley it seems to exhaust itself, and lie almost dormant for the hundred years between the days of Wither and Suckling and the days of Burns and Cowper. - That the change from our early style to the modern brought with it at first a loss of nature and simplicity is undeniable: yet the bolder and wider scope which Poetry took between 1620 and 1700, and the successful efforts then made to gain greater clearness in expression, in their results have been no slight compensation.

LXXXV   (p. 79, l. 7) *whist*: hushed.

(p. 79, l. 31) *than*: obsolete for *then: Pan*: used for the Lord of all.

(p. 81, l. 5) *consort*; Milton's spelling of this word, here and elsewhere, has been followed, as it is uncertain whether he used it in the sense of *accompanying*, or simply for *concert*.

(p. 82, l. 29) *Lars and Lemurés*: household gods and spirits of relations dead. *Flamens* (p. 82, l. 32) Roman priests. *That twice-batter'd god* (p. 83, l. 3) Dagon.

(p. 83, l. 17) *Osiris*, the Egyptian god of Agriculture (here, perhaps by confusion with Apis, figured as a Bull), was torn to pieces by Typho and embalmed after death in a sacred chest. This mythe, reproduced in Syria and Greece in the legends of Thammuz, Adonis, and perhaps Absyrtus, may have originally signified the annual death of the Sun or the Year under the influences of the winter darkness. Horus, the son of Osiris, as the New Year, in his turn overcomes Typho. (p. 83, l. 19) *unshower'd grass:* as watered by the Nile only. (p. 84, l. 9) *youngest-teeméd*: last-born. *Bright-harness'd* (l. 13) armoured.

LXXXVII   *The Late Massacre*: the Vaudois persecution, carried on

in 1655 by the Duke of Savoy. No more mighty Sonnet
than this 'collect in verse,' as it has been justly named,
probably can be found in any language. Readers should
observe that it is constructed on the original Italian or
Provençal model. This form, in a language such as
ours, not affluent in rhyme, presents great difficulties;
the rhymes are apt to be forced, or the substance
commonplace. But, when successfully handled, it has a
unity and a beauty of effect which place the strict
Sonnet above the less compact and less lyrical systems
adopted by Shakespeare, Sidney, Spenser, and other
Elizabethan poets.

LXXXVIII   Cromwell returned from Ireland in 1650, and Marvell
probably wrote his lines soon after, whilst living at
Nunappleton in the Fairfax household. It is hence not
surprising that (st. 21–24) he should have been deceived
by Cromwell's professed submissiveness to the Parlia-
ment which, when it declined to register his decrees, he
expelled by armed violence: – one despotism, by natural
law, replacing another. The poet's insight has, however,
truly prophesied that result in his last two lines.

This Ode, beyond doubt one of the finest in our lan-
guage, and more in Milton's style than has been
reached by any other poet, is occasionally obscure from
imitation of the condensed Latin syntax. The meaning
of st. 5 is 'rivalry or hostility are the same to a lofty
spirit, and limitation more hateful than opposition.'
The allusion in st. 11 is to the old physical doctrines of
the non-existence of a vacuum and the impenetrability
of matter: – in st. 17 to the omen traditionally connected
with the foundation of the Capitol at Rome: – *forcéd*,
fated. The ancient belief that certain years in life com-
plete natural periods and are hence peculiarly exposed
to death, is introduced in st. 26 by the word *climacteric*.

LXXXIX   *Lycidas*: The person here lamented is Milton's college
contemporary, Edward King, drowned in 1637 whilst
crossing from Chester to Ireland.

Strict Pastoral Poetry was first written or perfected by
the Dorian Greeks settled in Sicily: but the conventional
use of it, exhibited more magnificently in *Lycidas* than

in any other pastoral, is apparently of Roman origin.
Milton, employing the noble freedom of a great artist,
has here united ancient mythology, with what may be
called the modern mythology of Camus and Saint
Peter, – to direct Christian images. Yet the poem, if it
gains in historical interest, suffers in poetry by the
harsh intrusion of the writer's narrow and violent theo-
logical politics. – The metrical structure of this glorious
elegy is partly derived from Italian models.

p. 95, l. 15 *Sisters of the sacred well*: the Muses, said to
frequent the Pierian Spring at the foot of Mount Olym-
pus.

p. 92, l. 21 *Mona*: Anglesea, called by the Welsh poets,
the Dark Island, from its dense forests. *Deva* (p. 92, l. 22)
the Dee: a river which may have derived its magical
character from Celtic traditions: it was long the bound-
ary of Briton and English. – These places are intro-
duced, as being near the scene of the shipwreck. *Orpheus*
(p. 92 l. 25) was torn to pieces by Thracian women.
Amaryllis and *Neaera* (p. 92 l. 35–6) names used here for
the love-idols of poets: as *Damoetas* previously for a
shepherd. p. 93 l. 5 *the blind Fury*: Atropos, fabled to cut
the thread of life.

Arethuse (p. 93 ll. 15–16) and *Mincius*: Sicilian and
Italian waters here alluded to as representing the pasto-
ral poetry of Theocritus and Vergil. p. 93 l. 18 *Oat*:
pipe, used here like Collins' *oaten stop* l. 1, No.
CLXXXVI, for *Song*. p. 93 l. 26 *Hippotades*: Aeolus, god
of the Winds. *Panope* (p. 93 l. 29) a Nereid. Certain
names of local deities in the Hellenic mythology render
some feature in the natural landscape, which the Greeks
studied and analysed with their usual unequalled in-
sight and feeling. *Panope* seems to express the boundless-
ness of the ocean-horizon when seen from a height, as
compared with the limited sky-line of the land in hilly
countries such as Greece or Asia Minor. *Camus* (p. 93. l.
33) the Cam: put for King's University. *The sanguine
flower* (p. 93 l. 36) the Hyacinth of the ancients: prob-
ably our Iris. *The Pilot* (p. 94 l. 2) Saint Peter, figura-
tively introduced as the head of the Church on earth,

to foretell 'the ruin of our corrupted clergy,' as Milton regarded them, 'then in their heighth' under Laud's primacy.

p. 94 l. 17 *scrannel*: screeching; apparently Milton's coinage (Masson). p. 94 l. 21 *the wolf*: the Puritans of the time were excited to alarm and persecution by a few conversions to Roman Catholicism which had recently occurred. *Alpheus* (p. 94 l. 25) a stream in Southern Greece, supposed to flow underseas to join the Arethuse. *Swart star* (p. 94 l. 31) the Dog-star, called swarthy because its heliacal rising in ancient times occurred soon after midsummer: p. 94 l. 35 *rathe*: early. p. 95 l. 16 *moist vows*: either tearful prayers, or prayers for one at sea. *Bellerus* (p. 95 l. 17) a giant apparently created here by Milton to personify Belerium, the ancient title of the Land's End. *The great Vision*: – the story was that the Archangel Michael had appeared on the rock by Marazion in Mount's Bay which bears his name. Milton calls on him to turn his eyes from the south homeward, and to pity Lycidas, if his body has drifted into the troubled waters off the Land's End. Finisterre being the land due south of Marazion, two places in that district (then through our trade with Corunna probably less unfamiliar to English ears), are named, – *Namancos* now Mujio in Galicia, *Bayona* north of the Minho, or perhaps a fortified rock (one of the *Cies* Islands) not unlike Saint Michael's Mount, at the entrance of Vigo Bay.

p. 95 l. 27 *ore*: rays of golden light. *Doric* lay (p. 96 l. 10) Sicilian, pastoral.

XCIII

The assault was an attack on London expected in 1642, when the troops of Charles I reached Brentford. 'Written on his door' was in the original title of this sonnet. Milton was then living in Aldersgate Street.

The Emathian Conqueror: When Thebes was destroyed (B.C. 335) and the citizens massacred by thousands, Alexander ordered the house of Pindar to be spared.

l. 12, *the repeated air Of sad Electra's poet*: Plutarch has a tale that when the Spartan confederacy in 404 B.C. took Athens, a proposal to demolish it was rejected through the effect produced on the commanders by hearing part of a chorus from the *Electra* of Euripides sung at a feast. There is however no apparent congruity between the lines quoted (167, 168 Ed. Dindorf) and the result ascribed to them.

XCV A fine example of a peculiar class of Poetry: – that written by thoughtful men who practised this Art but little. Jeremy Taylor, Bishop Berkeley, Dr. Johnson, Lord Macaulay, have left similar specimens.

XCVIII These beautiful verses should be compared with Wordsworth's great Ode on *Immortality*: and a copy of Vaughan's very rare little volume appears in the list of Wordsworth's library. – In imaginative intensity, Vaughan stands beside his contemporary Marvell.

XCIX *Favonius*: the spring wind.

C *Themis*: the goddess of justice. Skinner was grandson by his mother to Sir E. Coke: – hence, as pointed out by Mr. Keightley, Milton's allusion to the *bench*. l. 8: Sweden was then at war with Poland, and France with the Spanish Netherlands.

CIII l. 28 *Sidneian showers*: either in allusion to the conversation in the 'Arcadia,' or to Sidney himself as a model of 'gentleness' in spirit and demeanour.

CV Delicate humour, delightfully united to thought, at once simple and subtle. It is full of conceit and paradox, but these are imaginative, not as with most of our Seventeenth Century poets, intellectual only.

CX *Elizabeth of Bohemia*: Daughter to James I, and ancestor of Sophia of Hanover. These lines are a fine specimen of gallant and courtly compliment.

CXI Lady M. Ley was daughter to Sir J. Ley, afterwards Earl of Marlborough, who died March, 1629, coincidently with the dissolution of the third Parliament of Charles' reign. Hence Milton poetically compares his death to that of the Orator Isocrates of Athens, after Philip's victory in 328 B.C.

CXVIII A masterpiece of humour, grace, and gentle feeling all, with Herrick's unfailing art, kept precisely within the peculiar key which he chose, – or Nature for him, – in his Pastorals. l. 2 *the god unshorn*: Imberbis Apollo. St. 2 *beads*: prayers.

CXXIII — With better taste, and less diffuseness, Quarles might (one would think) have retained more of that high place which he held in popular estimate among his contemporaries.

CXXVII — *From Prison*: to which his active support of Charles I twice brought the high-spirited writer. l. 7 *Gods*: thus in the original; Lovelace, in his fanciful way, making here a mythological allusion. *Birds*, commonly substituted, is without authority. St. 3, l. 1 *committed*: to prison.

CXXVIII — St. 2 l. 4 *blue-god*: Neptune.

CXXXIII — *Waly waly*: an exclamation of sorrow, the root and the pronunciation of which are preserved in the word *caterwaul*. *Brae*, hillside: *burn*, brook: *busk*, adorn. *Saint Anton's Well*: below Arthur's Seat by Edinburgh. *Cramasie*, crimson.

CXXXIV — This beautiful example of early simplicity is found in a Song-book of 1620. [Added later] These stanzas are by Richard Verstegan (– c. 1635) a poet and antiquarian, published in his rare *Odes* (1601), under the title *Our Blessed Ladies Lullaby*, and reprinted by Mr. Orby Shipley in his beautiful *Carmina Mariana* (1893). The four stanzas here given form the opening of a hymn of twenty-four.

CXXXV — *burd*, maiden.

CXXXVI — *corbies*, crows: *fail*, turf: *hause*, neck; *theek*, thatch. – If not in their origin, in their present form this, with the preceding poem and CXXXIII, appear due to the Seventeenth Century, and have therefore been placed in Book II.

CXXXVII — The poetical and the prosaic, after Cowley's fashion, blend curiously in this deeply-felt elegy.

CXLI — Perhaps no poem in this collection is more delicately fancied, more exquisitely finished. By placing his description of the Fawn in a young girl's mouth, Marvell has, as it were, legitimated that abundance of 'imaginative hyperbole' to which he is always partial: he makes us feel it natural that a maiden's favourite should be whiter than milk, sweeter than sugar – 'lilies without, roses within.' The poet's imagination is justified in its seeming

extravagance by the intensity and unity with which it
invests his picture.

CXLII   The remark quoted in the note to No. LXVI applies
equally to these truly wonderful verses. Marvell here
throws himself into the very soul of the *Garden* with the
imaginative intensity of Shelley in his *West Wind*. – This
poem appears also as a translation in Marvell's works.
The most striking verses in it, here quoted as the book
is rare, answer more or less to stanzas 2 and 6: –

> Alma Quies, teneo te! et te, germana Quietis,
> Simplicitas! vos ergo diu per templa, per urbes
> Quaesivi, regum perque alta palatia, frustra:
> Sed vos hortorum per opaca silentia, longe
> Celarunt plantae virides, et concolor umbra.

CXLIII   St. 3 *tutties*: nosegays. St. 4 *silly*: simple.

CXLIV–CXLV   *L'Allégro* and *Il Penseroso*. It is a striking proof of
Milton's astonishing power, that these, the earliest great
Lyrics of the Landscape in our language, should still
remain supreme in their style for range, variety, and
melodious beauty. The Bright and the Thoughtful as-
pects of Nature and of Life are their subjects: but each
is preceded by a mythological introduction in a mixed
Classical and Italian manner. – With that of *L'Allégro*
may be compared a similar mythe in the first Section of
the first Book of S. Marmion's graceful *Cupid and Psyche*,
1637.

CXLIV   *The mountain-nymph*: compare Wordsworth's Sonnet, No.
CCLIV. p. 147, l. 16 is in *apposition* to the preceding,
by a syntactical license not uncommon with Milton.

p. 148, l. 24 *Cynosure*: the Pole Star. *Corydon, Thyrsis*,
&c.: Shepherd names from the old Idylls. *Rebeck* (p. 149,
l. 38) an elementary form of violin.

p. 150, l. 2 *Jonson's learned sock*: His comedies are deeply
coloured by classical study. p. 150, l. 6 *Lydian airs*: used
here to express a light and festive style of ancient
music. The 'Lydian Mode,' one of the seven original
Greek Scales, is nearly identical with our 'Major.'

CXLV   p. 150, l. 3 *Bestead*: avail. p. 151, l. 14 *starr'd Ethiop
queen*: Cassiopeia, the legendary Queen of Ethiopia,
and thence translated amongst the constellations.

> p. 152, l. 18 *Cynthia*: the Moon: Milton seems here to
> have transferred to her chariot the dragons anciently
> assigned to Demeter and to Medea.
> p. 153, l. 10 *Hermes*, called Trismegistus, a mystical
> writer of the Neo-Platonist school. p. 153, l. 21 *Thebes*,
> &c.: subjects of Athenian Tragedy. *Buskin'd* (p. 153, l.
> 24) tragic, in opposition to *sock* above. p. 153, l. 26
> *Musaeus*: a poet in Mythology. p. 153, l. 31 *him that left
> half-told*: Chaucer in his incomplete 'Squire's Tale.'
> p. 154, l. 1 *great bards*: Ariosto, Tasso, and Spenser, are
> here presumably intended. p. 154, l. 8 *frounced*: curled.
> *The Attic Boy* (p. 154, l. 9) Cephalus.

CXLVI · Emigrants supposed to be driven towards America by
the government of Charles I.

ll. 23–24 *But apples*, &c. A fine example of Marvell's
imaginative hyperbole.

CXLVII · l. 6 *concent*: harmony.

CXLIX · A lyric of a strange, fanciful, yet solemn beauty: –
Cowley's style intensified by the mysticism of Henry
More. – St. 2 *monument:* the World.

CLI · Entitled 'A Song in Honour of St. Cecilia's Day: 1697.'

Summary of Book Third

It is more difficult to characterize the English Poetry of the Eighteenth
century than that of any other. For it was an age not only of spontaneous
transition, but of bold experiment: it includes not only such absolute
contrasts as distinguish the 'Rape of the Lock' from the 'Parish Register,'
but such vast contemporaneous differences as lie between Pope and Collins,
Burns and Cowper. Yet we may clearly trace three leading moods or
tendencies: – the aspects of courtly or educated life represented by Pope and
carried to exhaustion by his followers; the poetry of Nature and of Man,
viewed through a cultivated, and at the same time an impassioned frame of
mind by Collins and Gray: – lastly, the study of vivid and simple narrative,
including natural description, begun by Gay and Thomson, pursued by
Burns and others in the north, and established in England by Goldsmith,
Percy, Crabbe, and Cowper. Great varieties in style accompanied these
diversities in aim: poets could not always distinguish the manner suitable for
subjects so far apart: and the union of conventional and of common

language, exhibited most conspicuously by Burns, has given a tone to the
poetry of that century which is better explained by reference to its historical
origin than by naming it artificial. There is, again, a nobleness of thought, a
courageous aim at high and, in a strict sense manly, excellence in many of
the writers:—nor can that period be justly termed tame and wanting in
originality, which produced poems such as Pope's Satires, Gray's Odes and
Elegy, the ballads of Gay and Carey, the songs of Burns and Cowper. In
truth Poetry at this, as at all times, was a more or less unconscious mirror of
the genius of the age: and the many complex causes which made the
Eighteenth century the turning-time in modern European civilization are
also more or less reflected in its verse. An intelligent reader will find the
influence of Newton as markedly in the poems of Pope, as of Elizabeth in
the plays of Shakespeare. On this great subject, however, these indications
must here be sufficient.

CLIII   We have no poet more marked by rapture, by the
                   ecstasy which Plato held the note of genuine inspiration,
                   than Collins. Yet but twice or thrice do his lyrics reach
                   that simplicity, that *sinceram sermonis Attici gratiam* to
                   which this ode testifies his enthusiastic devotion. His
                   style, as his friend Dr. Johnson truly remarks, was
                   obscure; his diction often harsh and unskilfully la-
                   boured; he struggles nobly against the narrow, artificial
                   manner of his age, but his too scanty years did not
                   allow him to reach perfect mastery.
                   St. 3 *Hybla*: near Syracuse. *Her whose ... woe*: the
                   nightingale, 'for which Sophocles seems to have enter-
                   tained a peculiar fondness'; Collins here refers to the
                   famous chorus in the *Oedipus at Colonus*. St. 4 *Cephisus*:
                   the stream encircling Athens on the north and west,
                   passing Colonus. St. 6 *stay'd to sing*: stayed her song
                   when Imperial tyranny was established at Rome. St. 7
                   refers to the Italian amourist poetry of the Renaissance:
                   In Collins' day, Dante was almost unknown in Eng-
                   land. St. 8 *meeting soul*: which moves sympathetically
                   towards simplicity as she comes to inspire the poet.
                   St. 9 *Of these*: Taste and Genius.
CLIX   *The Bard.* In 1757, when this splendid ode was com-
                   pleted, so very little had been printed, whether in
                   Wales or in England, in regard to Welsh poetry, that it

is hard to discover whence Gray drew his Cymric allusions. The fabled massacre of the Bards (shown to be wholly groundless in Stephens' *Literature of the Kymry*) appears first in the family history of Sir John Wynn of Gwydir (cir. 1600), not published till 1773; but the story seems to have passed in MS. to Carte's History, whence it may have been taken by Gray. The references to *high-born Hoel* and *soft Llewellyn*; to *Cadwallo* and *Urien*; may, similarly, have been derived from the 'Specimens' of early Welsh poetry, by the Rev. E. Evans: – as, although not published till 1764, the MS., we learn from a letter to Dr. Wharton, was in Gray's hands by July 1760, and may have reached him by 1757. It is, however, doubtful whether Gray (of whose acquaintance with Welsh we have no evidence) must not have been also aided by some Welsh scholar. He is one of the poets least likely to scatter epithets at random: 'soft' or gentle is the epithet emphatically and specially given to Llewelyn in contemporary Welsh poetry, and is hence here used with particular propriety. Yet, without such assistance as we have suggested, Gray could hardly have selected the epithet, although applied to the King (p. 141-3) among a crowd of others, in Llygad Gwr's Ode, printed by Evans. – After lamenting his comrades (st. 2, 3) the Bard prophesies the fate of Edward II, and the conquests of Edward III (4): his death and that of the Black Prince (5): of Richard II, with the wars of York and Lancaster, the murder of Henry VI (*the meek usurper*), and of Edward V and his brother (6). He turns to the glory and prosperity following the accession of the Tudors (7), through Elizabeth's reign (8): and concludes with a vision of the poetry of Shakespeare and Milton.

p. 173, l. 13 *Glo'ster*: Gilbert de Clare, son-in-law to Edward. *Mortimer*, one of the Lords Marchers of Wales.

High-born Hoel, soft Llewellyn (p. 174, l. 10); the *Dissertatio de Bardis* of Evans names the first as son to the King Owain Gwynedd: Llewelyn, last King of North Wales, was murdered 1282. p. 174, l. 11 *Cadwallo*: Cadwallon (died 631) and Urien Rheged (early kings of Gwynedd and Cumbria respectively) are mentioned by Evans (p. 78) as bards none of whose poetry is extant. p. 174, l. 15 *Modred*: Evans supplies no *data* for this name which Gray (it has been supposed) uses for Merlin (Myrddin Wyllt), held prophet as well as poet. – The Italicized lines mark where the Bard's song is joined by that of his predecessors departed.

p. 174, l. 17 *Arvon*: the shores of Carnarvonshire opposite Anglesey. Whether intentionally or through ignorance of the real dates, Gray here seems to represent the *Bard* as speaking of these poets, all of earlier days, Llewelyn excepted, as his own contemporaries at the close of the thirteenth century.

Gray, whose penetrating and powerful genius rendered him in many ways an initiator in advance of his age, is probably the first of our poets who made some acquaintance with the rich and admirable poetry in which Wales from the Sixth Century has been fertile, – before and since his time so barbarously neglected, not in England only. Hence it has been thought worth while here to enter into a little detail upon his Cymric allusions.

p. 175, l. 3 *She-wolf*: Isabel of France, adulterous Queen of Edward II. – p. 175, l. 33 *Towers of Julius*: the Tower of London, built in part, according to tradition, by Julius Cæsar.

p.176, l.3 *bristled boar*: the badge of Richard III. p. 176, l. 9 *Half of thy heart*: Queen Eleanor died soon after the conquest of Wales. p. 176 l. 19 *Arthur*: Henry VII named his eldest son thus, in deference to native feeling and story.

CLXI   The Highlanders called the battle of Culloden, Drumossie.

CLXII   *lilting*, singing blithely: *loaning*, broad lane: *bughts*, pons: *scorning*, rallying: *dowie*, dreary: *daffin'* and *gabbin'*, joking and chatting: *leglin*, milkpail: *shearing*, reaping: *bandsters*, sheaf-binders: *lyart*, grizzled: *runkled*, wrinkled: *fleeching*, coaxing: *gloaming*, twilight: *bogle*, ghost: *dool*, sorrow.

CLXIV   The Editor has found no authoritative text of this poem, to his mind superior to any other of its class in melody and pathos. Part is probably not later than the seventeenth century: in other stanzas a more modern hand, much resembling Scott's, is traceable. Logan's poem (CLXIII) exhibits a knowledge rather of the old legend than of the old verses. – *Hecht*, promised; the obsolete *hight: mavis*, thrush: *ilka*, every: *lav'rock*, lark: *haughs*, valley-meadows: *twined*, parted from: *marrow* mate: *syne*, then.

CLXV   The Royal George, of 108 guns, whilst undergoing a partial careening at Spithead, was overset about 10 A.M. Aug. 29, 1782. The total loss was believed to be nearly 1000 souls. – This little poem might be called one of our trial-pieces, in regard to taste. The reader who feels the vigour of description and the force of pathos underlying Cowper's bare and truly Greek simplicity of phrase, may assure himself *se valde profecisse* in poetry.

CLXVII   A little masterpiece in a very difficult style: Catullus himself could hardly have bettered it. In grace, tenderness, simplicity, and humour, it is worthy of the Ancients: and even more so, from the completeness and unity of the picture presented.

CLXXII   Perhaps no writer who has given such strong proofs of the poetic nature has left less satisfactory poetry than Thomson. Yet this song, with 'Rule Britannia' and a few others, must make us regret that he did not more seriously apply himself to lyrical writing.

CLXXIV   With what insight and tenderness, yet in how few words has this painter-poet here himself told *Love's Secret!*

CLXXVII   p. 193, l. 1 *Aeolian lyre*: the Greeks ascribed the origin of their Lyrical Poetry to the Colonies of Aeolis in Asia Minor.

Thracia's hills (p. 193, l. 17) supposed a favourite resort of Mars. *Feather'd king* (p. 193, l. 21) the Eagle of Jupiter, admirably described by Pindar in a passage here imitated by Gray. *Idalia* (p. 193, l. 27) in Cyprus, where *Cytherea* (Venus) was especially worshipped.

p. 194, l. 22 *Hyperion*: the Sun. pp. 195–6 allude to the

Poets of the Islands and Mainland of Greece, to those of Rome and of England.

p. 196, l. 15 *Theban Eagle*: Pindar.

CLXXVIII   p. 199, l. 2 *chaste-eyed Queen*: Diana.

CLXXIX   From that wild rhapsody of mingled grandeur, tenderness, and obscurity, that 'medley between inspiration and possession,' which poor Smart is believed to have written whilst in confinement for madness.

CLXXXI   *the dreadful light*: of life and experience.

CLXXXII   *Attic warbler*: the nightingale.

CLXXXIV   *sleekit*, sleek: *bickering brattle*, flittering flight: *laith*, loth: *pattle*, ploughstaff: *whyles*, at times: *a daimenicker*, a corn-ear now and then: *thrave*, shock: *lave*, rest: *foggage*, after-grass: *snell*, biting: *but hald*, without dwelling-place: *thole*, bear: *cranreuch*, hoar-frost: *thy lane*, alone: *a-gley*, off the right line, awry.

CLXXXVIII *stoure*, dust-storm; *braw*, smart.

CLXXXIX   *scaith*, hurt: *tent*, guard: *steer*, molest.

CXCI   *drumlie*, muddy: *birk*, birch.

CXCII   *greet*, cry: *daurna*, dare not. – There can hardly exist a poem more truly tragic in the highest sense than this: nor, perhaps, Sappho excepted, has any Poetess equalled it.

CXCIII   *fou*, merry with drink: *coost*, carried: *unco skeigh*, very proud: *gart*, forced: *abeigh*, aside: *Ailsa craig*, a rock in the Firth of Clyde: *grat his een bleert*, cried till his eyes were bleared: *lowpin*, leaping: *linn*, waterfall: *sair*, sore: *smoor'd*, smothered: *crouse* and *canty*, blithe and gay.

CXCIV   Burns justly named this 'one of the most beautiful songs in the Scots or any other language.' One stanza, interpolated by Beattie, is here omitted: – it contains two good lines, but is out of harmony with the original poem. *Bigonet*, little cap: probably altered from *béguinette*: *thraw*, twist: *caller*, fresh.

CXCV   Burns himself, despite two attempts, failed to improve this little absolute masterpiece of music, tenderness, and simplicity: this 'Romance of a life' in eight lines. – *Eerie*: strictly, scared: uneasy. This poem, under the title *Absence*, has been set to an air worthy of its beauty, by Mr. F. H. Crossley (published 1889: Augener, London).

CXCVI   *airts*, quarters: *row*, roll: *shaw*, small wood in a hollow, spinney: *knowes*, knolls. The last two stanzas are not by Burns.

CXCVII   *jo*, sweetheart: *brent*, smooth: *pow*, head.

CXCVIII *leal*, faithful. St. 3 *fain*, happy.

CXCIX   Henry VI founded Eton.

CC   Written in 1773, towards the beginning of Cowper's second attack of melancholy madness – a time when he altogether gave up prayer, saying, 'For him to implore mercy would only anger God the more.' Yet had he given it up when sane, it would have been 'maior insania.'

CCIII   The Editor would venture to class in the very first rank this Sonnet, which, with CCIV, records Cowper's gratitude to the Lady whose affectionate care for many years gave what sweetness he could enjoy to a life radically wretched. Petrarch's sonnets have a more ethereal grace and a more perfect finish; Shakespeare's more passion; Milton's stand supreme in stateliness; Wordsworth's in depth and delicacy. But Cowper's unites with an exquisiteness in the turn of thought which the ancients would have called Irony, an intensity of pathetic tenderness peculiar to his loving and ingenuous nature. – There is much mannerism, much that is unimportant or of now exhausted interest in his poems: but where he is great, it is with that elementary greatness which rests on the most universal human feelings. Cowper is our highest master in simple pathos.

CCV   Cowper's last original poem, founded upon a story told in Anson's 'Voyages.' It was written March 1799; he died in next year's April.

CCVI   Very little except his name appears recoverable with regard to the author of this truly noble poem, which appeared in the 'Scripscrapologia, or Collins' Doggerel Dish of All Sorts,' with three or four other pieces of merit, Birmingham, 1804. – *Everlasting*: used with side-allusion to a cloth so named, at the time when Collins wrote.

Summary of Book Fourth

It proves sufficiently the lavish wealth of our own age in Poetry, that the pieces which, without conscious departure from the Standard of Excellence, render this Book by far the longest, were with very few exceptions composed during the first thirty years of the Nineteenth century. Exhaustive reasons can hardly be given for the strangely sudden appearance of individual genius: that, however, which assigns the splendid national achievements of our recent poetry to an impulse from the France of the first Republic and Empire is inadequate. The first French Revolution was rather one result, – the most conspicuous, indeed, yet itself in great measure essentially retrogressive, – of that wider and more potent spirit which through enquiry and attempt, through strength and weakness, sweeps mankind round the circles (not, as some too confidently argue, of Advance, but) of gradual Transformation: and it is to this that we must trace the literature of Modern Europe. But, without attempting discussion on the motive causes of Scott, Wordsworth, Shelley, and others, we may observe that these Poets carried to further perfection the later tendencies of the Century preceding, in simplicity of narrative, reverence for human Passion and Character in every sphere, and love of Nature for herself: – that, whilst maintaining on the whole the advances in art made since the Restoration, they renewed the half-forgotten melody and depth of tone which marked the best Elizabethan writers: – that, lastly, to what was thus inherited they added a richness in language and a variety in metre, a force and fire in narrative, a tenderness and bloom in feeling, an insight into the finer passages of the Soul and the inner meanings of the landscape, a larger sense of Humanity, – hitherto scarcely attained, and perhaps unattainable even by predecessors of not inferior individual genius. In a word, the Nation which, after the Greeks in their glory, may fairly claim that during six centuries it has proved itself the most richly gifted of all nations for Poetry, expressed in these men the highest strength and prodigality of its nature. They interpreted the age to itself – hence the many phases of thought and style they present: – to sympathise with each, fervently and impartially, without fear and without fancifulness, is no doubtful step in the higher education of the soul. For purity in taste is absolutely proportionate to strength – and when once the mind has raised itself to grasp and to delight in excellence, those who love most will be found to love most wisely.

But the gallery which this Book offers to the reader will aid him more than any preface. It is a royal Palace of Poetry which he is invited to enter:

Adparet domus intus, et atria longa patescunt –

though it is, indeed, to the sympathetic eye only that its treasures will be visible.

CCVIII	This beautiful lyric, printed in 1783, seems to anticipate in its imaginative music that return to our great early age of song, which in Blake's own lifetime was to prove,–how gloriously! that the English Muses had resumed their 'ancient melody': – Keats, Shelley, Byron, – he overlived them all.

CCX   *stout Cortez*: History would here suggest *Balbóa*: (A.T.) It may be noticed, that to find in Chapman's Homer the 'pure serene' of the original, the reader must bring with him the imagination of the youthful poet: – he must be 'a Greek himself,' as Shelley finely said of Keats.

CCXII   The most tender and true of Byron's smaller poems.

CCXIII   This poem exemplifies the peculiar skill with which Scott employs proper names: – a rarely misleading sign of true poetical genius.

CCXXVI   Simple as *Lucy Gray* seems, a mere narrative of what 'has been, and may be again,' yet every touch in the child's picture is marked by the deepest and purest ideal character. Hence, pathetic as the situation is, this is not strictly a pathetic poem, such as Wordsworth gives us in CCXXI, Lamb in CCLXIV, and Scott in his *Maid of Neidpath*, – 'almost more pathetic,' as Tennyson once remarked, 'than a man has the right to be.' And Lyte's lovely stanzas (CCXXIV) suggest, perhaps, the same remark.

CCXXXV   In this and in other instances the addition (or the change) of a Title has been risked, in hope that the aim of the piece following may be grasped more clearly and immediately.

CCXLII   This beautiful Sonnet was the last word of a youth, in whom, if the fulfilment may ever safely be prophesied from the promise, England lost one of the most rarely gifted in the long roll of her poets. Shakespeare and Milton, had their lives been closed at twenty-five, would (so far as we know) have left poems of less excellence and hope than the youth who, from the petty school and the London surgery, passed at once to a place with them of 'high collateral glory.'

CCXLV   It is impossible not to regret that Moore has written so little in this sweet and genuinely national style.

CCXLVI   A masterly example of Byron's command of strong thought and close reasoning in verse: – as the next is equally characteristic of Shelley's wayward intensity.

CCLIII   Bonnivard, a Genevese was imprisoned by the Duke of Savoy in Chillon on the lake of Geneva for his courageous defence of his country against the tyranny with which Piedmont threatened it during the first half of the Seventeenth century. – This noble Sonnet is worthy to stand near Milton's on the Vaudois massacre.

CCLIV   Switzerland was usurped by the French under Napoleon in 1800: Venice in 1797 (CCLV).

CCLIX   This battle was fought Dec. 2, 1800, between the Austrians under Archduke John and the French under Moreau, in a forest near Munich. *Hohen Linden* means *High Limetrees*.

CCLXII   After the capture of Madrid by Napoleon, Sir J. Moore retreated before Soult and Ney to Corunna, and was killed whilst covering the embarkation of his troops.

CCLXXII   The Mermaid was the club-house of Shakespeare, Ben Jonson, and other choice spirits of that age.

CCLXXIII   *Maisie*: Mary. – Scott has given us nothing more complete and lovely than this little song, which unites simplicity and dramatic power to a wild-wood music of the rarest quality. No moral is drawn, far less any conscious analysis of feeling attempted: – the pathetic meaning is left to be suggested by the mere presentment of the situation. A narrow criticism has often named this, which may be called the Homeric manner, superficial, from its apparent simple facility; but first-rate excellence in it is in truth one of the least common triumphs of Poetry. – This style should be compared with what is not less perfect in its way, the searching out of inner feeling, the expression of hidden meanings, the revelation of the heart of Nature and of the Soul within the Soul, – the analytical method, in short, – most completely represented by Wordsworth and by Shelley.

CCLXXVII	Wolfe resembled Keats, not only in his early death by consumption and the fluent freshness of his poetical style, but in beauty of character: – brave, tender, energetic, unselfish, modest. Is it fanciful to find some reflex of these qualities in the *Burial* and *Mary*? Out of the abundance of the *heart* . . .
CCLXXVIII	*correi*: covert on a hillside. *Cumber*: trouble.
CCLXXX	This book has not a few poems of greater power and more perfect execution than *Agnes* and the extract which we have ventured to make from the deep-hearted author's *Sad Thoughts* (No. CCXXIV). But none are more emphatically marked by the note of exquisiteness.
CCLXXXI	st. 3 *inch*: island.
CCLXXXIII	From *Poetry for Children* (1809), by Charles and Mary Lamb. This tender and original little piece seems clearly to reveal the work of that noble-minded and afflicted sister, who was at once the happiness, the misery, and the life-long blessing of her equally noble-minded brother.
CCLXXXIX	This poem has an exultation and a glory, joined with an exquisiteness of expression, which place it in the highest rank among the many masterpieces of its illustrious Author.
CCC	*interlunar swoon*: interval of the moon's invisibility.
CCCIV	*Calpe*: Gibraltar. *Lofoden*: the Maelstrom whirlpool off the N. W. coast of Norway.
CCCV	This lovely poem refers here and there to a ballad by Hamilton on the subject better treated in CLXIII and CLXIV.
CCCXV	*Arcturi*: seemingly used for *northern stars*. *And wild roses, &c.* Our language has perhaps no line modulated with more subtle sweetness.
CCCXVI	Coleridge describes this poem as the fragment of a dream-vision, – perhaps, an opium-dream? – which composed itself in his mind when fallen asleep after reading a few lines about 'the Khan Kubla' in Purchas' *Pilgrimage*.
CCCXVIII	*Ceres' daughter*: Proserpine. *God of Torment*: Pluto.
CCCXXI	The leading idea of this beautiful description of a day's landscape in Italy appears to be – On the voyage of life

are many moments of pleasure, given by the sight of Nature, who has power to heal even the worldliness and the uncharity of man.

Amphitrite was daughter to Ocean.

CCCXXII   p. 387, l. 17 *Maenad*: a frenzied Nymph, attendant on Dionysos in the Greek mythology. May we not call this the most vivid, sustained, and impassioned amongst all Shelley's magical personifications of Nature?

Plants under water sympathize with the seasons of the land, and hence with the winds which affect them.

CCCXXIII   Written soon after the death, by shipwreck, of Wordsworth's brother John. This poem may be profitably compared with Shelley's following it. Each is the most complete expression of the innermost spirit of his art given by these great Poets: – of that Idea which, as in the case of the true Painter, (to quote the words of Reynolds,) 'subsists only in the mind: The sight never beheld it, nor has the hand expressed it: it is an idea residing in the breast of the artist, which he is always labouring to impart, and which he dies at last without imparting.'

p. 390, l. 26 *the Kind*: the human race.

CCCXXVII   *the Royal Saint*: Henry VI.

CCCXXVIII   st. 4 *this* folk: *its* has been here plausibly but, perhaps, unnecessarily, conjectured. – Every one knows the general story of the Italian Renaissance, of the Revival of Letters – From Petrarch's day to our own, that ancient world has renewed its youth: Poets and artists, students and thinkers, have yielded themselves wholly to its fascination, and deeply penetrated its spirit. Yet perhaps no one more truly has vivified, whilst idealising, the picture of Greek country life in the fancied Golden Age, than Keats in these lovely (if somewhat unequally executed) stanzas: – his quick imagination, by a kind of 'natural magic,' more than supplying the scholarship which his youth had no opportunity of gaining.

THE MAKING OF *THE GOLDEN TREASURY*

I

In the summer of 1860 a young man in his thirties, a civil servant who worked in the Education Department, was on holiday in Cornwall with a friend whom he had known for ten years or so. The young man was Francis Turner Palgrave, Frank to his friends, and his travelling companion was the Poet Laureate, Alfred Tennyson, then fifty.

Four months earlier, in April 1860, Palgrave had published in the vigorous new journal *Macmillan's Magazine* an essay 'On Readers in 1760 and 1860'. He had deplored the new scurry: 'We read at once too much and too little.'

Reading tends to become only another kind of gossip. Everything is to be read, and everything only once; a book is no more a treasure to be kept and studied and known by heart, as the truly charming phrase has it, if deserving that intimacy.[1]

A treasure, and thence a treasury. As Palgrave and Tennyson walked, their talk of poetry must have turned at some point to an anthology which had been published only nine months earlier, for Christmas 1859, by a friend of theirs, the Irish poet William Allingham. *Nightingale Valley* (1860) had as its subtitle 'A collection, including a great number of the choicest lyrics and short poems in the English language'. Like everything of Allingham's, the anthology is charming, idiosyncratic and supple. But it is of the nature of an anthology never to seem to any of its readers, let alone its reviewers,

---

1 *Macmillan's Magazine*, I, April 1860. This essay is reprinted in the present edition (p. 451), as is J. W. Mackail's account of Palgrave's life and work, from the *Dictionary of National Biography* (p. 455).

to be altogether satisfactory in its exclusions and inclusions, or even in its principles. Palgrave decided to create his own anthology of the best songs and lyrical poems in the English language.

It was during this expedition [in Cornwall, at the end of August 1860], 'while traversing the wild scenery of Treryn Dinas' [quoted from Palgrave's Dedication to Tennyson], that the scheme of the 'Golden Treasury' was first brought forward, and received that encouragement and help from the Poet Laureate which caused the work to be immediately begun on F. T. Palgrave's return to London [in September 1860].[2]

The making of *The Golden Treasury* should first be told in the words of those who collaborated in it. Palgrave was to enlist the advice not only (though it was paramount) of Tennyson, but of two other friends. George Miller worked with Palgrave in the Education Department and was still, like him, a non-resident Fellow of Exeter College, Oxford. The sculptor Thomas Woolner was a friend of Palgrave as well as of Tennyson (whom he was soon to furnish with the stories from which the poet created *Enoch Arden* and *Aylmer's Field* in 1864). Woolner accompanied Palgrave and Tennyson for part of the Cornish holiday.[3]

A letter from Woolner to Tennyson's wife, Emily Tennyson, shows that by 8 October 1860 Palgrave was already hard at work on his pleasurable accruing.

Palgrave called in this evening; he is busy reading all the Poets for the purpose of making a collection which he intends to beat that of Allingham. I am rather fond of such books, for I can dip from gem to gem without the trouble of getting up to take books down from the shelves.[4]

At the end of the month, Palgrave was in a position to report to Tennyson:

Since I returned I have worked steadily for two or three hours a day at making the collection of English Lyrical Poems which we discussed in

2 Gwenllian F. Palgrave, *Francis Turner Palgrave: His Journals and Memories of His Life* (1899), p. 63.

3 Noted by Kathleen Tillotson in her excellent essay on *The Golden Treasury*; see the Bibliography (p. 466).

4 Amy Woolner, *Thomas Woolner* (1917), p. 199.

Cornwall; and I have spoken about it to Macmillan, who gives a conditional assent to act as publisher.[5] I have gone through the whole of Chalmers' Collection, and through several of the writers not included in it, and have thus made a preliminary list of contents, which I am going over with Woolner. Whenever this is in order I hope you will let me go through it with you. Besides many special points of doubt, I hesitate whether *Elegies* such as Gray's, and *Sonnets* should properly be included. They are lyrical in structure, and sonnets have always ranked as lyrical; but their didactic tone appears to me not decisively lyrical in a whatever strictness of sense so vague a word can bear. What do you think? The Greeks classified elegies as non-lyrical, and they had no sonnets.[6]

Tennyson proved strongly in favour of including Gray's 'Elegy' and sonnets such as Shakespeare's.

The letter makes clear that all the preliminary enterprise of selection was carried out by Palgrave. He turned then to his advisers, particularly to Tennyson, on two counts: general points of principle (as here, what should be ranked as lyrical), and final judgments, by the four readers, on each poem's candidacy. These judgments are reported in the manuscript (now in the British Library, thanks to the generosity of Palgrave's daughter), and are recorded in the notes to the present edition.

Woolner sent word of Palgrave's progress, on 9 December 1860, to Emily Tennyson:

Palgrave has nearly finished making his selections from the Poets, and has throughout shown the most extraordinary interest in his work; in fact he scarcely seems to think of anything else than the work he is engaged upon. He certainly has an astonishingly acute and quick mind in reading an enormous amount and extracting the best things.[7]

In addition to what he wrote in May 1861 in his Dedication to

5 Unfortunately the correspondence between Palgrave and Macmillan about *The Golden Treasury* does not survive. Nor does any letter from Tennyson to Palgrave about it. Macmillan did not become Tennyson's publisher until the last years of the poet's life, though Alexander Macmillan early sought the honour; but Tennyson had published 'Sea Dreams' in *Macmillan's Magazine* in January 1860, and it was there that Palgrave had published 'On Readers in 1760 and 1860' in April 1860.

6 30 October 1860; G. F. Palgrave, *F. T. Palgrave*, p. 64.

7 Amy Woolner, *Thomas Woolner*, p. 203.

Tennyson, Palgrave left three accounts of the enterprise. The first was contained within the dedication (complementary as well as complimentary) to Emily Lady Tennyson, in January 1885, of a volume which Palgrave had selected and annotated, *Lyrical Poems of Alfred Lord Tennyson*. Palgrave writes of his happy fortune in having been allowed the honour of dedicating *The Golden Treasury* to Tennyson, and then recalls, a quarter of a century later, not only Tennyson's assistance but a crucially influential insistence:

During a walk near the Land's End, which is still fresh in my memory, I had placed the scheme of the book before him: – but, on hearing that my plan included the best lyrics by writers then alive, and only the best, he at once barred any pieces by him from insertion within an anthology bearing a title which, in itself, seemed to claim the honours of excellence for the contents. And so very large a portion of admissible contemporary song was banished by this decree, that limitation to the poetry of those no longer alive became inevitable.[8]

At which point Palgrave expressed his confidence in this later venture, his selection of *Lyrical Poems* by Tennyson (who was then in his mid-seventies), this 'Treasury, not less worthy the title Golden, with the formation of which I have been entrusted'.

In his 'Personal Recollections' of Tennyson printed in 1897, the year of Palgrave's death, Palgrave told again of how Tennyson had 'encouraged me to proceed, barring only any poems by himself from insertion in an anthology whose title claimed excellence for its contents', and then summed up the next stage: 'And at the Christmas-tide following [1860], the gathered materials, already submitted to the judgment of two friends of taste (one, the very able sculptor, T. Woolner, lately taken from us), were laid before Tennyson for final judgment.'[9]

The story had been told more fully in the note which Palgrave set down in the manuscript in 1861, the month before the first publication:

8 See p. 469 for the paragraph from the Preface of 1861 which Palgrave dropped in 1883: 'It would obviously have been invidious to apply the standard aimed at in this Collection to the Living . . .'

9 Hallam Tennyson, *Alfred Lord Tennyson: A Memoir* (1897), ii, 500.

In putting the book together, all poems which appeared at all available or likely were gone through, after my [the *deleted*] selection, by George Miller and Thomas Woolner, sometimes alone, but perhaps oftener in courts of poetry held here[10] and elsewhere. The mass thus diminished, but retaining all that stood near admission, was gone through by Alfred Tennyson during ten days at Xmas 1860 at Farringford [the Tennysons' home on the Isle of Wight]. He read almost everything twice over generally aloud to me. The book as it stands fairly represents his taste, as his opinion was the final verdict: but so severe and strict was his judgment, that if the scheme of the book had been his, it would probably have held less.

June 1861

[As a postscript] Some few poems were added after Tennyson's rescension: but about most I knew that he would have approved.

On 1 January 1861, Woolner had written to Lady Trevelyan about Palgrave's having returned from this stay with Tennyson at Farringford:

I think I told you of a collection of English lyrics that Palgrave has been making: he took his batch of poems for the Poet to give his opinions on, and says that well as he knew Tennyson's powers of insight into poetry he was nevertheless astonished at the precision and profundity of his judgments in each poem, in giving its characteristics without any hesitation, and compares his judgment to the fine touch of Dürer or Leonardo.[11]

Palgrave was more than gratified by the reception of *The Golden Treasury*. Published cautiously in July 1861 in only 2,000 copies, it was reprinted in October (1,200 copies), and again in November (3,800 copies, so 7,000 by then). In October 1861, Palgrave wrote to Tennyson. The letter makes clear not only his hopes for the book but his sense of its mission, while going on to the prospect of another anthology less constrained by such Victorian decorum as had led him not to include Spenser's 'Epithalamion' even while indicating by

10 Kathleen Tillotson suggests that this refers to the Education Department.

11 *Letters of Tennyson*, edited by Cecil Y. Lang and Edgar F. Shannon, ii (1987), 270n. Palgrave wrote in the same spirit to Sir Alexander Grant: 'Tennyson's remarks on the different poems as he went over them and selected were admirable – a kind of school of fine judgment' (22 February 1862; G. F. Palgrave, *F. T. Palgrave*, p. 71).

a note in *The Golden Treasury*[12] in 1861 that he thought it better than the 'Prothalamion'.

I hope you are really pleased with the 'Treasury' – dedication included. It sells well, and seems not only to give pleasure, but to arouse thought and discussion about poetry, which I regard as the *causa finalis* of such a book much more than mere acquiescence in any one person's selection. I have received gracious messages about it from her Majesty and from old Carlyle ... [G. F. Palgrave's ellipsis] The making the book suggested many thoughts on our poetry, some of which I have set down in a little paper which you will find in the just-published 'Quarterly',[13] and which I hope may more or less please you ... [G. F. Palgrave's ellipsis] I have now a fancy to make a collection of English love poems only, of all dates: to include a few omitted from the 'Golden Treasury' as too high-kilted – i.e. such as Spenser's 'Epithalamion', some of Sidney's Sonnets, Moore, etc. – all to be called 'Under the Rose'; the tone being never coarse, but decidedly amorous. What do you think? 'Pueris' rather than 'Virginibus'.[14]

The reading public in 1861 was preoccupied with what might bring a blush to the cheek of the young person, whether youth or maiden. *The Golden Treasury* therefore made such sacrifices as were called for if the anthology were to appeal to, and bring into being, the most stable mid-Victorian readership for poetry. Queen Victoria and Carlyle, whose praises Palgrave relished in the letter to Tennyson, were at one with many other eminent Victorians. Benjamin Jowett, the Master of Balliol College, wrote to Palgrave: 'It is the best collection I have ever seen.'[15] Frederick Temple, the headmaster

---

12 The 1861 note on the 'Prothalamion' said: 'Although beautiful, it is inferior to the "Epithalamion" on Spenser's own marriage, – omitted with great reluctance as not in harmony with modern manners.' In 1883 Palgrave replaced these words with some thoughts on Beauty and long poems.

13 'The Growth of English Poetry', a review-article on Bell's Annotated Series of British Poets (29 vols.); *Quarterly Review* CX, October 1861, 435–50. There are later essays by Palgrave which are likewise relevant to *The Golden Treasury*: 'English Poetry from Dryden to Cowper', *Quarterly Review* CXII, July 1862, 146–79; and a review-article on Alexander Gilchrist's *Life of William Blake* (1863), *Quarterly Review* CXVI, January 1865, 1–27.

14 G. F. Palgrave, *F. T. Palgrave*, pp. 64–5.

15 24 July 1861; G. F. Palgrave, *F. T. Palgrave*, p. 68.

of Rugby who later became Archbishop of Canterbury, gave it the highest praise compatible with the need to maintain the highest hedging: 'I like the book exceedingly: nearly everything that I cared for is in it; hardly anything that I did not care for.' The headmaster's past tenses skilfully play the anthology-reviewer's ploy of intimating that nothing in the book was actually *new* to one's very well-read self.

Matthew Arnold, bent on rebuking the 'freaks and violences' in the criticism written by Palgrave,[16] was both generous enough and canny enough to reach such a rebuke only after praising the anthology itself:

Again, there is Mr. Palgrave, certainly endowed with a very fine critical tact: his *Golden Treasury* abundantly proves it. The plan of arrangement which he devised for that work, the mode in which he followed his plan out, nay, one might even say, merely the juxtaposition, in pursuance of it, of two such pieces as those of Wordsworth and Shelley which form [1861's CCLXXXV and CCLXXXVI][17] in his collection, show a delicacy of feeling in these matters which is quite indisputable and very rare.

Arnold was right, and Palgrave was not so much modest as disingenuous when he wrote to Sir Alexander Grant: 'I hope you liked the arrangement and my notes &c. In this sort of paste-and-scissors authorship these trifles are all one can call one's own.'[18]

The anonymous review in *Fraser's Magazine* in October 1861 was direct, patriotic and alive to the fact that the book was not only a delight but 'a primer of poetical education'.[19] In *The Education of Henry Adams*, Henry Adams was to pay Palgrave a tribute such as

16 His censure is given in the note to XCIII (p. 481). As R. H. Super points out in his indispensable edition of Arnold's prose, Arnold sent a copy of *The Golden Treasury* to Sainte-Beuve, who praised it as that 'Charmant petit livre', 'tout un trésor, en effet, de forte ou suave poésie'.

17 Finally CCCXXXV and CCCXXXVII, Palgrave having removed the juxtaposition which Arnold praised, by adding CCCXXXVI in 1883.

18 22 February 1862; G. F. Palgrave, *F. T. Palgrave*, p. 71.

19 *Fraser's Magazine* LCIV, October 1861. This review is reprinted in the present edition (p. 459). Kathleen Tillotson: 'No Victorian anthology has had a longer life or a wider influence – more truly educational than anything else that came out of an Education Department.'

many would happily pay: 'His literary taste, condensed into the "Golden Treasury", helped Adams to more literary education than he ever got from any taste of his own.'[20] Such literary education was not only a gift to Britain but a gift from Britain to its far-flung empire. Palgrave wrote to Sir Alexander Grant in Bombay in February 1862, seven months after the first publication:

It seems to have pleased people here, and has revealed an ignorance of poetry and an interest in it – both of which rather surprised me. That it should be of any real use is exactly what I wish.[21]

Sir Alexander's reply from India must have fortified Palgrave's confidence in one such real use:

The Golden Treasury is an immense comfort out here. Hughlings and I had been talking of it for some time, and were waiting to see if it would not be suitable as an English class-book for the higher native students. I hope you won't think this a degradation. English poetry is to these people what Homer is to us.[22]

The accents of this should no longer be deemed sensitive, but it would be a misguided hyper-sensitivity which would find ignoble the thought, the impulse, itself.

The Golden Treasury won not only the field but the world. The four printings in the year of publication, 1861, were succeeded by reprintings in 1862, 1863, 1865, 1870, 1872, 1874, 1875, 1877, 1878, 1880, 1881, 1882, twice in 1883, 1884, 1885, 1886, 1887, 1888, 1890, 1891, 1892, 1894 and 1896. Until the Second World War, sales then averaged over ten thousand a year, with more than 650,000 copies printed by that time.[23]

In 1897, the year of his death, Palgrave published *The Golden Treasury: Second Series*. This, too, he dedicated to Tennyson, or rather, 'To the Memory of Alfred Lord Tennyson'; he included

20 *The Education of Henry Adams* (privately issued 1907, published 1918), chapter XIV.

21 G. F. Palgrave, *F. T. Palgrave*, p. 71.

22 G. F. Palgrave, *F. T. Palgrave*, p. 73.

23 This information by the kindness of John Handford of Macmillan Publishers Ltd.

twenty-three poems by Tennyson (and sixteen by Tennyson's brothers); and he chose to end the collection with two elegiac poems by Tennyson in memory of Arthur Hallam, who had been recalled, with his father Henry Hallam, in the Dedication of the original *Golden Treasury*. 'In the Valley of Cauteretz' and 'Break, Break, Break' invited the reader, in closing, to think elegiacally of Tennyson himself, who had died five years earlier and of whom the *Memoir* by his son, which included 'Personal Recollections' by Palgrave, was published in this same year 1897. Readers have never found *The Golden Treasury: Second Series* as inspired as the original volume. But then it lacked not the poems but the living presence of Tennyson, in himself 'a kind of school of fine judgment'.[24]

II

Palgrave brought energy as well as sensibility to his initial selection. Of the multi-volume editions of the English poets which supplied his first quarry, the primary ones were Alexander Chalmers' *The Works of the English Poets* (1810) and Robert Bell's *Annotated Edition of the English Poets* (1854–7).[25] He availed himself, too, of other recent selections and anthologies: Robert Bell's *Songs from the Dramatists* (1854) and, as has been suggested above, an impetus for the whole undertaking: William Allingham's *Nightingale Valley* (1860).

Robert Chambers's *Cyclopaedia of English Literature* (1844) led Palgrave to some good things, as did the better-known compilations, Sir Walter Scott's *Minstrelsy of the Scottish Border* (1802–3) and Thomas Percy's *Reliques of Ancient English Poetry* (1765). Palgrave knew too, the Elizabethan collections, among them *England's Helicon* (1600) and Francis Davison's *A Poetical Rhapsody* (1602).[26]

---

24 Quoted on p. 441. Palgrave's Preface, February 1897, to *The Golden Treasury: Second Series* is very pertinent to the original anthology, and is therefore reprinted in the present edition (p. 461).

25 Palgrave mentions Chalmers not only in a letter to Tennyson (p. 439) but in his Preface, and he reviewed Bell in *Quarterly Review*, October 1861.

26 Kathleen Tillotson notes that Palgrave's marked copy of the 1812 edition of *England's Helicon* is in the British Library, and that he probably used the 1826 edition of *A Poetical Rhapsody*.

But more important than tracking Palgrave in other scholars' and anthologists' terrain is an understanding of his great good sense in the principles of selection.

Allingham had included in *Nightingale Valley* nearly twenty poems by Tennyson, including sections of *In Memoriam* unattributed to him. It proved a mercy that Tennyson forbad Palgrave his poems and therefore, in Palgrave's eyes, forbad any work by poets still alive. (Of the poets included, Rogers was the most recently dead, in 1855; and then Wordsworth in 1850). There is no reason to believe that Palgrave would have been perceptive in selecting contemporary poetry, and some reason to believe the opposite, judging not only from the undiscriminating *Second Series* (1897) but from Palgrave's own practice as a poet, derivatively inferior, say, to Allingham's art.

Tennyson's taste was discriminating, catholic, and in both senses decisive. Palgrave did all the initial sifting, true, but then Palgrave's own taste had been formed on Tennyson's poems and by Tennyson's friendship. Robert Graves and Laura Riding, in their witty assault on anthologies, were genially grudging about *The Golden Treasury* (it 'has become the Dean of Anthologies, its original liberalism ossified'), and they went so far as to say that 'it was as much Tennyson's influence through *The Golden Treasury* as the direct influence of his poems which gave the next two generations a Tennysonian view of the progress of English poetry'.[27]

Yet it was not just the fact that Tennyson was diversely well-read, confident and generous of sensibility that made his influence on *The Golden Treasury* so strong and so benign. For the crucial critical fact about Tennyson is that, almost alone of our great poets in recent centuries, he did not engage in literary criticism. He left no critical essays, let alone books; his letters are almost entirely vacant of criticism, whether of his own poems or of others'; and though there are indeed some penetrating remarks about poets and poems recorded in Hallam Tennyson's life of his father, most of them and the best of them are to be found there within the account of . . . the making of *The Golden Treasury*.

The tradition of the poet-critic has been so miscellaneously strong

27 *Anthologies* (1927); Robert Graves, *The Common Asphodel* (1949), p. 177.

– Dryden, Pope, Johnson, Wordsworth, Coleridge, Keats, Byron, Shelley, Hopkins, Eliot, Empson . . . – as to make it worth pondering the poet who eschews literary criticism whether formal or informal. What Tennyson gave to Palgrave was evident enough. What Palgrave gave to Tennyson was handsome: an opportunity to vent the pent, and to exercise taste, engaging with one of the most specific and most welcoming kinds of criticism – this giving of hostages worth a king's ransom. We might adapt for the occasion furnished by Palgrave in 1860 the description which Henry Taylor wittily gave of Tennyson the poet in this very year: 'He wants a story to treat, being full of poetry with nothing to put it in.'[28] Tennyson wanted too this other story to treat, being full of criticism with nothing to put it in. No doubt he was gruffly grateful to Palgrave, as Palgrave was more lavishly to him, and as we should be to the pair of them as well as to the other pair, Miller and Woolner, all of them manifesting such creative acumen in the critical enterprise.

Palgrave's mid-Victorian taste, though it has lasted much more than it has faded, is not ours in some respects.[29] Donne, for instance, though he was known to and appreciated by the Victorians,[30] was not for them among the indisputably great English poets. Palgrave included only one poem, and it is a poem no longer accepted as Donne's. Blake, again, was not unknown or unappreciated; Allingham had included in *Nightingale Valley* four poems, among them 'The Tiger', and had added two pages of notes on Blake with very high praise of his genius. Palgrave, who was to review in 1865 Alexander Gilchrist's life of Blake (1863) with fervour and with extensive quotations, included in 1861 not a single poem.

But by 1891 there were four poems by Blake. By 1891 there were five poems by Marvell where there had been three. The year 1861, though it issued *The Golden Treasury*, did not see the final form of it. For Palgrave's imaginative dedication is nowhere clearer than in the revisions which he effected over the next thirty years, revisions

---

28 *Autobiography* (1885), ii. 192.

29 On Palgrave and Victorian taste, see the two informative articles listed in the Bibliography (p. 465), by B. Ifor Evans and Colin J. Horne.

30 See Kathleen Tillotson, 'Donne's Poetry in the Nineteenth Century' (1959), *Mid-Victorian Studies* (1965).

which not only further the greatness of the anthology but make it a fascinating organism in the evolution of taste. Over the years, Palgrave added sixty poems and dropped ten. It was the first Book (Elizabethan Poetry) which was most expanded, from sixty-one poems to eighty-four, thanks largely to the scholarly rediscoveries by Edward Arber, Alexander Grosart, and above all A. H. Bullen in the years after *The Golden Treasury* was first published.

The substantial changes came in three editions: 1883, when the newly added poems were gathered together at the end of the whole sequence; 1890, when they were distributed through the four Books; and 1891 ('revised and enlarged'). Often when Palgrave added a poem he furnished too a Note of approbation. The present edition, unlike others, includes every poem which at some stage formed part of the sequence, with a headnote indicating that a particular poem was added or dropped and when. Palgrave revised his Notes, too, often in a way which carries political and religious weight as well as more strictly literary judgment; the most interesting cases are recorded in the notes to this edition, together with notice of the liberties (usual then and for some time later) which Palgrave took in supplying titles and in excerpting from poems.

'The Golden Treasury of the Best Songs and Lyrical Poems in the English Language': Palgrave did not rack himself or cramp his possibilities by any exacerbated concern with what exactly a song or a lyrical poem is. 'The Editor is acquainted with no strict and exhaustive definition of Lyrical Poetry.' Nor is anyone else. As he well knew, his working definition may be open to objection but it works: 'Lyrical has been here held essentially to imply that each Poem shall turn on some single thought, feeling or situation.'[31]

Palgrave was explicit in his Preface about what then would fall outside his bounds: narrative, descriptive, and didactic poems, as well as humorous, occasional, religious and dramatic ones. He conceded, without flummery, that readers will differ from him about this and that case. But in general he was saved from flabbiness and dogmatism, his own or others', by three virtues: his having a good

---

31 See p. 439 for Palgrave's letter to Tennyson about whether to include elegies and sonnets.

ear, especially when it listened to Tennyson, who had the finest ear of all of our poets; his not having an axe to grind; and his holding in happy tension the two necessary aspects of a definition – a firm sense, with its danger of being narrow, and a broad sense, with its danger of being slack. Taken together, each mitigates the other's propensity to do less than justice.

Defining the lyric was not primary to Palgrave's purposes. Richard Holt Hutton, who in the year of *The Golden Treasury*'s publication became joint editor of the *Spectator*, asked in that journal the question 'What is a Lyric?', and stayed for Johnson's answer and for his own.

The passage which Johnson selected from Dryden to illustrate the meaning of the word 'lyric' is equally to the point for the purposes of definition: 'Somewhat of the purity of English, somewhat of more equal thoughts, somewhat of sweetness in the numbers; in one word, somewhat of a finer turn, and more lyrical verse'. 'I should define a true lyric as a poem expressive chiefly of emotion which makes the hearer long for music to help him to utter its very heart.' [32]

If there are poems here such as few readers would now assign to the song or the lyric, *The Golden Treasury* has been profoundly effective just because it at once ministers to and mitigates the ordinary reader's belief that essentially poetry *is* the lyric. This belief has long ebbed and flowed through the sea-changes of English poetry. A price has always been paid for it, for taking the lyric to be not just an excellent starting-point in the appreciation of poetry but the consummation and the essence. In the world which succeeded Tennyson, it was pre-eminently the poetry and criticsm of T. S. Eliot which needed (and was needed) to recover a more open sense of the forms and impulses which the greatest poetry may have. But Palgrave included much that pointed towards such a sense: Milton's 'Lycidas', Marvell's 'Horatian Ode', Henry Carey's 'Sally in Our Alley', John Gay's 'Black-Eyed Susan', John Collins's 'Tomorrow', Southey's 'The Battle of Blenheim', Wordsworth's 'Ode on Intimations of Immortality' . . . Inevitably there were timbres which Palgrave kept far thence, but not, remember, the lines which were to mean so much to T. S. Eliot:

[32] *Brief Literary Criticisms* (1906), pp. 106, 108.

> But keep the wolf far thence, that's foe to men,
> For with his nails he'll dig them up again.
>
> [Webster, LXVI]

In the month in which *The Golden Treasury: Second Series* was published, October 1897, Palgrave died. In the month in which *The Golden Treasury* itself was published, July 1861, there died Palgrave's formidable father, the historian Sir Francis Palgrave. The younger Francis Palgrave may have recalled, in the years following 1861, his father's growls about anthologies before the publication of the book which has given the name of Palgrave to the annals of English literature:

Excerpts, selections, pieces picked for quaintness or curiosity, pall the intellectual appetite. Elegant extracts, Anthologies, are sickly things: cut flowers have no vitality – the single growing violet lives sweetly, and lasts: the splendid bouquet decays into unsavoury trash, and as trash is thrown away.[33]

Trash? But it is now the father's, not the son's, achievement which might find itself disparaged as the olden trashery.

---

33 *The History of Normandy and of England* (1851), i, 119.

ON READERS IN 1760 AND 1860

BY F. T. PALGRAVE

[*Macmillan's Magazine*, I, April 1860]

Comparing the last century and this, we may notice a curious change in the common estimate of literature and of its readers. The line was strongly drawn in Johnson's time between those who read and those who counted, without shame, as not readers, and far more decidedly of course between the class of authors and the world at large. They seemed to form opposite camps, contrasted as practical and helpless, fashionable and low, or again, as trivial and studious, learned and ignorant, ephemeral and immortal, as gay or serious thought respectively dictated men's criticisms. Literature in popular judgment oscillated between Glory and Grub Street. Student was then a word not so confined to youth or to special pursuits; the student or author were looked on at once with a respect and with a contempt unknown to our judgment – more liberal, but less accurate and sensible. For no one who knows Boswell's book (and to know this is to know more of the last century than we can of any before it) will fail to acknowledge that just grounds existed for some portion of the contempt and for a large portion of the honour. The tone of that century was, in a certain sense indeed, as we have often been told of late by rather violent voices, shallow and worldly, and certain special studies (philology and mathematics, mainly in England) were unsatisfactorily followed. Yet, in contrast with this, there is abundant proof that men read and wrote then, though not on such deep or earnest subjects altogether as now, yet in a deeper and more earnest spirit. We need not, now, much value many of their results; the 'process of the suns' has rendered it certain that perfect poetry was written before Cowley, and left us quite indifferent to the Warburtonian theory of government. Yet men gave their best thoughts and long labour to the books alluded to; they were written for and found real readers; they influenced men's opinions, more or less, for many years. Any moderately well-informed man would smile if it were pretended here, that all the writers and all the readers of 1760, were of that uniformly intelligent class which we know authors now are privileged to address; yet the line then drawn between the studious and the world was traced by the knowledge that those who wrote were more or less the separate class who were qualified and trained to teach others, and that readers came to learn new thoughts or information, or to find amusement of a kind higher and more amusing than could be expected from living gossip. Books were then a 'substantial world' by themselves. They now become daily more and more a voice from another speaker who does not happen to be by. They were then apparently objects of a special belief; they were oracles conveying something not to be found elsewhere, or to be approached casually. No doubt the cave was often dingy, the tripod perhaps two-legged, the Pythoness drunk and declamatory, and the god altogether of a material order; yet there lay a genuine worship of the Muses in it all, an honest recognition of industry, and earnestness, and genius.

We have given up this superstition in great measure, and speak without any flattery of the ages which held it. Nay, to the writer, the attitude of the present century to the eighteenth, seems often to be not quite after the fashion of the folks in the parable; but rather a derisive gesture towards that Pharisee – thanking God that we are not like him, so proud, formal, worldly, and overwell dressed. We have proclaimed liberty of writing and reading, and in many obvious ways find this other free-trade much to our advantage. Nor would it be just to say that the respect generally wrung at last from the world for genius is paid at the present time with more than its usual reluctance. Do we not boast, in fact, that in our century a Johnson or a Chatterton would never have starved and struggled, that genius is at once crowned and welcomed, that our Miltons cannot complain of falling upon alien days? We believe what we boast, and think there is something very favourable to gifted natures in this universal diffusion of literature. But genius, meanwhile, is very passive under these advantages.

'Some books,' said one of the greatest human authorities, '*are to be tasted*, others to be swallowed, and some few to be chewed and digested.' Amongst our many facilities and gains in this matter, there is reason to fear that Lord Bacon's first class not only passes the others (as perhaps it always must) numerically, but threatens more or less to absorb them.

There seems no reason to think the froth of this day frothier than of old, and I am very grateful for novels and any good easy reading; it is not in the much extended attention such books now receive that the danger lies. One should differ from an authority so high as Mr. J. S. Mill with a rare hesitation; yet it does not seem to me that it is in a marked degree the mere number of new books, or the over-influence of advertisements, which renders good books scarce and good readers almost scarcer. Genius and Industry will not naturally heed the crowd in the market, nor is the difference between their works and the wares of the crowd less than at any former period. The root of the wrong appears to be, that people, unless profession or scientific interest influences them, go to books for something almost similar to what they find in social conversation. Reading tends to become only another kind of gossip. Everything is to be read, and everything only once; a book is no more a treasure to be kept and studied and known by heart, as the truly charming phrase has it, if deserving that intimacy. People expect no longer an art in writing – a genuine vocation in the author for his work, a real accuracy, a clear condensation of fact or fancy, a language suitable to the thought, and thoughts worthy of choice language. Almost all but first-rate writers (and this majority includes many who were once first-rate) meet the fashion: their works are only to pass over drawing-room tables for the season, far indeed from that 'possession for ever' which one of the books most justly so described was named by its author. The 'Run and Read Library' only too accurately fits the popular feeling. It is here that the multitude of books tells injuriously.

Really, the more books, the better possible selection for the readers; but each fills so little time in an age when every one reads, that it is natural to turn to the next on the table. I may notice that this summary process, this inability to read even novelties more than once, leads to a truly mean and miserable false judgment on many books once justly studied and enjoyed. Byron, it appears, is too shallow, Scott too popular of old, Wordsworth too dull for the Athenians of the moment. And yet any one of these volumes, to those who read in a more purpose-like and higher spirit, will give far truer pleasure than libraries only 'tasted.' We read at once too much and too little.

Multum, non multa. I have tried to say in many words what the proverb says in three. Without a pedantic exclusion of lesser and lighter matters, let a man, or a woman who wishes to claim her natural mental rights and position, read mainly the best books, and begin again when the series is ended. Life is not long; but the available list is briefer still. Putting aside the books which give special information or discuss points of theory, a few shelves would hold all the modern master-works – how few the ancient! Yet these are enough. For a good book not only puts the thoughts of its age in the sweetest and highest form, but includes, by a natural implication, the thousand lesser works contemporary. And these again we read with far more gain and amusement through familiarity with master-pieces. Knowledge of these supplies taste and judgment and standards for the pleasant work of comparison. It is books thus read which 'give growth to youth and pleasure to age, delight at home, make the night go by, and are friends for the road and the country.'. . . How modern the words seem! yet they tell that 1,900 years ago there were men who comprehended reading.

J. W. MACKAIL ON PALGRAVE
from the *Dictionary of National Biography*

Palgrave, Francis Turner (1824–1897), poet and critic, eldest son of Sir Francis Palgrave, the historian and antiquary, was born at Great Yarmouth, in the house of his maternal grandfather, Dawson Turner, a banker of that town, on 28 Sept. 1824. His childhood was spent partly there, but chiefly in his father's suburban residence at Hampstead. He grew up, in both houses, amid an atmosphere of high artistic culture and strenuous thought. He was familiar from infancy with collections of books, pictures and engravings, and when he first visited Italy with his parents at the age of fourteen, was already capable of appreciating, and being profoundly influenced by, what he saw there both in art and nature. This gravity and sensibility beyond his years was further reinforced by the fervid anglo-catholicism of his family. His earlier education was at home; he was afterwards (1838–43) a day boy at Charterhouse, from which in 1842 he gained a scholarship at Balliol College, Oxford, and went into residence there in 1843. There he joined the brilliant circle which included Arnold, Clough, Doyle, Sellar, and Shairp, and which has been commemorated by the last-named of these in the posthumous volume of poems entitled *Glen Desseray*, prefaced and edited by Palgrave himself forty years later. He took a first class in classics in 1847, having already, some months previously, been elected a fellow of Exeter College; he did not graduate until 1856, when he took both his B.A. and M.A.

Early in 1846 Palgrave had been engaged for some months as assistant private secretary to W. E. Gladstone, then secretary of state for war and the colonies. Soon after completing his probationary year at Exeter he returned to the public service by accepting an appointment under the education department, in which the rest of his active life was spent. From 1850 to 1855 he was vice-principal, under Dr. Temple, the present Archbishop of Canterbury, of Kneller Hall, a government training college for elementary teachers at Twickenham. Tennyson was then living in the neighbourhood, and the acquaintance begun in 1849 between the two grew into a warm and lasting friendship. In 1855 Palgrave returned to London on the discontinuance of the training college, and served in Whitehall, first as examiner and afterwards as assistant secretary of the education department, till his retirement in 1884. In 1854 he had published *Idyls and Songs*, a small volume of poems which has not achieved permanence. He was for several years art critic to the *Saturday Review*, and contributed a large number of reviews and critical essays dealing with art and literature to the *Quarterly Review* and other periodicals.

Much of the inner history and not a little also of the outward incident of his life up to this time is recorded in the remarkable volume published by him pseudonymously in 1858, under the title *The Passionate Pilgrim*, the *Dichtung und Wahrheit* of a highly cultured and delicately sensitive mind. The work is now little known, but is notable for the mingled breadth and subtlety of its psychology, and is only marred by a slight overloading of quotation. This was, however (and the same may be said of much of his later writing), no ostentation of learning, but the natural overflow of unusual knowledge and a power of critical appreciation which was in excess of his own creative faculty. Here, as so often elsewhere, the imaginative precocity fostered in him by his early surroundings had to be paid for by a certain lack of sustained force in his mature work.

During annual holidays spent with Tennyson in England or abroad, the scheme and contents of the *Golden Treasury* were now being evolved. It was published in 1861, and obtained an immediate and decisive success which has continued for over forty years. The enterprise was one often attempted before, and often renewed since; but it at once blotted out all its predecessors, and retains its primacy among the large and yearly increasing ranks of similar or cognate volumes towards which it has given the first stimulus. In itself, it is, like all anthologies, open to criticism both for its inclusions and its omissions. In later editions some of these criticisms were admitted and met by Palgrave himself. But it remains one of those rare instances in which critical work has a substantive imaginative value, and entitles its authors to rank among creative artists.

In 1862 Palgrave was employed in the revision of the official catalogue of the fine art department of the exhibition of that year, and the compilation of a descriptive handbook to the art collections there, and also wrote a memoir of Clough, who had died the autumn before. In 1866 he published a volume of *Essays on Art*, and a critical biography of Scott prefixed to a collected edition of his poems. Among other productions of this period were an edition of *Shakespeare's Poems* (1865), a volume of *Hymns* (1867), another of *Stories for Children* (1868), and one of *Lyrical Poems* (1871). *The Children's Treasury of English Song*, a companion volume for children to the *Golden Treasury*, and the result, like it, of many years of thought and selection, appeared in 1875. The other anthologies made by him may be mentioned here together: *Chrysomela*, a volume of selections from Herrick (1877), *Tennyson's Select Lyrics* (1885), and the *Treasury of Sacred Song* (1889). A second series of the *Golden Treasury*, the response to many appeals for inclusion of later poets, was published only in the year before [read *of*] his death. In it the selection made failed to give general satisfaction; and indeed the judgments in poetry of a man of seventy are likely to have lost much and gained little in the years of declining life. By that time too the way he had opened thirty-five years before was thronged with followers, and the new volume took a place only as one among the crowd. Two more volumes of original poems, the *Visions of England* (1881) and *Amenophis* (1892), complete the list of his own contributions to English poetry.

In 1884 Palgrave resigned his assistant secretaryship in the education department. The remainder of his life was divided between London and the country house at Lyme Regis which he had bought in 1872, with almost annual visits to Italy. In 1878 he had been made an honorary LL.D. of Edinburgh University, and in 1885 he was elected to the professorship of poetry at Oxford, vacated by the death of John Campbell Shairp. He had already declined to be put in nomination for that chair in 1867 as Arnold's successor, and had actually been a candidate in 1877, but had withdrawn then in Shairp's favour. He held the chair for two quinquennial terms

(1885–95). It is singular that during nearly forty years its successive occupants from Arnold to Palgrave were all contemporaries, and all members of the same group of Balliol scholars.

A volume of his Oxford lectures, *Landscape in Poetry* (1897), collected and revised by him after he vacated the chair, was Palgrave's last published work. His health had been for some years failing, and he died after a brief illness on 24 Oct. 1897. He had married, in December 1862, Cecil, daughter of J. Milnes Gaskell, M.P., who predeceased him on 27 March 1890, and left surviving him a son and four daughters.

Palgrave was one of those men whose distinction and influence consist less in creative power than in that appreciation of the best things which is the highest kind of criticism, and in the habit of living, in all matters of both art and life, at the highest standard. This quality, which is what is meant by the classical spirit, he possessed to a degree always rare, and perhaps more rare than ever in the present age. Beyond this, but not unconnected with it, were qualities which only survive in the memory of his friends – childlike transparency of character, affectionateness, and quick human sympathy.

[*Francis Turner Palgrave*, by G. F. Palgrave, 1899 (a Memoir by his daughter); Boase's *Reg. Coll. Exon.* (Oxford Hist. Soc.); personal knowledge.]

J. W. M.

AN ANONYMOUS REVIEW OF
THE GOLDEN TREASURY

Fraser's Magazine, LXIV, October 1861

There are some poets, not of the year, but of all years, whose choicest productions have recently been collected and presented to us, in the most precious casket that ever accompanied traveller in his roamings, or laid beside the pillow, or on the table at home. Mr. Palgrave's labour has not been that of an ordinary compiler, and the *Golden Treasury* deserves notice as something beyond a common volume of 'Beauties' or 'Elegant Extracts.' The judgment of the editor has, in the first place, been shown by his adherence to that class of poetry which admits of being printed in entire pieces; and his taste is well seen in the final process of taking from the priceless stores at his disposal, the best specimens to illustrate so much of the poetry of England as falls within his conditions. Mr. Palgrave tells us that he has carefully read through the great collection of Chalmers and other anthologies twice, in the express purpose of collecting the materials for this charming little book. With a view to illustrate the successive developments of English poetry in the most authentic manner, the contents of this rich treasure-house have been garnered up in four distinct chambers. Book I. contains the poems of the ninety years ending about 1616; II. from thence to 1700; III. to 1800; and IV. is devoted to the deceased poets of the present century. 'Or,' in Mr. Palgrave's words, 'looking at the poets who more or less gave each portion its distinctive character, they might be called the books of Shakespeare, Milton, Gray, and Wordsworth;' and in placing the contents of each book, a certain unity and harmony has been aimed at, which will increase the pleasure of using the volume to all, and will make it instructive, so to speak, as a primer of poetical education, to those who may be commencing their studies among the great English writers of songs and lyrics.

The volume includes all the most popular and favourite pieces, and in printing these, Mr. Palgrave's only difficulty must have arisen from the wish perhaps to omit them, as almost certain to be found in every house where there are any books at all, in order to make room for other choice but less celebrated pieces. He is right, however, to retain them. The crowns of poetry in his jewel-house would have been marred by spoiling them of their Koh-i-noors; we are all glad to have the ready means of turning to the best and most familiar works; nor would the collection be what it is meant to be – 'a storehouse of delight to labour and to poverty' – if its greatest valuables had been omitted.

In selecting the pieces of less universally acknowledged merit, the task must indeed have been difficult and delicate. In what golden scales must Mr. Palgrave have weighed them – how rigidly and yet how lovingly he must have watched the quivering needle of his balance – how joyfully he must sometimes have heaped up the dish – and how sorrowful he must sometimes have been when rejecting a favourite that would not bear the scrupulous test.

The few notes are excellent, but of a most exemplary and self-denying brevity. The preface is beautiful, and contains more thought in its four too-short pages, than is often found spread over forty. We cordially repeat the wish expressed in its last sentence for the destinies of this volume; that 'wherever the poets of England are honoured, wherever the dominant language of the world is spoken, it is hoped they will find fit audience.'

PALGRAVE'S PREFACE TO
THE GOLDEN TREASURY:
SECOND SERIES (1897)

IN the former volume of this selection our lyrical poetry was brought down to 1850 (including hence six of the greatest poets who have ennobled the century), but limited also to the work of writers no longer alive in 1861. We have hence now to retrace the stream, beginning with a period nearly corresponding to what has been called the Victorian, during part of which Wordsworth in solitary grandeur was the one surviving link between those whom we now almost think of, as poets ancient and modern. The two ages in fact overlap. And it was therefore my first wish to include in the same volume the later risen of our stars.

But this plan proved impossible. A decided preference for Lyrical poetry, – to which in all ages the perplexed or overburdened heart has fled for relief and confession, – has shown itself for sixty years or more; an impulse traceable in large measure to the increasingly *subjective* temper of the age, and indeed already in different phases foreshown by Shelley and by Wordsworth. From this preference (whilst the national or commemorative Ode has become rare), followed also a vast extension in length of our lyrics: their work is apt to be less concentrated than that of their best predecessors, classical or English: whilst, concurrently, they have at the same time often taken a dramatic character, rarely to be found before; though Dryden's *Alexander's Feast* and Gray's *Bard* are splendid exceptions in our earlier poetry. Lastly, while during the first quarter of the century Keats, Shelley, Byron, died in actual or comparative youth, within my present range England has been favoured with the long lives and persistent powers of our two most eminent singers, whilst few of real promise have been cut off prematurely.

Hence, also, despite this whole volume dedicated to a harvest of song more copious than even that famed Elizabethan outflowering, it has not been possible to renew the attempt made in the former book, wherein with but three or four exceptions on the ground of length, all our best lyrics (so far as I could judge) were gathered: and a selection only from the finest work of our greater Victorian poets (so far as my choice may have been happy) can alone be offered here. It should therefore be remembered that many famous and favourite beauties must inevitably be wanting from the present portrait gallery: but I have tried to make the specimens characteristic of each writer's genius. Despite, however, the wide difference between the work, for example, of Browning and Tennyson, the present series, as representing only the spirit of less than a single century, wears a certain monotony of character compared with the vast range of style exhibited in the earlier volume. Yet – and yet – after all, this little book, as I turn the pages over, seems to have a variety and wealth of power and beauty, which, its range considered, is wonderful.

This second Treasury has cost thrice the labour of the first. For nothing, it need scarcely be said, is harder than to form an estimate even remotely accurate of our own contemporary artists, whatever the sphere of their art. This difficulty, in the former book, was far less. For its contents, the verdict of Time had been already largely given, and I had also that invaluable assistance which my Dedication acknowledges. I may however add (asking pardon for egotism) that the best endeavour within my power has been made to hold the balance even between substance and form, the figure or the drapery, – and beauty always the last impression, – by spreading the choice over three or four years during which the poets have been searched and read over, and the results noted at many months' interval. Some check on a choice necessarily imperfect, and indeed convincing only when the verdict of Time has been given, – it is hoped may thus have been gained. But a personal element always remains, too often refusing to be excluded; especially in case of early favourites, and the haunting music which has seized on our youth, and passed perhaps physically into the very nerves or whatever may be that mysterious organ of Memory which transacts its secret and inexplicable life within the soul's furthest recesses.

The selection has been brought, near as I can venture, to our own day. But, especially in case of those later singers whose course is not yet run, it is all too soon even to attempt a valuation. Many indeed and bright are the blossoms springing up among us, though night-shade and yewberries be not absent. It were, however, presumption if we attempted with the microscope of criticism to classify these growths, or decide whether they belong to the children's 'Adonis Garden' of cut flowers, or the true 'immortal amaranth.' This I leave to other hands than mine in the far-off summers. I have however tried my best to fill the book with such *Underwoods* (to take Jonson's phrase) as the early Roman poet Naevius spoke of 'wherein the copse-wood is sown by natural process, not planted;'

Ingenio arbusta ubi nata sunt, non insita:

– a definition, more than two thousand years old, of the strange spell which lifts verse into poetry which it would be difficult to improve. – But here that wearisomely familiar 'tastes differ' warns that no invitation to its critical exercise more liberal and alluring can be held out, than is offered by a selection like the present. One of the worldly-wise Goethe's best aphorisms was that his opinion on any matter was immensely strengthened if he found it accepted by any one fellow-creature. But I cannot hope even as much acceptance for this book. Varieties in taste, often deeply rooted and strenuously held, will lead every reader to condemn me for omissions and inclusions: inevitably, and rightly. For such judgments reveal the power which poetry, our own recent poetry in especial, holds over us. They testify to life. All the leniency that can be asked is the reflection that to love the rose need not carry with it scorn of the lily; while the flowers of the Victorian domain are so multitudinous and so nobly large in the blossom, – like those sixty-leaved roses which Herodotus, two thousand and more years since, heard of in the king's garden below Mount Bermion, – that a limited, an imperfect garland only can be collected within the garth allowed me.

It is my pleasant duty here to give thanks once for all to the copyright proprietors or publishers who have kindly permitted me to transfer their treasures, sometimes almost too graspingly, to the enrichment of this Anthology. Should any claims have been over-looked by inadvertence I ask forgiveness. Special acknowledgments will be found in the notes.

I deeply regret, and every reader will regret with me, that I am not able to adorn my pages with examples of Mr. A. C. Swinburne's brilliant lyrical gift.

After the lapse of six-and-thirty years to complete a book brings with it an inevitable sadness: the longing for the irrevocable; the sigh for the old familiar faces; – of his, perhaps, here above all, who privileged me to dedicate to his honoured name that first volume to which he gave such invaluable aid: it is a feeling such as that to which Goethe, in one of his most beautiful lyrics, gave expression, –

> Sie hören nich die folgenden Gesänge,
> Die Seelen, denen ich die ersten sang: –

Yet I may hope perhaps for new friends to replace the lost. Kind readers! – if I have the fortune to find such – may this little selection, like the former, with whatever deficiencies, be the draught tempting you to approach, in their free fullness, the inexhaustible and invigorating fountains, old and new, of England's Helicon.

F. T. P.

February 1897

BIBLIOGRAPHY

On Palgrave

Gwenllian F. Palgrave, *Francis Turner Palgrave: His Journals and Memories of His Life* (1899)

Writings by Palgrave relevant to The Golden Treasury

'On readers in 1760 and 1860', *Macmillan's Magazine*, I, April 1860 [included in the present edition, p. 451]

'The Growth of English Poetry', *Quarterly Review*, CX, October 1861

'English Poetry from Dryden to Cowper', *Quarterly Review*, CXII, July 1862

Review article on Alexander Gilchrist's *Life of William Blake* (1863), *Quarterly Review*, CXVII, January 1865

A Selection from the Works of William Wordsworth (1865)

Lyrical Poems (1871)

Selected Lyrics of Alfred Lord Tennyson (1885)

The Treasury of Sacred Song (1889)

Landscape in Poetry from Homer to Tennyson (1897)

'Personal Recollections', in Hallam Tennyson, *Alfred Lord Tennyson: A Memoir* (1897)

The Golden Treasury: Second Series (1897)

On The Golden Treasury

B. Ifor Evans, 'Tennyson and the Origins of the *Golden Treasury*', *Times Literary Supplement*, 8 December 1932. [On the MS, which had been given to the British Museum, now the British Library, by Palgrave's daughter, 11 October 1930.]

Colin J. Horne, 'Palgrave's *Golden Treasury*', *English Studies*, New Series ii (that is, *Essays and Studies*), 1949. [Further reflections on the MS, and on changing tastes in the nineteenth century.]

Kathleen Tillotson, 'Palgrave's *Golden Treasury* and Tennyson: Another Source', *Tennyson Research Bulletin*, vol. 5, number 2, November 1988. [A report and analysis of the markings in Palgrave's copy of Bell's *Songs from the Dramatists*, used by him in selection and consultation.]

NOTES TO THIS EDITION

The title-page

The title was a brilliant stroke. Perhaps Palgrave recalled a work by Lodge from which he selected a poem in 1861 (and added another in 1891): *Euphues' Golden Legacy*.

Palgrave slightly changed his full title. In the proofs of the first printing (British Library), July 1861, it was 'The Golden Treasury / A collection of the best songs and lyrical poems in the English language'. When first published, it was 'The Golden Treasury / Of the best songs [etc.]'

'Fellow of Exeter College Oxford' (1861) was duly replaced by 'Professor of Poetry in the University of Oxford', an honour which came to Palgrave in 1885 in consequence of *The Golden Treasury*.

In his choice of poems, Palgrave was aided by the artist Thomas Woolner, of whom Kathleen Tillotson says, 'his visible share in the anthology is the exquisite vignette of the flute-player on its 1861 title-page'.

The epigraph

The Greek epigraph (p. 9) on the back of Palgrave's Contents page was not in the first printing, July 1861; it was added in December 1861. Euripides, frag. 754: 'He sat in the meadow and plucked with glad heart the spoil of the flowers, gathering them one by one.' An *anthology* is from the Greek for flower-gathering; hence, a collection of the flowers of verse.

The MS gives a 'motto proposed for Book First':

> huc ades, O Galatea; quis est nam ludus in undis?
> hic ver purpureum, varios hic flumina circum

> fundit humus flores, hic candida populus antro
> imminet et lentae texunt umbracula vites:
> huc ades; insani feriant sine litora fluctus.

(Virgil, *Eclogues* ix, 39–43: 'Come to me, Galatea! What sport can there be in the waves? Here is rosy spring; here, by the streams, Earth scatters her varied flowers; here the white poplar bends over the cave, and the clinging vines weave shady bowers. Come to me; let the wild waves lash the shore.')

For Book Second:

> continuo ventis surgentibus aut freta ponti
> incipiunt agitata tumescere et aridus altis
> montibus audiri fragor, aut resonantia longe
> litora misceri et nemorum increbescere murmur.

(Virgil, *Georgics* i, 536–9: 'From the first, when the winds are rising, either the sea's straits begin to heave and swell, and on mountain-heights is heard a dry crash, or the shores ring a confused echo afar and the woodland murmur waxes loud.')

For Book Third:

> sunt hic etiam sui praemia laudi,
> sunt lacrimae rerum et mentem mortalia tangunt.

(*Aeneid* i, 461–2: 'Here, too, virtue has its due rewards; here, too, there are tears for misfortune and mortal sorrows touch the heart.')

For Book Fourth:

> largior hic campos aether et lumine vestit
> purpureo.

(*Aeneid* vi, 640–41: 'Here an ampler ether clothes the meads with roseate light.')

Palgrave wrote of these epigraphs in the MS, June 1861: 'Macmillan would have these struck out, lest they should give the book a learned look – as well as Sappho's [122:] Πόλυ πάκτιδος ἀδυμελεστέρα, χρυσω χρυστέρα. [*Far sweeter of tone than harp, more golden than gold*] from the title page and the fragment of Euripides [quoted] which was to have been on the back of the Contents Page.'

The dedication

Palgrave revised the dedication. His praise of the historian Henry Hallam's 'heroic magnanimity' (MS) became 'high-hearted patriotism'; and for publication he added, to open the final sentence, 'If this Collection proves a store-house of delight to Labour and to Poverty'.

The preface

Palgrave revised his preface. The substantial changes are these:

(a) Preceding the second paragraph, there was in July 1861 a brief paragraph, dropped in October 1861:

For those who take up the book in a serious and scholarly spirit, the following remarks on the plan and the execution are added.

(b) Preceding the paragraph which begins 'Chalmers' vast collection', there was in 1861 a paragraph, dropped in 1883:

It would obviously have been invidious to apply the standard aimed at in this Collection to the Living. Nor, even in the cases where this might be done without offence, does it appear wise to attempt to anticipate the verdict of the Future on our contemporaries. Should the book last, poems by Tennyson, Bryant, Clare, Lowell, and others, will no doubt claim and obtain their place among the best. But the Editor trusts that this will be effected by other hands, and in days far distant.

(c) In the paragraph which begins 'Chalmers' vast collection', the statement that 'The poems are printed entire, except in a very few instances' had in 1861 been followed by the assurance '(specified in the notes)'; this was dropped in 1890.

(d) Preceding the paragraph which begins 'In the arrangement', there was in 1861 a paragraph, dropped in 1883:

For the permission under which the copyright pieces are inserted, thanks are due to the respective Proprietors, without whose liberal concurrence the scheme of the collection would have been defeated.

(e) In the paragraph which begins 'In the arrangement', there had been in 1861 the sentence (following '. . . or subject.'): 'The development of the symphonies of Mozart and Beethoven has been here thought of as a model, and nothing placed without careful consideration.' This was dropped in 1883.

The poems

Palgrave's Notes (capitalized here to distinguish them) to the poems
are more than helpful. The further notes in the present edition are
devoted to Palgrave's editing:

(i)   Palgrave's adding or dropping a poem between 1861 and
       1891;

(ii)   his proffering an unauthorized title (see his Note to
       CCXXXV), by modifying the title, by dropping or by supply-
       ing one, or by continuing an inauthentic title (for instance
       from Robert Chambers's *Cyclopaedia of English Literature*); all of
       these are recorded simply as 'Palgrave's title';

(iii) a poem's being from a longer work such as a narrative poem,
       play, masque or novel;

(iv)   a provenance for poems given as 'Anon.';

(v)   an attribution no longer accepted;

(vi)   a poem's having been abridged by Palgrave (see particularly
       the note to CCLXX); the omitted lines are supplied in the
       notes where the scale makes this practicable, as unfortunately
       it is not for XCVI, CIII, CXXXIV, CXXXVII, CXLI, CL,
       CLXXIX, CCXXIV and CCCXXI;

(vii) interesting cases where Palgrave revised his Notes on particular
       poems after 1861 (his notes being given in their final form in
       the present edition);

(viii) the judgments of the four readers, Palgrave, Tennyson, Wool-
       ner and Miller, as shown by the MS.

Palgrave translated his MS markings:
o.w. = on the whole   P? = [Print] not decidedly
P X = [Print] decidedly   P = Print
He did not give a translation of O, which must be Out or Omit; it is
taken as Omit here, in parallel with the injunction 'Print', as in
Miller's 'I should *O* the answer decidedly' (VII). Contractions are
expanded ('would' for 'wd.'), and 'ditto' is given as the judgment it
intends.

No attempt is made to indicate the innumerable occasions when
Palgrave's text of a poem diverges from what would now be taken as

a text of greater authority. Over the years, Palgrave made a great many small improvements to his texts, which are given here in their final form.

In the body of the book, the poets are spelt as Palgrave spelt them (thus, Wyat); in the index, in their usual modern form.

I Palgrave's title. From *Summer's Last Will and Testament*. MS: 'Chosen by A.T'; Tennyson and Palgrave, 'Print'. In his copy of Robert Bell's *Songs from the Dramatists* (1854), Palgrave recorded 'A. T. XX (Dec. 1860)', XX being for Tennyson a doubled 'decidedly'. (The markings in Bell were reported by Kathleen Tillotson, *Tennyson Research Bulletin*, Nov. 1988.)

II Added 1883, when it was among the poems grouped together at the end of the main sequence; 1890 placed II and III between what became IX and X; this final placing, 1891. Palgrave's title. From *The Tempest*, V, i.

III Added 1883; see previous note. From *The Tempest*, I, ii.

IV Palgrave's title. (Drummond, 'Song'.) Before the line 'Now, Flora . . .', Palgrave (see his Note) omits:

> Nay, suns, which shine as clear
> As thou when two thou did to Rome appear.

And before '– The winds . . .':

> Kissing sometimes these purple ports of death.

MS: the four readers, 'Print'; Tennyson compared *Romeo and Juliet*. Palgrave revised his Note. In 1861: 'It has been thought worth while to explain these allusions, because they illustrate the character of the Grecian Mythology, which arose in the Personification of natural phenomena, and was totally free from those debasing and ludicrous ideals with which, through Roman and later misunderstanding or perversion, it has been associated.' In 1883: 'This is one of that limited class of early mythes which may be reasonably interpreted as representations of natural phenomena.'

V Palgrave's title. Palgrave had doubted whether to include sonnets. He wrote to Tennyson on 30 October 1860: 'I hesitate whether *Elegies* such as Gray's, and *Sonnets* should properly be included.

They are lyrical in structure, and sonnets have always ranked as lyrical; but their didactic tone appears to me not decisively lyrical in a whatever strictness of sense so vague a word can bear. What do you think? The Greeks classified elegies as non-lyrical, and they had no sonnets' (G. F. Palgrave, *Francis Turner Palgrave: His Journal and Memories of His Life*, p. 64). MS: Tennyson, 'Print'. In Hallam Tennyson's *Alfred Lord Tennyson: A Memoir* (1897), ii, 500, Palgrave reports of Tennyson and the selecting: 'Between Shakespeare's Sonnets he hardly liked to decide, all were so powerful.'

VI   MS: Tennyson, 'Print'.

VII   MS: the four readers, 'Print'. The MS had included 'The Nymph's Reply' by Sir Walter Raleigh; Palgrave, Tennyson and Woolner, 'Omit on the whole', and Miller, 'I should omit the answer decidedly'; the 'Reply' was then deleted, with 'Omit'.

VIII   Added 1890. Palgrave's title. Anon., from Tobias Hume, *The First Part of Airs* (1605).

IX   Palgrave's title. There is no evidence that it is by Shakespeare; from *The Passionate Pilgrim* (1599). MS: Tennyson, 'Print on the whole'; Palgrave, 'Print'.

X   From *As You Like It*, II, v. MS: Tennyson and Palgrave, 'Print'. Palgrave omits Jaques' sardonic 'Ducdame' stanza which follows; William Allingham had done the same in *Nightingale Valley* (1860).

XI   From *As You Like It*, V, iii. Palgrave adopts the convention, here and elsewhere, of omitting the refrain from all but the first and last stanzas of a poem. MS: Palgrave and Woolner, 'Print'. Kathleen Tillotson records, from Palgrave's copy of Bell's *Songs*, that Miller was inclined to reject the poem as 'too coarse' (end-leaf); Miller 'was the youngest of the group and the most cautious in such matters'.

XII   Palgrave's title. In 1861, 'Anon.'; 1891 attributed it to Donne (following Grosart's edition, as is clear from a jotting in Palgrave's copy of 1884, British Library); the attribution is rejected by Herbert Grierson and Helen Gardner, and the poem is probably by John Hoskins. From Francis Davison, *A Poetical Rhapsody* (1602). Palgrave omits the third stanza:

> My senses want their outward motion
>   Which now within
>   Reason doth win,
> Redoubled by her secret notion:
>   Like rich men that take pleasure
> In hiding more than handling treasure.

His note acknowledges the omission. He revised the Note, which in 1861 specified the ten other poems so abridged; in 1890 this became 'a few other poems'. MS: the four readers, 'Print'.

XIII   Added 1890, with a long commendatory Note. Palgrave's title.

XIV   Palgrave's title. MS: 'Print'.

XV   MS: Tennyson and Palgrave, 'Print'. In the MS it is titled 'In Absence'.

XVI   Palgrave's title. MS (here dated 23 Jan. 1861): Tennyson and Palgrave, 'Print'.

XVII   Palgrave's title. MS: Tennyson, 'Print'.

XVIII   MS: Tennyson, 'Print'.

XVIII∧XIX   Following XVIII in 1861 there was 'Diaphenia', attributed to H. Constable (it is probably by Henry Chettle). Dropped 1891. It had been accompanied by a Note: 'This charming little poem, truly "old and plain, and dallying with the innocence of love" like that spoken of in *Twelfth Night*, is taken, with [VII, XX, XXVII, XLV, and LIII], from the most characteristic collection of Elizabeth's reign, "England's Helicon", first published in 1600.' MS: Tennyson, 'Print?'; Palgrave, Woolner and Miller, 'Print'. In Hallam Tennyson's memoir of Tennyson, ii, 500, Palgrave says that dropping this poem in 1891 carried out Tennyson's judgment in 1861.

XIX   Palgrave's title, as is the spelling Rosaline, for the rhyme, where Lodge had Rosalynde. From *Euphues' Golden Legacy* (1590). MS: the four readers, 'Print'; Palgrave reported of Tennyson: 'new to him and much admired'. Tennyson queried the readings 'like to' (stanza 2) – 'two?', and 'orbs' (stanza 3) – 'globes'. Palgrave added: '*orbs* however is the right reading – as given in Singer's reprint'.

XX   Palgrave's title. ('To Colin Cloute'.) Generally agreed to be by Anthony Munday. From *England's Helicon* (1600). MS: Palgrave and Woolner, 'Print'.

XXI   Added 1890. Palgrave's title. Anon., from John Wilbye, *Madrigals* (1598).

XXII   Added 1883. Palgrave's title. From John Dowland, *Third Book of Songs* (1603).

XXIII   Palgrave's title. MS: Tennyson, 'Print'.

XXIV   Palgrave's title. MS: Tennyson, 'Print'.

XXV   Added 1890. Palgrave's title.

XXVI   Added 1891. Palgrave's title.

XXVII   Palgrave's title. From *Love's Labour's Lost*, IV, iii. MS: the four readers, 'Print'.

XXVIII   Palgrave's title. MS: the four readers, 'Print', with Tennyson's X (decidedly). The recto is dated 6 Feb. 1861.

XXIX   From the sequence *Aurora*. MS: Palgrave, Woolner and Miller, 'Print'; Tennyson, 'Print on the whole I suppose but commonplace'. The MS, here dated 6 Feb. 1861, is also marked 'Omit??'

XXX   Added 1891. Palgrave's copy of 1890 (British Library) has a pencil note, deleted, which indicates that he thought at first of placing the poem after LVIII. Palgrave's title. Anon., from John Dowland, *Second Book of Songs* (1600).

XXXI   Palgrave's title; in the first three printings in 1861 (July, Oct., Nov.), Palgrave titled it 'Man's Love'. MS: Tennyson, 'Print'.

XXXII   Palgrave's title, but Puttenham introduced it as 'the ditty made by the noble knight Sir Philip Sidney'. MS: Palgrave, 'Print on the whole' and 'Print?'; the others, 'Print'.

XXXIII   Added 1890, when it was placed between LXXII and LXXIII; this final placing, 1891. Palgrave's title. Anon., from J. Danyel, *Songs for the Lute* (1606). Palgrave prints only the middle stanza of three. The first runs:

> Let not Chloris think, because
> She hath unvassel'd me,
> That her beauty can give laws
> To others that are free:
> I was made to be the prey
> And booty of her eyes!
> In my bosom, she may say,
> Her greatest kingdom lies.

And the third stanza:

> O then why
> Should she fly
> From him to whom her sight
> Doth add so much above her might?
> Why should not she
> Still joy to reign in me?

XXXIV Palgrave's title. From Davison, *A Poetical Rhapsody* (1602), where it is attributed to 'I.S'; there is no evidence that it is by Joshua Sylvester. MS: Palgrave, Woolner and Miller, 'Print'.

XXXV Palgrave's title. From *Twelfth Night*, II, iii. MS: Palgrave and Woolner, 'Print'. The MS had at first, then deleted, a title 'Against Delaying'.

XXXVI Added 1890. Palgrave's title. Anon., from Dowland, *Second Book of Songs* (1600). Palgrave omits the third stanza:

> Within this pack pins, points, laces and gloves
> And divers toys fitting a country fair,
> But my heart, wherein duty serves and loves,
> Turtles and twins, court's brood, a heavenly pair –
> Happy the heart that thinks of no removes!
> Of no removes!

XXXVII Palgrave's title. From *Love's Labour's Lost*, V, ii; this is the Winter half of the song, Spring not being included by Palgrave, 'presumably because of the *double entendre* of "Cuckoo"' [cuckold] (Kathleen Tillotson). MS: Tennyson, Palgrave, and Woolner, 'Print'; the marking in Bell's *Songs*, 'O.M.P', 'probably means that Miller said "out"' (Kathleen Tillotson).

XXXVIII   MS: Tennyson, 'Print'. In the MS it is titled 'Old Age'.

XXXIX   Palgrave's title in 1891; in 1861, he titled it 'Remembrance'. MS: Tennyson, 'Print'.

XL   Added 1883. Palgrave's title.

XLI   Palgrave's title. MS: Tennyson, 'Print'.

XLII   MS (dated here 20 May 1861): Tennyson and Palgrave, 'Print'. MS: 'To be substituted for "When, in disgrace . . ."' (Shakespeare's Sonnet 29); proofs of the first printing, 1861 (British Library), have XLII, 'Farewell!. . .', printed and pasted over 'When in disgrace . . .' (XVI; see the note).

XLIII   Palgrave's title. MS: Tennyson, 'Print'. The MS went through several titles: first, 'The Lord of Himself'; next, 'The Self-contained Nature'; finally, 'Apathetica'.

XLIV   Palgrave's title. Palgrave revised the Note. In 1861: 'It was long before English Poetry returned to the charming simplicity of this and a few other poems by Wyat.' In 1883: 'Renaissance influences long impeded the return of English poets to the charming realism of this', etc. MS (dated here 13 Feb. [1861]): Tennyson, 'Print on the whole'; Palgrave, 'Print?'; Woolner, '? too slight by far'; deleted, 'Omit'.

XLV   Palgrave's title. There is a version in fifty-eight lines in Barnfield's *Poems in Divers Humours* (1598); Palgrave follows *England's Helicon* (1600). MS: Tennyson, 'Print on the whole'; Palgrave, '??'; Woolner and Miller, 'Print'. Palgrave added: 'Would omit – too vague and formless: and doubtful whether it is the whole poem.'

XLVI   MS: Tennyson, 'Print X' (decidedly); Palgrave and Woolner, 'Print on the whole'; Miller, 'Print'.

XLVII   Added 1890 with a commendatory Note.

XLVIII   Palgrave's title in 1890; in 1861, he titled it 'Madrigal'. From *Measure for Measure*, IV, i. MS: Tennyson, Palgrave and Woolner, 'Print'.

XLIX   Palgrave's title. MS: Tennyson, 'Print X' (decidedly); the others, 'Print'.

L   Added 1890. Palgrave's title.

LI   Palgrave's title. MS: Tennyson, 'Print'.

LII   Added 1890 with a commendatory Note.

LIII   Palgrave's title. ('Philon the Shepherd. His Song'.) Anon., from William Byrd, *Songs of Sundry Natures* (1589), and *England's Helicon*. MS: Palgrave, Woolner and Miller, 'Print'.

LIV   Added 1890. Palgrave's title. Anon., from Robert Jones, *The Muses' Garden for Delights* (1610).

LIV∧LV   Following LIII in 1861 (LIV not yet being included) there was 'A Renunciation' ('If women could be fair'), by E. Vere, Earl of Oxford. Dropped 1891, when LV was added. Palgrave's title. It had been accompanied by a Note: '*haggards*: the least tameable hawks'. MS: Tennyson, 'Print X' (decidedly); the others, 'Print'.

LV   Added 1891, when 'If women could be fair' (given the same title by Palgrave, 'A Renunciation') was dropped.

LVI   From *As You Like It*, II, vii. MS: the four readers, 'Print', with Tennyson adding the injunction to print 'Sigh no more', from *Much Ado about Nothing*, II, iii. (This song was not included.)

LVII   Added 1891. Anon., from *The Arbour of Amorous Devices* (1597); possibly by Nicholas Breton (see Palgrave's Note).

LVIII   Added 1890.

LIX   Added 1890. Palgrave's title.

LX   Added 1891. A pencil note in Palgrave's copy of 1890 (British Library) shows that he thought of placing it to follow LXXIII.

LXI   Palgrave's title from 1891; in 1861, 'Madrigal' (Drummond's title), and in 1890, 'Lost Love'. MS: Tennyson, 'Print X' (decidedly); the others, 'Print'. Againt the phrase 'Who caitiffs scorns', Tennyson remarked 'harsh'.

LXII   Palgrave's title. From *Twelfth Night*, II, iv. MS: the four readers, 'Print'.

LXIII   Palgrave's title. In 1861, it followed XLIX; final placing, 1890. MS: Tennyson, 'Print ? – falls off'; Palgrave, 'Print'; Woolner, 'Print on the whole'; Miller, 'Print?'

LXIV   Palgrave's title (changed in the MS from 'Imogen'). From *Cymbeline*, IV, ii, omitting the final stanza:

> No exorciser harm thee!
> Nor no witchcraft charm thee!
> Ghost unlaid forbear thee!
> Nothing ill come near thee!
> Quiet consummation have,
> And renowned be thy grave!

MS: the four readers, 'Print'.

LXV   Palgrave's title (changed in the MS from 'A Dirge'). From *The Tempest*, I, ii. MS: Tennyson and Woolner, 'Print'; Palgrave and Miller, 'Omit', with Palgrave adding 'extract'. In Palgrave's copy of Bell's *Songs*, 'Miller was the only doubter: "beautiful but part of play"' (Kathleen Tillotson).

LXVI   Palgrave's title (changed in the MS from 'A Dirge'). From *The White Devil*, V, iv. MS: Tennyson and Palgrave, 'Print'; Woolner, 'Print?'; Miller, 'Print on the whole'.

LXVII   Palgrave's title. MS: no markings.

LXVIII   Palgrave's title. MS: Tennyson, 'Print'.

LXIX   Palgrave's title in 1890; in 1861, he titled it 'Madrigal'. From *The Merchant of Venice*, III, ii. MS: Tennyson, 'Print X' (decidedly); the others, 'Print', with Palgrave adding '? Is it not too much like an extract?' In Palgrave's copy of Bell's *Songs*, Palgrave twice queried it, and Miller asked 'Why not' (Kathleen Tillotson).

LXX   Added 1890. Palgrave's title. Anon., from John Wilbye, *Madrigals* (1598).

LXXI   Added 1891. From *Euphues' Golden Legacy* (1590).

LXXII   Palgrave's title. (Lyly, 'Song by Apelles'.) From *Campaspe*, III, v. MS: Tennyson, 'Print X *decidedly*' – 'one of the most elegant things in English'; Palgrave, 'Print'; Woolner and Miller, 'Omit', with 'clever mannerism' written below.

LXXIII   From *The Rape of Lucrece*. MS: Tennyson, 'Print X' (decidedly); the others, 'Print'.

LXXIV Palgrave revised his Note. In 1861 he followed the first sentence with this comment only: 'Although beautiful, it is inferior to the "Epithalamion" on Spenser's own marriage, – omitted with great reluctance as not in harmony with modern manners.' In 1883 this was replaced by Palgrave's thoughts on Beauty and on long poems. See his letter to Tennyson, October 1861, on the 'Epithalamion' and other love poems judged 'too high-kilted' for *The Golden Treasury* (above, p. 442). MS: Tennyson, Palgrave and (probably) Woolner, 'Print'.

LXXV Palgrave's title. From *The Pleasant Comedy of Patient Grissil*, I, ii. MS: Tennyson, 'Print on the whole'; Palgrave, 'Print'. The markings in Palgrave's copy of Bell's *Songs from the Dramatists* suggest that Palgrave queried it, Miller voted against it, and Tennyson (apparently) supported it decidedly (Kathleen Tillotson).

LXXVI Added 1890. Palgrave's title.

LXXVII MS: the four readers, 'Print'.

LXXVIII Palgrave's title. In the second line, *Sonnets* (1609) has 'My sinfull earth these . . .'; in 1861 Palgrave adopted the emendation '[Fool'd by]', and in 1891 '[Foil'd by]'. MS: Tennyson and (it seems) Woolner, 'Print'.

LXXVIII, LXXIX Following LXXVIII in 1861 was 'Life' ('The World's a bubble . . .'), by Lord Bacon. Dropped 1890, when LXXIX was added. Palgrave's title. It had been accompanied by a Note: 'A fine example of a peculiar class of Poetry: – that written by thoughtful men who practised this Art but little. Wotton's, [XCV], is another. Jeremy Taylor, Bishop Berkeley, Dr. Johnson, Lord Macaulay, have left similar specimens.' When he dropped the poem, Palgrave simply moved the Note to accompany Wotton's poem, XCV. MS (20 Feb. 1861): Palgrave, Woolner and Miller, 'Print'.

LXXIX Added 1890, when 'The World's a bubble . . .' was dropped (see the previous note and Palgrave's Note which mentions Bacon).

LXXX Palgrave's title. (Drummond, untitled till 1630, when 'The Book of the World'.) MS: Tennyson, 'Print on the whole'; Palgrave and Woolner, 'Print'; Miller, 'Print?'

LXXXI   MS: the four readers, 'Print'.

LXXXII   Palgrave's title. MS: Tennyson, 'Print'.

LXXXIII   Added 1890. Palgrave's title.

LXXXIV   Palgrave's title. (Drummond, untitled till 1630, when in the contents as 'For the Baptist'.) MS: Tennyson, 'Print on the whole'; Palgrave and Woolner, 'Print?'; Miller, '? or Omit'.

LXXXV   Palgrave revised his Note. In 1861 the commentary on Osiris and Horus ended: 'It suited the genius of Milton's time to regard this primaeval poetry and philosophy of the seasons, which has a further reference to the contest of Good and Evil in Creation, as a malignant idolatry. Shelley's Chorus in *Hellas*, "Worlds on worlds", treats the subject in a larger and sweeter spirit.' This part of the Note was dropped in 1883. MS: the four readers, 'Print'.

LXXXVI   MS: the four readers, 'Print'.

LXXXVII   Palgrave revised his Note. Compare the 1883 account of the sonnet form (see p. 419) with the 1861 Note: 'Readers should observe that, unlike our sonnets of the sixteenth century, it is constructed on the original Italian or Provençal model, – unquestionably far superior to the imperfect form employed by Shakespeare and Drummond.' MS: the four readers, 'Print'.

LXXXVIII   Palgrave revised his Note, adding in 1883 the commentary on Marvell's having been deceived by Cromwell (see p. 419), to replace the brief 1861 comment: 'Hence the prophecies, not strictly fulfilled, of his deference to the Parliament, in stanzas 21–24'. MS: Tennyson, Palgrave and Woolner, 'Print'. Palgrave added: 'First shown to me by A. Tennyson who had long admired it and read it to Carlyle'; at the end of the poem, 'Farringford [Tennyson's home on the Isle of Wight]. Xmas 1860'.

LXXXIX   Palgrave's subtitle, adapting Milton's introductory words of 1645: 'In this monody the author bewails a learned friend, unfortunately drowned in his passage from Chester on the Irish Seas, 1637.' Palgrave added the date '1637' in 1890. Palgrave revised his Note, adding in 1883 (following 'direct Christian images'): 'Yet the poem, if it gains in historical interest, suffers in poetry by the harsh intrusion of the writer's narrow and violent theological politics'. Along the same lines, he revised the gloss on 'the grim wolf', which in 1861 had read simply 'Popery', to become instead in 1883 'the Puritans of the time were excited to alarm and persecution by a few conversions to Roman Catholicism which had recently occurred'. And where his 1861 Note had run: 'to foretell "the ruin of our corrupted clergy, then in their heighth"', this became in 1883: 'to foretell "the ruin of our corrupted clergy", as Milton regarded them, "then in their heighth"'. There is an odd slip in his Note to 'the Cam': 'put for King's University' (Cambridge University / King's College). MS: Tennyson, 'Print XXX' (thrice decidedly) – 'he would not hear of the book unless it had this, the Allegro and Penseroso, and Gray's Elegy – how often he has read it aloud to me, – and how admirably!' The other readers, 'Print'.

XC MS: Tennyson, 'Print?? on the whole'; then '"decidedly" 2nd time'; Palgrave and Woolner, 'Print'; Miller, 'Omit – What is there to recommend it?' By the last line there is a comment (probably Palgrave's): 'Pity that this is obscure'. (Another, longer, version of the poem has this line as 'Forgotten, dead, disconsolate'.)

XCI Palgrave's title. (The MS titles it 'The Unavoidable'.) From *Cupid and Death*. MS: Tennyson, Palgrave and Woolner, 'Print'; Miller, 'Omit'. The comment added is probably Tennyson's: 'It is quite different from the other' (meaning XCII). In Palgrave's copy of Bell's *Songs*, Miller wrote 'No', and Palgrave wavered, apparently because of the similarity to XCII (Kathleen Tillotson).

XCII Palgrave's title. From *The Contention of Ajax and Ulysses*, scene iii. MS (Farringford, Xmas 1860): Tennyson, 'Print X' (decidedly); the others, 'Print'.

XCIII Palgrave revised his Note, dropping in 1883 the remark of 1861 about Alexander: 'He was as incapable of appreciating the Poet [Pindar] as Lewis XIV of appreciating Racine: but even the narrow and barbarian mind of Alexander could understand the advantage of a showy act of homage to Poetry.' In 'The Literary Influence of Academies', Matthew Arnold in 1864 had deplored this note: 'A note like that I call a freak or a violence; if this disparaging view of Alexander and Louis XIV, so unlike the current view, is wrong, – if the current view is, after all, the truer one of them, – the note is a freak. But, even if its disparaging view is right, the note is a violence; for, abandoning the true mode of intellectual action – persuasion, the instilment of conviction, – it simply astounds and irritates the hearer by contradicting, without a word of proof or preparation, his fixed and familiar notions; and this is mere violence. In either case, the fitness, the measure, the centrality, which is the soul of all good criticism, is lost, and the note of provinciality shows itself.' MS: Tennyson, Palgrave and (probably) Woolner, 'Print'.

XCIV   Not Milton's title but traditional. MS: the four readers, 'Print'.

XCV   MS: Palgrave and Woolner, 'Print'; Miller, '?'. In the margin is noted 'Allingham', meaning that the poem had been included in William Allingham's *Nightingale Valley* (1860), Palgrave's immediate precursor in his enterprise as anthologist; Allingham's subtitle is 'A collection, including a great number of the choicest lyrics and short poems in the English language'.

XCVI   Palgrave's title. These are lines 65–74 of 'To the Immortal Memory of Sir Lucius Cary and Sir H. Morison', a poem of 128 lines. Added to the MS (here dated 12 March 1861); no markings.

XCVII   Palgrave's title. (Herbert, 'The Pulley'.) The MS has the title 'Pandora' (revised from 'A New [Pandora?]'). MS: the four readers, 'Print'.

XCVIII   Palgrave revised his Note. In 1861: 'Vaughan's beautiful though quaint verses should be compared with Wordsworth's great Ode, No. [CCCXXXVIII].' In 1883: 'These beautiful verses should be compared with Wordsworth's great Ode on *Immortality*: and a copy of Vaughan's very rare little volume appears in the list of Wordsworth's library. – In imaginative intensity, Vaughan stands beside his contemporary Marvell.' MS: Tennyson, 'Print X' (decidedly), 'who admired it much' (deleted is the comment 'if not too theological'); the others, 'Print'.

XCIX   Not Milton's title but traditional. MS: Tennyson, '? lyrical'; the others, 'Print'.

C   Not Milton's title but traditional. MS: Tennyson, '? lyrical'; the others, 'Print'.

CI   Added 1890.

CII   From *Cynthia's Revels*, V, vi. MS: the four readers, 'Print'.

CIII   Crashaw's title: 'Wishes. To His Supposed Mistress'. These are sixty-three lines (their ordering changed on occasion) from a poem of 126 lines. MS: Tennyson, 'Print on the whole'; the others, 'Print'.

CIV   Palgrave's title. (Changed in the MS from 'The Great Adventurer'.) From Percy's *Reliques*. MS: Tennyson, 'Print X' (decidedly) – 'a very fine thing'; Palgrave, 'Print?'; Woolner, 'Print'; Miller, 'Print? or ?'.

CV   Added 1891 with a commendatory Note.

CVI   Palgrave's title. (In Chambers, 'Song'.) From *The Mulberry Garden*, III, ii. Palgrave's text follows that in Robert Chambers's *Cyclopaedia of English Literature* (1844) in omitting a final stanza:

> Though now I slowly bend to love
>   Uncertain of my fate,
> If your fair self my chains approve,
>   I shall my fortune hate.
> Lovers, like dying men, may well
>   At first disorder'd be,
> Since none alive can truly tell
>   What fortune they must see.

MS: Tennyson, 'Possibly print'; the others, 'Print on the whole'.

CVII   Added 1891. ('Song'.) Now believed to be not by Rochester but by Carr Scrope.

CVIII   Palgrave's title. (Herrick, 'To the Virgins, to make much of Time'.) MS: Tennyson: '?'; Palgrave and Woolner, 'Print?'; Miller, 'Print'.

CIX   MS: Tennyson, 'Print X' (decidedly); the others, 'Print'. 'A.T. after reading this said with perfect seriousness, I would rather have written this than all I have written – he admired its gallant highhearted tone so greatly.' Tennyson proposed 'lance' for 'horse' in the second stanza, 'but unhappily the original edition gives no warrant for this improved reading of his'.

CX   Title: 'On His Mistress, the Queen of Bohemia'. MS: Tennyson, 'Print on the whole'; Palgrave, 'Print' (from 'Print?'); the others, 'Print'.

CXI   MS: Tennyson, 'Print on the whole'; Palgrave, 'query lyrical', and Tennyson, 'hardly lyrical'.

CXI, CXII   Following CXI in 1861 there was 'It is not Beauty I demand'. Dropped 1891. The poem was subscribed 'Anon.', but is by George Darley (1795-1846). A Note in 1890 said: 'Archbishop Trench has kindly informed the Editor that this graceful poem is an imitation of early style by G. Darley: published circ. 1847.' It had been included, without attribution and with antique spelling, in Allingham's *Nightingale Valley* (1860). Palgrave's title, changed from 'The Pursuit of the Ideal' to 'The Loveliness of Love' in the third printing, November 1861. MS: Tennyson, Woolner and Miller, 'Print'; Palgrave, 'Print on the whole'. Palgrave noted 'about 1600'; Tennyson, 'circa 1650'.

CXII   Palgrave's title. (Carew, 'Disdain Returned'.) Palgrave omits the third stanza:

> No tears, Celia, now shall win
> > My resolv'd heart to return;
> I have search'd thy soul within,
> > And find nought but pride and scorn.
> I have learn'd thy arts, and now
> Can disdain as much as thou.
> Some power, in my revenge convey
> That love to her I cast away.

MS: Tennyson and Miller, 'Print'; Palgrave, 'Print?'; Woolner, 'Omit'.

CXIII   MS: Palgrave and Woolner, 'Print'.

CXIV   Added 1890.

CXV   MS: Tennyson, 'Print X' (decidedly) – 'who read it aloud twice from sheer admiration to Mrs Tennyson and me'; the others, 'Print'.

CXVI   MS: Tennyson, 'Print on the whole but the 2nd verse falls into sad hyperbole'; the others, 'Print'.

CXVII Palgrave's title. The poem is now attributed to Campion. MS: Tennyson, 'Print if the last line can be borne' (with !!! beside it); the others, 'Print'.

CXVIII Added 1883 with a commendatory Note. Title: 'Corinna's Going a Maying'.

CXIX Palgrave's title for this grouping of three poems, his earlier thought having been 'The Poetry of Clothes'. (Herrick's title for CXIX, 'Delight in Disorder'.) MS: Tennyson, 'Print X' (decidedly); Palgrave and Woolner, 'Print'; Miller, 'Print?'.

CXX Title: Herrick, 'Upon Julia's Clothes'. MS: Tennyson, 'Print on the whole'; Palgrave and Miller, 'Print'; Woolner, 'Print X' (decidedly).

CXXI Anon., from Francis Davison, *A Poetical Rhapsody* (1602), 'A Madrigal'. MS: Tennyson 'Print X' (decidedly) – 'new to him'; the others, 'Print'. Of 'But . . .' in the penultimate line, '*And* A. T. would prefer'.

CXXII MS: Tennyson, 'Print X' (decidedly); the others, 'Print'.

CXXIII Added 1883 with a discriminating Note. Palgrave's title in 1890; in 1883, he titled it 'Love Triumphant'. Palgrave omitted the last four stanzas:

> Nay more; if the fair Thespian ladies all
>   Should heap together their diviner treasure:
> That treasure should be deem'd a price too small
>   To buy a minute's lease of half my pleasure.
>   'Tis not the sacred wealth of all the nine
> Can buy my heart from him, or his, from being mine.
>
> Nor Time, nor Place, nor Chance, nor Death can bow
>   My least desires unto the least remove;
> He's firmly mine by oath; I his by vow;
>   He's mine by faith; and I am his by love;
>   He's mine by water; I am his by wine;
> Thus I my best-beloved's am; thus he is mine.
>
> He is my altar; I, his holy place;
>   I am his guest; and he, my living food;
> I'm his by penitence; he mine by grace;

      I'm his by purchase; he is mine, by blood;
          He's my supporting elm; and I his vine:
      Thus I my best-beloved's am; thus he is mine.

      He gives me wealth, I give him all my vows:
          I give him songs; he gives me length of days:
      With wreaths of grace he crowns my conqu'ring brows:
          And I his temples with a crown of praise;
              Which he accepts as an ev'rlasting sign,
      That I my best-beloved's am; that he is mine.

CXXIV   MS: Tennyson and Miller, 'Print on the whole'; Palgrave, 'Print'; Woolner, '?'

CXXV   Anon., from John Wilbye, *Second Set of Madrigals* (1598?). MS (24 Feb. 1861): Palgrave and Woolner, 'Print'.

CXXVI   Title (the MS titles it 'Fidelity'): Sedley, 'Song'. MS: the four readers, 'Print on the whole'.

CXXVII   MS: Tennyson, 'Print X' (decidedly); the others, 'Print'.

CXXVIII   Until 1890 Palgrave omitted the second stanza. MS (20 Feb. 1861): Palgrave and Woolner, 'Print'; Miller, 'Print?'; below, 'one verse omitted'.

CXXIX   Palgrave's title. (Suckling, 'Song'.) MS: Tennyson, 'Print X' (decidedly); Palgrave and Miller, 'Print?'; Woolner, 'Print'.

CXXX   Palgrave's title. From *Davideis*, Book III. MS: Tennyson, 'Print X' (decidedly) – 'to whom it was also new'; the others, 'Print'.

CXXXI   Palgrave's title. (Wither, 'The Author's Resolution in a Sonnet'.) It had been included in Allingham's *Nightingale Valley* (1860). MS: Tennyson, 'Print decidedly'; Palgrave, '?'; Woolner, 'Print' (from 'Print?'); Miller, 'Omit'; below, 'not truly poetry – and an extract – though no one reads the original whole'. (It is not clear what is in Palgrave's mind here.)

CXXXII   Palgrave's title. From *Nice Valour*, Act III. MS: Tennyson, 'Print on the whole'; Palgrave, '? Omit' (from 'Print'); Woolner, 'Omit on the whole'; Miller, 'Print'. Palgrave added: 'One-sided passion should be perfect if it is to be great. This has many blots and one unintelligible line.' In Palgrave's copy of Bell's *Songs*, the unassigned markings are twice 'Print' and once 'Print X' (decidedly) (Kathleen Tillotson).

CXXXII, CXXXIII Following CXXXII in 1861 there was 'To a Lock of Hair', by Sir Walter Scott. Dropped 1890. It had been accompanied by a Note: 'Inserted in Book II as written in the character of a Soldier of Fortune in the Seventeenth Century'. Title: 'Verses Found, with a lock of hair, in Bothwell's Pocket-Book'. From *Old Mortality*, chapter xxiii. MS: Tennyson and Palgrave, 'Print?'; Woolner, 'Print'; Miller, '? suitable?'. The unsuitability was its being an imitation, not an instance, of seventeenth-century poetry.

CXXXIII Palgrave's title in 1890; in 1861 he titled it 'The Forsaken Bride'. Anon., from Scott's *Minstrelsy of the Scottish Border*. It had been included in Allingham's *Nightingale Valley* (1860). MS: Tennyson, 'Print X' (decidedly); Palgrave, 'Print?' (from '?'); Woolner and Miller, 'Print'.

CXXXIV Added 1890. 'Anon.': for Palgrave's subsequent attribution to Richard Verstegan (or Verstegen), see his Notes, of which the later one was added in pencil to his copy of 1891 (British Library). 'The four stanzas here given form the opening of a hymn of twenty-four.'

CXXXV Anon., from Scott's *Minstrelsy of the Scottish Border*. MS: Tennyson, 'Print X' (decidedly); Palgrave and Woolner, 'Print'; Miller, 'Omit'; Miller, 'mighty little in it – only ancient [?]', with the word 'vulgar' (apparently) deleted.

CXXXVI Anon., from Scott's *Minstrelsy of the Scottish Border*. MS: the four readers, 'Print'.

CXXXVII Added 1891 with a commendatory Note. These are stanzas 1–2, 6, 10, 12, 14, 16, of a poem of nineteen stanzas.

CXXXVIII Added 1890. Palgrave's title. He omits the last three stanzas:

> If a star were confined into a tomb
>   Her captive flames must needs burn there;
> But when the hand that locked her up, gives room,
>   She'll shine through all the sphere.

O Father of eternal life, and all
    Created glories under thee!
Resume thy spirit from this world of thrall
    Into true liberty.

Either disperse these mists, which blot and fill
    My perspective (still) as they pass,
Or else remove me hence unto that hill,
    Where I shall need no glass.

CXXXIX   MS: Palgrave, 'Print?'; the others, 'Print'.

CXL   MS: the four readers, 'Print'.

CXLI   Added 1890 with a highly commendatory Note. Palgrave's title. (Marvell, 'The Nymph Complaining for the Death of Her Fawn'.) These are lines 47–92 of a poem of 122 lines.

CXLII   Palgrave's title, but from Chambers's *Cyclopaedia*. (Marvell, 'The Garden'.) Palgrave revised his Note. In 1861: 'these truly wonderful verses, which, like "Lycidas", may be regarded as a test of any reader's insight into the most poetical aspects of Poetry. The general differences between them are vast: but in imaginative intensity Marvell and Shelley are closely related.' (In 1890 he dropped the words 'which, like ... Poetry'.) In 1891: '... verses. Marvell here throws himself into the very soul of the *Garden* with the imaginative intensity of Shelley in his West Wind'. MS: the four readers, 'Print'. Against the last stanza Palgrave wrote: 'This stanza might have been transposed with advantage to follow "a green shade".' Palgrave added that Tennyson 'greatly pleaded for the *Lover* ["To His Coy Mistress"] – but I thought one or two lines too *strong* for this age'. In Hallam Tennyson's memoir of Tennyson, ii, 500–501, Palgrave records Tennyson's pleasure in Marvell: 'For some poems by that writer then with difficulty accessible, he had a special admiration: delighting to read, with a voice hardly yet to me silent, and dwelling more than once, on the magnificent hyperbole, the powerful union of pathos and humour in the lines "To his coy Mistress"' (from which Palgrave then quotes a dozen lines).

CXLIII   Added 1891. Palgrave's title.

CXLIV   Palgrave revised his note. In 1861, of Jonson: 'The gaiety of our age would find little pleasure in his elaborate comedies.' In 1883: 'His somewhat pedantic comedies exhibit one of the less fortunate results of the Renaissance movement.' In 1890: 'His comedies are deeply coloured by classical study.' MS: the four readers, 'Print'. For Tennyson's urging, see the note to LXXXIX.

CXLV   MS: the four readers, 'Print'. For Tennyson's urging, see the note to LXXXIX.

CXLVI   Palgrave's title, but varying that in Chambers's *Cyclopaedia*, 'The Emigrants in Bermudas'. (Marvell, 'Bermudas'.) MS: the four readers, 'Print', with Tennyson further urging to print the 'Lover', viz. 'To His Coy Mistress'; see the note to CXLII. Palgrave added that his text transposes lines 7–8, 9–10, 'so transposed by me on conjecture'. For such, there is neither need nor authority, but this is Palgrave's book and so the transposition is preserved in the text of this edition.

CXLVII   MS: the four readers, 'Print'.

CXLVIII   Added 1891.

CXLIX   Added 1890. Palgrave's title. (Norris, 'Hymn'.) Palgrave omits the last three stanzas:

> Tho' light and glory be th' Almighty's throne,
>   Darkness is His pavilion.
> From that His radiant beauty, but from thee
> He has His terror and His majesty.
> Thus when He first proclaim'd His sacred Law,
>   And would His rebel subjects awe,
> Like princes on some great solemnity,
> He appear'd in 's robes of State, and clad Himself with thee.
>
> The blest above do thy sweet umbrage prize,
>   When cloy'd with light, they veil their eyes.
> The vision of the Deity is made
> More sweet and beatific by thy shade.
> But we poor tenants of this orb below
>   Don't here thy excellencies know,
> Till Death our understandings does improve,
> And then our wiser ghosts thy silent night-walks love.

> But thee I now admire, thee would I choose
>   For my religion, or my Muse.
> 'Tis hard to tell whether thy reverend shade
> Has more good votaries or poets made,
> From thy dark caves were inspirations given,
>   And from thick groves went vows to Heaven.
> Hail then thou Muse's and Devotion's spring,
> 'Tis just we should adore, 'tis just we should thee sing.

CL   Added 1883. Palgrave's title. (Vaughan, 'The World'.) These are lines 1–7 of a poem of sixty lines.

CLI   MS (8 Jan. 1861): Tennyson, 'Print X' (decidedly); Palgrave and Woolner, 'Print'.

CLII   MS: Tennyson, Palgrave and (probably) Woolner, 'Print'.

CLIII   Added 1891 with a commendatory Note.

CLIV   Palgrave's title in 1890; in 1861 he titled it 'The Quiet Life'. MS: Tennyson and Woolner, 'Print'; Palgrave, 'Print?'; Miller, 'Print on the whole'.

CLV   MS: Tennyson and Woolner, 'Print on the whole'; Palgrave, 'Print'; 'A. T. however noticed that, like Millais' picture [*The Blind Girl*, 1856], this Poem clearly is the work of a man with eyesight.'

CLVI   Title: 'Ode on . . .'. MS: Tennyson and Palgrave, 'Print'.

CLVII   Title: 'To Miss Charlotte Pulteney in Her Mother's Arms'. MS: Tennyson, 'Print as it is a peculiar kind'; Palgrave, 'Print on the whole'; Woolner, 'Print' (probably, though it may be that Woolner concurred with Palgrave, and that Miller advised 'Print').

CLVIII   From *Alfred*. MS: Tennyson, 'Print?'; the others 'Print'.

CLIX   Palgrave revised his Note, adding in 1883 the details of Gray's allusions and the commendation of the poet. MS: the four readers, 'Print'.

CLX   MS: the four readers, 'Print'.

CLXI   MS: Tennyson, 'Print X' (decidedly); Palgrave, 'Print' (from 'Print?'); Woolner (probably), 'Print'.

CLXII   Palgrave's title. (In Chambers, 'The Flowers of the Forest'.) MS: Tennyson, 'Print on the whole'; the others , 'Print';

Palgrave noted that the poem was from Chambers's *Cyclopaedia of English Literature*, corrected from Scott's version.

CLXIII MS: Tennyson (apparently), 'Print on the whole'; Palgrave and Woolner, likewise; Miller, 'Omit' (deleted).

CLXIV Anon.; traditional, to be found in many collections, for instance W. E. Aytoun's *The Ballads of Scotland*. MS: 'A. T. allows'; the others, 'Print'; Palgrave added, '*Not* ancient', 'follow Scott – by whom T. takes it to be. Partly modern, perhaps by Scott, A. T. Ritson only gave verses 2, 8, 9, 10 as numbered here. I have rearranged it on the basis of his version.'

CLXV Palgrave revised his Note, adding the commendatory part in 1883. MS: the four readers, 'Print'.

CLXVI Title: 'Sweet William's Farewell to Black-Eyed Susan'. MS: Tennyson, 'Print'; Palgrave and Miller, 'Print?'; Woolner, 'Print' (from 'Print on the whole').

CLXVII See the note to CCVI. MS (13 Jan. 1861): Tennyson, Palgrave and Woolner, 'Print'.

CLXVIII Palgrave's title. (Burns, 'My bonnie Mary'.) MS: Tennyson, 'Print X' (decidedly) – 'who, I think, reckons it as Burns' best Song'; Palgrave and Woolner, 'Print'.

CLXIX From Scott's *Minstrelsy*. MS: Miller, 'Print?'; the others, 'Print'.

CLXX Title: 'Another [Comparison] Addressed to . . .'. MS: Miller, 'Print?'; the others, 'Print'.

CLXXI Palgrave's title. (Rogers' title has an ellipsis, 'On . . . Asleep'.) MS: the four readers, 'Print'.

CLXXII Palgrave revised his Note, dropping in 1890 the remark on Thomson: 'Yet he touched little which he did not beautify.' Title: 'Song'. MS: Tennyson, 'Print?'; the others, 'Print'.

CLXXIII Title: 'An Ode'. MS (30 March 1861): Palgrave and Woolner, 'Print'.

CLXXIV Added 1890 with an approbatory Note. Palgrave's title.

CLXXV   Title: 'Song'. MS: Woolner, 'Print on the whole'; the others, 'Print'; Tennyson 'struck out "The wretch" as false and weak', this being another eight-line song by Goldsmith, 'To the last moment of his breath / On hope the wretch relies . . .', from *The Captivity: An Oratorio*.

CLXXVI   MS: Tennyson, Palgrave and (probably) Woolner, 'Print'.

CLXXVII   Palgrave deleted the Greek epigraph (Pindar) from the printed text he was following. MS: the four readers, 'Print'.

CLXXVIII   MS: Tennyson, 'Print' (underlined); Palgrave, '?' (from 'Print on the whole'); Woolner, 'Omit' ('rather unpleasantly fantastic', probably his); Miller, '??'. Palgrave noted: 'A. T. insisted on this, and I now see, rightly. Collins' obscurity caused us with great regret to omit most of his other Odes.'

CLXXIX   Added 1883. Title: 'A Song to David'. These are lines 103–8, 121–6, 235–40, of a poem of 516 lines.

CLXXX   Added 1883.

CLXXXI   Added 1890.

CLXXXII   MS: the four readers, 'Print'.

CLXXXIII   MS: Tennyson, 'Print' – 'who especially admired its sweet flow – said he did not know why, but it seemed as if no such verses could be written now'. Palgrave, 'Print'; Woolner, 'Omit'; Miller, 'Print on the whole'. In Hallam Tennyson's memoir of Tennyson, ii, 501, Palgrave records of Tennyson: 'After reading Cowper's "Poplar Field": "People nowadays, I believe, hold this style and metre light; I wish there were any who could put words together with such exquisite flow and evenness."'

CLXXXIV   MS: Tennyson, 'Print on the whole'; Palgrave, 'Omit'. The further comment is probably Palgrave's: 'It is only tuneful and clever commonplace – verses 2 and 6 are the only good verses.'

CLXXXV   MS: Tennyson, 'Print' – 'who has often quoted it to me as a perfect thing in its way – especially praising the sweet simplicity of lines 3 and 4 of stanza 1'; Palgrave, 'Print?'; Woolner, '?'; Miller, 'Print'.

CLXXXVI   MS: the four readers, 'Print'.

CLXXXVII   MS: Tennyson, 'Print XXX' (thrice decidedly) – 'who would unfeignedly prefer it to all his own poetry'; the others, 'Print'. For Tennyson's urging, see the note to LXXXIX. For Palgrave's doubt about including 'Elegies such as Gray's' because 'not decisively lyrical', see his letter to Tennyson, 30 October 1860 (under V above, p. 471).

CLXXXVIII   MS: Tennyson, Palgrave and Woolner,'Print'.

CLXXXIX   MS: Tennyson and Palgrave, 'Print'.

CXC   MS: Tennyson and Palgrave, 'Print'; 'chosen by A. T.'

CXCI   MS: Tennyson, Palgrave and (probably) Woolner, 'Print'.

CXCII   MS: Tennyson, 'Print X' (decidedly); the others, 'Print'. It had been included in Chambers's *Cyclopaedia* and in Allingham's *Nightingale Valley* (1860).

CXCIII   MS: Tennyson and Palgrave, '?'.

CXCIV   Palgrave's title. (Mickle, 'Song'; in Chalmers, 'There's nae luck about the house'.) MS: Tennyson, 'Print X' (decidedly); Palgrave, 'Print' (from 'Print?'); Woolner, 'Print'. A stanza preceding the last one is deleted:

> The caul blasts of the winter wind
> > That thrilled through my heart,
> They're aw blawn by, I hae him safe
> > Till death we'll never part:
> But why should I of parting tauk,
> > It may be far awa;
> The present moment is our ain,
> > The naist we never saw.

Chalmers' *English Poets*, which Palgrave used, identified these lines as 'inserted by Dr James Beattie'. 'This verse totally spoils the tone of thought and shows that Beattie who interpolated it, and Burns, who praised it, did not feel the true key of the original – P: T:.'

CXCV   Added 1883 with an approbatory Note. Anon.; for Burns's version, 'How lang and dreary is the night', see the note in James Kinsley's edition of Burns.

CXCVI   MS: Tennyson, 'Print on the whole'; Palgrave and

(probably) Woolner, 'Print'. Palgrave added to his Note in 1897: 'The last two stanzas are not by Burns.' They are by a music publisher, John Hamilton.

CXCVII   MS: Tennyson, Palgrave and (probably) Woolner, 'Print'. 'A. T. decided that the note [which was to be in Palgrave's Preface] that Excellence lies in the whole *must* require the omission of "Ae fond kiss" [likewise by Burns] – after much consideration.'

CXCVIII   In the MS it was headed 'Anon.'. In Carolina Nairne's poems, it consists of Palgrave's lines 1–8; then his lines 13–16 followed by:

> But sorrow's sel' wears past, John [*so throughout*],
> And joy's a-comin' fast, John,
> The joy that's aye to last
>   In the land o' the leal.
>
> Sac dear's that joy was bought, John,
> Sae frae the battle fought, John,
> That sinfu' man e'er brought
>   To the land o' the leal.

Then Palgrave's lines 17–24. MS: Tennyson, 'Print' (underlined); Palgrave, '? Print?'; Woolner and Miller, 'Print?' Below, deleted: 'Last verse very weak'.

CXCIX   Palgrave deleted the Greek epigraph (Menander) from the printed text he was following. MS: the four readers, 'Print'.

CC   Added 1883.

CCI   MS: the four readers, 'Print'.

CCII   Palgrave's title. (Cowper, 'Verses, Supposed to be Written by Alexander Selkirk, During His Solitary Abode in the Island of Juan Fernandez'.) Palgrave omits Cowper's fourth stanza:

> Religion, what treasure untold
>   Resides in that heav'nly word!
> More precious than silver or gold,
>   Or all that this earth can afford.
> But the sound of the church going bell
>   These vallies and rocks never heard,

> Ne'er sighed at the sound of a knell,
>> Or smiled when a sabbath appeared.

MS: Tennyson, 'Print (omitting one verse)', and beside the stanza 'Omit A. T.'; the others, 'Print'.

CCIII   MS: the four readers, 'Print'.

CCIV   Title: 'To Mary'. Palgrave omits Cowper's tenth stanza:

> And then I feel that still I hold
> A richer store ten thousandfold
> Than misers fancy in their gold,
>> My Mary!

MS: the four readers, 'Print'; of Tennyson: 'to whom it is a kind of holy thing'. In Hallam Tennyson's memoir of Tennyson, ii, 501, Palgrave records: 'Presently we reached [Cowper's] stanzas to Mary Unwin. He read them, yet could barely read them, so deeply was he touched by their tender, their almost agonizing pathos. And once when I asked him for the "Lines on my Mother's Portrait", his voice faltered as he said he would, if I wished it; but he knew he should break down.'

CCIV, CCV   Following CCIV in 1861 was 'The Dying Man in His Garden', by G. Sewell. Dropped 1890. Palgrave's title. (Sewell, 'Soliloquy'.) It had been accompanied by a Note: '*fancied green*: cherished garden'. MS (3 April 1861): Palgrave, 'Print'; Woolner, 'Print?' In Hallam Tennyson's memoir of Tennyson, ii, 500, Palgrave writes that dropping this poem in 1890 carried out Tennyson's judgment in 1861; the MS does not record Tennyson's judgment.

CCV   Added 1883.

CCVI   In 1890 Palgrave revised his Note; in 1861 it had followed the words 'this truly noble poem' with very high praises:

It should be noted as exhibiting a rare excellence, – the climax of simple sublimity.

It is a lesson of high instructiveness to examine the essential qualities which give firstrate poetical rank to lyrics such as 'To-morrow' or 'Sally in our Alley' [CLXVII], when compared with poems written (if the phrase may be allowed) in keys so different as the subtle sweetness of Shelley, the grandeur of Gray and Milton, or the delightful Pastoralism of the

Elizabethan verse. Intelligent readers will gain hence a clear understanding of the vast imaginative range of Poetry; – through what wide oscillations the mind and the taste of a nation may pass; – how many are the roads which Truth and Nature open to Excellence.

MS: Tennyson, 'Print' (twice underlined); Palgrave, 'Print'; Wc ̇ ̇ ner, 'Print on the whole'.

CCVII   Title: 'Life'. These are the opening and closing lines; Palgrave omits:

> But this I know, when thou art fled,
> Where'er they lay these limbs, this head,
> No clod so valueless shall be,
> As all that then remains of me.
> O whither, whither dost thou fly,
> Where bend unseen thy trackless course,
>   And in this strange divorce,
> Ah, tell where I must seek this compound I?
>
> To the vast ocean of empyreal flame,
> From whence thy essence came,
> Dost thou thy flight pursue, when freed
> From matter's base encumbering weed?
>   Or dost thou, hid from sight,
>   Wait, like some spell-bound knight,
>   Through blank, oblivious years the appointed hour
>   To break thy trance and reassume thy power?
>   Yet canst thou, without thought or feeling be?
>   O say what art thou, when no more thou 'rt thee?

MS: Tennyson and Palgrave, 'Print'; 'Chosen by A. T. – but I don't know if he knew the whole'.

CCVIII   Added 1890 with an approbatory Note.

CCIX   In 1861 transposed with CCX; final placing, 1890. Palgrave's title. (Keats, 'Ode'.) MS: Tennyson, 'Print'.

CCX   See the previous note. MS: Tennyson and Palgrave, 'Print'.

CCXI   MS: the four readers, 'Print'.

CCXII   Palgrave's title. (Byron, 'Stanzas written on the road between Florence and Pisa'.) MS: the four readers, 'Print'.

CCXIII Palgrave's title. (Scott, 'Song'.) MS: Tennyson, 'Print X' (decidedly), with 'ballad' underlined; Palgrave and Woolner, 'Print'; Miller, 'Print?', with, deleted, 'query omit last verse?'.

CCXIV Title: 'Stanzas for Music'. MS: the four readers, 'Print on the whole'; of Tennyson: 'who greatly admires its music'.

CCXV Title: until 1890, Palgrave used the other Shelleyan title, Mrs Shelley's 1824 one, 'Lines to an Indian Air'. MS: the four readers, 'Print'. On the rhyme-word 'fail' in the second stanza, Palgrave noted: 'Allingham reads *pine*. Query MS. The conjecture of *pine* here A. T. held quite superfluous – poets are not bound by such rigid rules of rhyme.' This refers to a note by Allingham in *Nightingale Valley* (1860): 'The reading "pine", in the second verse, instead of "fail", must, for the present, rest on its own merits. We believe that the "fail", in the third verse, caused the same word to be slipt into the second, under the notion of making the iteration more exact; but such merely verbal and mechanical iteration is not in place here, and destroys the rhymic structure of the lyric in a very un-Shelleyan manner'.

CCXVI In the MS, Palgrave titled it 'The Perfect Woman'. MS: Tennyson and Palgrave, 'Print on the whole'; Woolner, '?'; Miller, 'Print'.

CCXVII MS: the four readers, 'Print'.

CCXVIII Title: 'Song'. MS: Tennyson and Palgrave, 'Print'.

CCXIX Title: 'To —' (1824). MS: Tennyson and Palgrave, 'Print?'; Woolner, 'Print'; Miller, 'Omit'.

CCXX In 1861, Palgrave titled it 'The Lost Love'; he dropped his title in 1890. MS: the four readers, 'Print'.

CCXXI MS: no markings. (The poem is at the foot of the page, following CCXX, and is presumably governed by the previous recommendations, as happens with CCXXII–CCXXIII.)

CCXXII Palgrave's title. MS: the four readers, 'Print'.

CCXXIII MS: the four readers, 'Print'.

CCXXIV Palgrave's title. (Lyte, 'Sad Thoughts'.) These are lines 17–32 and 77–84 of a poem of ninety-six lines. This poem (or extract) is not in the MS.

CCXXV   MS: the four readers, 'Print'.

CCXXVI   Added 1890 with an approbatory Note.

CCXXVII   MS: the four readers, 'Print'.

CCXXVII, CCXXVIII   Following CCXXVII in 1861 was 'Freedom and Love', by Thomas Campbell. Dropped 1891. Palgrave's title. (Campbell, 'Song'.) MS: the four readers, 'Print'; of Tennyson: 'to whom [this breaks off: supply "it was new", as elsewhere in the MS?]'. On the line 'Love's wing moults when caged and captured', Tennyson commented: 'A harsh line – how one wished one could have Tom Campbell or Burns in the room just to point out a few such slight blemishes – they would have corrected them in a moment!' (For a version of this remark, see the note to CCLI.)

CCXXVIII   MS: Tennyson, 'Print?'; Palgrave and Miller, 'Print'; Woolner, '?'.

CCXXIX   Palgrave's title. (Moore, 'Echo'.) MS: Tennyson and Palgrave, 'Print'.

CCXXX   Palgrave's title. From *Quentin Durward*, chapter iv. MS: Tennyson, 'Print?'; the others, 'Print'.

CCXXXI   MS: Tennyson, 'Print on the whole'; Palgrave, 'Print'; Woolner (probably), 'Print?'

CCXXXII   Title: 'To Night'. MS: Tennyson, 'Print X' (decidedly) – 'insisted on it'; Palgrave, 'Print?'; Woolner and Miller, '?'.

CCXXXIII   Palgrave's title. MS: Tennyson and Palgrave, 'Print'; 'chosen by A. T.'.

CCXXXIV   MS: the four readers, 'Print'.

CCXXXV   Palgrave's title. (Keats, 'Stanzas'.) In the MS, Palgrave titled it 'The Blessings of the Insensible'. MS: Tennyson, 'Print on the whole'.

CCXXXVI   From *Marmion*, canto iii. MS: Tennyson, 'Print on the whole'; the others, 'Print'.

CCXXXVII   MS: the four readers, 'Print'.

CCXXXVIII   Palgrave's title. From *Rokeby*, canto iii. MS: Tennyson, 'Print X' (decidedly); the others, 'Print'. Of the first two lines of the second stanza: 'When a boy I used to repeat these lines – and they seemed to me like a Heaven of glory – A. T. – who read this over and over again.'

CCXXXIX   Palgrave's title. ('Lines', 1824.) MS: Tennyson, 'Print on the whole'; the others, 'Print'.

CCXL   MS: Tennyson and Woolner, 'Print'; Palgrave, 'Print on the whole'; Miller, 'Print?' 'The close is almost *too* pathetic – hardly right for a poet not to suggest some relief– as Campbell does in his last lines – A. T.' Campbell's poem follows. (Palgrave reports this in Hallam Tennyson's memoir of Tennyson, ii, 502.)

CCXLI   Title: 'Song'. In 1861 this poem, like the previous one, was given the title 'The Maid of Neidpath'; this was corrected in 1890. MS: Miller, 'Omit'; the others, 'Print'.

CCXLII   In 1891 Palgrave revised his Note; in 1861 it had begun: 'This beautiful sonnet was the last word of a poet deserving the title "marvellous boy" in a much higher sense than Chatterton. If the fulfilment may ever safely be prophesied from the promise, England appears to have lost in Keats one whose gifts in Poetry have rarely been surpassed.' (The subsequent reference to Shakespeare and Wordsworth had in 1861 taken in Milton too, and in 1890 spoke of Shakespeare and Milton.) MS: the four readers, 'Print'. Palgrave records that Tennyson 'talked of it with me off Finisterre in Sept. 1860: we fancied that this was the coast Keats alluded to'.

CCXLIII   Palgrave's title. MS: the four readers, 'Print'. At the foot, Tennyson listed three poems by Keats; all were included (CCIX, CCX, CCXXXV).

CCXLIV   Palgrave's title. MS: the four readers, 'Print'.

CCXLV   MS: Tennyson and Palgrave, 'Print'; 'Chosen by A. T. who much admired its longdrawn music'.

CCXLVI   Palgrave's title. (Byron, 'Stanzas'.) In 1890 Palgrave revised his Note; in 1861 it had concluded, following 'wayward intensity': 'and [CCXLVIII] of the dramatic power, the vital identification of the poet with other times and characters, in which Scott is second only to Shakespeare'. Palgrave reports that 'Tennyson was much struck by the plain force' of this poem (Hallam Tennyson's memoir of Tennyson, ii, 502). MS: Tennyson, 'Print on the whole'; Palgrave and Woolner, 'Print'; Miller, 'Print?'.

CCXLVII   In the MS, Palgrave titled it 'Love and Adoration', then 'Love and Faith'. ('To —', 1824.) MS: Tennyson, 'don't [doesn't?] care much'; the others, 'Print'.

CCXLVIII   Title: 'Pibroch of Donald Dhu'. See the note to CCXLVI. MS: Palgrave, 'Print?'; the others, 'Print'.

CCXLIX   MS: Tennyson and Woolner, 'Print on the whole'; Palgrave and Miller, 'Print'.

CCL   MS: the four readers, 'Print'.

CCLI   MS: Tennyson, Palgrave and (probably) Woolner, 'Print'. Against the first two lines of the third stanza: 'What does this mean? A. T.' Palgrave records Tennyson's comment on the last stanza: 'the infelicitous "mermaid's song *condoles*" . . . tempted him to a "How easily could a little blot like this be cured! If we had but Tom Campbell in the room to point it out to him": adding, however, a tale how Rogers had done the same office for another poem; and how Campbell had bounced out of the room, with a "Hang it! I should like to see the man who would dare to correct me!"' (Hallam Tennyson's memoir of Tennyson, ii, 502-3). (For a version of this, see the note to CCXXVII, CCXXVIII.)

CCLII   MS: Tennyson, 'Print XX' (doubly decidedly); the others, 'Print'.

CCLIII   Title: 'Sonnet on Chillon'. MS: Miller, 'Omit'; the others, 'Print'; of Tennyson: 'to whom it was apparently new and who much praised the last six lines'.

CCLIV   Palgrave's title. (Wordsworth, 'Thought of a Briton on the Subjugation of Switzerland'.) MS: Tennyson, 'Print X' (decidedly); Palgrave, 'Print'; 'chosen by A. T.'.

CCLV   MS: Tennyson and Palgrave, 'Print'; below, 'query truly lyrical?'.

CCLVI Title: 'Written in London, September, 1802'. MS: the four readers, 'Print'; below, 'not lyrical'.

CCLVII Title: 'London, 1802'. MS: the four readers, 'Print'.

CCLVIII MS: the four readers, 'Print'.

CCLIX MS: the four readers, 'Print'.

CCLX Palgrave's title. (Southey, 'The Battle of Blenheim'.) MS: the four readers, 'Print'.

CCLXI Palgrave's title. MS: Tennyson, 'Print'; Palgrave and Woolner, 'Print on the whole'.

CCLXII Title: '... after Corunna'. MS: the four readers, 'Print'. 'The "Mary" was rejected by A. T. as a pathetic impostor: after careful study.' (But Palgrave added Wolfe's 'To Mary', as CCLXXVII, in 1883.) Palgrave reports that Tennyson 'wished the last line but two could be changed': 'From the field of his fame fresh and gory' (Hallam Tennyson's memoir of Tennyson, ii, 502).

CCLXIII MS: Tennyson, 'Print on the whole'; the others, 'Print'.

CCLXIV MS: the four readers, 'Print'.

CCLXV Palgrave's title. MS: Palgrave and Woolner, 'Print on the whole'.

CCLXVI Palgrave's title. (Byron, 'Stanzas for Music'.) MS: the four readers, 'Print'.

CCLXVII Palgrave's title. (Wordsworth, 'The Small Celandine'.) MS: Tennyson, Palgrave and (probably) Woolner, 'Print'; below, deleted, 'didactic'.

CCLXVIII Palgrave's title. MS: Tennyson and Miller, 'Print'; Palgrave and Woolner, 'Print on the whole'; Tennyson 'rejected "Inez" ["Fair Ines"] and several other things by Hood as what he called "invertebrate"'. 'Fair Ines' had been included in Allingham's *Nightingale Valley* (1860).

CCLXIX Palgrave's title. MS: Tennyson, 'Print X' (decidedly) – 'one of the most perfect things in the language'; the others, 'Print'.

Palgrave reports that Tennyson 'was much struck by the plain force' of this poem, saying of it, 'O si sic omnia!' (Hallam Tennyson's memoir of Tennyson, ii, 502).

CCLXIX, CCLXX   Following CCLXIX in 1861 there was 'Invocation' ('Rarely, rarely, comest thou'), by Shelley. Dropped 1890. Palgrave's title. (*Posthumous Poems*, 1824, 'Song'.) MS: Palgrave, 'Omit' (deleted) – 'I think rather weak and jerky'; the others, 'Print'.

CCLXX   Palgrave omits Shelley's last stanza:

> Some might lament that I were cold,
> As I, when this sweet day is gone,
> When my lost heart, too soon grown old,
> Insults with the untimely moan;
> They might lament – for I am one
> Whom men love not, – and yet regret,
> Unlike this clay, which when the sun
> Shall on its stainless glory set,
> Will linger, though enjoyed, like joy in memory yet.

MS: Palgrave, 'Print (4 verses)'; Woolner, 'Print'; Miller, 'Print?'. Palgrave, of Shelley's last stanza: 'I should say, Omit. It is fanciful and morbid, and weak in many lines – and also unintelligible': 'omit – breaks the leading idea'; 'A. T. agrees to omit'. Lord Lyttelton praised *The Golden Treasury* but resisted Palgrave's excerpting; Palgrave wrote to him, 5 February 1863:

Your objections, and others which have been made, have convinced me that in attempting to make omissions and to justify them, I have come upon perilous ground ... [G. F. Palgrave's lacuna] You will find that I *have* noticed the omission of the last stanza of Shelley's 'Lines at Naples', with all my other retrenchments in a note [to XII] ... It is, as I felt very strongly at the time, a serious responsibility to touch in any way the work of so great a master. If Shelley had lived to give an authentic edition of his works, or if I were printing one, or quoting the poem as part of his biography, I should not think of omitting stanza V. But the very beauty and personal quality of that stanza seemed to me to render the poem less *universal* in interest – to bring it more within the class of individual or occasional poems – to place it among those which require *biographical* notes, and thus to remove it from the class of poems which Tennyson and I wished to unite in the selection' (*Francis Turner Palgrave*, p. 66).

CCLXXI   Palgrave's title. MS: the four readers, 'Print'.

CCLXXII   Title: 'Lines on the . . .'. MS: Tennyson, 'Print decidedly'; Palgrave, 'Print'.

CCLXXIII   Palgrave's title. From *The Heart of Mid-Lothian*, chapter xl. In 1890 Palgrave revised his Note; in 1861 it had specified other poems which show this particular excellence: CCXL, CXCVII, and CLXV. MS: the four readers, 'Print'.

CCLXXIV   MS: the four readers, 'Print'. Palgrave reports that for Tennyson 'at the close of Hood's "Bridge of Sighs" "Her evil *behaviour*" was a slight defect in that masterpiece' (Hallam Tennyson's memoir of Tennyson, ii, 502).

CCLXXV   Palgrave's title. MS: the four readers, 'Print'.

CCLXXVI   MS: Tennyson, 'Print on the whole'; Palgrave and Woolner, 'Print'; Miller, 'Print?'

CCLXXVII   Palgrave's title. (Wolfe, 'Song'.) Added 1883 with an approbatory Note. See the note to CCLXII.

CCLXXVIII   From *The Lady of the Lake*, canto iii. MS: the four readers, 'Print'.

CCLXXIX   In 1861, Palgrave omitted the two central stanzas; he restored them in 1878. MS: Tennyson, 'Print on the whole – first and fourth verses are the only ones *good* however'; 'ingenuity misplaced. Goethe would have only printed stanzas 1 and 4. A. T.'; the others, 'Print'.

CCLXXX   Added 1890, with an approbatory Note, when it followed CCCLXXXI; final placing, 1891.

CCLXXXI   Palgrave's title. From *The Lay of the Last Minstrel*, canto vi. MS: Tennyson, '??'; the others, 'Print'.

CCLXXXII   MS: Tennyson, 'Print XX' (doubly decidedly) – 'to whom and Mrs T. it was new, and appeared excellent – as well as eminently true and affecting. They lost their first child thus at Twickenham' [still-born, April 1851]; Palgrave and Woolner, 'Print on the whole'; Miller, 'Print'.

CCLXXXIII Added 1891. Palgrave's title. (Lamb, 'Parental Recollections'.) The poem is attributed by Lamb's editor Thomas Hutchinson to Charles not Mary Lamb. (See Palgrave's Note.)

CCLXXXIV MS: the four readers, 'Print'.

CCLXXXV In the MS it is titled 'Reveillé'. MS: Tennyson, 'Print on the whole'; Palgrave, '? Print'; Woolner, 'Print?'; Miller, 'Print'.

CCLXXXVI Title: 'To a Skylark'. (Presumably Palgrave changed the article to 'the' to differentiate this poem from the next.) MS: the four readers, 'Print'.

CCLXXXVII MS: the four readers, 'Print'.

CCLXXXVIII MS: the four readers, 'Print'.

CCLXXXIX MS: the four readers, 'Print'.

CCXC MS: the four readers, 'Print'.

CCXCI Title: 'Composed upon . . .'. MS: the four readers, 'Print'.

CCXCII Added 1890.

CCXCIII Palgrave adds 'of Egypt' to the title. MS: Miller, '?'; the others, 'Print'.

CCXCIV Palgrave's title. (Wordsworth, 'Sonnet Composed at — Castle'.) MS: the four readers, 'Print'.

CCXCV Added 1891.

CCXCVI Title: 'Admonition: Intended more particularly for the perusal of those who may have happened to be enamoured of some beautiful place of Retreat, in the Country of the Lakes'. MS: the four readers, 'Print'; Tennyson 'greatly admired lines 3 and 4'.

CCXCVII Title: 'To a Highland Girl at Inversneyde, upon Loch Lomond'. MS: the four readers, 'Print'.

CCXCVIII Title: 'The Solitary Reaper'. MS: the four readers, 'Print'.

CCXCIX MS: Tennyson, 'Print XX' (doubly decidedly) – 'divine'; the others, 'Print'.

CCC Title: 'With a Guitar, to Jane'. MS: Tennyson and Palgrave, 'Print'. Tennyson marked for (presumably) commendation the lines 'For it had learned all harmonies' to 'And airs of evening'.

CCCI   Palgrave's title. MS: the four readers, 'Print'.

CCCII   MS: Tennyson, 'Print on the whole'; Palgrave and (probably) Woolner, 'Print'.

CCCIII   Title: 'To Autumn'. MS: the four readers, 'Print'.

CCCIV   MS: Woolner, 'Omit'; the others, 'Print'.

CCCV   MS: the four readers, 'Print (both)', to include CCCVI. 'A. T. however insisted on the omission of "Yarrow Revisited" with many others of Wordsworth's later poems – give the best of so great a man, – not what he wrote in old age etc.'

CCCVI   See the note to the previous poem.

CCCVII   Title: 'To Jane. The Invitation'. Palgrave omits lines 29–46 (deleted from the printed text he was following): 'query omit marked: which is not in the first edition'. (For the textual history of this and the next poem which were originally published as one piece, see Hutchinson's edition of Shelley.) Omitted:

> I leave this notice on my door
> For each accustomed visitor: –
> 'I am gone into the fields
> To take what this sweet hour yields; –
> Reflection, you may come tomorrow,
> Sit by the fireside with Sorrow. –
> You with the unpaid bill, Despair, –
> You, tiresome verse-reciter, Care, –
> I will pay you in the grave, –
> Death will listen to your stave.
> Expectation, too, be off!
> Today is for itself enough;
> Hope, in pity mock not Woe
> With smiles, nor follow where I go;
> Long having lived on thy sweet food,
> At length I find one moment's good
> After long pain – with all your love,
> This you never told me of.'

MS: Tennyson and Woolner, 'Print'; Palgrave, 'Print' (from '?'); Miller, 'Omit'.

CCCVIII   Title: 'To Jane. The Recollection'. See the note to the previous poem. MS: the four readers, 'Print'.

CCCIX   Palgrave's title: MS: the four readers, 'Print'. On the last two lines: 'she was thinking of herself and her dress etc. – A. T.'

CCCX   MS: Woolner, '?'; the others, 'Print'.

CCCXI   Palgrave's title, changed in the MS from 'Song'. From *The Doom of Devorgoil*. MS: the four readers, 'Print'.

CCCXII   MS: Tennyson, 'Print'; Palgrave, 'Print' (from '?'); Woolner (probably), '?'; Miller (probably), 'Omit'.

CCCXII, CCCXIII   Following CCCXII in 1861 was 'A widow bird . . .', by Shelley; it had been inserted in the MS (10 May 1861), and then moved in the proofs of the first printing, July 1861, from its place following CCCXIV. Dropped 1890. MS: Palgrave, '?'; the others, 'Print'.

CCCXIII   MS: the four readers, 'Print'.

CCCXIV   MS: Tennyson, 'Print on the whole'; the others, 'Print'.

CCCXV   Palgrave's title. (Shelley, 1822, 'A Dream'; *Posthumous Poems*, 1824, 'The Question'.) In the MS, Palgrave changed the title from 'The Unknown'. He followed 1824 and 1839 in omitting a line from the second stanza:

> and that tall flower that wets –
> Like a child, half in tenderness and mirth –
> Its mother's face . . .

The line (found in some MSS) is desired by the rhyme-scheme and is now incorporated by Shelley's editors. In 1883 Palgrave revised his Note on 'And wild roses'; in 1861 it went on: 'A good poet *might* have written *And roses wild*, – yet this slight change would disenchant the verse of its peculiar beauty.' MS: the four readers, 'Print on the whole'; below, 'not lyrical' (underlined).

CCCXVI   Added 1891.

CCCXVII   Palgrave's title. MS: Tennyson, 'Print on the whole'.

CCCXVIII   Palgrave's title. (Keats, 'Fancy'.) Before this, the

MS had gone through other titles: 'The Power of Fancy', 'The Empire of Fancy'. MS: no judgments.

CCCXVIII, CCCXIX   Following CCCXVIII in 1861 was 'Life of Life! thy lips enkindle', by Shelley. Dropped 1890. It had been accompanied by a Note: 'This impassioned address expresses Shelley's most rapt imaginations, and is the direct modern representative of the feeling which led the Greeks to the worship of Nature.' Palgrave's title. from *Prometheus Unbound*, II, v. MS (10 May 1861): Palgrave, Woolner and Miller, 'Print'. In Hallam Tennyson's memoir of Tennyson, ii, 500, Palgrave writes that dropping this poem in 1890 carried out Tennyson's judgment in 1861; the MS does not record Tennyson's judgment.

CCCXIX   Title: 'Lines Written …'. MS: the four readers, 'Print'.

CCCXX   Palgrave's subtitle. MS: Tennyson, Palgrave and Woolner, 'Print'.

CCCXXI   Title: 'Lines Written …'. Palgrave omits lines 27–65, 142–284. MS: Tennyson and Palgrave, 'Print'; '(*as abridged*) with A. T.'s concurrence – who said of the line "When a king etc." [l. 58, When a king in glory rides] "when Shelley comes to such passages, he seems to me to *burst*"'. (In Hallam Tennyson's memoir of Tennyson, ii, 500, Palgrave writes as if this comment, slightly differing, were made by Tennyson about Shelley's 'Life of Life!' [CCCXVIII, CCCXIX]: 'about which Tennyson remarked that it was one of those flights in which the poet "seemed to go up, and burst"'.) Beside the lines 'Far from passion, pain, and guilt' to 'That the Spirits of the Air', Palgrave wrote: 'A. T. often repeated.'

CCCXXII   Palgrave revised his Note, adding in 1890 his commendatory question. MS: Tennyson, 'Print on the whole?'; the others, 'Print'.

CCCXXIII   Palgrave's title. (Wordsworth, 'Elegiac Stanzas'.) MS: Tennyson, Palgrave and Woolner, 'Print'; below, 'didactic?'.

CCCXXIV   Palgrave's title. From *Prometheus Unbound*, I. Palgrave omits the Spirit's last two lines:

> One of these awakened me,
> And I sped to succour thee.

MS (10 May 1861): Palgrave and Woolner, 'Print'; Miller, 'Print?'.

CCCXXV   Added 1890.

CCCXXVI   MS: the four readers, 'Print'.

CCCXXVII   Title: 'Inside of. . .'. MS: Tennyson, 'Print X' (decidedly); Palgrave, 'Print'; 'chosen by A. T.'

CCCXXVIII   Added 1890, with an approbatory Note in 1891.

CCCXXIX   MS: the four readers, 'Print'.

CCCXXX   MS: Tennyson, 'Print XX' (doubly decidedly); the others, 'Print'; 'both', meaning this and the next poem.

CCCXXXI   See the note to the previous poem.

CCCXXXII   Palgrave's title. (Campbell, 'A Thought Suggested by the New Year'.) MS: the four readers, 'Print'; of Tennyson, 'to whom it was new, and admirable'.

CCCXXXIII   Palgrave's title, changed in the MS from his earlier thought, 'The Mortal Seasons'. MS: Miller, 'Print?'; the others, 'Print'. The eleventh and twelfth lines are marked: 'Like Wordsworth – yet with something more exquisite – A. T.'

CCCXXXIV   Added 1891.

CCCXXXV   Palgrave's title in 1891; 1861, 'A Lament' (as in *Posthumous Poems*, 1824). MS: Tennyson, 'Print'; Palgrave, 'Print' (from 'Omit').

CCCXXXVI   Added 1883.

CCCXXXVII   MS: Palgrave, 'Print?'; the others, 'Print'.

CCCXXXVIII   MS: the four readers, 'Print'. Palgrave chose not to publish an interesting Note which is among those he pencilled into a copy of the second issue, October 1861 (British Library):

that imperial palace: compare Horace's

> Regium certe genus et Penates
> Maeret iniquos.

We have probably here an example of that interesting transfusion by which the thoughts of one great Poet are reproduced with a new significance by his successor. Horace was Wordsworth's special favourite.

(*Odes*, II, iv, 15–16: 'Surely her lineage must be of royal origin, and she mourns the cruelty of her household gods.')

CCCXXXIX   Title: 'To —' (1824). MS: the four readers, 'Print'.

The Notes by Palgrave

Palgrave revised his Notes. Many cases of interesting revision are given above in this edition's notes to particular poems; given here are cases when Palgrave revised the Summaries (provided within his Notes) for the four Books of *The Golden Treasury*.

Summary of Book First: Palgrave added in 1890 the sentence: 'For the didactic verse of the century, although lyrical in form, yet very rarely rises to the pervading emotion, the golden cadence, proper to the lyric.' He also changed the ending. In 1861 it ran: '. . . neither modern nor ancient, but true in all ages, and like the works of Creation, perfect as on the first day'. In 1890: '. . . neither modern nor ancient, but true and speaking to the heart of man alike throughout all ages'.

Summary of Book Third: Palgrave revised his sentence on European civilization. In 1861: '. . . the genius of the age; and the brave and admirable spirit of Enquiry which made the eighteenth century the turning-time in European civilization is reflected faithfully in its verse'. In 1890: '. . . the genius of the age; and the many complex causes which made the Eighteenth century the turning-time in modern European civilization are [also *added* 1891] more or less reflected in its verse'.

Summary of Book Fourth: Palgrave revised his account of the French Revolution. In 1861:

Exhaustive reasons can hardly be given for the strangely sudden appearance of individual genius: but none, in the Editor's judgment, can be less adequate than that which assigns the splendid national achievements of our recent poetry to an impulse from the frantic follies and criminal wars that at the time disgraced the least essentially civilized of our foreign neighbours. The first French Revolution was rather, in his opinion, one result, and in itself by no means the most important, of that far wider and greater spirit which through enquiry and doubt, through pain and triumph, sweeps mankind round the circles of its gradual development;

In 1883:

... individual genius: that, however, which assigns the splendid national achievements of our recent poetry to an impulse from the France of the first Republic and Empire appears to the Editor [*replaced by* is *1890*] inadequate. The first French Revolution was rather one result, – the most conspicuous, indeed, yet itself in great measure essentially retrogressive, – of that wider and more potent spirit which through enquiry and attempt, through strength and weakness, sweeps mankind round the circles (not, as some too confidently argue, of Advance, but) of gradual Transformation:

Palgrave revised too the closing sentence of this Summary. In 1861: 'For, as with the Affections and the Conscience, Purity in Taste is absolutely proportionate to Strength . . .'. In 1890 he dropped the first eight words.

Some poems specifically considered but rejected

Shakespeare, (i) 'Who is Silvia? What is she?', from *Two Gentlemen of Verona*, IV, ii. (ii) 'How should I your true love know from another one?', from *Hamlet*, IV, v. In her study of Palgrave's copy of Bell's *Songs from the Dramatists*, Kathleen Tillotson notes that these 'went out on the first round' because of 'Palgrave's reasonable exclusion of "pieces markedly dramatic"'.

Jonson, 'Slow, slow, fresh fount', from *Cynthia's Revels*, I, ii. From Palgrave's copy of Bell's *Songs*, Kathleen Tillotson notes that it 'had no clear votes'.

Greene, 'Doron's Description of Samela', from *Menaphon*. Kathleen Tillotson notes from Palgrave's copy of Bell's *Songs* that it was 'rather unexpectedly submitted to [Tennyson] as a borderline case although Palgrave had queried it and Miller said "No"', and 'was firmly rejected – "only manufacture A T"'. Perhaps Palgrave submitted it to Tennyson because of Bell's words: 'This charming song, which, in its structure, will remind the reader of one of Tennyson's popular lyrics'.

Fletcher, (i) 'Weep no more, nor sigh, nor groan', from *The Queen of Corinth*, III, ii. From Palgrave's copy of Bell's *Songs*, Kathleen Tillotson notes that Palgrave at first favoured it but was persuaded by 'No' from Miller and Woolner. (ii) 'Now the lusty spring', from *Valentinian*, II, v. In Bell's *Songs*, Miller voted 'No'.

Herrick, 'The Night-piece, to Julia'. In a pencil note by Palgrave in a copy of the first printing, July 1861 (British Library), this is listed, as 'Her eyes', together with 'Corinna Maying'; Palgrave added the latter (CXVIII) in 1883.

Milton, 'On Time'. MS (under CXLVII): Tennyson, 'Omit'; 'and B. Jowett' (Palgrave).

Congreve, 'Prithee fill me the glass', from *The Way of the World*, IV. From Palgrave's copy of Bell's *Songs*, Kathleen Tillotson notes: 'None of Bell's songs from dramatists after 1660 were chosen; not even Sheridan's, no doubt on the principle stated in the Preface of not including "humorous poetry". Palgrave hankered after the drinking song in *The Way of the World*, writing "very clever" both on p. 255 and the end-leaf; it did not get as far as Farringford.'

Goldsmith, 'Air'. See the note to CLXXV.

Burns, 'Ae fond kiss'. See the note to CXCVII.

Wordsworth, 'I watch, and long have watched, with calm regret'. MS, verso, deleted, of CCXIX.

Coleridge, (i) 'Sonnet to a Friend who Asked . . .'. MS, verso, deleted, of CCXXVIII. (ii) 'Epitaph on an Infant'. MS, verso, deleted, of CCXXIX; Palgrave, 'Print?', then 'Omit' in line with Woolner and Miller; 'slight and physical fulsomeness'.

Byron, 'Stanzas' ('If sometimes in the haunts of men'). MS, verso, deleted, of CCXXXIX.

Keats, 'Fairy's Song'. MS, verso, deleted, of CCXLV. Palgrave, '?', then 'I should omit – too slight and fanciful'; Woolner, 'Print'; Miller, '? or Omit'.

P. J. Bailey, 'The rose is weeping for her love', from *Festus*. MS, verso, deleted, of CCLIV. Palgrave, 'Print?', then 'Omit' in line with Woolner and Miller; 'on whole too slight'.

Hood, 'Fair Ines'. MS, under CCLXVIII: Tennyson 'rejected "Inez" and several other things by Hood as what he called "invertebrate"'.

Campbell, 'To the Rainbow'. MS, under CCCIV: '*Rainbow* probably'.

Shelley, (i) 'Sonnet: Political Greatness'. MS, verso, deleted, of CCXLVII. Palgrave, 'Omit'; Woolner, 'Print'; Miller, '?'
(ii) 'Time' ('Unfathomable Sea!!'). MS, deleted, following CCXII. Tennyson and Miller, 'Omit'; Palgrave, '?'; Woolner, 'Print'.
(iii) 'A Bridal Song' ('The golden gates of Sleep unbar'). MS, deleted, following CCCXXV. Woolner, 'Print'; the others, 'Omit'.

Bernard Barton, 'The Solitary Tomb'. MS, deleted, verso of CLVI. Palgrave, 'Omit?'; Woolner and Miller, 'Omit'.

INDEX OF WRITERS

INDEX OF FIRST LINES

READ MORE IN PENGUIN

In every corner of the world, on every subject under the sun, Penguin represents quality and variety – the very best in publishing today.

For complete information about books available from Penguin – including Puffins, Penguin Classics and Arkana – and how to order them, write to us at the appropriate address below. Please note that for copyright reasons the selection of books varies from country to country.

In the United Kingdom: Please write to *Dept. EP, Penguin Books Ltd, Bath Road, Harmondsworth, West Drayton, Middlesex UB7 ODA*

In the United States: Please write to *Consumer Sales, Penguin USA, P.O. Box 999, Dept. 17109, Bergenfield, New Jersey 07621-0120*. VISA and MasterCard holders call 1-800-253-6476 to order Penguin titles

In Canada: Please write to *Penguin Books Canada Ltd, 10 Alcorn Avenue, Suite 300, Toronto, Ontario M4V 3B2*

In Australia: Please write to *Penguin Books Australia Ltd, P.O. Box 257, Ringwood, Victoria 3134*

In New Zealand: Please write to *Penguin Books (NZ) Ltd, Private Bag 102902, North Shore Mail Centre, Auckland 10*

In India: Please write to *Penguin Books India Pvt Ltd, 706 Eros Apartments, 56 Nehru Place, New Delhi 110 019*

In the Netherlands: Please write to *Penguin Books Netherlands bv, Postbus 3507, NL-1001 AH Amsterdam*

In Germany: Please write to *Penguin Books Deutschland GmbH, Metzlerstrasse 26, 60594 Frankfurt am Main*

In Spain: Please write to *Penguin Books S. A., Bravo Murillo 19, 1° B, 28015 Madrid*

In Italy: Please write to *Penguin Italia s.r.l., Via Felice Casati 20, I–20124 Milano*

In France: Please write to *Penguin France S. A., 17 rue Lejeune, F–31000 Toulouse*

In Japan: Please write to *Penguin Books Japan, Ishikiribashi Building, 2–5–4, Suido, Bunkyo-ku, Tokyo 112*

In South Africa: Please write to *Longman Penguin Southern Africa (Pty) Ltd, Private Bag X08, Bertsham 2013*

READ MORE IN PENGUIN

A SELECTION OF POETRY

American Verse
British Poetry Since 1945
Caribbean Verse in English
Contemporary American Poetry
Contemporary British Poetry
English Poetry 1918–60
English Romantic Verse
English Verse
First World War Poetry
German Verse
Greek Verse
Irish Verse
Japanese Verse
Love Poetry
The Metaphysical Poets
Modern African Poetry
New Poetry
Poetry of the Thirties
Scottish Verse
Spanish Verse
Women Poets

READ MORE IN PENGUIN

POETRY LIBRARY

Arnold	Selected by Kenneth Allott
Blake	Selected by W. H. Stevenson
Browning	Selected by Daniel Karlin
Burns	Selected by Angus Calder and William Donnelly
Byron	Selected by A. S. B. Glover
Clare	Selected by Geoffrey Summerfield
Coleridge	Selected by Richard Holmes
Donne	Selected by John Hayward
Dryden	Selected by Douglas Grant
Hardy	Selected by David Wright
Herbert	Selected by W. H. Auden
Jonson	Selected by George Parfitt
Keats	Selected by John Barnard
Kipling	Selected by James Cochrane
Lawrence	Selected by Keith Sagar
Milton	Selected by Laurence D. Lerner
Pope	Selected by Douglas Grant
Rubáiyát of Omar Khayyám	Translated by Edward FitzGerald
Shelley	Selected by Isabel Quigley
Tennyson	Selected by W. E. Williams
Wordsworth	Selected by Nicholas Roe
Yeats	Selected by Timothy Webb

READ MORE IN PENGUIN

A CHOICE OF CLASSICS

Matthew Arnold	**Selected Prose**
Jane Austen	**Emma**
	Lady Susan/ The Watsons/ Sanditon
	Mansfield Park
	Northanger Abbey
	Persuasion
	Pride and Prejudice
	Sense and Sensibility
Anne Brontë	**Agnes Grey**
	The Tenant of Wildfell Hall
Charlotte Brontë	**Jane Eyre**
	Shirley
	Villette
Emily Brontë	**Wuthering Heights**
Samuel Butler	**Erewhon**
	The Way of All Flesh
Thomas Carlyle	**Selected Writings**
Arthur Hugh Clough	**Selected Poems**
Wilkie Collins	**The Moonstone**
	The Woman in White
Charles Darwin	**The Origin of Species**
	The Voyage of the Beagle
Benjamin Disraeli	**Sybil**
George Eliot	**Adam Bede**
	Daniel Deronda
	Felix Holt
	Middlemarch
	The Mill on the Floss
	Romola
	Scenes of Clerical Life
	Silas Marner
Elizabeth Gaskell	**Cranford and Cousin Phillis**
	The Life of Charlotte Brontë
	Mary Barton
	North and South
	Wives and Daughters

READ MORE IN PENGUIN

A CHOICE OF CLASSICS

READ MORE IN PENGUIN

A CHOICE OF CLASSICS